THE EMPATH

The Above & Beyond Series

Book 1: The Empath
Book 2: Blind Trust
Book 3: Untrained Eye
Book 4: Hindsight
Book 5: Midas Touch
Book 6: Black Ridge Falls
Book 7: Full Circle

THE EMPATH

THE ABOVE AND BEYOND SERIES • BOOK 1

JODY KLAIRE

BInk

Bedazzled Ink Publishing Company • Fairfield, California

978-1-939562-66-1 paperback
978-1-939562-67-8 ebook

Cover Design
by
TreeHouse Studio

A Mindancer Book

BInk
a division of
Bedazzled Ink Publishing Company
Fairfield, California
http://www.bedazzledink.com

To Hoody, Ollie and Uncle Terry—
You live in my words always.

For:
Mum and Em who go above and beyond.

And
For anyone who is that little bit different.

Acknowledgements

There're so many people I need to thank that it's hard to know where to start. One thing I will state first is that I may have put the words down alone but without the support and guidance from so many people, I would not have found the strength or knowledge to get my book released. If you're a reader, yup you who has taken the chance on me, thank you. I really hope that you love Aeron and enjoy her story. To anyone who is starting to write and are unpublished as yet, you can do it. Don't give up, work hard, learn, and love it. There's nothing better than letting your imagination free.

Okay . . . For the people on FB (especially the Clubhouse ladies!) and Twitter who have been so supportive, I really appreciate your kind words. To the Cloudies who have also been right behind me all the way, there're so many of you but namely Katherine Hetzel, Louise Walters, John Taylor, Brenda Woodford, Ian, Emma D, there're so many more but I could take a tome to list you! Britta Murasaki who helped me out with some of the finer points of Missouri life, thank you for your time. The Writers' Workshop, you guys have given so much to us and I am so very grateful to have been pointed in your direction. Nikki, Laura, Harry and the team, extra chocolate for you!

To Pat and Ian Griffiths, you help me to be able to keep writing. Without your expertise, my hands may have fallen off by now!

Gerri Hill, Georgia Beers, your support of newbie authors and warmth towards me was very much appreciated! To the GCLS who work tirelessly to offer great opportunities and to their education team and faculty (Liz M and Liz G especially). Wonderful organisation, wonderful ladies.

To my Betas: Sarah Rickman, Moira Spence, Glenda Davies (and Mel Oglesbee!) Joy Fry your lovely words and gentle encouragement really mean the world to me. To Mary Buchanan who beta read for me, thank you very much!

To Team Truth, Gena Ratcliff and Dani Dixon-Bradshaw, what can I say? I am so very lucky to have stumbled across you both.

Your fervent love, belief in my work and joy really do make a difference to me. Thank you for all the uplifting chats, lessons in southern speak and pie recipes too!

Casey and Claudia at Bedazzled Ink for taking the chance on me and my work, I couldn't imagine a better home for Aeron. Thank you for helping me to share my stories with the world. To Sandra Moran, you know I think you rock, SFH, but your encouragement, your help and your patience for me mean the world. To Ann McMan, thank you for the wonderful cover, it is perfect for Aeron. To my fellow Binkies who have been welcoming and always ready to help and chat. TOTS!

Brie Burkeman, you may need to be canonised for your patience with a wide-eyed naive Welshwoman. Having the fortune to receive all your guidance, time, and energy was and is truly a blessing. Debi Alper, I have never met such a passionate advocate for writers learning their trade. You have been an elite mentor who has taught me so much and yet has inspired me more. Everytime I have the pleasure of learning from you, it seems another facet of writing illuminates before my eyes.

To those who guarded me when that cloud hovered overhead: Fr Mike Komor, Mr B & Revd. Sue Beverly, Moira Spence, and all in the CNB parish, it was in the depth of darkness that I truly found a welcome. Your teachings, love and support mean an immeasurable amount to me. You are warmth, welcome and light.

My family: Uncle Terry, you were a blessing that I will treasure always, there is no tenor that even comes close to you. Aunty Heddwyn, you inspired so much of Aeron's experiences and I adore you for it, it was also nice to know that spiritual is in the genes. A special thank you for the armour too! Dad, whose stories and weaving of tales seemed a mark of my childhood. Those days of spooky tales, the castles, the love of the sea and the wonder of the stars at night ignited my imagination, thank you.

To two very special people that I could not be without yet no words can quite bring to life just how important you are to me: Em, home isn't home without you, thank you for your eagle-eye, your constant patience, and your love for Aeron.

Mum, for the love of literature you share, for the love and comfort that you give, for the endless cuddles and undying support. From reading me stories, to encouraging every creative whim I had, for the hours of queuing outside auditions and for your belief in me even when mine faltered. Thank you for loving my books, for sharing the stories, and never giving up on me. Thank you for helping me to construct a sentence and for being as passionate about my writing as I am.

To the both of you for being there no matter what. I'd need more than words to express what you mean to me.

To THS, there is no Word greater, thank you for giving me Aeron and thank you for the light.

Jody Klaire
July, 2014

"Stand firm then, with the belt of truth buckled around your waist, with the breastplate of righteousness in place, and with your feet fitted with the readiness that comes from the gospel of peace. In addition to all this, take up the shield of faith, with which you can extinguish all the flaming arrows of the evil one. Take the helmet of salvation and the sword of the spirit which is the Word of God."

—Ephesians 6:14 - 17 (NIV)

Chapter 1

MY PROBLEM IS that I know too much.

I see things. I can tell a person's life from their jewelry, I can read other people like you would read the morning newspaper. Plus, I can displace ailments, heal and wound . . . and none of it is voluntary.

I'm different and for some people being different is what makes the world love them. They have talents that everyone else wishes they had. Hell, they might even be a genius of some kind.

I don't know how to stop it and I sure as hell can't control it. When I try to explain these "burdens" to people, I either become a freak-show, a threat, or they think I'm just another crazy person, which is why I am now in a secure mental facility and have been since the age of sixteen. I murdered someone—at least, I think I did. The authorities found me guilty of manslaughter.

My name is Aeron Lorelei. Aeron, because right up until birth, the family thought I was a boy and my father wanted a boy more than anything, a son called Aaron. They were all pretty disappointed when I appeared and at a loss of what to name me, they changed the A to an E and so I got a name that stuck out as much as I did.

Not that any of that matters anymore since I was convicted as no one in my family will admit I exist. Aeron, the odd runt who talked to animals and wandered around telling people things about themselves they didn't want known. Who'd want that kind of gossip?

I mean, my family tried . . . really tried. I was even sent to a priest once. They thought some holy water and chanting was going to fix me right up but the priest was actually kinda nice. Still, I didn't tell him a thing. Even back then I knew that my family and the local folks figured me for a freak.

They were probably right all things considering. Look where I ended up, wearing orange and sitting 'round in a concrete tomb with a bunch of other misfits.

I share my cell with a woman named Lori. She's a bulky

woman with mad professor hair. Now, Lori murdered her entire family as they slept and I don't think she even knows why. I can see this nasty dark cloud over her, its slimy tentacles leeching away her sanity. I could get rid of it for her but then I'd have to figure out what to do with it. Besides, it's been attached for so long that it would leave a great big crater in her mind. Sure, they'd free her, they would say she had responded to whatever "miracle drug" they were dishing out this month. Then, when she was out in the world, that great big hole would attract a different leech . . . Someone else could get hurt and it'd be my fault, like always.

So I do nothing but watch her getting fed on by the cloud over her head. It sounds cold, doesn't it? I know, but I don't believe in messing with the future, in messing with people. No one should have that kind of power or knowledge.

So, like I said, I know too much, and the last thing I want is to have more blood on my hands.

Chapter 2

AT LUNCHTIME, I sat in the usual spot on the bench in the cafeteria. It was me and the four other inmates I called friends. We'd been here the longest but if you thought that bought us any kind of dispensation, you'd be wrong. I didn't really think that we were particularly devious, or violent but somehow we fell into a category that the Head Shrink would class as ringleaders.

In other words, if there was trouble of some sort, generally we were at fault . . . and when I say we, it was normally me.

The shrink told me that I liked to incite unrest. I'd call it standing up for human rights and objecting to being treated like a guinea pig but whatever name you gave it, that was us . . . well, more me . . . but guilt by association and all that.

My buddies were Aimee, Nora, Yasmin, and a girl originally from China. Her name was too difficult for us to pronounce without her breaking out into fits of laughter, so we called her Tiz. We'd stick together to stop some of the more vicious offenders targeting us. I may be tall and overly muscular but some inmates were so sucked into their pain that I could have the strength of ten men and not survive it.

"So how's the new girl?" Tiz asked.

I looked at Lori for a moment, that nasty cloud sucking at her. "Desperate . . . she's thinking about attacking Sheila."

"She told you that?" Nora asked, picking at her thumbs.

I shook my head and tapped her hands until she stopped. I hated it when she did that.

"Ah, so third eye, huh?" Aimee chimed in.

I looked at Aimee. "Somethin' like that . . . I think she's had enough."

Aimee and me, well, we had hated each other for years, right up until we'd been trapped in the laundry room with an inmate in a full psychotic rage. Fear, and the need to survive, had melted the ice. Although to hear us talk to each other, you would never believe it.

"If she takes on Sheila . . . Hell, she won't make dinner," Yasmin said.

I nodded, looking at Lori's fierce expression. The cloud pulsated over her, black and soulless. I felt for her, and that was why I wouldn't do a thing to stop her.

It was her choice.

As I thought it, she got up as if by my command and walked over to Sheila. Sheila spent most of her days locked in restraints, the woman was a walking mass of anger.

"Should we stop her?" Tiz asked.

"You kidding me?" Aimee scowled. "She'd rip your freakin' heart out."

The five of us sat there and watched. I guess you would call it morbid fascination. I wanted to turn away, I did. I wanted to lock myself in my cell and hide but instead I sat there watching.

Lori picked up a simple plastic fork from the table and jabbed it into Sheila's face, right into the left cheek. Blood splattered out over Lori's hand and the cloud pulsed over her.

Nora started fiddling with her hands and Tiz gripped my arm tight as Sheila exploded with fury. I felt my entire body ripple under her anger. She was like standing beside the mouth of an angry volcano—that was what normal people would feel.

For an Empath, it was like being burned by the spewing lava. My chest tightened as she roared. Tiz gripped harder. Lori jabbed the fork again and caught Sheila in the shoulder. The middle fork prongs snapped. Blood poured out. It was deep. I tensed, getting the burst of her pain as I sat there. Deep and agonizing.

Sheila pulled the fork off Lori, jammed it into her chest, and hauled Lori over two sets of tables. I winced, clutching my own chest, it had hurt.

The cafeteria was in chaos, people screaming and others chanting, the frenzy of violence stirring everyone up. Nora started biting her skin, Aimee scratched her neck, Yasmin hugged herself, Tiz squeezed the life out of my bicep.

I sat there, numb. Their pain thudded through my heart. I wanted to get up, to go over there and stop what I knew was going to happen. I could see both women's intentions like they were picture books but it wasn't my place to do anything.

It was their choice, not mine, theirs.

Unable to tear my eyes away, I sat still and awaited the inevitable crescendo.

Lori wasn't done. She got up and hurled herself, a jagged half of the fork in hand. The guards sprinted over. I held my breath. Sheila lifted up her half . . .

Then calm.

I watched the chaotic scene in silence as Sheila and Lori fell to the ground with a thud. The guards tore at them as they tried to save them.

But it was too late.

The five of us exchanged looks. After ten years of being trapped in here with the tortured and unloved, we understood. I understood and that was why I'd done nothing.

They were free now—something I would never be.

Chapter 3

I ENTERED THE psychiatrist's office for my daily session less than an hour after the incident. I was surprised to find that the elderly Doctor Bison was now a thirty-something woman with the brightest shade of lipstick that I had ever seen.

"Come in, take a seat," she said, not once looking up from her notes.

I did as I was told and noted the differences in the office from that of her predecessor. Doctor Bison had been in residence here for longer than most of the inmates had been alive. He had been the kind of man that Freud would have loved but more as a specimen than a fellow psychiatrist.

This woman, on the other hand, emanated a different energy. She was in love with her job, in love with her books and her certificates. She was proud of all she had achieved and she had not wanted, in the slightest, to be stuck in this institution with the likes of me.

"Aeron Lorelei. Unusual name."

I nodded, slightly transfixed by the energy dancing around her. A go-getter.

"You were Lori's cellmate?"

I nodded again and chose to stare at the large certificate of the Doctorate instead of the woman who so clearly couldn't be bothered to look at me. Doctor S. Llys. So she went to Yale, Ivy League then.

"It says on your file that you believe you can see the future."

I sighed. Most people who started off with "you believe" generally finished by saying "delusional." I may be many things, but I know what I see.

"You saw Lori attack Sheila?"

I folded my arms. "In what context?"

Llys looked up, her steel-gray eyes unnervingly clear. She thought I was trouble. If she kept up her attitude, I would be.

"Is there more than one?"

"You start by saying I see the future, then asked if I saw Sheila and Lori. Therefore it ain't too obvious to assume you're referring to my foresight other than the actual events."

She raised her eyebrows.

Yeah, I read, lady. I can throw out a sentence when I need to, I thought. *Stick that, Ivy League.*

"Did you see it . . . beforehand?" she asked.

Human curiosity. All the degrees in the world couldn't suppress the inner-gossip.

"Yes."

She sat back and perched her hands together in a prayer-like pose. I half wondered if she was going to do just that. "You saw Lori attack Sheila, and you didn't stop her?"

"Correct."

"Why?"

I looked past her out of the window. When you're stuck inside four gray walls for years on end, it's funny how much greener the world always looks beyond . . . even if it was through bars and barbed wire.

"Freedom," I answered.

"Yours?"

I laughed. Now, she was just being dumb. The only thing it would offer me was peace from Lori's screaming all night long and her desperation coating the walls of the cell like thick black tar.

I didn't bother to answer and that seemed to rile Miss Ivy-League right up. "Did you convince her it was a good idea? Is that the way you work? Is that how you and your friends entertain yourselves?"

I raised an eyebrow. Did psychiatrists come off production lines? If they didn't get a satisfactory answer to shove you in box A, B, or C. They went for an attack instead.

"Nice of you to think so highly of me."

"I haven't come to any opinion of you yet," she answered.

"Haven't you? You sat for twenty minutes reading the notes of a man who should have been retired forty years ago. You borrow *his* opinion and he didn't know me."

Llys smiled.

I smiled back.

I'd just told her exactly what had happened and it confused the hell out of her. She would put it down to perception skills or guesswork. Doctors are like that.

"So who are you?" she asked.

I tried not to roll my eyes, if in doubt switch the question. "Aeron Lorelei . . . but then I thought you'd read it on the notes."

"Is this the way it's going to be, Aeron?" she asked. You know you're definitely irritating them when they use first names.

"That depends on you, Tess," I shot back.

She froze. How could I possibly know her mother's pet name for her?

I smiled. No use in trying to outplay an Empath. We can see all your cards.

And that's when our first session ended.

Abruptly.

She kicked me out.

It was the first time I'd been kicked out of a session.

I liked it.

Chapter 4

THAT NIGHT I managed to sleep for the first time in a month. I could feel that somewhere, wherever people go after they leave here, I could feel that Lori was happy. The next morning, however, Llys had decided to assert her authority in the hope of wearing me down. In short, she had separated me and the other so-called ringleaders.

I breathed in the biting cold of December and tried not to shiver with fear. She'd not only separated me but she'd stuck me in the yard with Sheila's fellow fury-fiends. All of which I knew instantly felt that *I* was responsible for Lori's attack.

In here that kind of attention would see you in the infirmary and that was if you were lucky. My neck prickled with the cold and the wave of hate as I wandered over to a pile of fallen snow. Pure, pristine, gleaming snow undisturbed by the boots of the inmates.

I knelt in front of it. There's something magical about snow, at least to me. It reminds me of how my childhood *should* have been. The days spent building snowmen and riding sleighs, the warm toasty fires and the sweet hot chocolate.

My childhood had been nothing like it. Pushed from pillar to post as my parents worked longer and longer hours. The brief promises of how, when Daddy got his promotion, he would be home more or when Mommy won this case she would take time off.

Neither did.

I spent most of my time with Nan. I'm not even sure if she was my grandmother and that was a pet name or if she was an elderly woman who had nothing better to do than babysit a misfit. When I look back, I can't ever recall her talking much, she would either be fishing, tending to her vegetable garden, or reading. Nan loved to read.

An angry voice broke me from my trip into memories. "Lei—A word."

I sighed. Whenever someone shortens my last name or asks for a word in here, it means they want to rip my head off.

"What's up?" I asked.

I knew the second I turned around, the woman belonging to the huge shadow on the snow was going to swing for me. The longer I delayed, the harder it would be for the guards to ignore what was happening. One was already itching to intervene, I could feel her.

"You Lori's friend?"

I shook my head. I was no one to Lori. Lori didn't know where the hell she was by the time she'd gotten into the cell. All I had met was a screaming shell.

"Are too . . . I know you bunked with her."

I rubbed the back of my neck. A flash of the woman's intentions made the hairs on my arms prickle. What was with all the violence?

"They put her in my cell," I said. "I didn't know her."

"Liar!"

She lunged. I rolled to the left and got to my feet, my attacker now sprawled in the snow. Three of her friends started to run over. Hell, they were going to tear me to pieces.

I looked up at the guards, who turned away. Thanks a lot.

Damn, I was in trouble. I looked around at the yard. Four massive walls, armed guards on top, a chain-link fence, penning me in like a turkey at Christmas. My eyes lifted to the guard who I could hear wanted to help, she was *desperate* to help and so I walked as calmly as I could back to the gate.

My heart thudded so hard that I thought my ribs were going to break. The sound of the heavy boots crunched on the grit and sludge behind me. My breath was loud and rapid.

"Get her!"

A little further, just a little bit further, come on. The clomping got nearer, my heart—*thud, thud, thud*—I could make it. The guard was itching to help. She was new, it would wear off.

I could hear the mob behind me shouting, their thoughts crystal clear. *Kill her, rip her apart, pound her head, stamp on it . . .*

"Please," I blurted as I got to the gate. The guard opened it instantly and locked it behind me as the three bear-like women charged into the solid iron.

I smiled at the guard, hardly able to hear over my heartbeat. "Thanks."

She nodded and moved me away from the flaying arms of the crazed trio. "Why did they put you out there with them if they hate you?"

I met her eyes for a moment. First day. She had a hell of a lot to learn. "They don't hate me, they just want to crush anything that moves. They'd happily crush each other."

"You aren't like them," she said.

"No, but the guards will tell you I'm trouble, which I probably am. They won't like that you just got me out of a hiding."

The guard frowned. "I'm sure they would never do that."

I smiled. "You'll see. Watch the rotation—my friends will all be in with the lynch mob at some point today."

"Why?"

"I dared to answer back. Crazy people ain't allowed opinions."

The guard wasn't completely convinced. I could see her running through the training that she had been given. The training that informed her that the inmates in this institution were as crafty and slippery as they came. Diligence at all times.

She took nearly half an hour to navigate the rabbit warren of corridors to take me back to my cell. Not that I minded, I needed the time to calm down.

I didn't say a word the entire time but listened to her feelings, her worries and I owed the woman. "Piece of advice. In these places it's you or us . . . outsiders or insiders. If they think you aren't completely one of them, you won't last long."

"I appreciate the honesty," the guard said.

I smiled. "It's an ear infection by the way . . . she needs to go to the doctors."

The guard tilted her head. "Excuse me?"

"Your daughter, she's not ignoring you, she has hearing problems. Right now, it's an infection."

The guard looked down the corridor and back to me as if to say, "Did I speak aloud?"

"You don't have to believe me but just think of it as me returning the favor. Oh, and stick her in front of a piano."

The guard looked at me in disbelief. I was used to it. "Maybe I'll try that."

"I would. Don't forget that you think I'm a troublemaker. They'll like that."

The guard smiled. "Noted."

I walked back into my cell and lay flat out on my bed. My friendly guard would be gone in six months, she was pregnant. I wanted to tell her but realized she already knew. She was working in this place to get enough money to see her through to the birth.

I wasn't sure how she was going to cope with life in here. It was hard enough when you lived in it day after day but to leave the world outside and spend time in the gloom of the institution, who the hell would want that?

They were more desperate than us.

Chapter 5

I FELL ASLEEP in my cell after my rescue. It was one of those odd siestas that left me feeling groggy and confused. I lay there between full sleep and awareness and tried to lift my consciousness. In that state, as an Empath, I'm in danger of visions and if there's one thing I hate more than anything, it's visions.

A simple person falls into sleep and processes the day before. Occasionally they have an odd dream where their husband becomes a monkey and dances the samba . . . but all in all, safe, sweet dreams, right?

For me, a person's odd dreams are my vision-time. I get wonderfully horrific glimpses of events that haven't yet happened. It never works on a simple level either. If, for instance, someone was going to find the love of their lives, I would see smashing heat and fire crushing everything in its path. Their passion, my inferno.

None of it even remotely pleasant.

Unable to drag myself from a doze, the dream began, only it was not future but past replayed.

I had always liked Jake. He was Sam's brother. Sam was my best friend and we were joined at the hip from the age of eleven. He had been the guy who every girl loved. I loved him but not in a cuddly way. Empath's have a bit of trouble in that area. We don't know if what we feel is us or simply a projection of someone else's emotions. At a very young age, I decided that it would be better for the world if I never attempted to find out.

So, Sam and I were as close as you could get. Jake, his junior by two years, followed us everywhere. I doted on him. Sam put up with him. Wherever one was, the others were.

A trio of terrors, that's what his mother called us. She was right. If we weren't breaking into the old soda pop factory to steal glass bottles to shoot at, then we were raking the floor under the machines in the arcade.

Coming from a small town in the middle of the Ozarks, prime tourist country, we had more than a few tricks to earn money.

Some of them a little more light-fingered than I like to remember but then I did end up a murderer so no use sweating the small stuff, I guess.

That night, the one I have replayed a thousand times, we were out by the old rail crossing on the far edge of town. Sam and I had come up with the brilliant idea to strip the copper from the signal posts and sell it for scrap. It seemed like fun and we had done it a million-and-one times. We could get a fair amount for scrap.

That night, Jake had followed us. Sam was furious because Jake could never keep his mouth shut about anything. I quite liked the trait in him. Jake was honest, sweet, and adored me. He detested Sam like an ogre. Brotherly love for you.

We stripped the signal and loaded up the pick-up truck that Sam had "borrowed" from the campsite out in the fields. I hopped in the passenger seat as Sam and Jake began to argue.

It's always at this point the dream gets foggy, confused, and out of place.

I'm in front of Jake, he's telling me it's illegal, that we need to stop stealing, that someone will catch us. The ground rumbles as a high-speed train hurtles around the corner. Jake tries to grab for me, my hands stretch out. He's gone. The blast of air hits me backwards.

I woke up and, as always, I sat bolt upright, clutching my pillow, desperately trying to pull Jake back. It was always too far, too late. Jake was gone and it was my fault.

"Doctor Llys would like to see you," I heard my friendly guard say.

I half turned and nodded.

"Do you need a few minutes?" she asked.

I shook my head and pulled myself to my feet. A quick splash of water on my face to wash away the past I couldn't change and I was off to meet Doctor Llys . . . round two.

Chapter 6

LLYS GAVE ME one of *those* looks as I wandered into her office. The "you're late" look. The one which people who are always early for everything give those of us who really don't give a damn. I gave her a look back, the one that said, "Yeah, I'm late. Deal with it."

"Did you enjoy your exercise?" Llys asked, attempting not to scowl.

"Oh yes," I said. "Especially the part where Uma landed on her ass."

Her real name wasn't Uma, but it was another of those very long and foreign names that none of us could manage. This time, I thought Scandinavian or maybe Polish, I wasn't really sure.

"You enjoy other people getting hurt?"

I sighed. She was back to borrowing Doctor Bison's opinions again. Bison felt that I was plotting to take over the prison. I'm not quite sure what he felt I would accomplish by this but the man was paranoid and way past his expiration date.

"You get she was attempting to take my head off at the time?"

Llys raised an eyebrow. Course she did. "Why, when you're so sweet and innocent?"

One piece of advice. Never bug a person who has been locked inside four gray walls for as long as me. We have a tendency to get testy. "Using patients to fight your battles only shows weakness. You wouldn't want the rest thinking that you were fallible now, would you?"

"Point made," Llys said.

Darn right it was. If she tried it again, she'd have to figure out how to remove her pen from . . . Well, you get the picture.

"I heard you were having dreams?"

I looked at the door. The friendly guard had been worried about me, she was too good for this place.

"You were in distress."

I shrugged. The dream still probed at my groggy senses.

"Do you have it a lot?"

I looked Llys in the eyes. "You've just spent the last session trying to beat me into submission. Why the hell would I tell you anything? You don't care. You don't even want to be here."

Llys looked at me for a moment or two and then nodded. "You're right. I'm sorry. I don't want to be here, but I am. I'm not too bad at my job either, so maybe . . . I could help."

Normally, I would have seen this change of tact as a subtle maneuvering but I could see the truth shining around her. When someone tells me something and means it, they shimmer like glitter has fallen from their lips. It's kinda pretty.

"Do we have a truce?"

Again Llys nodded. Again honesty.

I leaned back in the chair. It wasn't like I was really giving anything away. I'd told Ol' Bison the same dream a hundred times. He'd managed not to snore . . . once.

"I'm at the railroad crossing. Jake is there. The train comes and hits him."

Llys nodded. "Where was Sam?"

I frowned. "What do you mean?"

"I read the report . . . hazy as it is. Sam, Jake's brother was there, yes?"

"Yeah."

"So, where was he at this point?"

I replayed the dream but my entire focus had been on Jake. Every sound, feeling, every second suspended in time as I grab for him. "I don't know. I was too busy trying to save Jake."

"But it says in the file that you confessed to his murder."

I looked up. "I was sixteen and I'd just let my best friend's little brother get hit by a train. That's murder."

Llys made notes. I hated it when they made notes. I couldn't see what she was writing, which irritated the hell out of me. She wasn't as open to reading today, maybe she had taken me seriously. Some people are so good at blocking me from their thoughts that I can't read them at all.

Sam was one of those people. That's why it was so nice to be around him. I could be a person.

"Why did you run?" Llys probed.

"Because I was scared, because we had a stolen truck with

stolen signal wire . . . because I was in shock . . . I loved that kid. I mean, *really* loved him. Like he was my own little brother."

Llys's aura flickered. It resonated with her. So she was human. Go figure.

"The police said neither you or Sam told anyone what happened. Sam denied ever being there."

I nodded. I had told Sam to say it. It was bad enough that I couldn't stop Jake getting hit, the last thing Sam needed was to be looked at by his own family. It would make my story look weaker if Sam denied everything.

It worked too. No one believed a word I said. I was the loner, the odd one, the kid who no one wanted around. It was easy to blame me and believe that the son of the mayor was innocent.

"He lied?"

"Course he did. Sam had a big future ahead of him. I was just a thieving little runt."

Llys frowned. "You were the daughter of the local police chief."

"The only part he played was long before I was born."

"But it says your parents were married?"

I nodded. "Yeah, she had about as much input. They preferred their ambition. I rebelled."

Llys smiled. "Explains the thievery."

"What better way to get Daddy's attention than to make him look bad in front of his colleagues."

Llys sat back in her chair. "Did it work?"

I laughed. "I could have robbed the local bank and paraded the money on top of his desk and it wouldn't have made a difference."

"And why do you think that is?"

"I *know* it was for one reason alone. I wasn't a boy. He managed to produce one measly kid and not only was I a girl, I was his worst nightmare."

Llys looked at me for a moment. She liked to do that. I didn't mind, while she tried to decipher the messed up childhood, I read into why she was here when she didn't want to be.

"So, you believed he didn't want you?" she asked.

"I *know* he didn't want me. He told me. You know that my parents worked a crap load less than they said they did? They used to have dinner parties but they didn't want me there. They borrowed one of the girls from school if my mother's partners from the firm came around."

"Where were you?"

I closed my eyes. Nights spent in the watermill cabin with Nan. The smell of trout cooking and the crackle of the fireplace, the slosh of the water hitting the window from the wheel. "Nan's."

"Did you get along with her?"

I opened my eyes. "We never spoke. I'm not even sure if she could speak. I'm not even sure who the hell she was."

"You said she was your nan."

"No, I said she was Nan. Whether she was a nan, my nan, or her name was Nan, I have no idea."

Llys looked up at the clock on the wall. For some reason they felt bad when they checked the time. Like I cared that they needed me to leave so another poor soul could get the third degree. I'd have to have feelings of my own for that.

"If what you're saying is right, you didn't kill Jake, Aeron. I know you may not wish to acknowledge my opinion but you seem unable to grieve until you find a resolution in your mind."

I nodded. She was probably right but in my mind I was responsible. And, I would remain responsible, indefinitely.

"Enjoy the dinner," I threw her way as I wandered out the door.

"I thought we had a truce?"

"We do. Your cocktail dress." I pointed to the bathroom door, a glitzy twinkle came from the hanger-bag.

Llys laughed. "In that case, thank you."

Chapter 7

MONTHS PASSED AND Llys and I seemed to find a common ground. I started to tell her about my dreams and she started to trust that I was telling the truth. She didn't believe in my gifts, but she did accept that I did. So, when I told her about a dream I'd been having about Yasmin leaving, she came clean with me.

Now, I don't see the future, I'll swear blind to you that I don't. What I see is snatches, symbols and, like I mentioned before, all fiery infernos. None of it makes the slightest bit of sense but I'd been dreaming over and over about Yasmin. I could see a pair of shoes up on a wall, a gurney with a black bag, and Yasmin's hand hanging out of it. I could see a gun and it scared the hell out of me. These weren't symbols, these were pretty clear pictures and that's why I told Llys.

Llys told me that the parole board had indeed sanctioned Yasmin's release. Even the thought made my stomach clench. I had seen what would happen. Yasmin had it in her head that she would be the next superstar. She would quite happily tell you that she sang like a strangled cat, and there were tree trunks less wooden than her but, in spite of these drawbacks, she was still going to win every award.

That *ambition* had seen her end up on the streets at age thirteen.

Yasmin was a nervous sort. She came in not long after me for killing the man who handled her on the streets. She was from Farmington originally—a small town girl, like me, but she loved the city. She talked a lot about the life and the clubs and of course, the glamour of the stars and how if she could make a name for herself in St. Louis she could head out to L.A. in first class.

I saw through it all though, I never told her so, but I knew the truth. Yasmin had no one, nowhere to go and she was terrified that the people her handler had worked for would find her and shove her back out on the corners.

She chain smoked and drank black coffee by the barrel, her yellow-tipped fingers always adjusting her hair. Even in rec time, she would dress like she was off down some red carpet and that was pretty hard to do dressed like an orangutan.

Yasmin was a kind soul at heart. Her ash blonde hair, the mask of makeup, the dumb-blonde routine was all a cover. When you got past it, you got to see an intelligent, sweet-natured woman who had been given a crappy start. I didn't even think that she should ever have been sent here but she had told me, once, that it was to protect her from her life outside.

Today, Yasmin was getting out.

The others had hugged and whimpered and shed tears and murmured "write to us" requests but I had said nothing. I couldn't.

"You been silent, sweetie," she said as I walked her to the guards.

"Don't go back there. You can find money some other place. Hell, you can go to Nan's cabin . . . live there . . . you'll be safe there."

"And miss my shot at stardom?"

I pulled her around to meet my eyes. "I mean it, Yasmin. You know. You know what I see."

She kissed me on the cheek, wiped the lipstick off with her nicotine thumb, and started to waltz out of my life. I stood there helpless. Another person I cared for was about to be taken and I couldn't do a thing to stop it. I'm guessing that was why it happened. Before I could stop and think logically, I took a plate and threw it in Yasmin's direction. It clanged right off the bars next to her head.

"Don't do this!"

Three guards hurled themselves at me as I watched her heels clicking away.

I felt the friendly digs and lost it.

As I said before, I'm muscular. Really muscular. I have spent years in the gym trying to exhaust myself enough to sleep without dreaming. So, the guards had one hell of a time trying to subdue me. They were about to hit me with a shot when Llys's voice stopped them.

"Bring her to my office."

The guards muttered and I fought them every step of the way. I couldn't let Yasmin go, I had to stop her.

"Get off me!" I scrabbled out of their grasp to run, got tackled from behind, and hit the floor. "Yasmin. Please!"

She looked like she'd come back for a second but one of the other guards pulled her away and out of sight. I threw the heavy bulk of a guard off my back. I had to get to her . . . reason with her.

I got half way down the hall, then one of the grumpier guards, Val, smacked me into the wall and the lights went out.

Chapter 8

I CAME TO in Llys's office with her holding smelling salts under my nose.

"Glad to see you're back," she said.

I tried to get up, remembering with a burst of adrenaline, that Yasmin was getting away. I didn't get far, I was strapped down. "Please, you have to stop her. *Please*."

Llys sighed and walked to her desk. "Yasmin had no reason to be here anymore. She served her time, there was nothing I could do."

"You know she's going back. They'll pull her body out of the river. Please."

The flashes of what would be if I didn't stop it pulsed through me like venom. My skin dripped with it, my heart screamed as it beat, my stomach cried out in agony of what would happen. If Yasmin went back, she would never survive.

"I . . . can't. I tried, Aeron. I contacted the police department to see if I could find someone who would listen."

"And?"

She shook her head. "I think the exact words were, 'We have enough to deal with without pursuing crimes that *might* occur.'"

I hung my head. It didn't surprise me. It sounded like my father. I'd tried to help him with a case once, when I was, maybe, nine. A big case, one that no one else could solve. He was a detective back then, commuting to the same big city now sucking Yasmin into its claws. I had told him where to look and who to look for. He'd replied, "Enough of your fairy stories, don't you have dolls to play with?"

Two months later, he had solved the case, only after he had followed my visions. I know he'd done it out of desperation and when I had been right, I didn't get a hearty well done or a thank you. No, that's when I got sent to the priest.

"So, that's it?"

Llys sighed. "I know we disagree vehemently on your belief in foresight but my logical observations tell me that Yasmin is going to head straight back to where she thinks she can make her fortune."

"What the hell does she want for a fortune anyway? Yasmin wants kids, a perfect husband, and a white picket fence. What the hell is a fortune going to bring her?"

Llys offered me a warm smile. "Love, Aeron. That's what she thinks. Acceptance, adoration . . . attention."

I rolled my eyes. "I wanted love . . . attention. Look where the hell it got me. Strapped to your chair, knowing my friend is about to walk head first into a pistol."

"Why don't we just hope that both of us are overreacting and Yasmin will be sensible?"

It was a half-hearted consolation and Llys knew it.

"Because we both know Yasmin."

Chapter 9

THE SUN WAS shining down, beating heat through the bars of the cafeteria on the day the news filtered through about Yasmin. They had found her in the river. She had been free less than a week. It was the only time that I had ever known the cafeteria to fall silent. Even the monster mashers over in the corner dropped their heads.

Everyone had loved her.

Nora sobbed huge tears onto Tiz's t-shirt. Aimee hugged herself, head bowed. I stood staring at the friendly guard as she wiped a tear from her eye. I'm pretty sure Aimee had tried to console me, she didn't often but I registered her hand on my arm.

I wandered in a daze down the corridor, my head empty, everything so numb.

I didn't cry, I seem incapable of it, but I *wanted* to, I *willed* myself to, but nothing. Not a single tear would fall. That's why I figured it was all my fault like when Jake died. I should have said something more, fought harder, I should have forced her to stay.

Now it was too late.

I know days passed as I sat alone in my cell. I know that I stared for weeks at the solid brick wall opposite my bed. I know that I ate the food brought for me by the friendly guard and I know that I must have showered, must have slept, must have gone about in some routine because I didn't end up in observation. That's where people go who don't look like they are going to make it.

Whatever I managed to do, I wasn't present. I switched off. Another friend falling from my outstretched hands while I stood by helpless. Life became a blur, people, places, time, a wash of gray over an empty canvas. No details, no real emotion only a slideshow of life before my eyes.

I looked up then, one morning, to the high window in my cell and saw the sunlight stream gently onto the floor. The dust floated in kaleidoscope-colored shapes, dancing before my eyes. A form emerged, only briefly, but it was enough to break the numbness from my senses. It was a picture of Yasmin, she was happy, smiling . . . and she had new shoes.

The vision made me laugh. One thing Yasmin had always wanted was a pair of new shoes, mainly to buy them herself, it was her definition of success. Fancy shoes meant you must have it all.

I found myself waving at the dust, knowing that as I did, the vision would fade before I could see her wave back. I promised her then and there that if one day, I ever got out of this place, I would buy the most expensive pair of high heels I could find and display them on my wall just for her.

Her voice echoed in my mind. "Just make sure they're sparkly, sweetie!"

Chapter 10

LLYS HAD SEEN me a lot in the months I'd spent in a daze. I think I must have worried her because that day, as I sauntered into her office ten minutes late, she didn't scowl. In fact I thought she was going to get up from behind her desk and hug me senseless. I know she was seriously considering it, her aura danced like the Northern Lights.

"You're okay?"

I shook my head. "I don't think I'll ever be that. But I'm with it again, if that means anything."

She smiled. "It does. May I ask what sparked this?"

"Depends if you are prepared for me to talk about freaky stuff."

Llys smiled again. Hell, she *was* glad to see me.

"I will take it. Just don't expect me to buy it."

I nodded and sat in the chair. It felt like yesterday, not months ago, that I had been strapped to it. "I saw her—she's okay—she has new shoes."

Llys laughed. It was actually nice that she got Yasmin as much as I had. Whichever way we had got there, the conclusions were the same.

"You know, I don't agree that you have a gift, but I will concede that you were right. I only wished I could have convinced the police to listen to you."

I shrugged. "A tip off from a person locked up ain't really going to win you brownie points."

Llys sighed. "I guess not. Have you seen the others?"

I shook my head. "No. I just hope they're okay and they're speaking to me."

"They are. Nora has found an outlet."

I cocked my head. Nora was always fiddling with her hands, her nerves and her worries with nowhere to go, so they turned on her instead. "What did you convince her to do? And can you see her hands under the Band-Aids?"

Llys laughed. "She doesn't pick anymore."

I shook my head. That *couldn't* be possible, could it? "What did you do to her?"

"Art therapy."

I folded my arms. "Bison tried that . . . made her worse."

Llys nodded. "Very true. Mostly because he was unimpressed she wasn't Renoir at first try."

"You know he should have been committed too, right?"

Llys said nothing, she didn't have to, her thoughts sung like church bells on summer evenings.

"Thought so."

After that session, I started to get a sense that Llys trusted me. I was one of the longest servers there. I could help her to get a feel for the other girls. I was happy to help. I figured that as I hadn't been able to save Yasmin, maybe, somehow, I could help stop the others going the same way.

The institution where I lived wasn't easy to cope with. Most people got shoved from pillar to post. Lesser offenders flitted in and out. Then, they'd get shifted to another institution. It was unusual for anyone to stay more than eight years in one place.

The folks at the top had some kind of policy that shifted everyone around to stop them becoming institutionalized. Toward the end of their terms, some of the girls would go to half-way houses or minimum security places. It was always like watching salmon trying to get to the top of the river, some would make it and some would just come right back.

Thing is, you stay in a place long enough, it becomes a habit, you get in a routine and us humans love our routines. Makes us feel in control.

So, you can imagine what someone who has lived in one place for five or so years would feel like when someone says, "right, now we're going to move you someplace else." It was pretty distressing to watch and for days before the transfer list was announced, the whole institution descended into mayhem. I always expected to be on the list. I never was though, which was really odd. Not that I cared either way. I didn't really have strong feelings about anything much. I just hated the panic it stirred up.

Especially around a full moon.

Chapter 11

THE MOON IS so beautiful, she shimmers through the clouds or glows with the red of an unseen sunset. Sometimes I can even see a face on her. I think it's the sea of tranquility. Whatever it is, it's captivating and I ain't the only one to think so, I don't think. Her magnetic presence has been a source of fascination for mankind since someone looked up and saw it hanging there on a cloudless night.

Did you know that the moon apparently controls the tides of the sea? So, is it a surprise when the human brain with its squishy fluid gets affected by her pull? A pull so strong that it moves the earth's oceans? Some people seem fine with it. I don't know what it is exactly but I know that here, the effects of that pull fill me with dread. Not because the people here become monsters or nothing, but because of the torment.

You see, I feel them all . . . in here.

I'm trapped in a big concrete lump with hundreds of tortured souls. And during a full moon, especially before the transfer list, their pain roared through the halls like a giant wave of agony. The only place I could escape was the gym.

As dumb as it sounds, pumping, running, hauling, rowing helps me to focus on just the physical. It's my therapy, I guess. I stop thinking and receiving all the signals and relax.

Not that my mind ever calms totally. I've got too many scars, too many thoughts for that but here in this empty gym, I found a little solace. It was the only thing I ever asked for a little peace now and again. So, you can imagine my irritation when I felt someone wander into my little space.

"Mind if I join you?"

I turned at the sound of Llys's voice. She didn't look like the kind of woman who was a gym bunny.

"Sure, as long as you keep your emotions to yourself."

Llys raised her eyebrow. "I'm on nightshift . . . busy couple of days."

I nodded and went back to my set of fifty but I could sense her watching me. She wasn't here to work out, she was here to talk.

"Spit it out, Doc," I said.

"Am I that obvious?"

I nodded. "To me you are. Don't worry about Aimee, she's always uptight until she realizes she ain't leaving."

Llys slumped down on the weight bench next to me. "She's being moved."

I put down the weights before I threw them. "What?"

"They sent me the list today. She's being moved. They want to try integrating her back into society."

I got up, walked to the punching bag, and beat the crap out of it. "Let me guess, there's nothing you can do."

Llys was hurt by my comment. She pretended otherwise but she felt it.

"I didn't mean . . . I'm sorry . . . full moon and all that," I offered.

Llys nodded acceptance of the apology.

"You know, she won't cope with norms. Someone will say the wrong thing and—" I hit the bag hard to emphasize the point.

"I know but unless she can prove she's not ready . . ." Llys said.

I looked at her for a moment, realizing why she was paying a visit to the gym when no one else would be around. "And what kind of something would help convince?"

"She once told me she was a spaceman in a former life," Llys said. "If I think she believes that she is one . . . say now . . . then, I could put it down to the stress of her being moved and stop it happening again."

I turned to her. "I don't think she needs to be here for *that* long, Doc."

Llys smiled. "I agree, but until she has healed up enough she needs to be somewhere she feels safe, and for some odd reason, that's here."

I nodded. Aimee had been through most of the institutions in the country before ending up here. She was happy here, even when I had been zoned out for months. Aimee, Nora, and Tiz were really close now. They were all a couple of years younger than me and it felt really nice to know they could keep each other going.

"Spaceman," I started. "Got any spare fishbowls?"

Llys laughed and patted me on the shoulder.

When she was six, she fell off her bike, she had three stitches in her left arm. Her boyfriend in school was the prom king, she adored him. They married in the snow in front of a hundred friends and family. He left her two years later for a teenager he'd met at a club. She passed every exam with top grades in med school and flew into the top position at a leading university. Her "relationship" with her Dean had seen that come to an abrupt end and she was shunted into this job. She'd hated every second, first of all, but now after starting to see people beyond her medical assessments, she felt happy. Her mother always called her Tess, always. The reason why it irritated her so much was that it was her sister's name.

I shook the information free from my head. Too much data uploading causes my brain to freeze like a computer would.

"What just happened?" Llys asked, rubbing her hand.

"Are you okay?" I asked.

"Apart from the massive static shock you just gave me, fine."

I smiled, relieved that she didn't have a clue how much I had just learned about her. "Probably just the bag." I thumped it for good measure.

"So, you'll talk to Aimee?"

I nodded. "Doc's orders."

She smiled and started to leave.

"Hey, Doc?"

She turned and raised an eyebrow. "What's your name?"

The question seemed to catch her off guard, she worried if I was playing with her.

"Just a simple answer, Doc. You know my name."

"Serena," she answered.

I saw the uncomfortable wobble her aura gave off. "Serena's a really nice name. I knew you weren't a Tess."

"And how is that?" Llys folded her arms.

"Your certificate says S. Llys, not T."

Llys laughed and left me to my work out and I needed it. How the hell was I going to convince Aimee to go along with the plan? How was she going to pull it off? And how the hell had I managed to win the doc 'round?

Must have been the moon.

Chapter 12

BEING IN A secure institution wasn't a lot of fun, especially when it was for psychiatric reasons. Yet, there were times when somehow, we managed to make fun of the hell we lived in. That was going to be my pitch to Aimee anyway. It was bad enough knowing that you had a malfunction somewhere inside your head but being asked to play on it really pushed it.

And that's what I was asking Aimee to do.

I don't think that Aimee was wrong about being a spaceman in a past life. Even I couldn't tell that much about past lives, but she came out with feelings and quotes that were not in the least like the Aimee I know. I'm not sure what the medical name for Aimee was but she heard things. I couldn't see the people that whispered to her, and I can normally see spirits if they're present. Aimee believed what she saw and heard was real but I couldn't see any of those nasty black clouds with tentacles, and her brain seemed to work well, unlike many of the psychopaths here who seemed to have an entire section of their brains switched off.

Aimee, to me, seemed to be able to hear a hell of a lot better.

I told Llys that, and she smiled at my evaluation. See, the thing was, none of the psychiatrists had ever diagnosed her with anything definite. But one day Aimee woke up, took a rifle, and shot every adult male that she could find—which totaled five. Before that, she had been a happy-go-lucky kid with a loving family. A family that still visited her weekly. Aimee simply gave the reason, that the voice in her head had told her that these men were evil.

Now, normally when someone hears those kind of things, I can see the odd fluctuations they give off. I'm not sure if it's a short circuit or they really are picking up someone else's thoughts—but with Aimee—there was nothing. That was when Llys told me something.

"She's lying," she said.

"What do you mean?"

Llys smiled at me, she'd gotten warmer with her expressions after Yasmin. "There's nothing wrong with her. Well, there is. Just not the mental health issue she is portraying."

"I don't know what you mean?"

Llys wheeled her chair over to mine and dropped her voice. "She murdered someone and wanted to cover it up."

This news floored me. I had a million questions and none of them were pleasant. I felt cheated, why the hell would Aimee pretend to have problems?

Llys seemed to read my thoughts and placed her hand on the arm of my chair. "Aimee shot the man who attacked her sister. She then shot the other men who testified to his alibi. The police wouldn't help the family, didn't believe them, and so Aimee made sure her sister wouldn't have to live with seeing them."

What can you say to that? I'd have done the same. "Why crazy?" I asked.

Llys smiled. "Aimee is very intelligent. She worked out her defense before she committed her crime."

"You said she needed to heal. If she's so calculated, why?"

Llys met my eyes, gray, clear, baring her soul. "Aimee was in love with one of them."

I got a flash of Aimee in her normal pose, she would always fiddle with a gold ring she hung around her neck on a chain. A ring too big to fit her little hands.

"Didn't the police figure it out?"

Llys nodded. "They did, but they couldn't prove otherwise as the original complaint that Aimee's sister made had never been filed."

"How is her sister?"

Llys shook her head. "Moved away. That's all Aimee will say."

I rubbed my hand through my hair. "So, why did she want to come here?"

"I think Aimee knew she needed help to process what had happened. Now she's told me the truth, we're doing just that."

I grinned. "You know. You're not bad . . . for a doc."

"Thank you."

A couple of hours later, I sat next to Aimee while Nora showed Tiz her masterpiece. I'd thought about a million ways to break the news softly to Aimee but when I opened my mouth it was neither soft nor eloquent.

"You're getting shifted," I said.

Aimee launched into a tirade, screaming that her *voice* was angered. The scene normally tormented me as if I was going through the very same thing. To watch someone you care about suffer was hell on earth but this time, I knew better. Not only did I know better but it irritated the hell out of me.

I never raise my voice, I don't have outbursts unless I'm really upset and because of that, and the fact I'm tall and built like Samson, it seems to terrify everyone when I do and Aimee in particular was petrified. I grabbed the bench and hurled it across the cafeteria. I knew Llys would be watching and would keep the guards at bay for a moment.

"What are you doing?" she asked.

"I can't take it anymore. It's too much, those voices hurting you."

I flipped over another bench. Being destructive was actually quite fun.

Aimee grabbed me. "Stop, please . . . I'm okay now . . . stop."

I gripped her by the shoulders. "Of course *you're* okay . . . You're a spaceman."

Aimee looked at me like I'd grown three heads. "Aeron, you're scaring me."

"Why? You've seen loads of aliens, right?"

Aimee caught the glint of something in my eyes.

"You know spacemen can't leave the ship. Who the hell would fly this thing?"

A second later Aimee was on the table, using her dessert bowl as a helmet. "I will not leave my crew!"

"Never!" I yelled.

Nora and Tiz joined in. The wonderful thing about these places was that we made our own entertainment. The dafter the better. Within minutes the entire cafeteria was filled with inmates with dessert bowl helmets, some still with Jell-O inside and fork phasers.

Aimee merrily led the adventure for almost an hour before Llys finally sent in the guards to break it up.

Most of us hadn't had so much fun in years. Being locked up did have the occasional perk. As we were herded back to our cells, Aimee mouthed her thanks. She didn't need to, I knew how much it meant to her that someone shared her secret.

Chapter 13

LLYS WAS ON the phone as I got to the session. I could see that she was getting the kind of news she wanted to hear. I hoped it was Aimee getting to stay but I was quite happy to have another few hours of recreating space camp.

"Thank you, I'll be in touch," Llys told the other person and ended the call. She looked up and feigned a smile. "I was impressed at your little show earlier."

I shrugged, sensing that Llys wasn't happy about something.

"I've never seen you violent," she said.

I looked up at her. She thought she had spotted something and I knew it had set her alarm bells ringing. "I was trying to help Aimee."

"You threw that bench half the length of the room."

I nodded. "You know I work out."

"You were angry."

I sighed. "I was. She had been lying to me . . . for years. How was I supposed to feel?"

Llys tutted. "I thought you could see the future."

I frowned. "You breaking the truce?"

Llys nodded. "If you could see everything, you would have known."

I shook my head. "It doesn't work like that. I don't want to see or sense anything about anyone. Don't you understand? I don't want to know my friends personal thoughts."

"But you think you do, so why was Aimee different?"

"People who ain't emotionally charged can be harder to read. Some people are good at concealing it. I don't know how or why?"

Llys made the prayer-like pose with her hands again. "I thought you were an expert."

"No one gave me a freakin' handbook."

I jumped to my feet and paced. She'd tricked me, like Aimee, she'd used me to help and then used it against me. The truce was not only off, it was obliterated.

"You don't need one if you will just admit that it may not be real."

I turned to Llys. "You've been lying to me?"

"You. Tell. Me."

Provoking an Empath is probably a hell of a lot more dangerous than provoking any other inmate. Especially when you are scared of their gifts. I stomped over to her and snatched the pen she always played with in the sessions.

"You tell your friends that your favorite food is nouveau cuisine because you think it makes you look more sophisticated when your real favorite is a croque-madame. You wear high heels even when your feet are so sore that you can barely walk because your ex-husband left you for a girl over six foot—"

"Stop it!"

I shook my head. "Your mother calls you Tess, because she knows that to call you the name of the sister you hate makes you feel pathetic. She thinks it toughens you up but all it has ever done is rip away your self confidence."

Her desperation made me see past the barrier she'd erected, everything clear. She tried to snatch the pen away. "Your favorite color is blue, you have two dogs called Sasha and Misha, your dad was your hero, your first pet was a goldfish named George."

I leaned on the desk and threw the pen down. "And you are wearing red lacy underwear that you bought as a luxury to make yourself feel better when you're stuck in a hell hole day in, day out."

Llys looked at me, her face pale. There was a crap load more I could tell her and she knew it. I knew now I'd seen the truth.

"Forget the job. Get the hell out of my life," I barked and slammed the office door behind me as I left.

I stormed down the hall. The guard, Val, went to grab me. I turned around and pinned her against the wall. "You ever lay a finger on me again and I'll rip your tongue out and feed it to you."

She dropped to the floor with a thud as I let her go. I knew Llys was watching. I knew she didn't know what to think.

One thing was for certain. I was done helping.

Chapter 14

I STORMED into my cell, slammed it shut behind me, and the fury got worse. I felt like one of the fury-fiends. Over and over I kept re-running what Llys had said. Even after everything, after Yasmin, she still thought I was a whack job. I dropped to the floor, hoping that push-ups would help me to calm down but it didn't work.

Maybe I *was* responsible for everything. I mean, I had known what Lori would do. I didn't stop it. Was I the black cloud? Did I have tentacles? Was I a leech?

Stuff always happened around me. The weather got weird when I was in a bad mood. Mishaps always seemed to happen when I was near . . . that was why they thought I was a trouble maker. Was I? Was that what Llys could see?

I sped up my repetitions, the rain slammed against the window, the weather reflecting my mood.

Every catastrophe that had happened, I could see them, feel them, hear the screams, and I lived the fear and panic of the people involved. Places that I had never been, people I didn't know, rocketed pain into the deepest part of me. So had I caused them? What the hell was I?

Jake had suffered, he had suffered greatly. It wasn't instant when the train hit. I knew that but instead of running the mile or whatever down the track to attempt to save him, I did nothing. I had all this knowledge that I didn't want and I didn't ask for.

Well, no more. I wasn't going to live with this stupid crap a second longer. I wanted it gone. To do that meant I needed help from someone, someone who at least believed that these things could be possible. That meant going to the one place that scared me far more than any vision.

Chapter 15

DISCERNMENT IS THE ability to judge well. It's something that comes from experience. So, when I wandered into the chapel, my experiences had taught me that this chaplain was going to think I had a screw loose.

To my surprise I couldn't have been more wrong.

Now, I'm not a particularly religious sort. I understand all the billions of points of view and belief systems and I'm quite happy to think that there's good and evil in the world. I get that, I have seen the bad in action. What I wanted to know was, what the hell was I supposed to do with these *burdens*?

The chaplain wasn't actually a chaplain. The normal guy was apparently on a retreat but the man who was there instead was Father James McLaughlin. He was a Roman Catholic and a Jesuit, which was an Ignatian, too. I didn't know what that meant when he told me but, to summarize: St. Ignatius believed that you could discern what was good or bad by how it made you feel.

In a nutshell, if it made you feel all good things—joy, peace, happiness etc.—then it was from a good place. If it made you feel hate or violence etc., then it probably wasn't from a great place. It seemed pretty simple put that way. So, I asked him about fear. My visions terrified me, and I told him all about them. I expected him to start flicking water over me but the guy didn't. Instead he told me that some people in his faith were prophets, they had gifts and some of those gifts were scary.

He even told me that some people had been petrified when angels had appeared to them. I didn't blame them. People were scary enough. A vision of an angel hovering with its huge wings would more than likely convince me that I *was* crazy.

Then he gave me a passage. He told me that I had choices, that I should talk to the Big Dude about them. I wasn't quite sure about yabbering to the ceiling but I did take the passage and I used its principles to build a wall. It was all about armor and how the believer's faith could keep him or her safe.

That was when I built my own armor.

You see, every time I touch a door handle, a table, anything that someone has touched before me, I pick up their signals. I wander around battered by people's thoughts and feelings day and night. The only place I don't is my cell. So, I asked for gloves. I wore them everywhere. The barrier worked too. I stopped seeing Jean's obsession with jigsaws and Tiz's love for shiny objects. I refused to see Llys again too.

I had resigned myself to spending my days here. It was as good a place as any. The less people I had to press my buttons the better for my equilibrium. The fact that Llys didn't push it told me she was afraid of me. I was glad. If she was afraid, she would leave me the hell alone.

I did one other thing. I needed something other than a workout to take my mind off the world around me. I tried listening to music first but artists leave a part of their essence in their work. It's like listening to a life story on an audio book. No, I needed an outlet. So I requested a violin and as I had been in the prison for so long I got it without any arguments.

I didn't know if I was any good and I didn't care. I enjoyed it and hour after hour I learned every piece of music I could find. So my armor was in place and I found a little more solace than I had before.

Chapter 16

SERENA LLYS LOOKED at her appointment list and wrote in DNA—Did Not Attend—next to Aeron Lorelei's name. Aeron perplexed her somewhat. A fierce intelligence lay beneath her gentle eyes and under her impressive athletic stature lay a very large heart.

One thing Serena had learned about Aeron over the year she had been the head psychiatrist and that was Aeron Lorelei adored her friends. Aeron had no idea how much comfort she brought them. Not many inmates crossed her and that, coupled with her . . . talents . . . unnerved even her fiercest enemies.

In short, Aeron was a force of nature.

She had no idea how frightening she was. Aeron Lorelei in a temper was akin to a cyclone sweeping through the institution. And Serena had ignited that temper. Yet, at no point did this supposedly vicious murderess threaten her well-being. All Aeron had done was prove a point that had been obvious to Serena from day one. Aeron had no affliction of the mind that should see her in this place. Aeron *could* see everything that she said she did . . . and Serena had no doubt, much more.

Serena sighed and looked down at Doctor Bison's file on Aeron.

Unknown to Aeron, Bison had been a close friend of Mayor Roger Casey, Jake Casey's father. Bison had made very sure that Aeron would never be released. He had marked her as sociopathic, psychopathic, prone to inciting violence, and taking pleasure from the chaos. He had noted her as sadistic, had even fabricated several instances in support of his theories, and Serena had believed the entire thing. Only after being here for months and watching Aeron, did she change her opinion. Aeron suffered alone, protected her friends, and projected a calmness that gave strength and courage to all around her.

It had worn away at Serena's dislike. Then after seeing the affect Yasmin's death had inflicted on Aeron, she had resolved never to doubt Aeron again.

But, when Aeron had hurled the bench halfway across the

cafeteria, Serena had assumed the worst. She had assumed that Aeron had been toying with her all along and it had stung.

Serena looked at the pen on her desk. Professional pride, she was terrible for it. All insecurity based, she was honest with herself enough to admit that. And so, Aeron who had just helped her friend Aimee not to be thrown at the mercy of the world, had gotten the blunt end of Serena's bruised ego.

Unprofessional, unkind, uncalled for, and unnecessary. Serena added irredeemable to that list.

Whatever hurt she had caused Aeron, she was now isolated from everything. The gifts that she possessed, the ones that could help so many, had now been bound by barriers and solitude.

And it was up to Serena to fix it.

The problem was, Aeron Lorelei scared the hell out of her. Not only had she recited secrets that even Serena's closest friends didn't know but she knew why Serena was there in the first place. That, and she got under her skin and *no one* got under her skin. *No one.*

So far she had said nothing but she knew that Aeron had seen. She knew the truth and that was dangerous for them both. She tapped her pen against her notepad. What to do?

She got up from her desk and headed out into the corridor, ignoring Val and her cronies gossiping and taking bets on which newcomer would break first. She headed to the gym but it was empty and the only other place Aeron would be at this time was her cell. The closer she got to the cell, the more entranced she became by the beautiful strains of violin music wafting from someone's radio.

The tune was from the *Moonlight Sonata*. Breathtakingly beautiful and emotive on piano and now it was being sung by a lone violin and took on an eerie sorrow that gripped right at her soul. She got to Aeron's cell door and her heart lifted. She couldn't contain the gasp of delight that fell from her lips.

Aeron stood, in her tiny cell, her eyes closed as she produced the most heavenly sound that Serena had ever heard. The melody pulled at her, it's mournful, emotional release coursing into her, hypnotizing her into a meditative state, leaving her breathless. Her tears fell thick and fast as she listened to this lone soul pour out her heart to her wooden friend that reached places she never realized were possible. Far beyond this place they soared, higher and higher in a siren-like serenade. A lonely, lost angel in a world where no one understood her. What life had she known?

On and on it built, the crescendo of chorus, the dips and pauses, the mighty Beethoven's Sonata filling the air like moonlight dancing on the rippled sea of her emotions. The sweet solo finished and Aeron opened her eyes. She nodded curtly at Serena.

"Incredible," Serena whispered, her voice hoarse from tears. Her senses reverberated as though her own heart had been as bowed as the violin.

Aeron said nothing. She placed the instrument into its case and sat on the bed.

"I didn't know it had been done on violin."

Aeron shrugged. "I liked the music, so I adapted it."

Serena walked into the cell to look at the music notation. She had played a little cello in school and she knew enough to know that the elaborately written manuscript was the work of a virtuoso.

"It's just for me," Aeron said, as if reading her mind. "I ain't playing to a theatre full of people . . . even if they are ten feet away."

"Have I hurt you that badly?"

Aeron met her eyes for the briefest of moments. Yes she had. Serena had wounded her. Aeron had put her trust in her and it had been shattered.

"It's too late to apologize to you, the damage is done," Serena said, placing the score back on top of the tiny dresser. "But, for what it's worth, I am truly sorry."

Aeron nodded but her eyes were fixed on the wall, the same as when Yasmin had died.

Serena knew that Aeron thought that she felt nothing, but about herself, she was always wrong. Aeron felt *everything*, that was her problem. She felt so fiercely that her brain simply couldn't cope with the onslaught. Serena was going to have to do something drastic in order to show her exactly how much of a hero she could be. But, for now, simple words would have to suffice.

Serena looked Aeron long and hard in the eyes, so that she would know every single word was true. "I believe you."

Chapter 17

I HAD PRETTY much figured that I was in for life, that my gifts would forever mark me as someone to be kept from society. So imagine my surprise when the transfer list announced that I was getting out. I had to ask the warden to read it again when she said it. I was being thrown out. I had been inside for over a decade, for my *entire* adulthood. What the hell was I going to do out there?

Tiz, Aimee, and Nora celebrated like I had just won a fortune but I was too terrified to move a muscle. Where the hell would I go?

A load of thoughts shot through my head about how I could convince Llys to let me stay. Was that why she'd come to see me? The statement of belief a mere parting gift? What the hell would I do in the real world? Who would give someone like me a job? How would I feed myself? I'd end up a hobo, I'd end up cold and alone, I'd end up like Yasmin.

"You'll be just fine," Llys said from behind me.

I spun around, fighting the urge to grip her and shake the sense back into her. "Don't do this. I did everything you asked."

"It's not a punishment—"

"Ain't it? Where the hell will I live?"

I heard my voice echo off the walls, the guards edgy. My friendly guard had been gone for months and was well into motherhood. There were no comrades on the other side now.

"You've served your sentence—"

"So you abandon me? Like Yasmin?"

"Calm down," Llys said.

"Calm down? You just signed for me to get thrown into a world where I don't know how the hell to exist!"

The guards all had their hands on their new weapons—stun guns.

"Why don't we just go to my office?"

I backed off. Oh no. She'd suckered me in for the last time.

She'd fooled me good too. I didn't know who she was but she sure as hell could fake her signals.

"What if I commit another crime?" I said.

"Then you will go to a mainstream prison."

"What?" Aimee said, stomping over. "Are you nuts?"

Tiz and Nora were at Aimee's shoulders, all three in various states of worry—Aimee scratching, Nora picking, and Tiz rocking on the balls of her feet. Llys surrounded.

"Ladies, my office . . . please," Llys urged, shooting a glance at the guards drawing their guns.

"No! I've heard enough of your lies."

I ran. I ran so fast that none of the guards could catch me. I ran to the only place that I could hide. I was on the roof before anyone realized. Not to jump, just to think. The place was littered with old pallets and plastic crates but I could breathe here . . . breathe in fresh air. Hell, I was going to faint. I couldn't process it. The panic hammered through my heart like nails in a coffin. I'd never survive out there. Out there hated me, in here was bad enough but I knew in here, I knew how it worked. Out there I didn't know, I didn't know a damn thing.

"Aeron, please. Calm down. Listen to me . . . for a moment."

I spun to look at Llys. The guards were all gathered down in the yard below.

"What did I do to you? What the hell did I ever do to you?" I picked up a broken crate and hurled it down at the guards below, making them scatter.

"Nothing, Aeron. You should have never been here for this long. You could go to Nan's cabin. Maybe she—"

"She's dead. That's why I met Sam. Nan abandoned me too!" I picked up a pallet. "How the hell am I gonna feed myself?"

Llys moved forward. I hurled the pallet from the roof. "You'll find a way. You can find peace there. Nature . . . fishing . . . Do you like fishing?"

"I hate fishing! I know what it does to them." I hurled another pallet.

"How about gardening? Hiking in the woods? Aeron, there's a beautiful world of nature out there . . . waiting for you."

I rubbed my arms. I felt cold all of a sudden, really cold and tired. My jaw trembled and I lost every ounce of energy I had. I slumped onto the ground. There *was* a world out there. A world that I had resigned myself that I would never see. Now Llys was offering it to me. I looked past the concrete to the patchwork of fields beyond—so green, so bright, so vivid. Life in abundance.

"What if I end up on the street?"

Llys sat beside me and took my gloved hand. "It won't be easy but I will have to see you once a month to satisfy parole requirements. The girls will expect letters and I'm pretty sure that there's a set of high heels waiting for you to hang."

I squeezed Llys's hand. Then I felt something warm on my cold cheeks. I took off my glove and touched it. I looked down and my fingers were wet. I rubbed them together and looked up to the sky—was it raining? Warm rain? No—I was crying. I was free.

Chapter 18

I STOOD OUTSIDE the prison gates with enough money in my pocket to buy food for a week and the clothes that I had on eleven years ago when I arrived. They didn't fit but I didn't have nothing else. Llys had prepped me session after session for my release. She had helped me to plan a route back to the place where I had lived and she'd even tried to make contact with my parents.

The route we had figured out easily. There was a bus that could take me the entire journey. It wasn't a massive distance. Probably less than an hour but after my life had existed within half a square mile for so long, it seemed like another continent.

As for my parents, neither dignified Llys with a response. I expected as much. It wasn't like they had wanted me in the first place. I was pretty sure that they had hired someone to take my place so that their social status hadn't been affected.

The bus wouldn't arrive for a while. I turned and looked at the place that I'd lived in for so long. Why was I going back home? The simple answer was that I had to. The "powers" demanded that I remained within a set distance of the institute, mainly so I could be visited at any time and inspected. I also had a great big ol' piece of plastic stuck to my ankle, so disobeying that command was not really much of an option.

Within that radius, I had three options. The first, St. Louis, was a non-starter. Even if Yasmin hadn't died there, it was too crowded, too many people, and way too much noise.

The second option, Fredericktown, was a small town. A mass of houses, happy folks, and pristine lawns and no one there would want an ex-con working or living nowhere near them.

I had no money and so my only real option was Oppidum—and more to the point, Nan's cabin. The stretch of river that it was perched on was isolated from everything. Nowhere near tourists, too wild and cut off for anyone to want to set up home. There, I could just keep to myself. I guess, pretty much like Nan had.

I felt a wriggle in my stomach and rubbed my hand across the bare skin. I looked like I'd been marooned on a desert island. I shivered, but not from the cold. For all I knew, there could be a hotel on Nan's cabin now. I know my mother really wanted to cash in on the tourist trade. There could be a great big ol' lodge with canoes and ATVs tearing up the country in summer and snowmobiles thundering through the mountains in winter.

I felt sick at the thought.

Well, there was only one way I was going to find out. The bus pulled up, I took the backpack my life was piled in and boarded the bus. I had never been so terrified in my entire life.

Chapter 19

NOW, BUS JOURNEYS for ordinary folk are pretty straightforward. You get on, you read or fall asleep, you arrive at your destination, disembark, and go on your way, *simple*. When you are like me and you've been involuntarily secluded for so long, it's like climbing Mount Everest with a toothpick. Although Llys felt I wasn't suffering from an affliction that should keep me locked up, I do have scars and even she would admit that I was so institutionalized I probably couldn't cope with living on the outside.

Spending so much time in Serenity Hills pretty much had gotten me into a single routine, my days were routine. And, if I'm honest, having spent so long confined inside the walls, being outside them felt kinda freaky. Every sense told me that being outside wasn't allowed.

Llys had rehearsed the entire thing with me to help. Each day we'd walked out the gates and back in, a couple of steps further each time, the guards keeping a beady eye. Today, the guards hadn't even glanced in my direction. I wasn't their concern no more. Llys had walked me up to the gates, she'd even stayed a while until her next appointment had called her away. So she drummed the baby steps way into me. Positive visualization, she called it. Take it step-by-step was the mantra.

After one last lingering glance back at the gates, I turned and walked onto the huge, cranky bus. The smell of car freshener and that unique bus odor made my head swim. The driver looked at me bored. He was clearly used to crazies. My chest tightened. What was I doing? I shouldn't be out here, I should be safe, in my cell, with my violin. *Don't look up . . . just focus on the driver . . . one . . . step . . . at a time.*

I pulled out the ticket that Llys had helped me buy and watched in slow motion as my gloved hand stretched out, shaking like I was standing on a fault line.

He took my ticket and looked up at me. He tapped his newspaper. "No trouble. Got it?"

This hadn't been part of our rehearsal routine. My skin sprung a leak, soaking my t-shirt in sweat, my heart pounded in my ears. "I . . . what?"

The driver picked up the newspaper and gave it to me. "I want the sports section when you get off."

I nodded as I took the paper and stumbled down the aisle. A group of teenagers sat in the back. Their voices were booming, harsh, and aggressive.

In their bid to impress each other, they hurled abuse at a few people passing by the bus. Their hormones were thick like summer air coating the atmosphere in tense frustration. I looked up. I knew one of them thought about taking a shot at me until he gauged my size and where I had just been picked up. *Not a good idea, buddy.*

The bus was filled with people, some were inmates from the main prison. They lifted their eyes with knowing looks. One guy was dabbing his head with a hanky. He had been in longer than I had. He met my eyes and I smiled, seeming as I knew how he felt. He nodded and turned back to dabbing his forehead.

I found a seat next to the middle door, where the bus drivers slept on long journeys. I sat beside the window and placed my backpack—its logo showing people where I had been let out from–beside me. I hoped it would put off anyone who felt friendly.

As I'm not exactly small, the seat felt like being buried alive while sitting on one of those plastic chairs for toddlers. How the hell I was going to last the hour, I didn't know. I unfolded the newspaper, thinking at least I could read. I stared at the headlines and my mouth turned into a desert.

Town's outrage as violent killer released.

It was me. For long seconds I thought about jumping from the bus and running back to the prison but I didn't. Instead, I read on, which made everything worse.

> The population of Oppidum was in an uproar last night as news broke of the release of Aeron Lorelei. Lorelei was convicted of killing one of the town's children, Jake Casey, luring him to a secluded area and throwing him in front of a high-speed train.

There was further evidence, not submitted at the time of trial, that Lorelei was trying to derail the express-line train and that Casey had tried to stop her. Unable to prove what was so obvious to onlookers in court, Lorelei was convicted of manslaughter and sentenced to a mere eight years in a mental institution. However, due to several incidents of Lorelei's violence, the sentence was increased to eleven.

The town's mayor petitioned the prison officials to keep Lorelei from returning to Oppidum but the official responded saying, "Individuals who have served their sentences have the same rights as those within society. We will not comment on individual cases but every prisoner who is released is carefully monitored."

Mayor Roger Casey responded to the statement in a speech to the town meeting. "Lorelei, returning to the place where the family of her victim still lives, not only proves the need for the overhaul of the law in this country but it shows that this government, our government, has a blatant lack of respect for the rights of the average taxpayer."

Lorelei's return to Oppidum has caused concern in local schools who fear that the predator may strike again.

The local police chief Eli Lorelei, Aeron's father, said, "All evidence regarding Aeron Lorelei has been dealt with through the right channels. There is no proof to the unsubstantiated claims in the media that Lorelei did anything more than of what she was convicted. As for all offenders re-introduced into society, myself and my officers will be on hand to support, assist, or enforce as necessary."

These words ring hollow for many residents who believe that Chief Lorelei was aware of his daughter's sadistic nature long before the murder took place. Only time will tell if Lorelei has been cured of her love for violence or if she has simply been let free to kill again.

My stomach felt like someone had poured concrete into it. The story was ten pages. The newspaper had interviewed everyone they could find, including some "insiders" at the prison. I knew who the insider was, it was Val. She had delighted in telling the press how I had threatened to cut out her tongue and shove it down her throat.

I closed my eyes. The image of my sixteen-year-old self being hauled from court with a blanket over my head, the pictures of me looking "inhumane" and "unrepentant" as the verdict was read out. A mock-up of what I may look like now was even included with the words emblazoned in bold black ink: THE FACE OF A KILLER.

I buried my head in my hands. Llys thought that she had done me a favor. She was wrong. All she had done was send me to hell.

Chapter 20

I DID HAVE one thing in my favor. Thankfully, the media had no idea when I was due to arrive back. That, and I was nearly a foot taller than I had been at sixteen and, as I've said a few times, Samson-like. Which was weird in itself. I don't know where I got it from. My father was five-ten on a tall day and my mother was shorter than that. If Nan was related to me then she was even smaller. So I guess I'm a freak of nature . . . in every sense.

I handed the driver back his paper when we had stopped and turned to walk down the steps but something flickered from him and I couldn't ignore it, so I turned around.

"Get it checked out," I told him.

He looked at me.

I nodded. "You need it treated. Soon."

He searched my eyes for a moment and then smiled. "Some evil blight you are, huh?"

I shrugged. I know that he didn't believe a word of the story. Why, I didn't know, but maybe he could see through it.

"Linda wants a cruise. Make sure it ain't alone," I said.

"I will. Thanks, kid."

I walked off the bus and heard him laugh in disbelief, but I knew he'd listen.

Oppidum started at the transport hub. The bus station and private airport were stuck in a clump on the edge of town.

As the place was primed for tourists, for those who loved the outdoors, it was busy, filled with people in too much of a rush.

For that, today, I was thankful.

I passed by the newsstands splashed with my baby-faced self and wandered a mile down Main Street. Lodges and attractions towered in various Tudor-esque forms, some with thatched roofs for that little extra effect. Their signs flashed "vacancy" like they were a distress signal. Oppidum had started life as a Welsh settlement way back when a few folk felt they missed home so much that they decided to recreate it in the middle of the Ozarks. It's funny how being away from a place would make them so fond of it. Who was I to argue? I hadn't ever been out of the state.

It was not yet summer and most of the tourists would not arrive for another month or so. The sun had a gentle warmth to it and the few clouds glowed pink in the deep blue. The weather was nice enough for a lot of off-season tourists to be wandering around. It also meant that the locals had to get in tourist-mode and pretend they were happy, carefree, friendly people with a smile plastered on their faces instead of remembering how miserable and angry at the world they really were.

And right now, they were angrier than normal, despite the sunny smiles they showed the tourists.

I'd thought about trying to get to Nan's without telling a soul but I had to report to the police department to have my ankle bracelet checked. Years of experience had armed me with the knowledge that I would be kept waiting until somebody plucked up the courage to deal with me. No one wanted to be seen anywhere near me let alone get close enough to touch me.

Deciding that I didn't want to sit around on an empty stomach, I stuck my threadbare baseball cap on and hoped I looked different enough at nearly twenty eight to get served at the Ty Coch café.

Ty Coch was set up like an old cottage, with a fake stone fireplace on one side and a knitted Welsh Dragon sitting next to it. There were little ornaments of Welsh ladies in big black hats and shawls. A love spoon was proudly painted up on the big window with signs declaring that inside, folks could have all manner of weird foods they couldn't pronounce. It sure looked like the kind of place I'd find a hearty welcome but the second I stepped through the door, a wave of hostility ripped away my dumb-ass wishing for peace and brought me headlong back into reality.

Now, I knew that no one had figured out who I was but their judgment was quick and like a hammer blow. I wasn't a tourist, so they didn't have to fake it. I wasn't one of them, so they didn't like me, and I looked like a hobo, so they hated me. Bags, wallets, anything of value were tucked under protective arms as I wandered to the wooden counter filled with chocolate love spoons, tiered cake stands filled with Jell-O Welsh Cakes, and other drool-drawing stuff. Funny that the sign overhead said "Croeso" which meant Welcome but I sure as shoots felt anything but. It was like I was contagious—kinda amusing in a surreal and horrible way.

"We're closed," Mrs. Stein announced in a shrill voice. She looked like an angry crow guarding her nest behind the counter, the lines on her face seemed to mark her permanent frown. She puffed up her shoulders, arms folded, her eyes narrowed until it looked like her eyebrows might block her view.

"Takeout?" I asked, hoping my voice sounded alien from the teenager they had known.

"I said, we're closed." She stuck her nose in the air like I smelled or something. I lifted my eyes to meet the old bat's. She froze on the spot. She wasn't the only one, the entire place was still. Hell, talk about playing dodge ball.

Now, Mrs. Stein had terrified me as a kid. She had chased me with a broom when I had been barely five for dropping a milkshake on the floor. How that had changed. Her fear was so acute that I knew if I stood there a second longer her heart would good as give out.

I rubbed my palm across my chest, trying to soothe the sharp dagger of pain she was feeling. I winced as it worsened. Her panicky thoughts saying I was causing her pain . . . the freaky kid was clearly into some kind of hocus-pocus.

I wanted to tell her to take her tablets but I knew she was far too involved in her hate and fear to see anything but a threat. That knowledge made me feel sorry for her and for all of them. Imagine going through life hating everyone who didn't look, act, or feel like you? I mean, even the fury-fiends liked *some* people.

"I'm leaving," I said, hoping it would prevent her coronary.

"Good. Take a long walk off a short pier while you're at it," she snapped.

I turned. I recognized many of the faces and I was guessing there was no doubting they recognized me. Everyone was locked onto me, forks frozen half way to mouths, men wrapped protective arms around their wives, and every one of them narrowed their eyes and glared at me. A few huddled closer together as if to prove that I was alone, I wasn't one of them.

Now, fear could make people aggressive. Only years of being exposed to people who were tormented into rage stopped me from biting.

"It's nice to see you too, Mrs. Stein."

I opened the door, knowing that she had nothing to shout in response. So I left, calmly trying to ignore the bolts of hate that were being fired at me like lightning. One thing about aggression I have learned, is that it only builds if you feed it and the only thing I wanted to feed was my growling stomach.

Chapter 21

THE OTHER CAFÉS in town were closed. I hoped that if, or when the owners opened for the summer, they wouldn't turn away my business. I couldn't cook and I really wanted a good hot meal. There were two grocery stores in Oppidum. A really nice one half way down Main Street was Casey's Mart but it was run by Sam and Jake's mother. The last thing I wanted to do was face her. The only other option was my Uncle Abe's shop near the police department. It was a crooked short building—one of the original buildings in Oppidum. It was painted up all nice in red and green. But, to me, it looked more like a novelty store than the pretentious statement Abe had been shooting for. It used to be really nice when my grandfather owned it—simple stone work and a thatched roof. But Abe didn't do pretty. So the roof wasn't thatched like the others but corrugated steel. He was tight with his money to the point where his wife wandered around in hand-me-downs while he held an exclusive membership to the golf club. And, as you've probably guessed, Abe felt even less warmly toward me than Mrs. Stein did.

Uncle Abe, my father's brother, had three kids. The two girls were way older than me and pretty much escaped to the city the second they could drive. Both were high flyers and seemed to blossom out from under Abe's cloud of gloom.

The third kid, I had never met. All I knew was that his name was Uri. He was born not long before I got convicted but no doubt being a son, he was doted on like a prince. He'd probably end up a professor or something but right now he was nearly twelve.

I walked into the store, the bell tinkling my arrival, and kept my head down. I wandered to the shelves at the back and stared at all the food. Note to self—never shop when I'm hungry. Seriously. Everything looked like a three course meal—a three course meal that I couldn't cook. I settled for sandwiches and a bag of chips. Although, I didn't know what the hell had happened to chips since I'd gone inside. I picked the bag up, thinking it was a multi-pack, like twelve bags in one but no, it was *one* bag. Even the chocolate bars were twice the size.

Now, I knew Abe was watching from his counter. Old Hawkeye hovered over his store like you were about to raid his nest and he thought everyone was a pilfering little thief. In my case, this had always been right but it was down to the fact that the grumpy ol' tool would never serve me so what did he expect?

I kept my head down as I walked toward the counter and handed him my haul. He bagged them and charged me, all the while shooting to catch a glimpse of my face. He was as nosy as a crow. I could feel his little guesses. Was I a useless hobo? Was I a rich eccentric? Was I scoping out the store to break into the safe under his desk?

When I got my receipt and my goods and they were unequivocally mine, I looked up and let him see my face.

He went purple. "What the hell are you doing here?"

"Nice to see you too, Uncle Abe." Everyone was so sweet, so welcoming in this town.

"You're nothing to me. Crawling back here—"

"Pa?"

We looked at the spotty kid poking his head around the door to the back room.

"What is it, Uri?" Abe asked.

I could feel his panic, his face a picture. Uri, the prince, had revealed his hiding place. The big bad monster would surely devour him now. I looked at my uncle and would have laughed if I couldn't feel the severity of his fear. What the hell did he think I was going to do to Uri?

"Who's this?" Uri asked.

I looked at him. Oh, he was spoiled. He was spoiled, sneaky, and every bit as messed up as I had been. Only, he didn't have my burdens so I could read him like a book.

"I wouldn't if I were you," I warned.

He cocked his head. A girl talking to *him* like this? *Yeah, kid . . . you take a picture and post it and I will string you up.*

"Don't talk to Uri like that," Abe snapped.

"Unless you want the world knowing that I shopped in your store . . ." I raised an eyebrow.

Uncle Abe knew enough about my peculiarities to know I was right about the runt's intentions. "Uri, go help your mother."

Uri looked at his father with more disgust than Uncle Abe normally looked at me. "But—"

"Go!"

The kid ignored him and pulled out one of those smart phones. I knew enough from watching the guards in Serenity Hills that tapping away meant trouble. My hand was over the phone before he could snap the photo. I ripped it off him and threw it on the floor, then stamped on it for good measure.

Uri was heading the same way I had but for different reasons and no way was I letting him think he could get one over on me. Abe slipped off the stool and pulled a now sobbing brat away from me. With one hand secured around Uri, he picked up the receiver and called the police. He probably had them on speed dial.

Abe's wife, Sara, rushed in from the back and took her son away from dangerous old me. I waited patiently for the police to arrive and ate my sandwiches much to Abe's irritation. At least I could say that my homecoming had been memorable.

Chapter 22

UNSURPRISINGLY, MY FATHER answered the call. He always did follow Abe's orders but I had managed to eat my sandwiches and half the monster bag of chips before he hurried in through the door. I was unprepared for how old he'd gotten since I'd been in Serenity Hills. He'd never had masses of hair but now it was more gray than black and his face looked a lot grayer too. The best way I could've described him was weathered. He looked like I felt.

My father thought very little of me, this I knew from his words, 'cause I couldn't read a darn thing off him. Sometimes I could sense his immediate feeling, but it wasn't any more than ordinary people could sense.

One thing I had known was that my father did not believe that I had murdered Jake. He had disowned me yes, but because I had lied, I had run away from the scene and all the stupid nonsense that I believed in. That was in spite of the nonsense helping him catch a killer and gain a promotion.

"Evenin'," I said as cheerfully as I could.

My father looked ready to explode. Glaring at me, he ripped his brimmed hat off his head. "You've been here two minutes . . . two damn minutes!"

I shrugged. "Not my fault Abe can't raise his offshoots."

Abe narrowed his eyes at me, I narrowed mine back. "Get her out of my shop!"

"If you hadn't been a drama queen, I'd have left ages ago," I said.

"I want her charged," he ranted.

"What for?" my father asked, looking like he wanted to head for the whiskey.

"Criminal damage. She broke Uri's phone."

My father looked at me with the same look I had seen a million times. The "why did *you* have to be my daughter?" look. It stung like acid to my heart every time.

"Did you?" he asked.

"I warned the kid not to take pictures of me. He didn't listen."

"So that gives you the right to assault him?" Abe protested.

I laughed, finished off my chips, and threw the wrapper past his head into the trash can. "Look at me. If I had assaulted the little brat, he'd be dead."

I knew the second I had said it, it would be seen as a threat not an observation. I had no intention of hurting a soul but I was a murderer so my intentions meant diddly squat and sweet applejack as Nan would say.

Seconds later I was in the back of the police car in handcuffs.

"I was merely pointing out that at my size an assault would have been pretty noticeable," I said.

My father slammed the door and started the car. "I know."

I'd lasted less than twelve hours on the outside. That had to be some kind of a record. "Y'know, if you'd answered the doc's letters, this wouldn't have happened."

My father scowled in the rear view mirror. "So, it's my fault again, is it?"

"Partly. The doc told y'all I was coming. I could have been at Nan's hours ago."

"You think I wanted to be seen with *you*?"

I bit down my anger, my stomach already unsettled from the upheaval was now churning, my hands clenched in frustration. "Well, now you get to prove I don't mean nothing to you. Just lock me back up and forget I exist."

He said nothing as we drove past city hall where the police department was tucked into a corner of the first floor, one of the original buildings in town made of rough sandstone. Expecting him to swing into the parking lot, I frowned when he carried straight on down the road. His eyes were focused on the black top as we headed past the shops selling fishing and hunting equipment.

We neared my parents' house which was one of the newer buildings nestled back in their own private world. I stared up at the too-neat hedges cut into pretty shapes. They were all too perfect and ordered for my liking, like all the folks were terrified of breaking free of the uniform neighborhoods. I'd always felt happier in Nan's cabin.

"Will she be there?" I asked, hoping like hell my mother wouldn't be. I'd had enough drama for one day.

Again, my father didn't say a thing. He kept on driving, out over the planked bridge across one of the creeks that flowed into the river. The forest hugged the road on either side, the waning sunlight flickering through the green. Maybe he was just going to drive me straight on back to prison. How many years was it for freaking out a snotty brat?

We turned off and headed down a narrow lane that opened up to freshly furrowed fields on either side. To the right, Mrs. O'Reilly's farm sat on the horizon, a dark smudge against the glowing sunset. I could see for miles that way, nothing but flat farm land snaking into the valley. Different from straight ahead as we disappeared into more trees. The surroundings became wilder as an army of white oak lined the road either side. I'd had some good times climbing those and one painful meeting between my front teeth and a trunk. We came to a dirt and gravel lane and turned down it.

I had to hang on to the back of the front seat to keep from slamming into the roof as we seemed to hit every neglected rut and rock. Each rocking motion felt like the place was welcoming me home, the breeze rippling through the leaves before us. I could feel her, Nan, out there in the shadow of Blackbear Mountain—every branch, every blade etched with the sense of her.

I spotted the silhouetted shape of the cabin and felt an ache inside me that she wasn't there no more. Would the place I'd called a sanctuary still feel that way without her? It was the oldest place in town. I ain't exactly sure how old but I knew that generations of Loreleis had splashed in the river, heard the rumble of the waterwheel, and ate trout from up stream. I couldn't help but smile as we passed the old tree stump that my grandpa had carved Nan as a wedding present. I was pretty sure that Loreleis must grow out of the ground on the banks of the river.

With those kind of roots, my heart should have soared at the sight of the place but instead I could just about keep my teeth from grinding. It was nothing but a shell.

And shell was a polite word for it. The roof was half rotted away. The wooden door was black from where the river must have flooded the place at some point. The windows had been smashed with rocks or stones from bored kids and the wheel, which had once gotten its power from the river, was smashed up and growing its own meadow.

"It needs work," my father said.

"Stating the freakin' obvious," I muttered. "Don't I have to sign in? State I won't eat any of the town's children?"

My father flashed an irritated look in the rear-view mirror. "It's all a joke to you, isn't it? A decade in prison and you still think everything is funny."

I fought the urge not to explode in anger. The car was getting smaller as claustrophobia set in, the seat squeezing in and out. "Funny? No, I don't think being locked in a mental institution is funny . . . now, let me the hell out."

My voice filled the car and the birds nesting in the tree nearby made a break for it. My father got out and opened my door. I climbed out. The night air whipped through my ill-fitting clothes but I wasn't cold. I was too pent up. My father let me stand there, still cuffed, as he threw camping equipment and a large trunk at my feet.

"I'm surprised you didn't just torch the place to emphasize your bruised ego," I said.

He walked to me and uncuffed me. "She left it to you."

I laughed—a hollow, raw laugh. "I bet that really bugged mommy dearest. No way to milk the tourists now."

My father pulled a box of supplies from the trunk and placed it on the ground. "Your mother left me. I have a new life . . . a new family now . . . so do everyone a favor and keep away."

I pointed to my ankle. "What about my monitor?"

He knelt down, took it off, and threw it into his car. "You want supplies. Order them, grow them, hell, hike to the city—"

"That's an hour by car."

"I don't care. Just stay the hell away from town."

I pumped my fists as I looked at him. I might not be able to read him but I wasn't a skinny little kid he could bully anymore. "I served my time. I have rights. I can go where the hell I like."

My father got in his car, hiding in his metal shield. "I'm serious. If I see you near the town, you'll be in prison by nightfall."

"Very touching, *Daddy*," I shot back. "At least mother came to her senses in the end."

The jibe hit him where it hurt and he blinked. Then he scowled and screeched off.

I watched the cruiser throw up dust as he hurtled off and kicked the hell out of the stupid water wheel. To stop myself from breaking a toe I hauled the equipment and the trunk into the leaky-excuse-for-a-cabin. I cracked open the door, the bottom half splintering as I did so, and walked into the rank interior.

It was a dank, rotting ruin. The river water had made it halfway up the walls at some point, coating it with foul-smelling sludge that made even my concrete stomach twinge. Where there had been the comfort of Nan sitting in her rocking chair now was an empty space. Where she had cooked trout and concocted her herbal cures was only decay. Where there had been the grinding rumble of the wheel was a solemn, echoing drip, drip, drip. It felt as hollow as I did in that moment—hollow, haunted, forgotten, and pretty much falling apart. Had my parents left this place to rot to punish me? Was this the payback for messing up their tidy little lives? How the hell was I going to fix this mess?

Trying not to think about it, I focused on the baby steps that Llys had drummed into me. First, I set up the stove, but the gas flame did little to warm my freezing fingers. So I pitched the tent and climbed inside the sleeping bag to fend off the increasing chill. I looked through the tent opening at the trunk and realized it was Nan's. It had sat next to her rocking chair in the corner.

I was too tired to check it out now. The day had battered every sense I had.

The past is a taxing thing. It waits around corners to leap out at you and gets heavier and heavier as the years go by. It made me wonder if that was why Nan had never spoken to me. Maybe she had known what a rotten future lay in store for me.

Chapter 23

ELI LORELEI WAS a simple man. He liked his job, his morning runs, and fishing on the weekends. What he hated was conflict and his prodigal daughter's return, coupled with the prospect of having to explain himself to his wife, Jenny, sat so heavily on his chest he could hardly breathe.

For some reason, whenever he and Aeron ended up in the same place they descended into a fight. They had fought ever since she had learned to talk. Eli's problem was that Aeron was too much like her mother. Not the woman that she had grown up with but his first wife. Yes, he was unfortunate enough to have watched two wives walk out of his life. The first, his true love, Lilia, was a girl he had met in boyhood. The strange little girl who had lived with Nan beside the river.

Untamable, Lilia's sheer presence could render him speechless. She had a gift, a mysterious connection with the world around her. They had been married for less than a year when Aeron was born and not a month later, Lilia got up one morning and left without a word to anyone.

Wife number two had been less than enamored with little Aeron. He had met Iris at work when he was a hotshot detective and she was a hotshot defense attorney. Their relationship had been fireworks and battles from day one. Iris had tolerated Aeron but she would not let the odd little girl be present if one of her beloved partners in the firm came to dinner. It took the refusal of Iris to defend Aeron in court to finally make him see how stone cold Iris was. Now she was married to one of those partners at her firm and had nearly bankrupted Eli in the process.

Listening to that woman had been the worst thing Eli had ever done. He had so wanted Aeron to have a mother figure, and had been so wrapped up in his own life that he let the rift grow. He had become weak in his desperation to make Aeron fit into the world around her.

He had been heartbroken over Lilia and sniped and snapped and told his beautiful daughter the most unimaginable lies. Then, when she dared show him, a grown man, how to solve his own case, not only had he reacted badly but he had told her something so hurtful and so untrue, that to think of it even now hurt him. He had said that he had never wanted her, that he had never wanted a girl, and that she should go and play with her little dolls.

From that moment on, Aeron was no longer his daughter. She distanced herself from everything that was him. Her gifts scared him and the angrier she seemed to grow, the more intense her connection with the gifts became.

Eli had watched Lilia tortured to the point of madness by visions and wailing at the pain of some stranger over a thousand miles away.

At a loss of what to do, how to help, and not understanding any of it, he became as distant from Aeron as she from him. Her abilities grew in adolescence and he ignored her distress. She responded in the way many abandoned children did and he had turned away. The older she got, the more she looked like Lilia and it was like a dagger to his heart.

Then when they found Jake Casey's body, it was too late.

Now, Nan had raised Lilia, her granddaughter, and she had pretty much raised Aeron too. Nan had never forgiven him for the way he treated his own daughter and he didn't blame her. Nan had all the same gifts and knew her girls, she knew them inside out. A woman of few words but with a tongue so sharp it could slice through any armor.

While Nan had been alive, Aeron had kept it together. She was always calmed by her time spent at Nan's but when Nan had died, Eli had pushed Aeron into mainstream education. If he hadn't, Aeron wouldn't have met Sam. If he'd just kept her home, then Jake might still be alive.

He'd gone to Nan's graveside when Aeron confessed to him point-blank in the interview room that she had killed Jake. He had begged Nan for a way to know that Aeron wasn't responsible.

Now, Eli was not a superstitious man, nor did he believe in ghosts or ghouls or any such nonsense, but when Nan visited him in his sleep and gave him the biggest tongue-lashing he'd ever received, he knew it was the truth.

"All she wanted was for you to pay attention," she said. "But no, you're as dense as a forest and you ain't half as pretty. As if Aeron . . . *my* girl, could harm another living soul."

Even the memory made him squirm in his seat.

"You failed her, over and over. And now you're just gonna wash your hands, bury your head, and hope that your butt will smell of roses. Well, it ain't."

Eli looked up at the house he lived in with his third wife Jenny. He had two girls with her, Louise and Ruth. He was a loving father to them but he had failed Aeron spectacularly. He had failed and he didn't know how the hell to fix it. Aeron didn't even know that she had two half-sisters. She had no idea about Jenny.

Jenny wasn't exactly a good woman, she was a stern woman, and the only woman who wanted him after Aeron had been convicted. He and Jenny were compatible in a lot of ways but she had her opinions. One of them was that any other daughter he'd had was not as important as the two he had with her. Aeron was not welcome in the home. She didn't want her girls or him anywhere near his messed-up kid.

So pretty much, if Jenny knew where he'd just spent his last few hours, she'd hit the roof. Eli sighed. He wouldn't tell her, it was easier that way. Yes, Eli Lorelei was a simple man. Simple and a coward.

Chapter 24

I AWOKE IN the middle of the night with the smell of lavender in my nostrils. My entire body went rigid and I was so cold I felt like a human glacier. That meant only one thing.

"Nan?"

I opened my tent and saw Nan sitting on her rocking chair, which was weird 'cause there hadn't been one there earlier. She tapped the trunk and nodded. I rubbed my eyes, shivering, and wandered to the trunk. I opened it and inside was a bottle of champagne with one glass, a logbook or diary of some sort, and a bunch of items I couldn't really make out.

"You gonna toast?" Nan asked. "I'm getting a thirst."

I raised my eyebrow. "You're dead, you don't get thirsty."

"How are you to know, Shortstop? Now, crack it open. Been waitin' around long enough."

I nodded and pulled out the bottle, which she had wrapped up tight in bubble wrap. "You know what a dozy your father is."

I couldn't really argue with that so I popped open the bottle with a corkscrew in the trunk and poured a glass. "What are we toasting?"

"Your freedom, what else?"

I nodded and clinked my glass through hers. "You know, I don't think I've ever heard you talk before."

Nan nodded. "I had my reasons."

"You mean you saw everything that was going to happen?"

Nan shook her head. "You know well enough that you can't see the whole picture and you see a hell of a lot more than I ever did." She tapped the trunk. "Read the letter in the morning and promise me one thing, Shortstop."

I nodded, knowing it had taken her years to stay for this long. "Of course I will . . . as long as you get some rest and stop chirping at me."

Nan smiled. "Done."

"So, what's the promise?" I asked.

Nan met my eyes and every ounce of love she felt came hurtling at me like a huge beam of warmth. "Don't give up, Shortstop, and don't turn your back on who you are."

I folded my arms. "That's two."

"One promise. Two parts."

I looked down at the bottle. How could you turn down a request from a spirit that had waited so long to welcome you back? "I promise."

Now, the weird thing with meeting ghosts is that I never do it when I'm conscious, so I wasn't surprised to find myself waking with the taste of champagne on my lips. I lay there for a moment but then came the sound of some noisy critter trying to scratch a hole through the wall. I rolled over and got out of the tent. I stomped to the window and glared at the shocked squirrel.

"If you want a place for your nuts, I'll build you one. Just less of the destruction, I got enough to do."

The squirrel looked at me. She was a little taken aback. Like I said, I sense a lot and animals do to, so between both sets of extra senses, I'm like a real-life Doctor Doolittle.

"I'll get to it later, I promise," I told her.

I walked to the trunk and pulled out a large bag of nuts that I'd seen in my dream.

"There you go. *Bon appetite*," I told the squirrel.

She sniffed at it, eyeing me like I'd catch her and roast her.

"Look at the size of me, you wouldn't make much of a snack."

The squirrel cocked her head, studying me like she was considering my words, then dived, head first, into the bag. She'd be the size of a house if I spoiled her. I wandered back to the trunk and sat beside it. The bottle of champagne was gone but there was a notebook perched on top with my name scrawled upon it.

I opened up the book and saw Nan's handwriting. The kind of flowery writing that was used by older generations. The kind I use because Nan taught me how to write.

> *Shortstop,*
> *Now you celebrated your first night. It's time to get to the hard work. Now I know you wanna scare the wildlife with that fiddle o' yours but you gotta set up the place before the storms start.*

*I'm gonna talk you through the small stuff, so don't
sweat it. Step by step like that head doctor says. In no
time at all the place will be fixed up and firing.*

*You remember the field next door? The one I
always tended? Well, it's yours now, Shorty, so if you
go in the ol' barn you'll find the tools I left. They ain't
none of that new fangled fancy stuff but they work.*

*Prepare the field for plantin' and then build the
box you promised the pesky squirrel cos otherwise,
if she's anythin' like her grandmother and ancestors,
she'll hammer a hole in your roof!*

Love,

Nan xxx

*PS - I'm your Nan you halfwit. Why the hell else
would I have put up with you?*

I laughed, feeling for the first time in years someone understood
me. Tears sprung to my eyes and I sobbed like I'd never done
before.

Through my tears, I saw another scribble at the bottom of the
page.

PPS - Stop blubbering and get on with it!

I placed the book inside the trunk, fired up the stove, and made
myself some freeze-dried stuff that my father had thrown in a
box.

In an hour, I was out in the field, digging through years of
bramble and vine. I scooted past the animals' nesting and opened
up the barn where Nan kept her tools.

I had always thought that the little field was the farmer's next
door and that Nan had worked for him but now I knew different.
I turned and looked at the higgle-piggle wheat field, its weeds
thicker than some sections of the cricked and cracked fence.

Even if it needed work, it was mine.

I spent the entire day ploughing and plucking and turning over
the field until it was looking something like Nan used to conjure
and felt as though I had never been away. I'd helped Nan in the

field so many times that it felt more like home than the large, empty house my parents had occupied.

After dinner I pulled out some wood from the back of the shed and built the box for Mrs. Squirrel with a flap and lever attached. The squirrel watched me attach the box to the wall in the waning sunlight. She investigated her new store as soon as I stepped away. Mrs. Squirrel seemed pretty pleased with it. She tested it for structure and safety, did a dry run with the nuts and tested out the lever I'd attached for her to keep her stash from the birds. Happy that I had appeased the resident nag, I boiled some water on the stove for supper.

I heard a scraping in one of the rotting kitchen cupboards. I opened it up and Mrs. Squirrel sprinted past with a sealed package of sponges. "Hey!"

If squirrels could snigger, she would have. It was a good thing those sponges had survived the flood and they'd been sealed up so tight. I could have used them.

"Thieving little—"

I stopped as she appeared on her box, trying to haul her loot through the gap.

"Hang on a minute." I opened up the window, reached through, and snapped off the packaging. I then helped the little thief to break up her bounty and stuff it into the box. "It's supposed to be for your nuts, not you," I told her.

She gave me a look, which told me that she wanted another box for that, preferably within reach and if I'd be so kind to fit a flap to the wall so she wouldn't have to keep finding holes to get into the house.

"Y'know, Nan was right . . . bossy," I told her.

The squirrel flicked her bushy tail into my face and closed the lid as she settled in to her new home. I looked around at the creaky, leaky shack of a place I had inherited.

"At least one of us has some comfort," I muttered. I wandered wearily over to my sleeping bag, ate my boiled slop, and was out as soon as my head hit the pillow.

Chapter 25

SOME PEOPLE'S WEEDS are another's prize blooms, and no more was this the case than with creeping Charlie–that little plant that covered the ground in a thick blanket of green, then, in spring, burst out into the most vivid splashes of purple you'll ever see. It could provide cures for all sorts of ailments and could be put in tea. It had a load of uses, *if* you knew what you were doing with it. Nan had. She'd cook up that little plant when I had a cough or a cold and in no time I'd be running around causing chaos. She had used the garden like a pantry, she knew every leaf on every tree and what she could use it for.

I'm not Nan. I ain't got no idea how to cook toast, let alone make up a nettle stew or a cough mixture from ground ivy. Still, that didn't make the display that greeted my eyes, as I walked out into the morning sunshine, any less soul soothing.

I sat there for at least an hour in the morning sun. I felt like a child that had just opened its eyes to the wonders of the world. The simple pleasure of touching the indigo bursts meant more than my simple words could ever explain. So long had I been in the tomb of gray, thick stone, that I never dreamed such simple moments would ever be mine to treasure again.

After some wrenching and a prod from Nan in my ear I walked to the field. I made up for my leisure by working through every meal until the scarecrows were dancing in the evening breeze and the field was sewn with every seed Nan had stowed in the trunk for me.

Now, in a perfect world, I would have let the ground settle, I would have turned it over a few times, perhaps adding some new rich fertilizer to boost the nutrients. I didn't have that kind of time. The belt of storms would be on their way soon enough and I needed the seeds to get growing.

In Oppidum the weather is so unpredictable in some months, that you can go out in the morning in shorts and return at night wrapped in a scarf and gloves. A lot of the politicians are saying it's the world warming up but I can feel how important it is that weather cycles fluctuate, that they gotta change and shift about. I ain't no expert on anything but I think that's how the world seems to work. It's always on the move, always growing and changing and evolving. It's us that has to go with it, not try and control it.

And that's pretty much how it seems to work in Oppidum. We get this really unique phenomenon which scientists say is all about different air meeting and having some kind of disagreement. Either way, the result is we end up with summer storms. Every mid-May till sometime mid-June the weather goes completely bonkers. Mother Nature seems to look in her box of weather and thinks, "this needs a good ol' spring clean," so tips the box and empties it right on top of us. We get everything from blizzards to persistent thunderstorms, to gales so strong they blow over cars. There was rain so heavy one year and the river got so high that Nan and I were trapped on the half floor overlooking the main floor for days. And I ain't even gonna go into twisters.

Then, as if Mother Nature decides she's happy she's emptied out her garbage, it all stops. Normally on my birthday.

I still had a couple of weeks until the storms would arrive and hoped it would be long enough for the seeds to get all nestled in before the kitchen sink got thrown at them. As I locked up the barn and sauntered back to the cabin for the night, a scream hit my ears at such a level that I braced myself for the blow from an attacker.

Sun setting, run, run faster, legs so tired, so wobbly, run, stumble, fumble, fall, crawl, run, have to run, hands, so tight, so large, pain, so much pain, run, please, run . . .

I rubbed my head, trying to fend off the panic thumping its way through my body. "That was a bad one," I told Mrs. Squirrel who was looking at me, nut in her mouth. "Just a vision, that's all. Must be tired."

Mrs. Squirrel wasn't convinced but then neither was I.

There are three kinds of visions that I seem to have. There's the flashes, like the ones I just had. They are like watching a minute of a blockbuster movie in 3-D.

Then, there's the dreams—the kind that gets me up close and personal. I experience all the sights and smells and feelings, I'm all tuned in like I am actually there. I find it really hard to figure out if it's something I am experiencing or a vision.

Then, the last, the prophetic ones. Like I said before, I hate them. All the fire and fury and strange symbolic things that I don't have the faintest idea how to decipher.

The flashes seem to be like a warning beacon, a feeling so intense that it ripples through the area like an aftershock.

The dreams are another's experience, as it's happening. Somehow I am living the event with the person, experiencing what they experience.

Then the prophetic are clearly what could be, or will be or may be. I don't know. I wasn't given an instruction manual. All I know is that they are terrifying and not very useful even if I could understand. Who the hell would listen to me anyway?

Mrs. Squirrel bounced up onto her box. She seemed happy that I wasn't going to faint before she got into her nut-store and I headed inside for the evening, trying and failing to rid the flash from my mind.

MARI, SUCH A sweet peach of a girl. Dark hair swaying behind you as you walk. You don't belong here, Mari. You don't belong anywhere. Your filthy mongrel roots and your promiscuous ways . . . you're all the same, all less than human. Like cattle, but you're not so worthwhile. It's not like you'd make much money if I sold you for meat.

How does nature let runts like you exist? What is your use? You're a nobody, Mari. You're vermin, a dirty, flea-infested, disease-ridden tramp.

I'm going to change all that Mari . . . right now . . . I'm going to change everything for you. How would you like to be special, Mari?

I've waited so long, you see . . . waited and waited to start my collection. I think you're the perfect test, Mari. A worthless guinea pig.

Yes, I'll collect you, Mari . . . sweet, disgusting, Mari. Oh what fun we'll have.

MARI SAID HER thank yous to Mrs. O'Reilly and headed out into the corn field. She hadn't expected anyone in this hole to even look at her for a job but her mother had told her Mrs. O'Reilly wasn't like the others in this small town.

She didn't care that Mari wasn't from here and she didn't care that Mari was from the gypsy train that had pulled into town for the summer.

Mari wasn't sure why here. The place was dead, boring. Who would vacation here? Besides the locals were all red-neck idiots who hated them.

At least she could get some money together this summer. Strawberry picking sounded like hard work but she didn't mind that at all, she loved the feel of dirt in her fingers, a connection to the earth.

She'd gotten it from her grandmother, the mysterious woman who everyone turned to. The woman who she half wished her mother would be more like. It sounded harsh in her own mind but Grandma was steady, calm, her wise nature soothing.

Mari's mother was anything but those things. She dragged them from town to town, sometimes for months away from the train, as if she was running from something, as if they were being chased by a nightmare.

Mari had asked why once in a fit of frustration and the only thing her mother could tell her was "nine-eight-four." She didn't even know what it meant. They were running from a number.

Mari had demanded this year that there would be no more running. She was going to have one summer in a single place and that was final.

Something cracked behind her and she turned. A bar smashed into her temple. The ground hard. The blood tasted metallic as it dribbled into her mouth.

She reached out to crawl. A rope jolted her neck, she scrabbled for it, clawed at it, ripped her skin to pull free.

Air, she needed air, breathe!

The rope loosened. Not by much. She gasped, spluttered.

A rope rubbed roughly at her ankles and the sound of a machine roared into life.

Chapter 26

ELI SAT AT the old wooden desk he had insisted on keeping after the major renovations to the department two years ago. The door to his office was open and he listened to Gladys type reports into the computer as Sam Casey dealt with a complaint.

He was in work far later than usual today. He didn't want to face Jenny's inquisition when he got home.

It had taken Abe all of a day to send his wife Sara over to Jenny and fill her in on the details. To tell Jenny all about Aeron's re-appearance and no doubt the pair sat jibing at how dangerous and devious Aeron was.

The thought made Eli's stomach ache. Aeron wasn't a bad girl. She didn't have a callous bone in that gigantic body of hers. Yes, she was messed up and that was his doing. Yes, she had those peculiar gifts but her nature was a soft one. He couldn't say he knew a lot about her but of that much he was sure.

Sam Casey on the other hand wasn't so sweet. Eli had believed Aeron when she had told him that Sam was at the rail line when Jake died. It didn't matter that Sam had denied the fact, point blank, to his face, Eli had known the boy was lying.

But Sam Casey was the mayor's golden son. The son who was now deputy chief, despite Eli's disapproval of him ever getting a badge. Eli had enough respect from the city council to keep him in office, mainly because the only other alternative was for someone from outside Oppidum to take the post. Many of the city council members still remembered how Sam had been as much of a troublemaker as Aeron but Mayor Casey had pulled a lot of strings.

The deputy chief in question was currently looking bored as a distressed woman ranted at him, tears staining her cheeks crimson. Sam never had much in the way of empathy. He could charm those he chose to with that politician's tongue he'd inherited but he couldn't care a less about the "little people." He was all about getting to the top as quickly, and effortlessly, as he could.

The woman got more and more frantic, pleading with Sam to listen, and at the third mention of her daughter, Eli sighed and walked out of his office.

"She's gone. Why won't you listen?" The tears streamed down the woman's cheeks and dripped from her chin. "Mari would never leave without a word."

Eli knew why Sam wasn't bothered and it made his anger bubble. The woman was one of the gypsy train that had pulled into town ready for the Summer Fayre. They were about as popular as Aeron.

"Why don't you come and talk to me about it?" Eli said, pointing to his office.

"I'm dealing with it," Sam snapped.

Eli leveled "the look" at him—the one that petrified most of his officers. "Did someone make you chief, boy?"

Sam looked around at Gladys, who quickly returned her attention to her typing. "Not yet." He smiled sweetly.

Eli scowled. What the hell had Aeron ever seen in the spoiled brat? "Never, if I get my way," he muttered under his breath. "Please. This way." He pointed to his office door.

The woman blinked at him, her eyebrows dipping, her puffy eyes searching his. She glanced back at Sam as she clutched her handbag closer, and Eli motioned for her to walk ahead of him. "Would you like something to drink?"

She snapped her eyes from Sam's. "No . . . thank you." She hurried into Eli's office.

Eli shot Sam a cold look before following her. The boy shouldn't have had a damn badge.

"Please, sit down." He closed the door and headed to his desk as the woman sank down onto one of the visitor's chairs. He pulled out a notebook as he smiled as warmly as he could at the sniffling woman and nudged forward a box of tissues.

"So how long has Mari been gone . . . Mrs.—"

"Miss. Just call me Natalia."

Her curly black hair fell down over her high cheekbones. Eli swallowed, dipping his eyes to stop from staring at her. She had an air of . . . something . . . exotic maybe? With her dark eyes, gold hoops in her ears and a tight top that left little to his imagination, it was hard not to look at her. Still, she didn't seem to be the kind of woman easily won over. Shaking the thought from his head, Eli nodded and noted down the names. Natalia hadn't trusted him enough for a surname and he understood why. Sam and the others treated her people like rotting wood, trust would not be easily earned.

"How long has Mari been missing?"

"Four hours," Natalia answered. "She's not a runaway and she won't have got lost. Mari wouldn't leave without saying. She's a good girl."

Eli smiled. "Where was she headed last?"

"O'Reilly's farm. She was going to try for a picking job."

Eli calculated the distance from the gypsy encampment to the farm was about three miles walking at most. "Did Mrs. O'Reilly say anything?"

"Mari turned up. She got the job and Mari was set to start next week." She trailed her manicured nails over her handbag and smiled down at a charm bracelet on her wrist. Her eyes twinkled as she stared at the metal.

"And?"

"Then she left and walked back toward home. That's what Mrs. O'Reilly said."

Eli frowned. Police procedure dictated that they could only deem her missing after twenty-four hours but his instinct was rattling at him, the girl could be hurt. The fact that Natalia had come into the station looking for help spoke volumes about how worried she truly was. Something was wrong.

"I'll tell you what," he said. "Why don't we go and take a drive over there and I can check out some of the places she could be, and you can give me a description that I can circulate to the patrol tonight?"

Natalia looked at him, her eyes narrowed in suspicion. "So, you'll help . . . just like that?"

Eli nodded. "Always trust a woman's intuition."

ELI DROVE THEM out toward the farm. The fields around them glowed in silver moonshine.

"I saw the papers—I saw what they said about your girl," Natalia said.

Eli sighed. The whole world had read that damn rag.

"She's innocent, but you knew that . . . didn't you?" she said. "I mean, even a fool can see that."

Eli glanced at her. "How so?"

Natalia pointed to the turn off next to O'Reilly's farm. "Felt her on the way past. She's out by the river. She's got more reception than a satellite dish."

Eli laughed. "Her mother was the same."

They drove for hours, scoping every field and lane that Eli could think of but Mari was nowhere to be found.

"Do you think she might have made it back home?" he asked eventually.

Natalia shook her head. "Drop me at the river, could you?"

Eli tensed. "Why?"

Natalia smiled, not a happy one but one of a woman whose hope was fading fast. "She'll know. Your girl will know what happened to her. That is if she'll help."

"What do you mean?"

"The size of the gift that she has been given . . . Well, it's hard enough when people around you can help . . . want to help."

Eli sighed and turned down the little dirt track to the mill. "She's never had anyone."

The truth stung but how could he deny it?

Eli stopped the car at the cabin and gazed at the rundown ruin that had once housed so much love and happiness. Aeron had been keeping herself busy by the look of the field next door. Again, something she was doing alone without so much as a word of help from him.

"Thank you," Natalia said. "I know it's not easy going up against your own, but thanks."

Eli shrugged. "It's my job. If Mari isn't back by morning, let me know and we'll get a search party in motion."

Natalia got out and pulled her cardigan around her shoulders.

Eli wanted to go with her, to see Aeron. Maybe Aeron could help and he could go and find the girl. He closed his eyes. Who was he kidding? Aeron and he couldn't be in the same room without it descending into fireworks. That, and he had to go home and face Jenny.

Chapter 27

I KNEW SHE was coming before I heard the knock on the door. I saved time for us both by leaving the door open and putting on some tea—an old Welsh tradition I picked up from Nan.

Natalia stepped across the threshold and stared at me, uncertain.

I nodded and waved her in. "Come in. I'm Aeron."

"Natalia," she said.

"Nice to meet you, Natalia." I picked up Nan's old tea pot, poured out a cup, and handed it to her. "I don't have sugar."

Natalia took the plastic mug and nodded her thanks. She cast furtive looks at the rotted shell I lived in. She wanted to know why my father left me in a dump, why I was staying, why I hadn't run the second my chains had been unshackled. She wanted to know a lot but she was too polite and far too worried to do anything other than stand in the center of what used to be Nan's kitchen and cuddle her tea.

"Your father just dropped me off," she managed.

I nodded. I couldn't read my father's thoughts but I could feel him.

Natalia was terrified, her fear was like waves of gray crashing out from her heart in all directions. I didn't blame her. A dark cloud of . . . something . . . had appeared over the town in the few hours since nightfall. When events seem to suck a whole place into darkness, into the depth of a world void of hope, a cloud appears over the place.

It was a lot like the clouds I saw over people, the ones with the long slithery tentacles that hung down, feeding off the despair. I didn't know what the hell it was, I didn't know where it came from or how the hell to make it go away but I saw it. I knew it could sense that I could see it. It had a wariness, like thousands of eyes watching me. The cloud seemed to keep its distance from me but I couldn't stop it from spreading out over the rest of the town.

"Mari," Natalia started. "Did you see?"

I sighed. The black cloud's appearance told me more than my flash visions ever could. "I just saw . . . she left her flip-flop behind . . . in the field . . . next to the turn off."

Natalia drank deeply from the cup, her hands shaking. "I can't feel her anymore."

I looked down at my own mug. I could feel her but I would never tell Natalia why.

"What happened to her?" Natalia asked quietly.

"Storm clouds are gatherin', thick 'n' black. Ain't none of you will be safe until the sun breaks on through."

Natalia shook her head. "I won't leave her behind. I won't go without Mari."

"There's nothing good or right that I can say to you. I'm just some crazy woman in a shack."

Natalia shook her head. "Denying what you are will never change it. She's gone . . . hasn't she?"

I ran my hand through my hair. It was one of those choices: which version of the truth would hurt less? I could be wrong, I could be delusional, who was I to make this kind of decision when I screwed up my own life so badly?

Natalia gripped hold of her empty cup, her eyes filled with shining tears. "Please, please. . . tell me . . . tell me."

It was one of those choices, whatever you said, it would break a heart beyond healing. "She's gone, Natalia. Mari's gone."

OH NATALIA, HOW easy you make this . . . too easy. I just had to wait for you to come looking, didn't I? Mari is having so much fun, she's quite the experiment. You are too old for fun, Natalia. You're too old to be collected.

No, women like you are only good for scrap. You won't be collected, Natalia, but I can play. What shall we do? I'll make it fun? You're no good to be dragged and roped, no, you're too slow at your age . . . too . . . saggy.

I know, I'll make you an exhibit like all the other ancient monuments in the museums, how is that? You old hag, that will be fun won't it?

Yes, that will be perfect.

NATALIA HURRIED UP the road, her tears still dribbling down her cheeks. She'd seen this coming, she'd tried to keep Mari safe and somehow she'd failed. Had they not run far enough? Why hadn't she outrun it by now? Her mother didn't see the number, didn't understand that nine-eight-four was everywhere, that it haunted her.

"Natalia," she heard someone call and spun around.

Nothing there, nothing but corn and trees. No Mari, no one.

She turned back, wrapping her cardigan around herself. Aeron had confirmed her nightmares, her dark nightmares. Natalia wasn't like her mother, she couldn't see like her but the wind of the darkness had whipped at her since Mari was a girl. She'd run but not far enough and now Mari was gone.

"Natalia," the voice called again.

She turned, the bar hitting her in the temple. The road hard, sharp in her back. She grabbed out to rip at the air, blinded by blood and anger. Another blow landed, then another, over and over, then she saw it swaying in the distance. Nine-eight-four.

That was when she found the strength to run.

Chapter 28

I CAN HARDLY breathe, air tight in my chest. Panic screaming through constricted veins . . . RUN! I can't keep up . . . laughter chases me. Strange laughter, hollow, soulless . . . like a ghoul, a glowering, faceless ghoul. Feet on grass, cold, divots, sharp stones, pounding, pounding, pounding heart. So loud, so loud, ground so hard on cheek, it stings, fingers in soil, dig in dirt, sharp scratches, scraping, clawing, run, I have to run.

No, rope on neck, burning, fibers like fire, pull, pull it off, I can't breathe, No, I can't breathe . . . tighter . . . world spinning, clutching, clawing, desperation, I can't breathe. Pounding louder, chest bursting, world fading, please . . . no . . . please . . . I can't—

I snap open my eyes, gasping for air as if I am drowning. I claw my way out of my tent and sprint faster than I ever have before. No, please, no. My bare feet on graveled dirt, the bitter air in my throat, forcing my pace to slow. I clutch my neck, I feel every second of struggle. I am on my knees screaming in agony as the wound is inflicted.

I crawl on hands and knees to her. She stands looking up at her own body. "I'm so sorry . . . please . . . I'm so sorry."

I say it over and over, pleading forgiveness from her.

She turns to look at me with lifeless eyes, eyes that burst into flame as her face melts into fire, she wails with such fury that I cower from her, my ears ringing and bleeding from the cry—

I woke up, sweat soaked, shaking, trembling with the emptiness of a life taken before its time. Natalia's spirit was angrier than I have ever felt from anyone. Angry that she had been lied to . . . that I had lied to her . . . angrier now she knew why . . . furious with the burning loss only a mother could understand.

I had told her Mari was gone. I had lied to her. I made that choice not knowing what would happen. Like Nan said, I could only see snippets of the future and Natalia's fate, I did not see. I made the wrong choice. I should have made her stay, I should have told her the truth. How could I? I didn't know where Mari was exactly but the young girl was not moving. Mari's spirit was half with me.

It's a peculiar thing that sometimes happens to the victim of such a crime. Like the universe shows mercy and removes them from the suffering. See, most peoples' reaction is, why do these things happen if there's good in the world? My simple explanation would be that whatever is out there—the good—it feels the wounds deeper than anyone of us can ever comprehend. So, when these things happen. I think the good, unable to control mankind, does the only thing it can do, comfort. And as I sat in my tent, shivering and sobbing like a lost child, it wasn't Nan who was by my side comforting me . . . but Mari.

Chapter 29

THE NEXT MORNING, when I was out in the field checking the fences, I heard sirens. I knew it was my father hurtling down the lane and so prepared myself for the onslaught before he came stomping over to me.

"What the hell did you say to her?" he barked.

I ignored him and turned back to the fence I was fixing. I didn't care who the hell he was—chief, father, or king of the freakin' world. If he wanted answers, he'd learn to talk proper.

"Did you hear me? What the hell did you do?"

I fixed the horizontal beam onto the post and hammered a nail into the join with one shot.

"They're baying for your blood, Aeron!"

I looked up at his face, ruddy from fury, and shrugged. "What's new?"

"She's dead. Don't you care? I drop her off at your place and the next thing I know she's hanging from the road sign."

I hammered in the second nail, walked to the middle post, and pressed the beam against it. "Which one?"

"What do you mean which one? Oh hell, they're both dead?"

My father pretended he didn't know about my "nonsense" but the tone in his voice betrayed him. Natalia had reminded him of someone he'd cared about, I felt that much from him.

"Yeah," I offered. "The girl's flip-flop is in the wheat field."

My father took his hat off and rubbed his hand over his receding hair. "Did she? Did Natalia do what it looks like?"

I hammered in the third nail, trying not to relive every second of the vision from last night. "I thought it was nonsense," I muttered.

"Just tell me."

I hammered the fourth nail in and walked down to the end post. "She didn't get up there of her own accord if that's what you're asking."

"You knew?"

I tried not to sigh out loud and fixed the beam against the post and hammered in the fifth nail. "What do you think?"

White-knuckled grip on his hat, he looked like he wanted it to be my neck instead. "So, you just left her? You just let her wander off to her death?"

The fact that my own father thought I could act so coldly stung. No matter how hard I tried or how many times I told myself that his opinion didn't matter, that he couldn't hurt me because I didn't care, it still stung . . . every damn time.

"What can I say?" I said, hammering in the last nail. "I'm a killer. What the hell do I care about some woman?"

He threw his hands in the air. "And you don't think that's what everyone wants to believe? You don't think that they will blame you for this?"

"Sure as hell, I know they will blame me. That's the easiest route and always has been." I picked up another beam and checked for bowing, making sure there were no knots where the nails needed to go. "If you don't believe my words, ask her people."

"They know?" he asked.

"Course they know. Their mutts got more intelligence than you."

My father put his hands on his belt, hat still in one hand. "You know who did it?"

I shook my head. I had spent most of the night reliving the events over and over and at no point could I see anything useful.

"I need supplies to fix the roof," I said.

My father took stock of the conversation change. I was done talking. "Fine. Give me the list."

"Haven't made it. I'll leave it on your windshield."

"I told you, girl. You're banned."

I stood up to my full height. His eyes flicked to the beam in my hand as I did so. "I'll do as I freakin' well please. So, I either leave it on your windshield or I'll walk into the hardware store myself."

He rammed his hat on his head and stormed off. I wasn't surprised to see the dust kicking up as he sped off moments later.

I leaned on the fence and dropped the beam. I felt shaky, faint, and my throat was still sore from the vision. Whoever had killed both Natalia and her daughter, Mari, had enjoyed the whole thing, that much I felt. Whoever it was had loved every second. And this would be just the beginning.

Chapter 30

AS I WALKED toward city hall, I felt the cloud over the town pulse. I glanced up and saw that it had grown. Natalia's screams still rang in my ears and made my heart beat too rapidly, it made me feel so breathless that even walking was a trial. I looked around, feeling someone next to me, and nearly flew out of my own skin when I saw Mari standing there. I was wide awake, that much I knew. I only saw ghosts in dreams, was I losing it?

"You feel better now?" I asked. It was a dumb question to ask a ghost, I know, but I didn't know what the hell I was supposed to say to her.

"It doesn't hurt anymore," she told me.

I was glad of that. She was one brave girl.

"Mamma's angry and I can't reach her," Mari said.

"You tried your people?" I asked, hoping she would go find someone else to drag into this horrible tragedy.

"They can't hear me," she said.

I wasn't surprised. It could take her a while to collect up all her energy. Even if her people knew where to look for her, they were too grief stricken to spot her.

"Will you tell Grandma that she needs to talk to Mamma?"

I shoved my hands in my too-tight pockets. The thought of waltzing in and telling people, who had thousands of years combined experience in these matters, just how to conduct themselves, did not seem like a great idea. There wasn't anyone else who could help Mari. I was it. Me and my stupid gifts.

I nodded. "Just go get your rest. And for what it's worth, I'm sorry."

Mari smiled at my words and disappeared.

I looked around, glad that there was no one about to see me rabbiting on to someone they couldn't see. I could imagine trying to explain that one to Llys. I definitely would be back in her care, permanently.

I crossed the street that separated the tourist part of town from the regular part and passed Rod's Plaice, one of the fishing shops, and rounded the old city hall building. This end was a lot quieter with most folk at their daily jobs. Last thing I needed was my father seeing me talking to thin air. Tensing at the side door entrance, I couldn't help but think about the last time I'd walked through it. There was no way I was heading in there if I could help it so I snuck past to the parking lot in the back. I found my father's car and placed the list under a windshield wiper. A car pulled up alongside me and I turned to it. My chest tighten—Sam.

Now, when we were kids, Sam was always so much bigger than me, yet when he got out of the car, I realized that I bested him a little.

Sam, as I've said, was the kind of guy women loved. His square jaw with a cleft in the chin sported brown stubble, his smile perfect like those guys you see plastered on billboards. His eyes were like the pit of a cave, so brown that you could only just make out the pupils. With his long eyelashes, his charm, and his chestnut wavy hair, he had a puppy-dog look about him and he drove women crazy. Right now, those eyes were narrowed as he realized just who was standing in front of him.

"You shouldn't be here, Aeron."

"Just leaving a note," I explained. "Compromise and all that."

Sam scowled. "You don't need compromises. You just need to do what you're damn told."

My heart sank. I was responsible for Jake's death and for that I had paid and taken every bit of guilt on my shoulders. But Sam had been there, he wasn't so innocent himself. I had a track record far longer than it should have been *because* I had covered for my best buddy. Sam sure as hell wouldn't be a cop if it wasn't for me and I realized just what a mug I had been.

"Maybe I should start then," I said. "Daddy always told me to tell the truth . . . how 'bout I start there?"

Sam said nothing but the sweat trickling down his forehead answered my question.

"Nice seeing you, Casey," I shot at him as I walked past. "Try not to trip over your own ego."

Lucky for his sake he stayed quiet. Sam Casey had seen me in a bad mood with him only once and clearly, he remembered how painful it was.

Chapter 31

MY TRIP TO Natalia and Mari's family didn't take the route I'd expected. The second I got to the circle of old trailers on a small bluff on the waste ground of Old Thomas's land, I was welcomed by two women who seemed to know I was coming. Although their hurt rippled off them, they still offered small smiles and led me to meet the grandmother.

I stumbled into the tiny trailer, having to bow my head just to fit my frame inside. The smell of incense hit me, making my head swim. A yapping ball of fluff sat on the floral patterned sofa, stroked by the grandmother's age-marked hand. It struck me as the kinda place you would fit to most grandmothers, a little dated, a little worn in places but filled with memories and love.

"Hi," I said, wondering why I'd come here. What could I say? "I . . . Well . . ." I rubbed my hand through my hair, trying to figure where I was going to start. "You see . . ."

The grandmother smiled, her eyes wrinkling with it. "Your name is Aeron Lorelei, you live on the river."

Focusing on the beads hanging in the doorway, I tried to understand how the hell she'd got that from me walking in. Was I that infamous? All I could manage was, "Sure."

"You also see things that others don't."

Shrugging was the only response I could think of. What the hell did I say to that? This was a bad idea, I should leave—

The grandmother gave me a soul-penetrating look. "Now tell me everything you saw and don't spare any details."

I fitted myself onto a chair and sighed. Here went nothing. I told her everything, and she sat listening to every soul-crushing point I could recall, ending with Mari talking to me in the town.

"She's a good girl. She's safe now," the grandmother said. "If she visits you first, tell her that I will help her mother, and not to worry."

"How?" I asked.

The grandmother tilted her head. "You didn't get given that part, did you?"

I shook my head. "I never get nothing helpful."

"No one has spoken to you about it, have they?"

I tried not to laugh. "No one speaks to me. I just got out. But I doubt any folk are gonna talk to me . . . ever."

The grandmother nodded. "Well, you protect yourself a lot better than most who don't understand."

"Ephesians," I answered.

Chuckling, the grandmother's eyes wrinkled up. "You don't seem the kind to seek solace in scriptures."

"I'm not. Not that I wouldn't. But a priest, he told me about armor . . . and well, it works . . . a little."

The grandmother smiled. "He was a wise man. Anyone who believes in something—in the right way—can help you in ways they never dream possible."

I looked around at the generations captured in frames of wood and bronze. One of Natalia and Mari smiling together caught my eye. "The cloud ain't leaving anytime soon . . . so all the armor, spiritual or otherwise, ain't gonna help me when I get accused of murder."

The grandmother took my hands in hers and held them tight. "You walk a path that no one can follow . . . but you will be the one who sets it all right."

"How?" I asked. My hands were hot like I'd put them over a flame.

"You have so many gifts. Gifts that heal or hurt, but you will be the one to burst the dark overhead."

My hands were so hot, like my skin was burning from her touch. I pulled them away, unable to keep them there a second longer. Flashes of faces, of places I had never seen before all plummeted through my mind like the crack of a gunshot.

"What happened?"

The grandmother smiled. "I helped you see . . . just a little bit. But you have a lot to do."

I rubbed my hands, feeling a bit like cotton wool had been rammed into my brain. "Me? How could I help anyone?"

The grandmother smiled. "You'll know, when you hold the heart of the killer in the palm of your hand."

Chapter 32

ELI LOOKED UP when he heard the click as his office door closed and frowned as Sam Casey cleared his throat.

"You need to learn to knock, boy."

Casey grunted. "Look, old man. I don't like you and you sure as hell don't like me but we both know that Aeron hasn't hurt a soul and she's going to be the focus of a witch hunt when this gets out."

Eli nodded. The one thing keeping the hounds at bay was that the victims weren't locals.

"She needs to stay away from town. They'll only think she's up to something. Hell, Mrs. Stein wanted me to arrest her for trying to use hocus-pocus on her," Sam said, folding his arms. "I mean the old bat is crazy but she's just saying what the rest of the town is thinking."

Eli sat back in his chair and rubbed the bridge of his nose. "You try telling Aeron to stay put and keep her nose clean."

Sam looked at him in a way that almost made him laugh. A look that said, "I tried and she told me where to stick my badge."

"I can't chain her to the cabin. She has rights."

Sam waved a hand. "She's on parole, she's not free yet."

Eli shook his head. "She *is* free. Aeron served out her parole inside." And then some. No one had ever explained to him why Aeron ended up with an extra four years on top of her original sentence.

"Leaving notes on your windshield is only going to get her in trouble. So, why don't you get her a cell phone . . . a computer . . . bring her out of the dark ages."

Sam laughed at his own remark. Aeron was never much for technology. Not so much that she didn't like it, more that it didn't like her. She'd blow electrics up in no time. Eli had punished her for it so many times.

"I just don't want to see her go down 'cause of some nobodies."

Eli tensed. The defense of Aeron shouldn't have surprised him. Sam was many things, but his infatuation with her had always been clear. The flippant disregard of two women, however, irked him.

"Mari and Natalia . . . not nobodies . . . and Mari may turn up."

Sam raised his eyebrows. "Oh, come on, her mother is being peeled off the road sign as we speak. Whatever the hell happened, the kid ain't coming home."

Eli looked at Sam. Now he sounded like Aeron.

"Don't even think it, old man," Sam chided. "It's just logic. Same damn logic that Aeron uses. Whatever she *thinks* she sees."

Sam slammed the door behind him, leaving Eli to stare into the empty office. Sam was right but what could he do? Aeron was never going to listen to him, even if it was for her own good. That, and she insisted on telling people *everything*.

Aeron could just say that she had a funny feeling, or the facts pointed her to her uncanny conclusion, anything but no. No, Aeron had to be honest, she had to tell people that she dreamt it, or saw it in some dumb-ass vision. Sometimes, she'd describe something in such detail, especially as a kid, that people had sworn she must have been there, watching.

It was enough to make a prosecutor drool. If anyone could be fitted up for a crime, she made herself the perfect scapegoat. Eli had hoped that a decade behind bars would have taught Aeron to keep her mouth shut.

To stop himself dwelling on what may or may not happen, he headed over to the hardware store with the list and picked up the supplies Aeron would need. He borrowed the flatbed truck and some part of him longed to be the kind of father who would be helping her renovate the cabin. Laughing as they worked in the late evening sun, Lilia bringing them tea and listening to their take on the repairs.

He turned off onto the dirt lane to the cabin and shook the thought from his senses. He was married, to Jenny, he had two other girls . . . proper girls. Girls that liked dolls and make-up and played at being mother.

"Just take the stuff to the cabin and leave her the hell alone," he muttered.

As he pulled the truck into the yard clearing, Eli was struck at how silly it was that everyone called the place a cabin.

It wasn't a cabin, it was a large watermill. Several topsy-turvy floors built around the internal mill workings. It was too large to be a cabin, too tall to be a house, too much of a working building to be a lodge and too empty to be a home. Nan's family had lived there for generations, long before Eli's forefathers had settled here and probably longer than most of the other inhabitants of Oppidum. This little patch of the world belonged to them, belonged to the women beside the river.

Eli had only ever known of Nan and Lilia living in the building in spite of the history. He'd never been told about Lilia's parents and he wasn't really sure why Nan had raised her alone. It was not because he hadn't asked or because he didn't want to know but neither Nan or Lilia would ever tell him, and when Lilia left, Nan stopped speaking altogether.

Eli looked around the cabin as he got out of the truck and heard Aeron work before he could see her. He ducked his head around the boarded-up main door that jutted out like a grand entrance but was crumbling so badly it had been unusable for years. Aeron was fixing a box to the wall.

He watched her, knowing that somehow she could feel him there but she didn't break the silence and so he leaned against the wall as she worked.

Aeron looked deep in concentration as she focused on the box. Her deep amber eyes were framed by her perfectly natural eyebrows. Her tongue poked out from the mouth she'd inherited from Lilia, her nose just as perfectly made. Her jaw she seemed to have gotten from him, along with her ears. Eli's ears and jaw, that was his entire contribution. The rest came from Lilia and if it wasn't for the jawline and her right ear that tipped over at the top, he would wonder if she had ever been his at all.

Aeron was every inch like her mother. Granted, her mother had not been as tall or broad but there was no doubt who she belonged to. The hair was shorter than Lilia's, more practical, but Aeron had the same habit of flicking her hands through it, sweeping the center up over the top, and tucking the errant strands behind her ear.

The color was the same too, the color of redwood tree bark—specks of gold and copper-red glinting when it caught the sunlight.

"Staring," Aeron finally grunted as she hammered the last nail into place.

Eli nodded, his heart once again ripped in two by the memory and lingering emptiness of Lilia reflected in Aeron. "Unload the damn truck," he snapped as the pang of loss jibed at his frazzled senses.

Aeron did as he asked and they worked quickly in awkward silence.

"Mari is in the river," Aeron said finally as they unloaded the last of the supplies.

"What?" Eli was still too lost in Lilia to make sense of Aeron's words.

"Mari," Aeron repeated. "Upstream. Say two, maybe three miles east."

Eli came back to reality with a thump. "Stop doing that."

"Doing what?"

"Your lies . . . your nonsense."

"Nonsense? You asked me the other day where she was. So, that's where she is."

Eli slammed his fist on the door of the truck. "Telling me only makes you look guilty."

Aeron flicked her hand through her hair and glared at him with her mother's eyes. "Just get the poor girl out of the freakin' river." She stormed off into the cabin.

Eli leaned his head against the truck, trying to remember when the hell life got so darn complicated. He knew when—when he'd seen Lilia. He got in the truck, slammed the door, wrenched the gear into place, and drove off. Where the hell was Lilia? Where was she now? Where had she been for all these years? It was one thing to rip his heart out and leave, but why abandon Aeron? Why the hell had she left him with a child that would rub salt in his burned heart every time he looked at her?

Lilia had ruined both their lives. She'd ruined any chance that he and Aeron ever had of finding the word "happy." It was her darn fault, everything was her fault. Stupid, disloyal, bewitching, incredible Lilia.

I need to get a life. What would Jenny think?

He sighed. He didn't really give a damn what Jenny thought. He was a terrible husband, a terrible father, and a terrible man. Whatever Lilia had done to him years ago, it wasn't illegal but it sure as hell should be.

Chapter 33

DARCY TOUGHTON TOOK her iced tea from the newly painted counter and walked out the door of the converted stable. It had been a long one. All day in high school then back to the café at Mrs. Jenkins farm. A normal day for Darcy after her dad had broken his back on the job. Her entire family had to work as soon as they could just to afford to eat. Her mother spent most of her nights pouring over the accounts, trying to figure out how they could keep a roof over their heads.

It had been this way for years and ever since Darcy turned fourteen, she'd been working in Mrs. Jenkins café, keeping up with her grades, and studying long into the night.

One more summer though, only one more and she would be starting Columbia University on a scholarship. One more summer and she could get away from this place. Not that she didn't want to pitch in. She loved her family, but something inside her just wanted out. She wanted adventure and a life of her own.

"I need you at five tomorrow," Mrs. Jenkins called from the doorway.

Darcy turned around to object. Mrs. Jenkins knew that she had asked for tomorrow off. Her mother's birthday was tomorrow and she wanted to do something special. Mrs. Jenkins gave her a look. How many times had she told Darcy that she could just as easily get another girl to work her job.

"Yes, Mrs. Jenkins," Darcy said, trying not to cry.

Mrs. Jenkins didn't notice. Nobody ever noticed. Darcy wondered if it would be any different in college or if she would always be overlooked.

Darcy turned away from the café, trudged up the road, and cut into the field. She sipped her iced tea, trying to soothe her sore throat. She'd better not be coming down with something, she couldn't afford to. The sky was that odd color it always turned before a storm and the air was heavy, so heavy that even walking felt like a marathon. Hopefully they didn't get this kind of weather in New York.

DARCY, OH DARCY. You work so hard. It's such a shame that you'll never get to see college or your sad, pathetic mother on her birthday.

These creatures are so easy, so predictable, like cattle wandering to slaughter. Keep walking, only a little further, out of sight from the old crow.

You think no one sees you, Darcy, but I do. Oh yes, I've picked you out, picked you to be part of a special collection. My collection. You'd like that wouldn't you, Darcy.

You aren't the main prize though. Oh no, you're far too plain for that. Too much baby fat on you. You should be thankful really, sweet, innocent Darcy. I'm going to save you from a life of disappointment.

You won't swell and bloat like your slob of a mother or lie around mooching from those who love you . . . no, you see I'm saving you, Darcy. Saving you from getting knocked up by the first jock who casts a smile your way. Ain't that nice, Darcy?

You're going to help me. Help me to get it right, just perfect for her . . . for my main prize . . . my life's work.

I THREW MYSELF into ripping out the rotted remains of the kitchen as my father drove off. I just didn't get it. He had stood there for the longest time, watching me fix the Mrs. Squirrel's nut store to the wall. He had the stupidest look on his face—serene and wistful and, well, like he gave a damn. Two seconds later he was snapping and snarling like a demented dog. What the hell was his problem? Why the hell did every rejection sting so much?

Slam, rip, crack, bang. The kitchen torn away piece by piece.

Why did he hate me so much? What had I ever done to him?

Bang, wrench, crunch.

What did he want from me?

Slam, snap.

Why couldn't he love me for who I was?

Crunch, crack.

Was I so repulsive? So vile? My gifts so dark that I deserved nothing but his scorn and hate?

Wallop, creak, bang.

Why me? Why the hell did I get to see everything? Why burden me with stupid visions? Why not give it to one of those evangelists or TV mediums who proclaimed they could see it all?

Slam.

Why not give them to someone, anyone but me? Why me? Why? I hauled the remains from the kitchen out into the yard and bellowed at the sky. "What the hell do you want from me?"

I slumped down next to the rubble, feeling so empty, so tired. What was the point in giving someone like me superpowers? I couldn't use them, I didn't know what to do. Why not endow a world leader or someone who counted with them? Why me? Who the hell was I?

"You're no one," I told myself.

I sat staring at the pile of rotted wood as though it represented my life. I was in a daze, and I don't often feel that way. I keep going, I don't even know why half the time but I do. Right now, though, I felt like asking the point of it all.

Everyone else seemed to play at life on an easier level—settling down, raising kids, a career, and vacations in the sun, laughter, happiness, friendship. It all seemed a given to them, some more than others. I felt like I was playing life on nightmare level. Everything I wanted to do, even the simple things were guarded by twenty-foot walls and the snarling hounds of fate. "You will not enter." Everywhere I turned, people turned away from me, their words sharp and jagged to my heart. "You don't exist." But, if I didn't exist then why the hell did it hurt so much?

"It gets better," I heard Llys's voice say.

I stood up so fast that I got stars in my eyes. "Doc?"

A hand on my arm told me I wasn't hallucinating but the blood was thudding in my ears like I'd pass out any second.

"Doc? How are you here?"

The evening air was setting in and the cool breeze wrapped around the shadowed corners.

"You missed your appointment," she said.

My vision cleared a little and Llys swayed into view. Her concern almost making her look angry.

"I had an appointment? When?"

"Today," Llys said. "At two. You didn't get the letter?"

I sighed. "Post office is run by Jake's Aunt Edna. No mail for a murderer."

Llys frowned even deeper. "So where are you staying while you fix this place up?"

I shrugged. I was starting to get the feeling that Llys's mood was heading south.

Her aura flickered as she stared at me, waiting for an answer. "Don't you dare tell me that you're living in there?"

I shrugged again. "Where else would I go?"

Llys muttered something under her breath as she looked up into the sky. Clearly, I wasn't the only one who yelled at the stratosphere.

"Your father could have at least put you up until it was livable."

I laughed. I could hear the bitterness in it blaring like a foghorn. "My father? *Mine?* And break the habit of a lifetime? Oh no, my father can kiss my—"

A slate from the top of the stacks of supplies smashed to the ground. Llys squealed as she jumped.

I couldn't help laughing.

"It's not funny. They are tied on . . . tight. How?" Llys walked over to the supplies and prodded at the bundles.

"Sorry. Nan hates it when I cuss."

"Nan? *Your* Nan?" She laughed, putting her hand on her chest and staring at me like I'd grown a set of antlers. "You said she died."

I nodded.

Llys paled and moved away from the stack like it would bite her.

"Relax, Doc. She's just scolding me."

Llys didn't look at all convinced, so I led her into the now stripped lower floor of the cabin. Only the cold stone floor and the damp stained walls remained of the place. All the furniture and goods had been sold years ago, leaving only the trunk with Nan's belongings for me. I walked to my camp in the center and watched Llys as she took in the place.

"It's huge," she said. "I've stayed in lodges smaller than this."

I looked around, trying to see the place through her eyes. The first floor was the length of a small field, its stone walls in odd shapes jutting out here and there. The entire place was built around the watermill that brought power and the flour mill that it linked to so the back part was pretty much all cogs and shafts and clunking mechanisms—when it was working.

The cabin provided everything Nan and I had needed. The river powered the place, provided food and the field and mill provided the income. Even if I couldn't fish, Nan had been the greatest at it and I loved her meals, I just didn't like murdering the poor critters.

The only one bathroom was on this floor at the back. I'd fixed it all up the day after I had arrived. The pipe to the septic tank sure hadn't been pleasant to sort out but it beat using the great outdoors.

"Upstairs is a few floors. They're all open so you can see right into the kitchen from the top," I said, walking to the wall that would hold the wheel again when I re-attached it. "This here used to be the living area. I used to love looking out as the water from the wheel splashed against the window."

I went to the steps as Llys smiled.

"If you trust the stairs, I'll show you 'round."

Llys nodded and followed me up the rotting staircase.

"See, Nan always slept there." I pointed at the large expanse of wood. The light marks from where her bed had been for years making the rest look dirty and worn. "Nan said she couldn't sleep without the whir of the wheel. she suffered with her ears . . . ringing or something. It used to drive her mad."

"Tinnitus," Llys said. "It's not pleasant . . . and I thought she didn't speak?"

I nodded. "She didn't, but then she didn't have to."

I walked to iron steps that curled around the huge drive-shaft that would normally be rotating. It stretched right through every floor to the roof where the hot water and electrical box had been set up.

"What does it do?" Llys asked as she joined me.

"Runs the electricity. It's like the spine. If you could see the mechanism back there, it runs the flour mill."

"Why all the way up?"

"Well, the further you get from the point of power, the less output you get. The river gets pretty strong in winter so I guess it made sense to keep the electrical box up top and keep it from surging."

Llys stepped closer, eyeing the edge nervously. "It's a bit dangerous, isn't it?"

I raised my eyebrows. "What do you mean?"

Llys pointed to the cast-iron steps. "If your Nan was sleeping here, you were upstairs, correct?"

I nodded and made my way up to the next floor, followed by Llys.

"And at no point did a great big hole in the floor worry anyone?" Llys gave me an incredulous look. "There's not even a guard rail."

I laughed and stepped out onto what had been my floor. It was more cramped than I remembered. The absence of furniture made it feel even more neglected. It was all used to pay for Nan's funeral. A funeral that she hadn't wanted. No, Nan had wanted to be burned on a pyre and scattered over the mountain but my father wasn't having any of her wishes. He had rules to follow . . . as always.

"Nan would have known if anything was going to happen. Health and safety wasn't necessary."

"With you tearing around the place? Your Nan could have had a siren on her head and not stood a chance."

The echo of a laugh swept through the drafty windows and Llys shivered.

"No wonder you see things. This place is enough to make anyone feel like they can communicate with the dead."

The laughter whispered through the breeze again.

"What *is* that?" Llys asked, hugging herself.

I looked at her. I felt lifted by the fact she was paying attention to my mischievous Nan. "She likes you. Let's go back downstairs. I can make you some tea or somethin' . . . if you have time?"

Llys smiled. "Actually, I do. I'm on vacation and I was off to the mountains after your appointment. But it's late so I might just pitch outside if it's okay with you?"

I folded my arms. "You hike? As in wander lonely as a cloud?"

"Very droll, Wordsworth, and yes, I like hiking. I grew up in the Rockies."

The picture of the prim-and-proper doctor trudging up mountains dressed in flannel and a windbreaker made me chuckle out loud.

"Don't judge a book . . ." Llys said as we climbed back down to the first floor.

"You're more than welcome to pitch in here," I offered. "It seems odd but the wood keeps the heat in and it shelters you from the creeping crawlers."

Llys raised an eyebrow, skeptical. I saw a flash of a little girl holding her daddy's hand, his medal in the box.

"He was a great man," Llys whispered more to herself than me.

I nodded, not really knowing what to say.

"Is that why you joined?" I asked.

Llys broke from her thoughts and looked at me. "I thought we had a truce."

I wagged my finger. "Uh uh, you broke that truce. Remember?"

"You shouldn't know any of it. I'm serious. Hell, Aeron, you freak me out." She folded her arms and shuddered.

I shrugged. It was probably true and if anyone ever asked, they would never believe that Llys hadn't told me herself. "You don't have to answer. It's just—"

"What?"

"It ain't exactly professional . . . you being here and the fact you just happen to have your equipment with you. You're here for a reason."

Llys sighed and walked out the door. Had she gone? Was she coming back? Did she want me to go after her? I stood there wondering what I was meant to do and walked to the door to follow her and stopped. I'd look silly if she was coming back. I went back to the middle of the room. I did this a couple of times until, a few minutes later she came back in with a fully packed hiker's backpack.

Thankful that she hadn't seen my dumb wandering 'round, I watched her set up. First came her tent, then her sleeping bag, a camp stool, and finally some kind of luxury camp stove. I'd never seen nobody, not even Nan, erect a camp at that speed. It was like breathing to her. I knew better than to ask if she wanted help. One, I'd get in her way and two, she had a *system*. I learned quickly from Nan that when a woman's got a system, you leave her to it.

"So, you gonna spill it, or we just gonna ignore the obvious?"

Llys sighed. "I don't know how much you can tell, but your talents have me intrigued."

I nodded. "That and you're waiting for the investigation team to hit the institution and you need to get out of their way in case you need to go back."

Llys opened her mouth and then closed it. "Can you read everything?"

I shook my head. "I get a glimpse . . . flashes."

Llys motioned to my hands. "No gloves. You don't need them here?"

"Perceptive, and you're avoiding the question."

Llys walked into her tent and I set about starting the sludge that would be dinner. Boiled goop. Yum.

I toyed with telling Llys about Mari and Natalia but if I was honest, I didn't want to. I was too grateful of the company, I wanted to forget the reality around me and pretend.

"I have somethin' to show you," I said when she re-emerged in sweatpants and a sweater.

"You do?"

I nodded and walked over to Nan's trunk. I opened the journal she'd written for me and pulled out a sealed note. It had on the front: *Dr. Serena Llys—no peeking, Shortstop.*

"It's from Nan," I told her as I handed it over.

"Are you serious?"

I smiled.

Llys shook her head. "She knew I'd be here? She knew my name?"

"The one you're using, yeah."

"This is surreal, you know that?"

"You ain't seen nothing yet," I mumbled as I left her to read the note in private.

Chapter 34

ELI WALKED DOWN the river bank to the white tent where the forensic team from the sheriff's department was working. The county sheriff had happily agreed for Eli to take charge because he'd served in the city in homicide for so many years. All his experience, however, seemed to count for very little. It made him sick to his core that Aeron had been right and even sicker that he hadn't kept his temper to himself.

"Hey, Chief," Jeff, the medical examiner, said as Eli walked into the tent.

"Is it the girl?" Eli asked.

"No standing on ceremony today, huh?"

Eli scowled.

Jeff sucked in his neck like a turtle. "Guess not. It's the missing girl—"

"And?"

"Geez, give me a chance to speak, will you?"

Eli forced himself to relax and to unhinge his sore shoulders but he was panicked. How long before Aeron was hauled in for this? "Sorry. Go ahead."

"Strangulation marks were extensive but not the cause of death. Extensive wounds to her legs and arms, not to mention her front is consistent with being dragged for some distance."

"By what?"

"Car, horse . . . something with power."

Eli tried to swallow but he couldn't. The picture of his own daughters swam before his eyes.

"You want me to sum up? It only gets worse."

Eli nodded. If he looked like he felt, he was probably all shades of pale.

"Cause of death is drowning. She suffered . . . a lot and whoever did it is a sick son-of-a-bitch."

"Any clues?"

Jeff shook his head. "Wiped clean. I don't know how the hell the killer did it either. The boys are tracking the fields to take dirt samples. If we can find out where . . . maybe we can find a tread or something."

Eli looked up into the sky, an ominous-looking cloud slid over from the mountains. "You'd better work fast."

"No pressure. No pressure at all," Jeff muttered as Eli left the tent.

Jeff was good at his job but he didn't go too much for haste. His too-methodical-for-his-own-good pace was only going to wind Eli up more.

Eli pulled at his shirt collar and felt the sweat trickle down the back of his neck as Mayor Casey stomped across the field toward him.

Mayor Casey shook a finger at him. "She's been out less than a week!"

Eli tried to calm himself. It would do Aeron no good if he lost it now. "This has nothing to do with Aeron," he said as steadily as he could.

"No? She gets out after murdering my son and then two women just happen to end up dead?"

Eli gripped his belt to control his urge to knock sense into the ranting idiot. "Causing a panic will do the tourist trade no good, so why don't you leave it to the professionals and go on home?"

Mayor Casey sneered. "You think I trust *you* to keep an objective eye?"

Eli frowned. "I locked Aeron up once. If she is guilty of anything I'll do the same again. I am going to follow the facts and look at this logically, and do my job."

He didn't bother to remind the fool that he was chief by merit and not just popularity. He'd earned his damn position not bribed his way into it.

"She's a killer. She'll always be a—"

"Save your whining for someone who has time." Eli turned to Skip, his only full time officer. "Escort the mayor from the scene."

"Sir!" Skip kept his face stoic but Eli could see the twinkle in his eyes. He felt as warmly about the Casey family as Eli did.

Eli watched Casey Sr. leave as Casey Jr. pulled up. Sam got out of his car and hurried down to the river bank, his cheeks flushed.

"Where the hell have you been?"

Sam pulled him out of earshot of everyone. "Another one is missing. Toughton's girl."

Eli took his hat off and closed his eyes. "When?"

"Mother said she didn't come home from work, but you know the family."

Eli frowned. Oh yes, little people with no importance. Big family, small income. "We take it seriously. The last thing we need is three."

"Will do. Just make sure Aeron has an alibi . . . anything."

Eli nodded and watched Sam march across the field to his car with a determined stride. Sam could have radioed through and let the cat out of the bag but he hadn't. Maybe there was hope for the boy yet.

Chapter 35

LLYS WAS QUIET, real quiet after she had read Nan's letter. Her guarded mind got even harder to read as her eyes veiled. I didn't know what to think or what Nan had said in that letter but it made me feel edgy.

"Did it scare you?" I asked after what felt like forever.

She nodded. "Yes, but that isn't why I'm quiet."

"What is?"

"You didn't tell me about the girls."

I felt my hands get clammy. Had Nan seen it all? No wonder she never spoke. I could still feel Natalia's anger jarring at me in every quiet moment and I couldn't block it out.

"Nan's a rat," I muttered, getting a gust of icy wind in response.

"Why didn't you tell me?"

I looked at the floor, feeling like I'd committed a crime. "You have your secrets. I have mine."

Llys sighed, her eyes focused on the letter in her hands. "Aeron, they could fit the evidence to you . . . the same as they did with Jake."

I shrugged. "What am I supposed to do?"

"For a start, wear your monitor. It's to stop things like this from happening."

I got up, the frustration bubbling in me. I hated feeling guilty, and for what? I hadn't hurt anyone . . . had I? "My father took it. So I wouldn't go into town."

Llys scowled and her aura leapt a mile. I'd never seen her this mad, not even when I rattled her in the institution, but then this was outside, and she had no more control than I did.

"I'm staying. I'm staying until they catch the killer," she announced.

"What?"

Biting her lip, Llys nodded, her eyes intense. "I'm entitled leave. I've earned it and I'm not just going to let you get thrown to the wolves."

I stared at her. I didn't know what to say. What do you say to someone who is putting their entire career on the line for you? "It ain't necessary . . . really. I'll be—"

"Don't spout a load of lies, Aeron. Unless I'm here, you have no alibi and no chance of stopping this."

I folded my arms. "They could make you an accessory."

"They can't," she answered.

Ah yes, the elephant in the room that neither of us could discuss. "What makes you so sure that your superiors will back you up? It could take months, years. Who knows how long—"

"It'll be over by your birthday apparently." She offered me a wry smile as if she couldn't quite trust the words herself.

I rolled my eyes. "So, are you gonna fill me in? 'Cause I'd really like to know what the hell is going on."

Llys smiled. "She said you'd act like this. But I can't, she doesn't know."

"Then what did she know? What did she say?"

Llys looked away, her eyes veiled again.

"Just how bad is it?" I asked, my hands shaking.

"It's nothing like that, but we have to get moving on repairs."

I looked around, wondering how the hell she was going to repair anything. She'd chip a nail for a start.

"Why?" I asked after a long silence.

Llys gazed at the place where the wheel should be. "Nan said that this year's storms would be the most vicious yet."

DARCY STOPPED AND turned, hearing the whisper of her name. Her skin prickled yet it was warm. Was it the wind?

Her heartbeat thudded so forcefully in her chest. It was just the storm . . . or her exhausted mind playing tricks.

She needed a break that was all. Not that she'd get one. All the rich kids in school had gone on vacation during spring break. It must be nice being a—

Darcy screamed as white hot heat ripped through her leg. She looked down. Steel jaws of a snare clamped around her calf. Her body shook with the agony. She screamed for help, for someone. Her hot tears streaked her cheeks, dribbling into her mouth, her shaking hands clutched at the metal.

Sharp pain in her shoulder, she yelped, her hands grabbing at it. A dart? A hunter's dart . . . what?

The pain of the dart spread out across her shoulder, her head funny, she couldn't see, the ground hard on her back, had she fallen? What? . . . Why?

Chapter 36

WHEN I WOKE up, I smelled bacon frying and my stomach growled so loudly that I heard Llys chuckle somewhere outside the tent. I opened the zipper, and Llys was standing over an expensive-looking camp stove and cooking up breakfast.

Now, I've never been a morning person. I'm grumpy until past noon and grumpier if I haven't eaten but right then I smiled so broadly that my cheeks ached.

"Please tell me I can share," I said, rubbing my now roaring insides.

Llys flipped over an egg and flashed me a grin. "You think I'd just let you starve on that rubbish while I fed myself?"

I smiled. We both knew she'd more than likely give up her own food when starving than do that.

"Nan say I couldn't cook?" I asked as she handed me the plate. I sniffed in the aroma of eggs and bacon and toast and smiled. My stomach smiled with me, adding a loud rumbling groan.

"No, you did. When you were hysterical about leaving you asked how you'd feed yourself."

I nodded, shoved a forkful into my mouth, and closed my eyes as it hit my tongue. It was like eating heaven, after a decade of prison food and a week of slop . . . I could have hugged Llys half to death.

"It's not that good," Llys stabbed her fork into a piece of bacon, "but it'll keep you going a bit better."

I murmured, too entranced by the salty bacon dipped in sinfully delicious egg yolk on my taste buds.

Llys raised her eyebrows and laughed. "You'd think you'd never eaten bacon before."

"Not good bacon . . . not good food . . . since . . . well . . . since Nan."

Llys sighed as she ate her own breakfast.

"Y'know you're supposed to be a vegetarian, right?"

Llys's eyes flew to mine and she looked down at her plate in horror.

"I'm guessing that's an oops moment?"

Llys groaned.

"It's okay. Who would believe me anyway."

"How do you do that?" she muttered.

I looked at her, wondering what she meant now. It was no secret in the institution that she was supposed to be a vegetarian. "Do what?"

"Disarm me. No one ever does that."

I smiled. "Not even the fake husband who left you or the fake reason you took the job in the prison?"

Llys shoved her food in her mouth, which I knew was to stop herself speaking.

"Can I stop calling you Doc now?"

"No. No . . . you can't." She wagged her food-filled fork at me, a frown on her face. "Aeron. I don't know how you know—"

"Yes, you do."

Llys let her shoulders drop. "Okay, so I do but you can't. I'm Doctor Serena Llys. It's that simple and that complicated."

"So, you gonna blame the bacon on me?"

"I need protein. If I'm doing manual labor I have to eat enough to keep me going."

"And the fact you aren't wearing lipstick and you've scraped your hair back, and that T-shirt says Harvard on it when your certificate said Yale?"

Llys finished off her food, walked over to a plastic bowl full of water, and washed up her dishes. "What's first on Nan's list?"

I finished my own breakfast and washed up my plate. "Roof. Got to strip off the broken tiles and replace them."

"Sounds pretty high up."

"For a rock climber? You'll be just fine."

Llys scowled at me and walked out into the sunshine. Mrs. Squirrel had clearly introduced herself. When we passed by she didn't even cast us a second glance.

"We could use the climbing gear in your trunk to make it safe," I suggested.

"I don't know what you mean," Llys said.

I walked to her car, popped the trunk, pulled out the gear, and shoved it into her hands.

"Must have put it in your trunk by mistake . . . sorry, Doc."

Llys threw her hands in the air and pulled ropes from the rope bag.

"If you grew up in the Rockies, you can climb," I said.

"You aren't meant to know that." Llys took hold of the static rope and ran her hands over it, her eyes searching for any worn parts on the sheath.

"You told me yourself."

Llys sighed, looking up from her task. "Yes, and I'm also a bad vegetarian. Like I said . . . disarming."

I shrugged and picked up a rope. I ran my hands over it, felt a nick in the sheath, and tossed the rope aside. "Ever thought that maybe you don't have to pretend with me 'cause I already know?"

She took the rope bag and walked back inside. I looked at Mrs. Squirrel who cast a look at me that said, "She's tied up in knots."

"She was when I met her," I answered.

Mrs. Squirrel flicked her tail in agreement.

I walked inside. Llys was waiting for me.

"Fine," she said. "I'm clearly slipping up but let's get this straight. The second anyone approaches I'm Doctor Serena Llys."

"And what's the story why you're here?"

"I was concerned about the events, and concerned about you. So, I stayed and will stay until you feel . . . more settled."

I tried not to laugh. "You think they'll buy that?"

"They have to. Otherwise I'm blown and you'll be back in Serenity."

"Good point." I took the rope from her and tested the knot. "It's not bad for a first-timer."

I walked up the stairs with Llys behind me. She then pulled herself up into the rafters with me following close behind. At the far end was a window that led up onto the roof. Llys lifted herself up onto the roof with too much ease for someone who wasn't supposed to do any sport. I suppressed a chuckle.

She looked down at me with narrowed eyes. "Not a word."

Pulling myself up was easier said than done. Trying to squeeze my bulk through a window was even harder—flexibility was not a strong point of mine. As I scrabbled onto the roof, the breeze picked up and buffeted me as I tried to stand. I looked up at the clear blue sky, wondering if I could really smell rain. It didn't look stormy.

"You need to be careful up here," I told her as I attached the harness to her. "Take it easy, sure steps, anything feels creaky just stop and wait for me."

Llys smiled at me, a genuine warm smile that showed the real woman. "Thank you," she whispered.

"Can't have my psychiatrist take a dive off the roof now, can I? How the hell would I explain that one to Daddy dearest?"

Llys laughed and squeezed my hand.

It was raining when she found out he was never coming home. Her mother cried every day for a year. She pinned his medal onto her uniform and had never once missed the parade. She loved to ride horses, fast horses. She hated the city and loved the feel of the wind on her face, the quiet of the mountains . . .

"Static shocks are awful," she said and smiled as she started to walk down the roof.

I nodded, understanding that she'd let me see, just a little, of what she couldn't say. At least not now, but then, sometimes silence spoke far louder than words.

Chapter 37

ELI SHOVED HIS toast into his mouth to stop himself from answering Jenny as she jabbed at him about Aeron for the umpteenth time.

"Y'know they should never have gone an' let her out. Bad news, that's what she is."

Eli looked at his plate. *Keep chewing, don't rise to it, anything for a quiet life.*

"I mean come on." Jenny slammed the kids' lunch boxes onto the table, one hand waving the butter knife. "The girl is so freakin' weird that what'd they expect?" She slapped the knife into the peanut butter and slopped it onto the bread. "First Jake, then the oddballs . . . who's next?" She squashed the sandwich closed and licked the peanut butter off her finger. "No one is safe until she gets locked up. No one."

Eli picked up his plate and walked to the sink. He soaped it, the water warm. *Don't rise to it. Don't. She's picking a fight, ignore it.*

"It ain't really surprising when the girl was raised by the witch on the river."

Eli felt the plate strain under his white-knuckled grip. He rinsed it, methodically, slowly, he had a lot to do today. There wasn't time for a domestic spat.

"You listening, Eli? Hell, you're deafer than your father was."

Eli turned around and did the only thing he could trust his voice to do without exploding into a rant. He grunted.

"That it? The freak is threatening your career and all you can do is grunt?"

Eli smiled, a forced, placating smile, and kissed Jenny on the cheek, while wondering when she had become a stranger to him. Did she not care that she was talking about his daughter? Aeron, his own flesh and blood?

"Girls need a father with a purpose, don't want them ending up with a bum like the Toughtons now do you?"

Eli snapped. Shoot the easy life. "Their daughter is missing. What the hell is wrong with you?"

Jenny smiled that triumphant smile she got when she'd cornered him into a fight. "I'm not the one pretending the freak ain't guilty."

"The freak has a name. Aeron *Lorelei* the same name you have."

"And why is that, Eli? Why don't we share the same name as Abe and the rest of your family?"

"You know damn well why. I'm going to work."

"Oh no," Jenny countered, stepping in front of him, hands on her hips like he was a naughty school boy. "No one else wanted you . . . I gave you two girls. You don't get to march out when you don't like the truth."

"The truth?" he barked. "You're talking about my daughter. Aeron is *mine*. I love her like I love our girls. I don't care what anyone thinks of me, her, or our girls. I *love* them."

Jenny wagged her manicured finger. "Love? How can you love a murderer?"

Eli grabbed his jacket off the chair, sending the chair clattering onto the floor, making Jenny jump. He didn't turn around to look at her, he just got the hell out and slammed the door.

Not for the first time, Eli wondered why the hell he had married her. *Because no one else wanted you and she could cook.*

He was that great a guy that he'd married so he wouldn't end up eating frozen dinners for the rest of his life. He'd never pretended he was capable of loving any other woman but Lilia, he never pretended that he'd feel happy ever again.

He would have left, years ago, but Jenny had gotten pregnant with the girls, and they were everything to him. He'd done it right with them. Every mistake he'd made with Aeron, he'd corrected with them and every time he'd done that . . . it had stung like hell.

Eli got in his car and started the engine, the morning sun weak against the clouds that were threatening. Neighbors walking dogs or their kids to school waved as he past. It was a quiet little place, every house the same as the next, long green lawns with sprinklers whizzing around on them. A quiet place that housed good people, people who needed to be kept safe from whoever lurked out there.

They would need to find Darcy, the Toughton's girl fast. No doubt that cloud was the start of the storms and there was no way they could search when the weather closed in.

As he got to the main road into town, he looked right and thought of going to Aeron's. She'd know exactly where the girl was, she'd know if the girl was alive.

"And how the hell you gonna explain that one, man?" he asked the empty car.

What would he say when everyone asked how he'd gone straight to the spot and found the girl? "My daughter, the one you all hate and fear said she'd be here. But she's not a killer, she just gets visions."

He laughed at how absurd it sounded to his own ears. Aeron would be locked up by noon. He turned left, staring into his rearview mirror, wishing he'd had the courage to go to her. "So, you just play with the young girl's life because you're too gutless."

He turned into the city hall parking lot, his blood pressure sky high. If he wasn't careful he wouldn't be around to do anything at all. He rubbed his chest and popped the tablets he kept hidden in his dash. He'd gone to see a doctor in the city, who he'd known on the job, to get his blood pressure medication. A good guy, who wouldn't tell the mayor that the chief wasn't as fit as he used to be.

Eli rubbed his stubbled chin in an effort to find some kind of motivation to go inside. He was pretty certain that if Darcy was taken by the same person who killed Mari and Natalia, they would find her, but it would be far too late.

DARCY, YOU COULDN'T stay awake for me? All the wonderful things I have planned for you and this is how you reward me? You can't think I'd let you sleep just yet, oh no . . . you don't get to sleep now.

Ungrateful, that's the trouble with you and all your filthy muck . . . you don't appreciate the effort, the sweet attention I'm giving you. You're lucky . . . you know?

For that, we'll take a little ride in the woods, that will be fun, won't it? And I've got you something very special, Darcy . . . oh, so special. It's a new rope . . . far nicer than the one I used on the mutt . . . you get a proper one . . . ain't that nice?

Chapter 38

WE HAD SPENT a good hour on the roof checking the damage, and I was relieved that it didn't need a complete overhaul. The main problem seemed to be one section, which had been caught by debris in a waterspout, a funnel that shot up from the river in high winds.

A lot of the folk around town said they were mine and Nan's true forms, that we were nothing but water furies waiting for people to prey on. A lot of the folk had way too much time on their hands. If I could turn myself into all sorts of things, why the hell would I bother staying in Oppidum?

"Hey, Aeron," Llys called from the far side of the roof.

I got up and walked over the tiles which clanked beneath my ripped sneakers.

"This section needs fixing too," she said, tapping another hole.

"That's not too bad, considering." I made my way to her. It was another debris wound but it could be fixed within the day.

"How 'bout we stop for a snack before we start repairs?" Llys suggested.

I nodded my agreement and my stomach lurched.

Motor roaring, the ground hard, stinging, clawing, dirt, sore, the pain, agony, ankle snapping, the roaring motor, rope stinging, clawing, stop, stop, stop—

I knew I was falling but my legs wouldn't work and I toppled so fast that I was sure I'd hit the ground in seconds.

SERENA WATCHED IN horror as Aeron's eyes flickered in her head. It looked like she was having some kind of a seizure and there was no way the rope holding her would stop her before she did herself damage.

Serena was in broad daylight, on the roof. She should under no circumstances do what she was about to. Every bit of training she had been through told her who she was, and her agenda was far more important than this woman. It was too important to jeopardize for any one person, even if that person was Aeron Lorelei.

Serena looked around, though she knew no one was around for miles.

She lassoed the rope around Aeron's chest and held it tight as she controlled the fall until they were both lying side-by-side on the roof tiles, inches from the hole's jagged edges.

"Some psychiatrist you are," Aeron said groggily.

Serena checked Aeron over. Did she suffer from fits?

"Vision, Doc. Just a vision."

Serena looked at Aeron's ashen face. "That could have killed you."

Aeron nodded. "Good thing I have a novice up here with me."

"Can you move?"

Aeron wiggled her fingers and toes.

Serena winced at Aeron's tight clothes. Hell, she needed something that fitted.

"Chest is a bit tight," Aeron said.

"Probably the rope."

"Oh." Aeron's face paled again.

"What's wrong?"

"Can we get off the roof first?"

Serena nodded and pulled Aeron up. She helped Aeron put on a looped climbing rope harness and eased her down into the watermill. By the time she climbed down, Aeron was free of the ropes and shivering on the top step of the death-trap stairs, the ones she still couldn't believe had no guard rail.

"Asking if you're okay is a dumb question, but are you?" Serena asked.

Aeron nodded then shook her head. "Another girl," she mumbled. "Getting worse."

"Can you see who it is?"

Aeron looked down at the steps. "Darcy Toughton."

"Is this a flash or is she gone?"

Aeron rubbed her hand over her face like she was trying not to cry.

Serena stopped herself from comforting her, knowing that all she would do was give Aeron more visions.

"Same as Mari. not gone . . . not here . . . just . . ."

Aeron's eyes shimmered with unspilled tears.

"Do you know where she is?"

Aeron shook her head. "Why can't I get something that will help?"

Serena stood up, her training taking over. "You may have. We eat, we'll go over what you did see, and then we'll fix the roof."

"It probably ain't a good idea to make notes, Doc. Evidence an' all that."

Serena smiled. "I don't need notes." She held out her hand. "Trust me."

Aeron nodded and pulled Serena's sleeve over her hand before taking it.

"You might get a little freaked out," a shivering Aeron told her as Serena steadied her.

"I have no doubt about that, but I am good at my job. If you trust me, I can help."

Aeron laughed as they headed down to the camp on the first floor.

"What's so funny?"

Aeron plonked herself onto a camp chair as Serena walked to the cooler she'd bought. "You said that before. *After* you'd kicked me out and tried to get me mauled in the exercise yard."

Serena opened the cooler and pulled out a can of soda. Aeron had scared her out of her skin that day. Not only had she not believed Aeron could see things but she had wondered if Aeron was in fact a plant. "I have nowhere to kick you out of now, so you'll be safe this time."

Aeron took the can, and Serena opened one for herself. She drained it, the fizz refreshing her senses and making her eyes water.

"You are the worst undercover agent I've ever met," Aeron said.

Serena snapped her eyes open and stared at Aeron. "What?"

"You're meant to be a prim-and-proper doctor, remember?"

Serena nodded. "I *am* a prim-and-proper doctor."

"Really?"

"Yes."

"Then why are you drinking straight out of a can? Why haven't you noticed you're covered in dirt and where did your highly polished nails go?"

Serena looked down at herself. She was covered in muck from

the roof, her hair was half hanging out of her band, and somewhere between the roof and the kitchen half the stick-on nails had ripped off, revealing her neatly cut ones underneath. At a loss of what to say, her favorite cuss word fell from her lips.

"Nice," Aeron said and sipped her soda. "Real ladylike."

Serena sighed. She'd been deep undercover for nearly fifteen years and at no point had she ever even come close to being revealed. She was so good at being someone else, she had forgotten who she had been originally. At least until Aeron Lorelei had wandered into her office.

"Who *are* you?" Serena muttered, trying to ignore the smug look on Aeron's face.

"I think it's *your* identity that's in question."

Serena's mind flashed back to the note. Aeron couldn't know everything. Not yet, it was too dangerous. The murders were one thing but there was the bigger picture to think about, the bigger picture of keeping Aeron safe. And Aeron would not be safe if she knew the truth. That, and Aeron would never trust Serena the second she learned it either.

For some strange reason that bothered Serena. She'd protected countless people without their knowledge and kept them safe and well. It didn't matter that most of them despised her when they understood why she had been so close, why she had gained their trust. It was part of the job, *this* was just part of the job. Aeron knew Doctor Serena Llys, and when this was all over, Doctor Llys would no longer exist, she'd be another person in another place protecting another person of interest. Simple, right?

"So what did you see?" Serena asked after noticing that Aeron was watching her.

"Okay. Darcy was in woods, maybe near the tourist lodge out by the rapids. She got caught, same as Mari. She was running but the rope hit her feet. The killer likes to do that—to lasso them like they're cattle."

Serena tried to mark out the possible positions in her mind's eye as she stared at the ordinance map she'd brought.

"Darcy was dragged . . . a mile . . . maybe more, then she passed out. That's it."

Serena looked at Aeron who fiddled with her toeless sneaker. "What kind of trees?"

Aeron closed her eyes. "I smell pine . . . there were needles on the ground . . . a motor roaring . . . I can't tell what kind."

"What did the rope feel like?"

Aeron tensed, her shoulders tightening as she gripped the chair. Serena waited, disconnecting herself from emotion until she saw only facts of something familiar and easier than trying to fake who she was to Aeron.

"Big . . . Darcy's not a tall girl . . . a tow rope maybe?"

"What kind of rope?"

Aeron frowned and opened her eyes. "I don't know. How many kinds of rope are there?"

"Hundreds, what kind?"

"I don't know!"

Serena shook her head. "You do know. You know because you were there."

"What?"

"You know because you did it, don't you?"

Aeron shook her head. "I don't think so. I don't know. I don't know . . ."

Serena nodded. "And that's why you need to stop digging for information on me. The only way you know that you aren't the killer is if I'm here to tell you that you aren't."

Aeron glared, her eyes were so piercing when she was angered.

"If I didn't believe in you, I would have hauled you in myself." Serena sighed. She hated this situation, she hated feeling so out of control. Why did Aeron do that to her? "But, I do believe in you and I need to make sure that these yokels can't lock you up."

Aeron cocked her head. "You reading my mind now?"

Serena flashed her a smile. "I'm a psychiatrist remember. Mind reading is my thing."

Aeron said nothing, instead she looked down at the map. "Do you have an idea? I mean I like trees but one pine is like the other and I know there're a lot of them in the forest."

"Well, the thick smell and the carpet of needles would probably rule out yellow pine, they're too tall and if Darcy is being dragged, then the trees can't be dense . . . the motor, if it's a car maybe, would rule out deep forest."

Aeron nodded. "It was a roaring motor. Like . . . like a quad or a dirt bike."

"See, that's useful. Did she get hit?"

Aeron winced. "What do you mean?"

"By trees. Did she hit any trees?"

Aeron leaned over, paling as though she would be sick at any moment.

"Try and think. I know it's hard."

"Now you do sound like a shrink."

Serena didn't laugh. She was too busy thinking. If the girl was in dense forest, that could be anywhere. Aeron seemed to think instinctively it was over by the rapid lodges which catered to the water sports industry. The lodges wouldn't be open for another month according to her map. A perfect place to take victims.

"No, she didn't. She broke her ankle though."

Serena pulled her keys out of her pocket.

"Where are you going?"

Serena put her keys away. Exactly, where was she going? To charge off into the forest and take down a killer? To save a girl's life and blow her cover permanently?

"Can you tell anyone? Your people?"

"My people? Like Val and the other guards?"

Aeron closed her eyes and hung her head. "I hope it's worth it."

Serena shoved her hands in her pockets. "That's not my call to make."

"Ain't there anyone? She's going to suffer. It won't stop there."

"Will it make you have a fit again?"

Aeron opened her eyes and frowned. "What?"

Serena walked to Aeron and handed her a chocolate bar from the cooler. "Will it make you have another fit, will you keep seeing her?"

Aeron nodded. "I'll live every second if she's like Mari."

Serena nodded and pulled her keys back out of her pocket on the way to the door.

"Where are you going?"

"If your safety is in question I need to get advice from another doctor. Help stop the fits."

"Thank you," Serena heard Aeron whisper as she walked out of the door.

Serena walked to her car completely confused at how unraveled she had become. She'd heard of other agents who got to a stage when the lies all rolled into one and they couldn't operate anymore. Is that what was happening?

Aeron was a friendly, a protectee that Serena had no doubt wouldn't harm anyone intentionally but what about the next placement? What if the protectee wasn't a friendly? What if she slipped up then? She got into her car and pulled out the hidden flap in the dash. She took out the phone inside and hit her boss's number.

"What is it?"

"Reference 0128428, subject had a 3-2-4, nearly fell off the roof. The Unsub may be in or near the Rapid Lodge."

"Did anyone see you?"

"No."

Serena only prayed that was true. They were miles from anywhere.

"At no point will you allow the subject to get near."

"Will you send someone to clear it up?"

"It's none of our concern."

Serena bit her tongue. Her boss was silent for a moment before sighing. "Fine. I'll send someone . . . keep the subject at the mill."

Her boss disconnected, and she breathed out slowly. She was asking a massive favor, she was putting her career on the line. "What career? If you can't play doctor in a lonely mill with one woman then how the hell can you pull off anything else?"

Serena got out of the car and walked into the mill.

Aeron was already stacking up the tiles they would need to put on the roof. "We need to fix the holes first, the boards, then the tiles. It's hammer and nails, I'm afraid . . . Nan didn't do nail guns."

Serena nodded, remembering helping out her father when he fixed the roof after the winter. She had fond memories of good old hammer and nails.

"Doc, you coming?"

Serena looked up and nodded, shaking her memories from her mind. "Just don't expect me to talk to you if I break a nail."

Chapter 39

WHEN DARCY OPENED her eyes, the storm was almost upon her. Her vision so blurred, her body so beaten that she couldn't move. She was so tired, so worn. A blurred figure seemed to hover over the ground. It was in front of her but when she tried to focus, her eyes flickered in her head.

Darcy tried to speak, the words in her head saying one thing, her own voice in her ears, strangely saying something different. Something that made no sense, just noises.

The figure walked over to her. She tried to ask it for help, again more noises, again only strange sounds.

It spoke back, loud and booming, so much so that the tone rattled the walls of her mind and made her sick.

She heard it laugh at her as she retched on the ground and it spoke to her again. It was near now, and in a fit of anger she pushed out. It thudded against something nearby.

The reward was a rope sliding around her neck.

ELI TRIED NOT to sigh as Mayor Casey and his lawyers bustled into his office after lunch. So far the search for Darcy Toughton had yielded nothing. Mrs. Jenkins had seen her leave work and walk in the direction of home. A home she had never reached.

Eli had every on- and off-duty officer and a posse of volunteers out looking for her, scouring every inch of land between Jenkins' farm and her home. They had found nothing, not even a sign that she'd ever been there at all.

Jeff had found no DNA, no trace evidence, and no drag or tread marks anywhere and the last thing Eli needed right this moment was a run in with the mayor.

"Chief Lorelei, allow me to introduce my legal team," Mayor Casey said.

Eli nodded at the paid vultures. He was surprised his ex-wife Iris wasn't among them. "What can I do for you?"

"I want Aeron Lorelei out of this town."

Eli sat back, his fist balled under his desk. "You may be the mayor, but you do not own the entire town."

"I will buy the cabin from you, whatever the cost and you can just send your little freak show someplace else."

Eli laughed. "Oh, you think I own the cabin? Unfortunately, Mr. Mayor, I don't. Aeron does, along with the field and all the rest of the town . . . or have you forgotten?"

Mayor Casey narrowed his eyes. "What?"

Eli nodded to the lawyers who stopped smiling and scrabbled through the paperwork they had with them.

"The Lorelei family founded the place. It was their gold mine. It's been handed down since then, every right, every blade of grass belongs to Aeron."

The Mayor sneered. "It doesn't—"

"Sir, actually Chief Lorelei is correct," one of the lawyers said. "He ensured the line was not broken by taking the Lorelei name on marriage. It's all legal. Aeron Lorelei is the sole owner of Oppidum."

Eli tried not to enjoy watching the mayor turn as purple as a prune. "You can lock her up if she commits a crime, you can hound her and heckle her and make her life hell but you cannot force her to move because you're on her land. We all are."

"She's a murderer. A freak. A witch. That's what she is!" Mayor Casey said.

Eli looked at the lawyers who were trying to usher a ranting Mayor Casey out of the office.

"You mark my words, Lorelei. I'll see her behind bars. I'll see she pays."

Eli closed the door to his office and slumped back into his chair. Aeron didn't have a clue how rich she was, she didn't have a clue how much power she held. He had never told her anything.

Eli opened his desk drawer and pulled out the picture that he'd spent years drinking over. Lilia had been a clever woman. She'd seen that the town would remain in the family's hands by persuading him to take her last name.

It had all been completely secret of course. The fact that the Lorelei family lived in the mill from the start had prevented them from being targets. They'd never demanded anything from the people on their land, but the steady income had filled their pockets. Time had forgotten the township belonged to them.

As long as someone carried the Lorelei name, the land was safe. It was the sole reason why Eli had taken Lilia's name, and the reason why he had never relinquished it.

A bad father he no doubt was, a bad husband and man, but he would never take Aeron's roots from underneath her. That and he would never throw that kind of weight onto Aeron's shoulders. He was starting to understand that he may hold the name but it was Aeron who held the future in more ways than she realized.

Chapter 40

WE WERE EATING lunch after making great headway on the roof on an old bench in the front yard.

I sighed as I heard a car crunching up the lane. The squad car emerged from a cloud of dust and stopped on the edge of the grass. I knew it had to be about Darcy and I was pretty sure that I would be arrested. The sight of my father and Sam made me tense in expectation.

Llys touched my knee. "Let me handle this."

Sam and my father climbed out of the car and exchanged glances, both looking a little baffled that I had company. Her presence made them shuffle and shrug, which eased my nerves, if only a small amount.

"Aeron, I need to ask you a couple of questions," my father began.

Llys squeezed my knee again. "Keep it zipped." She looked up. "Good afternoon, Chief Lorelei. My name is Doctor Serena Llys, Aeron's psychiatrist."

I noticed that she did not get up to greet them but forced them to walk over to us. She had begun some kind of psychological battle that I didn't know much about.

My father nodded and smiled pleasantly. "I need to speak to Aeron alone, Doctor Llys."

Llys shook her head. "I am Aeron's legal representative. She's been in my care for some time and so she assigned me as such."

My father frowned and looked at me as if to question it. I simply nodded. No one would represent me when I was convicted, so it made sense that I'd ask someone I trusted.

"Very well, Doctor Llys, this is Deputy Chief Sam Casey. We would like to ask Aeron a couple of questions about her whereabouts over the past few days."

"Isn't that a conflict of interest?"

My father put his hands on his hips. "I'm quite capable of doing my job, Doctor."

Llys seemed unfazed. "I didn't mean you. Deputy Chief Casey is the brother of Jake Casey is he not?"

Sam tensed at the sound of his brother's name. I felt my stomach roll like a winter avalanche.

"Yes," my father said. I could see his irritation in his mannerisms—hands on belt, frown deeper than the colors in fall.

"Don't you think that's a little inappropriate that Aeron was convicted of Jake Casey's murder, yet you bring his brother to question her in another matter?" Llys asked.

"The mayor requested it," Sam snapped.

I could see Llys pulling in her trap. "And does the mayor often command the local law enforcement?"

My father took his hat off and sighed. "Sam, go wait by the car."

"What?"

"Just do it."

Sam stood there in defiance for several moments. He had never been much for obeying the orders of someone else and he'd spent the entire time avoiding looking at me. Now he glared at me as if I should stick up for him.

My father glared at him. "Sam—"

"Going!" Sam stomped to the car, got in, and slammed the door.

My father turned to Llys. "He didn't want to be here."

"Then perhaps you should remember who is the police officer and who is being policed."

My father scowled. I thought he was going to launch into a full blown argument but instead he turned to me. "Where were you between the hours of seven last night and ten this morning?"

I looked at Llys who nodded. "Here."

"Can anyone verify this?"

"I can," Llys answered.

"You?"

She nodded. "Me."

My father scowled, looking at me as if I would deny it. "What the hell were you doing here?"

I kept my mouth well and truly shut, knowing that all I'd do was end up tangling me and Llys in some kind of web.

"Aeron contacted me, she was distressed at the events in the town and the way in which she was being treated by the officials," Llys said. "She was worried that the murder of a woman who you dropped outside her cabin would be linked to her. I immediately came here to ensure that Aeron could not be the focus of a witch hunt of any kind."

My father did bite at that. "Officials? I guess that means me, does it?"

"You, your deputy." She nodded at the car. "It was you that removed her monitor and dropped the victim outside the cabin, was it not?"

My father's face turned red. "I didn't know that Natalia would get hurt . . ."

I heard the deep regret echo in his voice. Llys was making it sound like he was trying to frame me. I felt too lost at her argument to utter a word. Would he? Was he trying to get rid of me permanently? Would my own father do that?

"And the monitor?"

"To stop her coming into town."

Llys looked like a cat about to pounce on a cornered mouse. My father was being tied up in knots.

"Doesn't that play very nicely into someone's hands who may wish to rid the town of both of you?" she asked.

My father opened and closed his mouth a few times. He looked at me, then he looked at Llys. "You think that's . . ." He looked down at the ground with his tongue poking out. "Aeron, Darcy Toughton is missing," he whispered. "You got any ideas?"

Llys shot me a look to tell me to shut the hell up. "Perhaps that flare may help you, Chief."

My father looked up, as did I. She was pointing at a flare shot high over the forest quite a way from us.

My father looked at Llys, looked at me, and nodded as though he now understood something that was completely beyond my grasp.

"Thank you for your time, ladies," he said as he sprinted to his car.

"Take your tablets," I called after him.

He turned as though I'd just shot him. His eyes locked on mine. A second later he nodded again, got in the cruiser, and screeched off.

"Well, that went better than expected," I said.

Llys looked at me like I'd just missed the entire conversation. She got up, walked to where the car had been, picked up a rock, and threw it into the river.

"What are you doing?"

"My job." She brushed her hands together. "Now, let's fix up the roof because I want to go and get you some clothes that fit."

THE ROOF TOOK half the time I had expected it to. Llys and I worked really well as a team. Whoever she had been before she ended up here, she knew her way around a roof repair as well as I did. So, by mid afternoon I was fixing the axle on the side of the building and preparing it to get the wheel back on. With the roof fixed and the wheel working, the cabin would be up and running in no time and with electricity, we wouldn't have to rely so much on the cook stove for warmth. I didn't mind it, but the less propane I had hissin' at me in a confined space the happier I would be.

As I was hanging on my climbing rope fixing up the wall, I ran over all Llys and my father had said to each other. I didn't know what was going on, and the three people—Sam, my father, and Llys, I couldn't read.

When you're used to knowing too much, not knowing anything feels like running blind through a mine field. I didn't like it, not even a bit.

My thoughts kept going back to the almost lawyer-like arguments that Llys threw at my father. How he'd taken my monitor off and dropped off Natalia to me. I was shocked cold by that thought. My father was many things in my eyes but did he hate me enough to frame me for murder? And was he himself capable of such a thing?

I hoped to heaven he wasn't.

And what did Llys mean by the fact that someone could be trying to set both of us up? Who would want to get rid of my father? I mean, sure, he had me—I was an outcast but the folk around town liked him—didn't they? I mean, why would they keep him as chief if they didn't?

I looked down at the swirling clear waters. Llys had said she was doing her job. Doing what job? What was her job? As a defense attorney she would have trumped my mother any day.

As a doctor, she must be amazing because in the last twenty-four hours, I felt more normal than I ever had—if I didn't count the vision of Darcy.

I looked back down at the river. She'd thrown a stone into it, a stone that had been where the car had been. Why? I finished up the wall, trying not to think about it. The snatches I had from Llys told me that she was on my side, for whatever reason, and that she was trying to keep me from harm. I should leave well alone, shouldn't I?

She kept saying that to push and prod at her mask would put us both in danger. She didn't realize just how little I saw. Most of my questions about her being an agent were pretty much guesswork. Why would an agent be following me? Why would her duty here be more important than the murders of Natalia and Mari?

A gust of a bitter wind hit me out of nowhere and I swung on the end of the rope like a wind-chime.

"What?" I asked it, figuring it was Nan or Natalia.

The trees nearby howled with a gust leading my eye up to the sky. A huge, black, storm cloud was heading in. Not the cloud of despair over the town, no, even that was heading for cover. This storm cloud was the beginning of storm season. Nature had a way of trumping any other presence with its sheer force.

I climbed over to the side of the cabin and detached myself from the harness. We had a few hours yet but I needed to get the place storm proofed.

I looked at the wide eyes of Mrs. Squirrel as she sniffed the air. "You can camp inside with us. Okay?"

Mrs. Squirrel seemed relieved, and I detached her box and store, and placed her in the sturdiest and safest part of the house.

"You'll be safe here," I told her.

For that she sniffed my hand in thanks but my senses were starting to prickle. If a full moon can affect the fluid inside a human mind, then the might of Mother Nature, about to rage, most definitely affected the human heart. And my heart was thudding, this one was a big one.

Chapter 41

ELI LOOKED UP at the growing thunderheads, an ominous turret of white pluming up into the darkening sky. Anything to take his mind off the black zipped body bag being wheeled past him. The building columns looked as unsettled as he felt. Darcy had been found an hour too late by the hiker who had shot up the flare.

The whole situation tugged at his heart. He had worked big cases in the city, he had tracked down serial killers and seen their handiwork close up but this wasn't the city. Out here, in Oppidum, it was safe, wasn't it? Its people were small-minded folk who bickered and sniped yet stuck together like they'd been fixed with glue. To think one of them, and it could be one of them, had committed these sick crimes made his entire view of the world wobble.

Was it someone from the gypsy train trying to cover their tracks? Oh, the local folk would love that wouldn't they? Blame the entire thing on the outsiders they hated. Could it be one of the people in town? The victims were all undesirables in most folks eyes, the Toughtons weren't a liked family. Was someone trying to get rid of those they disliked?

Was it someone from out of town? Had someone scoped out Oppidum as a target? Was the killer out in the trees watching? Was the killer striking where the ground was already shaky with Aeron's return?

And what about Aeron? He wanted to believe with all his heart that the girl wouldn't and couldn't do a thing to hurt anyone. Those were the thoughts he had as a father, but what about as police chief? He'd arrested her for Jake's death and she'd recounted the whole thing in detail. There wasn't even a lot of emotion. He'd figured it for shock but what if she was as bad as everyone said?

What if it *was* Aeron?

Eli shook his head. No, he wouldn't even entertain the idea. She had that doctor with her to prove it now. A doctor that seemed a lot more filled in on the workings of the court and the town council than she should be.

He was glad that Aeron had someone to fight in her corner. Someone who had run rings around him. Was she right? Was the doc right about someone trying to rid the town of the Lorelei name? Who stood to benefit from that? The only way it would be up for sale was if there were no Loreleis alive.

Eli's heart skipped a beat. What better way to ensure that than to have Aeron stand trial for serial killings.

The clouds grew grayer, darker, more menacing as the flashes sparked a rumble of thunder. Eli pulled out his radio. "Update from the weather center, Skip."

"Storm force winds, flash floods, and maybe some electrical storms . . . ETA two hours," Skip answered in seconds.

Eli looked up at the greenish-yellow light in the sky. He prayed it would only be that. His instinct told him not to take the chance and he surveyed the crime scene around them. Whatever evidence was there would have to be left. The entire town needed to be locked down and readied.

"I want everyone prepped, roads cleared."

"Sir!" Skip answered.

Eli walked over to Jeff and his team. "Anything you haven't already got, it gets left."

Jeff looked like he was about to object. The ground trembled from a rolling rumble from the heavens. "Will do. You heard the chief. Move!"

Eli watched the men hurry around, clearing the last of their equipment. He noticed Michael, the forensics guy, was not moving from his spot.

"Hey, move it," Eli told him.

Michael waved it away. "I found something. I need maybe fifteen minutes."

Eli nodded and the rest of the team packed up the vans and drove off. Sam went ahead with Jeff, leaving just Eli and Michael.

"What did you find?" Eli asked.

Michael gently pulled something off a tree trunk. "I don't know, but it's not a part of the trunk."

Eli looked over Michael's shoulder. It looked like a hair or maybe a fiber of some sort. "Think it's from the girl?"

Michael shrugged. "For all I know it could be from a critter of some sort . . . but . . . it caught my eye."

Eli nodded and patted Michael on the shoulder as the sky let out another rumble, much louder—the storm was fast approaching.

"Got it," Michael said and bagged up the piece. "Let's get the hell out of here."

Eli nodded, and they hurried to his cruiser. A flash forked out across the sky and the roar deepened.

"Don't know about you," Michael said. "But I wouldn't want to be outside when she hits."

Eli looked in his rear-view mirror at the monstrous black-and-gray fist gliding down over from the mountains. The cloud filled the sky like an avalanche hurtling toward the town. He couldn't help but agree with Michael.

Anyone foolish enough to be out when that crashed through the town would be lucky to survive. Eli looked up at the thunderhead once more and floored it. Luck had nothing to do with it. If anyone was caught up in that, they'd need a miracle.

Chapter 42

I MOVED THE last of the supplies into the old corn store at the side of the mill and looked up at my work. It hadn't taken long to storm proof the place and I was quite pleased at how quickly it had all come back to me.

A few of the windows were already smashed so I boarded them up completely. The wheel which was still growing its own meadow, was now bolted down with chains, the barn an' everything was locked up and steadied.

I'd moved the camp, including all of Llys's things and Mrs. Squirrel up the metal safety stairs into the storm shelter that I'd built in amongst the colossal pipe work on the first floor at the back. The metal landing gave us enough room to get out of the cramped space should we be in there for any amount of time. It would keep us safe and dry from any flooding . . . I hoped.

I could feel the heaviness in the air, my chest protesting the weight of the atmosphere. It was like breathing in thick, hot water. The forest was in panic mode. Birds crying out their warnings fled the tree tops in numbers. Flash floods, a thunderstorm that was what my senses were telling me. No doubt there'd be a few waterspouts. I just hoped the roof would hold out.

As I sat down on the old bench to eat something before my final checks, the unease covered me like a cold, dark blanket. I couldn't shake the feeling no matter how much I tried to concentrate.

It wasn't so much the killer or Natalia's raging spirit but something else was nagging away in my mind, something unknown to me, something which was thumping through my veins faster than blood.

I looked up at the dirt track, hoping that Llys would hurry up. This storm was a bad one and for the first time I was a little scared to be alone.

"Come on, Doc. Come on," I muttered as I looked up at the thick black thunderheads.

A warning rumble rattled through my body and mind, shaking me in more ways than one.

"Hurry up, Doc. Don't make me ride this out alone."

SERENA PULLED ONTO the main road and looked at the backpack and clothes she had gotten Aeron. She'd had to go to the tourist outdoor supply store in order to find anything in Aeron's size. One pair of hiking boots and some sneakers on top of that had been like trying to pan for gold in Times Square.

The sky overhead darkened and Serena flicked on the headlights. Her instincts from childhood caused her to feel as though she needed to burrow for safety like a small animal. She hated storms. The vast column spilled toward her like lava, its igneous intentions evident. It was all too painful, too raw.

This was not the time to dwell on her father's death but even so, the cloud above represented loss and heartache. This storm looked the same as the one that took him, as though it was coming for her now.

"When did you become superstitious? Get over it," she told herself.

Even so, she took the phone from the dash and stowed it in her jeans, put the clothes and shoes in the pack and slung them on her back, along with her gun, ready to haul herself from the car. It was a stupid, childish reaction but one that enabled her to keep driving toward her worst nightmare.

As she got to the dirt track turn off, she glanced in her rear-view mirror. "What the—?"

Bang.

Serena clung onto the steering wheel as a huge pickup slammed her from behind.

She pumped the brakes. Nothing. The pickup was too big. Too powerful. The river too close. Oh, God, she couldn't stop. She gripped the wheel and yanked up the handbrake. The tires screamed as she hauled the steering wheel with all her strength, crashing her elbow into the door as the car flipped around. She pushed open the door, threw herself out, and thudded to the ground and rolled as the car crunched into a utility pole.

The momentum catapulted Serena off the edge of the road onto the mud-slick bank as her car fizzed somewhere above.

A sickened crunch sounded through her ears as something hard hit her head. The world spun violently, the mud sucking her down, down into swirling dark waters.

I LOOKED UP the road as I paced on the wet grass. The rain started to hammer down. Where the hell was she? She should be back by now. I didn't know Llys well, but I knew enough to know that she understood how deadly storms could be. So where was she?

I looked at the bulging river, the rain hammering down into it, the raging waters bubbling. the stone that Llys had thrown still called me like some kind of forbidden treasure. I knew that to touch it was wrong, to touch it would tell me more about her, more than she wanted me to know.

I stood there warring with myself, the rain dripping from my hair into my eyes. What if she was hurt . . . ? What if she had been taken by the killer?

"Listen to yourself. She could probably handle herself a lot better than you," I muttered.

All the while, that stone beckoned to me. I waded out, knowing exactly where it was. Her essence seemed to coat it until it glowed. I picked it up and flicked it over in my hand. The water dried in a strange way. I rubbed my eyes, wondering if I was hallucinating. The numbers nine-eight-four formed on its surface.

Slam, the brakes screech, the wind howls, bank scrapes and scratches, smell of gas and fire, the rain hammering, the water rising.

I scrambled through the waters and fought my way up the muddy bank, then I bolted up the lane, my toes catching on the gravel, the mud thickening under the might of the rain. The sheer power of it swept in waves across my path. I couldn't catch my breath. I couldn't stop. I had seconds to get there.

I saw the explosion from the car before I heard the tires of whoever did it spin in the gravel and mud as they drove off. They must have thought Llys was in the car, but she wasn't.

The car smoldered, hissing at me as I reached it. The driver's side was open. Blood was on the door. I looked around. Empty. She was out but where was she? Llys was face down in the river, somewhere. The river was rising so fast, the mud coming with it, that I couldn't see beneath the surface.

"Doc!" I yelled.

I knew there wouldn't be a response. She was drowning, she was unconscious. I closed my eyes, willing every gift I had ever been burdened with to help me.

"Where are you, *Renee Black*?"

The moment I said her name, I knew. I hurtled down the bank, scrambling over the sharp rocks and glass from the crash. She was there head down. The muddy water splashed into my face as I ploughed into the river. I gripped hold of her shoulders and hauled her upward, the blood gushing from a wound in her head. I lifted her into my arms, the river now hitting my knees, the current strengthening.

"Nan, if you're around. I need help."

A lightning flash rippled overhead and I pushed off through the river.

A gush of water smashed into me, sending me sprawling sideways. The current swept my feet away as I clung onto Llys, not daring to let go. The water sapped my strength as I found a foothold. So cold, so tired.

"I mean it, Nan. Help!"

A surge hit my back like a large hand pushing me and I got a foothold on the bank. I scrambled up, losing a shoe as the river bubbled below me. I got to a stable grassy patch and collapsed onto my knees, my body pounding with cold and adrenaline.

Llys was cold, not moving. Her breathing had stopped. I rolled her onto her back and frantically pulled at the debris in her mouth, clearing the airway. I didn't know how the hell to do CPR, I didn't know how to help her.

"Please."

A shallow breath hissed out at me. The rain mixed with the blood from her head wound. A roar overhead sparked a monstrous tremble through the ground and I staggered to my feet, hauling her up into my arms.

"Stay with me. Please."

I looked up into the raging storm and gasped for breath. The trees swayed like grass beneath her fury. I had no choice but to walk headlong into that storm. I fell forward. The silence deafening. The wind ceased. The entire forest seemed to still in that moment.

Oh no, oh no. I started to run, to pound down the road, gripping hold of Llys, praying I would get us back to the cabin before—

"God help us," fell from my lips as a crashing roar ripped through the air and I realized what was coming for us.

Chapter 43

ELI WALKED DOWN the steps into his basement. The house sat on a hill two miles or so from the river and he hoped that would stop the flood from reaching them.

He stopped for a second before he walked into the room where Jenny and the girls were sitting. He wanted to go and check on Aeron. Every bone in his body begged him to but he wouldn't. What right did he have to become the overprotective father all of a sudden?

Aeron knew the drill with the storms. Hell, the girl could fix wood faster than he ever could. Nan had taught her well. What use was he? Plus, she had the doctor to keep her company so she wasn't going to ride out the storm alone.

Eli leaned his head against the wall. The urge to get out there felt like a wildcat clawing its way out of his stomach.

"You and the girls okay?" he called to Jenny.

"Yeah, you coming?"

Eli looked up the stairs and at the door of the room where his family was. "I just got a call—O'Reilly—I got to check it out. You know she's on her own."

He didn't wait for a response. He didn't peek into the room either. His face always gave him away when he lied.

Eli rushed out the house and jumped into his secondary cruiser, a truck, and shook off the rain from his hat. "Take your tablets." Aeron's voice echoed in his head. He smiled and pulled out the bottle. The words, however sharp, gave away that maybe, just maybe, she didn't hate him completely.

He started the truck up and eased out onto the road now shimmering with the pooling rain. The clouds had massed into a bank of murky black, towering into the sky and for a brief second, he wondered when he'd gotten so crazy.

As he got to the turn off, every part of his body pulsed with panic. That was the doctor's car crashed into the utility pole.

Eli stopped, got out, and ducked as a branch hurtled from the trees to his left and nearly took his head off. The doctor wasn't in her car, and the river was like a torrent, crashing and straining against the banks.

Eli studied the saturated dirt track. Another branch hurtled through the air at him and crashed into his truck. He looked up and stared at the horizon, his heart nearly stopping. Beyond the O'Reilly farm, way in the distance, right on the horizon, he saw a funnel appear. Aeron, he had to find Aeron . . . and the doctor.

I COULDN'T BREATHE each time the wind smacked into me. It was so fierce I felt as though I was being rammed by an invisible car over and over again. It swept my feet from under me, the mud sucking at them like quicksand.

I fell again, the rain blinding me, my breath stolen from my body, the energy sucked from me. Every step I took felt like I'd hurled myself through a brick wall. The roar of the wind was deafening, and I was thrown forward, Llys landing in front of me. I heard a siren somewhere, faint, and my body tensed so painfully that my calf cramped.

I stared at the approaching tornado, trying to find something left to get both of us to the cabin. Sure, I'd seen one before, but from much further away. This close . . . Hell, it was huge.

I got to my knees and dragged myself through the mud to Llys. She was cold, alive, I knew, but for how long? I looked behind, the funnel moved closer. We stood no chance, no way would we get even close to safe. The lightning forked just above me, scoring a direct hit on the tree to my left. It slumped toward us. I tried to dodge it, dragging Llys to safety, but a branch caught the back of my leg. I collapsed onto my front with a mind-splitting pain.

I had nothing left, I couldn't do this. So tired . . . so tired.

A hand touched my own. I couldn't see, I couldn't hear who it was.

I found myself in a truck, Llys hauled in beside me and we were hurtling down the slippery mud road to the cabin. All I could do was look out of the back window as the twister gained on us.

ELI CLUNG TO the wheel and fought the truck as it was buffeted by the winds. His heart hammered so hard that he knew, if he hadn't taken his tablets, he'd be in trouble.

Eli looked into his rear-view mirror. He *was* in trouble. The twister was gaining fast and the only hope he had was that she would change course.

The road slid and slipped under the tires. The debris slammed every part of the truck. Twisters. He hated damn twisters.

Not only a twister but this monster had a base that now stretched across the width of a quarter of a field.

Eli hurtled into the yard and slid to a stop, thankful to Nan that she had re-enforced the first three floors. The river had burst its banks, and no doubt would sweep away the truck if the funnel didn't get it first. He ripped open the door, dragged a limping Aeron into the building, and headed back out into the wind. The twister would be on them in minutes. He lifted the doctor into a fireman's lift and used every ounce of fight he had to get to the door.

The wind sucked away his feet. He grabbed for the handle. Aeron was there. Her hand gripped his, and she had a rope around her, no doubt tethering her to the center driveshaft of the building.

She pulled with him and he broke free of the suction and slammed the door behind him.

"Bolt it. Bolt it," he shouted.

Aeron limped to him and they threw brace against brace over the door. Eli hammered the nails into the wood. The cabin rattled and he looked down at the floor. They were ankle deep in river water.

"Shelter," Aeron slurred as she tied the rope around him and the doctor.

They slogged through the water to the pipe room and Eli nearly cried in joy. Aeron had made a storm shelter there. She'd used the housing of the machines to build a makeshift fort almost, bolted to the main structure of the building.

"Ingenious," he said.

They dragged the doctor into the room and Aeron bolted the door. The room was set up like a base camp—sleeping bags, food stores, everything they would need.

"Med kit?" Eli shouted to Aeron over the roar like a freight train outside.

Aeron grabbed a box, and he helped her to open it. He saw her hands were grazed and swollen.

"Doc . . . Doc . . . Come on, please." Eli moved over to the prone doctor and checked her vitals. He heard barely a heartbeat.

"Warmth, she needs warmth," he told Aeron as he started to search through equipment.

Eli heard the rattle-like gasp from the doctor and tried to shake her. "No . . . no . . . Don't you die on us now!" He started CPR and Aeron scrambled back seconds later. "We're losing her!"

Aeron scrambled to the doctor's head and started mouth-to-mouth. They worked in a frenzied rhythm—desperate, panicked bursts.

"Please. Come on!" Eli said.

Eli stopped and looked at Aeron whose eyes spilled tears and made streaking light lines over her mud-battered face.

"No . . . don't give up . . . no!" Aeron said.

Eli tried to grab for her arm but Aeron moved around to the doctor's chest and pumped her fists.

"Please . . . breathe . . . Please," Aeron pleaded.

A huge crack of something hit the roof. Eli ducked but Aeron didn't even wince.

"Please!" she shouted.

Eli straightened and his vision seemed to dance in front of his eyes. Aeron had her hands over the doctor, her head resting in hopelessness on the doctor's shoulder but the room seemed to pulse with something. Not from the storm but from Aeron herself.

Eli sat rooted as Aeron continued to beg the doctor to breathe.

"Aeron, Aeron. Let go . . . please, sweetheart . . . let her go."

He went to Aeron and pulled her away. Aeron collapsed into his arms and sobbed so hard that he could do nothing but cry with her.

Chapter 44

I CRIED SO hard that my head pounded with grief. I held on so tightly, the pain wracked my body, mind, and spirit. It was my fault that Llys was here at all. It was my fault.

"Ow," came a very quiet whisper from behind me.

"What's hurting?" I heard my father ask.

I looked up at him, shaking my head. "I didn't say anythin'."

He frowned. "You said your head hurt."

"No, I didn't."

We looked at each other, then I spun around. Llys was breathing steady and calm and she was awake.

"Doc!"

We went to her, and she looked up at me with a confused look. "Did you slug me?"

I laughed and shook my head.

"Wow, you take a mud bath?"

Llys tried to sit up. My father went to stop her but she grumbled until he let her. "Where are we?"

I looked up at my version of Fort Knox. "Storm room."

"Hell, it hit us?"

My father and I nodded. I hoped it had switched lanes or blown itself out, but the scared child inside me made me feel like it was just waiting for us to step outside again.

"How's your head?" I asked.

Llys rubbed the dried blood off her forehead. She had one hell of a nasty gash.

"I feel fine . . . cold . . . groggy . . . like I had too much liquor and I'm paying for it, but oddly I feel fine."

I looked at my father.

His eyes were veiled. "You were dead . . . I don't . . ."

"Does it matter?" I asked.

"Did you? . . . you . . . the room . . ."

I shook my head. "No, I didn't do nothing. I swear it."

Llys looked from me to my father and back. "I died?"

"No, you didn't die. I wouldn't believe it. I kept going. It was because I kept going."

"You did. Yes, Aeron kept going." My father nodded as if wanting to believe it.

Llys touched my hand, just to thank me, but the world was sucked from before my eyes.

The killer was there watching, she pulled out of the parking lot, it was easy, no one would see, by the time they realized, the storm would destroy the evidence, easy, so easy.

"They're going to hit, brakes, brakes! No, No, swerve, swerve, I'm going to hit it, have to jump have to . . .

"It wasn't an accident," I managed to blurt out before I blacked out.

Chapter 45

ELI RUBBED HIS stinging eyes as he sat in the dim light of the lamp. The doctor and Aeron were resting but he couldn't. Aeron's words that someone had tried to kill the doctor, that the car hitting the pole hadn't been an accident, rolled around and around in his exhausted mind.

The storm had abated somewhat over the hours he'd sat there but the storm inside his own heart was only just beginning. He had left Jenny and the girls on instinct, he'd driven to Aeron and abandoned them to the storm. He hoped with every ounce of his being that they were okay but there would be repercussions from this, massive ones.

Eli looked at Aeron. She shivered in her sleep, so he looked for another foil blanket, like the one they had wrapped around the doctor. He searched in the boxes but found none. He saw the soaked bag tossed in the corner of the room and went to it. Shoes and boots. He took them out and put them next to the oil burner to dry out along with the clothes, which looked new, tags attached. He frowned as he felt something cold, hard, and familiar at the bottom.

"Probably a good idea if you don't pull that out," the doctor said.

Eli looked up and met the doctor's steady gray eyes. "I don't know many doctors who carry guns."

"There's a killer on the loose."

"It's not the kind of gun you buy at a store, Doctor."

The doctor raised her eyebrow. "Really, you can tell what it is by the feel?"

"I'm not an idiot and I know military spec when I feel it. Who are you?"

"I'm Doctor Serena Llys," the doctor answered. Her voice carrying an unmistakable warning tone.

"And are you the one I should be looking for?"

The doctor shot him a scornful look. "If I was harming anyone, it wouldn't be public now, would it?"

Eli felt the gun. He'd only ever felt one other like it. His childhood friend, Dan, had joined up with some hush-hush force and showed it to him. Dan had never come home. Years later his bereft mother had been sent a simple telegram. There was no visit, no phone call, no letter, just an impersonal telegram from a military source that informed her of her worst nightmare.

This gun was an upgraded version, but unmistakably the same make.

"So, what are you here for?"

The doctor looked at Aeron. "She's too important to leave to villagers and their pitchforks."

Eli frowned. "You may think you know the people in this town, but they are good people, quiet people—"

"Who hang outsiders from road signs and butcher young girls. Yes, citizenship of the highest regard."

Eli couldn't argue with the facts. "Is that why you were run off the road?"

The doctor sighed. "That, I don't know. In my line of work, the past has a way of ramming you into poles when you least expect it."

"So, you don't think it's the killer?"

"I don't know. Either way, someone is rattled."

Eli kept his hand on the gun. "How do I know you are on her side? That you won't just fire when our backs are turned?"

The doctor's gaze was steady, calm, unwavering. "You don't. You don't know me, assurances are hollow."

"But?"

The doctor smiled. "I won't let her come to harm."

Eli nodded. He had no idea why he was lifted by the doctor's words but perhaps someone out there was looking after the Lorelei name.

"Does she know?"

The doctor shook her head. "At least I haven't *told* her. Your daughter sees too much."

Eli looked at Aeron, who shifted in her sleep. He couldn't argue with that, not at all.

Chapter 46

I WOKE UP feeling like my head had been removed and tumble dried on high power. My tongue was stuck to the roof of my mouth and my nose was so stuffy that it stung when I breathed. I sneezed and yelped with a side-splitting pain in my ribs. I rubbed like crazy at the spot, feeling like I'd been in a fight with a truck.

"Let me take a look," I heard Llys say somewhere nearby and peeled my eyelids open. "We need to wash out your eyes."

My blurry vision made arguing pointless.

Llys ran her hands over my rib cage and the pain shot like a knife through my side again. "Nothing broken, but definitely bruised . . . hang on."

I waited as Llys clattered around beside me. "Where's my father?"

"Downstairs in the cellar. He's trying to budge the flood release lever. Last thing I heard he had resorted to swearing at it."

I went to sit up, to try and go help, but the room swayed like a pendulum, my stomach swaying with it.

"Lie back down," Llys said.

"I thought you were the one with a bad head?"

Llys's warm hand touched my side as she rubbed something gunky onto my ribs. "It's healing up pretty well, it was only a scratch."

"Lying to me is a bit pointless, you know."

Llys chuckled. "Well, unless you want to explain to me and your father how I rose from the dead. Maybe you should go with it."

"You weren't *completely* dead," I protested.

"There's more than one stage?"

I smiled. "Can I say you were just *mostly* dead?"

Llys laughed. "Not unless you're looking for a six-fingered man."

I lay back as Llys checked me over. She found more sore spots than I thought possible.

"Maybe you should try working on yourself," she said eventually.

"Doesn't work like that. Other people can. For some reason, I can't. Like I can't see nothing about me."

Llys helped me to sit up a little and began bathing my eyes, the cold damp cotton soothing. I swore that the mud, debris, and wind must have stripped away my eyeballs for the pain I was in.

"You can't see anything about you?"

I shook my head. "I am not sure if the universe has rules, but one of them seems to be that I can't have an unfair advantage."

A cool wet cloth touched my face and I winced, my skin felt on fire too.

"Wind burn," Llys told me. "Nasty too."

"Think I must have done somethin' to my ear too. I can hear all rushing and high-pitched squealing."

"You haven't perforated it, so that's good news, but it's definitely going to be sore."

I grunted. "No kidding."

Llys continued to bathe my face and then she opened up something that smelled like yoghurt.

"Hungry?" I asked.

"I'm going to put it on your face," she told me.

I wasn't quite sure how plastering my face in yoghurt would help but she seemed to have more of a clue than I did. I couldn't say that it was very pleasant having the goop splodged onto my burning skin but after only a few seconds the relief was immense.

"So why can't you see things that concern you? Surely, there are people who have your . . . er . . . talents . . . that aren't selfless."

I shrugged. "I don't really know anyone else . . . unless you count Mari's grandmother and Nan . . . but I don't think it's a choice."

"Maybe that's how you can discern it's a good gift," Llys said, her hands now on the leg that had been hit.

"How do you figure that?"

She touched my calf where the log had made contact, and I jumped.

"Sorry," she mumbled and continued to check it over. "I'm no expert, but if your gifts only allow you to help others, then that seems pretty good to me."

I wiggled my toes, thankful for the movement. "I'm not really sure if it's quite that black and white." I managed to open my eyes a little. "I look at it as we all can receive signals. Maybe its electricity and my brain can decipher it."

"Like some people can read body language better?" Llys asked.

"Exactly. Maybe it's just a sense, and genes dictate if that part of you works or not."

She smiled at me. "So you're saying that being able to see the future is as normal as rolling your tongue?"

I shrugged. "To me it is. And I can't see the future. if I had I would have stopped you going to get me clothes. I would have seen the huge twister that nearly got us."

Llys peeled off my threadbare socks, and dabbed disinfectant onto my feet. "What are you then?"

"A freak?"

She tutted. "You can't see the future, so I guess that means you aren't a mystic. Although you did see Yasmin."

"For all the good it did."

She sighed. "You tried your best. So, you can't help yourself, you can't read everyone, and you can't control it."

"Like I said . . . useless."

Llys shook her head. "You can read the past though, you can see past events and you can see what is happening to people in the present. Right?"

I nodded. "Sounds about right, that's why I say Empath. I can see most present things and maybe if I really try, the immediate future but mainly if anything is future it's all in symbols and bizarre pictures—a language I sure as hell can't read."

Llys tilted her head. "So you are admitting you *can* see the future?"

"No, I see jumbled crap I don't understand that *could* happen."

She gave me a look that said more than her words ever could. She had it figured that I *was* able to see glimpses of the future, I just didn't want to. Maybe she was right. Maybe I could have predicted a huge funnel would drop from the sky and try to demolish the entire town. I'd felt *something* wasn't right but so had every animal in the forest.

"Ever thought that you could actually help?"

I tensed, my ribs jarring as I did so. "No, I can't help. Even if I wanted to help, all I would be doing is fishing for something, and you know how I feel about fishing."

"Using your gifts isn't killing fish."

"Ain't it?" I asked, feeling sorer the more tightly wound I got. "I'm not just throwing some information around that you will meet a tall dark stranger who will turn your world upside down . . . I'm seeing girls being murdered . . . in detail."

Llys took my hands and put ointment on them.

"Was there anywhere I didn't bust up?"

"Nope."

I groaned. "Some hero I am."

"You saved my life," she whispered.

"My *father* saved your life, like he saved mine. All I did was get you muddy."

I knew that she didn't believe my protest for one second but she didn't push anymore. I had preferred it when she had discounted my gifts altogether, that way she felt as unhappy about them as I did. Under no circumstances did I want to use them . . . for anything.

Chapter 47

THE ENTIRE TIME we spent locked up together in the cabin made me so jittery that I didn't trust myself to speak. My father had pretty much busied himself the minute he woke, trying to shift the flood lever that would open the flood gates below the cabin to divert the chest-high water into a relief channel that had been built especially for that purpose.

In spite of all I had done to prepare the place, I hadn't gotten around to opening it and now the mechanism was under water and the already contrary crank had seized up. That meant most of the day, Llys and I were holed up in the storm room with Mrs. Squirrel, who was starting to get cabin fever the same as me. Unlike me, the squirrel wasn't injured. I've never been a great patient but being hurt and stuck in the aftermath of a storm, I could feel the panic from the town. The pulsing worries of people searching through debris flashed into my mind in rapid succession.

"You've been quiet," Llys said after dinner. My father had resumed his lever diving only moments before.

"Tired," I mumbled as an excuse.

"Tired in general or of the company?"

I looked up at her. "No, my father's keeping out of the way and you're never any bother."

"Did you have another vision?"

I shook my head.

"You know, I may not have a sixth sense but I do have some empathy."

I smiled. "Eight not six."

"Eight what?"

"Eight senses, not six."

Llys counted out her fingers. "Okay, I got five . . . six, you can see the future."

I frowned but didn't bother arguing. "I can see your past and present. Six, I can heal you. Seven . . ." I stared at the floor.

"And the eighth?"

I looked at my hands, now a mixture of scabs and red graze marks. "I can do the opposite."

Llys sipped her coffee quietly, her intense eyes flicking over me. "You can hurt people?"

"Like I said, nothing is intentional."

"So, how can you hurt? How do you hurt someone?"

I sighed. "Same way I fix you. I displace ailments. They have to go somewhere, so if someone is hurt badly enough and I heal, I wander around with it stored in my hands."

"Explains the mood," she answered.

I nodded, what else could I say?

"So how do you get rid of the ailment?"

I looked down at my hands. "It ain't really like that. It's not like if I touched you, your head would split open or nothing. But the hurt and damage, like a negative force, is just there."

"And how do you remove it?"

I wasn't really sure. That was the problem, the only time I'd ever wandered around after helping someone, I ended up really hurting someone else. I was only eight. One of the girls that had come to Oppidum on vacation fell into the river and broke her arm. I touched her to help and next thing I knew I was passed out on the bank and she was fine, like nothing had happened.

I was pretty happy with myself, thinking I'd done a good thing but then one of the other tourists, an older boy made me angry. I pushed him when he teased me and he was on the floor cradling his leg and screaming.

Lucky for me, the parents who had seen this didn't believe for a second that the little midget had pushed their son hard enough for his leg to snap in two like a twig. They assumed he'd gotten it caught. He was of the same thinking.

Nan wasn't.

I'd had my fair share of Nan's wrath over the years when I'd been up to some kind of mischief. Even though she didn't speak, her eyes were sharper than a sword.

That time, when I went home and told her, scared out of my wits, she gave me the biggest hiding I'd ever had.

I knew I'd scared her, as unintentional as it was. I learned my lesson. Under no circumstances was I to heal anyone. It wasn't my place, and people would only get hurt.

"What does Nan say about it?" Llys asked.

I knew I was scowling from the tight feel of my healing skin.

"In her diary, you said she spoke to you. Maybe there's something in there to help?"

I looked at the trunk. "You think?"

Llys shrugged, walked to the trunk, and brought me the book. I opened it, not quite sure that Nan had been *that* good.

> *Shortstop,*
> *You need to wash your hands of the wounds. The river is the best place, good cold water but wait till it's clear again.*
> *Listen to the doc, cos she knows what she's doin'*
> *. . . and you know it.*
> *Love*
> *Nan xxx*
>
> *PS Don't be so daft—course you can heal yourself, Dimwit.*

I laughed, shaking my head at the note. If it wasn't written out in front of me, I would swear blind that it couldn't be true. I handed the book to Llys who sat staring at it with wide eyes for the longest time.

"I just . . . how . . . ? My head hurts."

I nodded. "You'll have to get used to that when you're around me." My chest twinged. I got to my feet, and hobbled over to the railing. "Take your damn tablets!"

My father looked up with a guilty look on his face. "They're in the truck."

I looked at Llys who shook her head. "Oh no. Don't you even think about going in that water. Your wounds will get infected with I don't know what."

I sighed. Nan's warning in my head. "What do we do then, Doc? 'Cause my dear daddy needs to take his medication before he has an attack."

Llys frowned. "What the hell is he doing in the water then."

I grabbed her before she hurtled off into the sludge and grime below us. "Relax, Doc. Angina."

"Can he get out?"

I looked down at my father. "Think you can squeeze through the kitchen window?"

My father looked at the large window, nailed shut, and nodded. "Got a crowbar?"

I sighed. "In the barn."

Llys fumbled about in the back of the room as I tried to figure out some way to escape my own fort.

I turned to her. She held a metal brace from the old machine. She crawled out of the room onto the landing next to me.

"How 'bout this?" she called.

"That'll do," my father said.

Llys dropped the brace down to my father, and we watched him wade over to the kitchen window and start hammering. The swoosh of fresh air hit us seconds later and we stared at the sun streaming through the gap where the window had been.

My chest eased considerably and I nodded to Llys. "Let's hope he doesn't just leave us here, huh?"

Llys looked at me. "Would he do that?"

I heard a creaking and cracking and looked at the door. It flung open and the flood water poured in and out as my father waded through it. He had a crowbar in his hand.

A few seconds later the flood gate mechanism opened and the water flowed out, leaving a thick layer of mud and grime.

"I got to go check on the others. You two be okay now?" my father said.

I shrugged, knowing that he was itching to escape. "We'll be fine. Will your truck start?"

My father laughed. "It's upside down in the willow tree. Kept my meds dry though."

"Just keep them on you . . . and go to your appointment."

He saluted and turned to leave.

"Hey," I called out, making him turn to me. "Thanks."

He stood there for a couple of minutes, emotions running across his face like a movie on a screen until finally he nodded. "I'm your father. It's my job."

Chapter 48

ELI TOOK NEARLY two hours to walk the few miles to his house from the cabin. Between the utility lines littering the highway, the flood water, and the devastation, it was like negotiating a battlefield. The clean-up crews were out in force, picking through the remaining debris of their homes and possessions. He finally turned onto the block where he lived and stopped and stared at his house. The top floor had been ripped off. Why he'd ever let Iris talk him into building a half-timber house, he didn't know.

He didn't even want to think about the phone calls to the insurance company, let alone how to fix the damn place. At least the lower half had stayed solid. "Thank God for bricks and mortar," he whispered as he opened the door.

He heard Jenny and the girls in the kitchen talking to Skip. They sounded like they'd lost hope. "Sorry, Jenny . . . Eli's truck . . . we can't find it and Mrs. O'Reilly said he never got there . . ."

Eli took a deep breath and then stepped around the corner. "I got here soon as I could."

The girls ran to him and attached themselves to him. Skip laughed with joy but Jenny . . . Jenny was scowling, curled up like a snake ready to strike.

"What the hell happened to you?"

Eli sighed. "Twister nearly landed on my hood, just as I got to the farm, crash. Hell, the thing chased me."

"Chased you where?"

Eli knew that it would come out eventually. May as well be now. "Cabin. Just got to safety, truck's in the damn willow."

Skip whistled. "Hell, that was close. Aeron let you in?"

Eli nodded. Skip was from out of town. He had no clue about Aeron and no judgment either.

"Convenient," Jenny snapped.

Eli folded his arms, the girls still limpets. "I was at Aeron's, not a damn strip joint."

Jenny's eyes darkened with her anger and Eli felt all the fight leave him. Did she care that someone had tried to run Doctor Llys off the road or that he'd nearly been taken by a twister? Did she care that Aeron had tried to carry the doctor to safety not caring that she was in peril herself?

Did Jenny care that the doctor had died, right in front of his eyes, that somehow, some way, Aeron had helped her come back?

No. Jenny cared about when her next manicure was coming up and what her handicap at the golf club said about her pedigree.

Skip shifted on the balls of his feet.

Eli turned to him. "Got running water anywhere?"

"Mine and Sandra's has. Hot too. Benefits of being on the other side," Skip said.

Eli nodded. "Girls, you okay?" He kissed them both on the head. The eldest, Ruth, was just nine and was his girl through and through.

"We're okay," she said. "Do you have to go to work?"

Eli smiled, the guilt was nagging at him for leaving but if he stayed, they would just get to see Jenny and him in yet another yelling match. So, he'd run. Like the coward he was.

"Yup, got to make sure everyone is safe and sound."

Ruth kissed him on the cheek, her younger sister Louise waved a hand in front of her nose.

"And you smell . . . bad," she said.

Eli nodded. "Real bad." He went toward her as if to hug her again and she ran and hid behind the still fuming Jenny.

"Come on, Skip. Shower and then I want a full run down on how bad it is."

Chapter 49

LATER THAT NIGHT I watched Llys fixing the food. I wanted to go help her but I'd been ordered out of the kitchen—well, the cooking area.

"You cook real good for a doc," I said.

She lifted her eyes from her cooking and smiled. "I'm glad you like it." She went back to her task, and I rested my hands on my knees and tucked them under my chin.

Llys was so organized, every part of the process timed to perfection. I figured that she'd make a great TV chef. Tons of folks would tune in to watch her.

"Did you enjoy your meal after?" I asked, getting raised eyebrows in response. "Back in the institution. You had a sparkly number on the back of your door."

Her eyes veiled like I'd said the wrong thing. "I don't find it easy." She looked up at me. "Sharing, that is."

"I only asked about the meal, Doc," I answered. "I wasn't going for trade secrets."

Llys smiled. "Then, no. I didn't."

She went back to the food and I watched her, thinking about the dress. It had been a fancy dress, like the ones stars wore when they were on the red carpet. The kind that Yasmin would have dreamed of wearing.

"Why?"

Llys laughed. "I thought you didn't want trade secrets?"

"We're stranded after a twister nearly got us," I answered. "I guess I kinda figured that you would trust me a little more."

"Touché," she said, prodding at the food.

"So, you gonna spill it?"

She sighed. "You really want to know?"

I nodded as she stared with intent at the camp stove.

"I was meeting someone for dinner," she said.

I shot her a "duh."

She laughed. "But as I've just said, I don't find sharing easy."

"Then why didn't you get separate meals?"

She threw a scrap of food at me. "It started off well but someone commented that we would make a great couple."

I frowned. "I thought you were there with that other doctor. What was her name—?"

"Susan," Llys answered. "And yes, I was."

She went back to cooking while I stared at the floor. For some reason what she had told me made her feel on edge. I couldn't figure out why. "A couple of what?"

She stared at me, looking as confused as I felt. "What?"

I frowned. "Agents, hairdressers, doctors?"

"Aeron, what are you talking about?"

I folded my arms. "You're the one who didn't finish your sentence. You said someone thought you and Susan would make a great couple." I raised my eyebrows. "A couple of?"

"Oh hell, you have no idea, do you?"

"You trying to confuse me on purpose?"

Llys went back to cooking and I could see the feelings whirring around her. She was quiet, deep in thought. So I waited, hoping I'd get where she was going or this could be a long conversation.

"Is there anyone in town who is a little . . . different?" she asked.

"You mean like me?"

"More like two guys or girls who happen to live together."

"Like me and Nan?"

Llys rolled her eyes. "*Not* related."

I thought about it, real hard. I could feel her watching me. "No."

Llys muttered under her breath. "Well, what would you think if there were, don't you think it would be . . . different?"

"I'd have to know what the hell normal was first."

She beamed at me with such warmth that I wondered what I'd said to cause it. My head was starting to hurt with the twisting conversation and I just didn't get it. What did people living together have to do with a cocktail dress?

"Okay, I'm going to be blunt," she told me.

I nodded, focusing on her gray eyes and bracing myself for the nugget of wisdom she was about to unleash.

"Susan and I were on a date."

The answer not only flattened my thought process but I was pretty sure that my brain cells up and left for greener pastures. "Huh?"

"A date," she repeated.

"Like . . . huh?"

Llys's eyes faltered, her aura dimmed. I knew what it meant all too well. She was afraid, afraid I'd hate her. I tried to collect my remaining intelligence to say something uplifting that would ease her worries and inspire her trust in me. But when I opened my mouth only, "Oh," came out.

Her aura dimmed even further and I groaned internally.

"You're freaked out, aren't you?"

"I ain't freaked," I squeaked.

What the hell was wrong with my voice? I cleared my throat, seeing that she was getting upset. I wasn't freaked out or afraid of her. I was more afraid of saying something dumb—kinda like I had already.

Knowing I had to do something before she thought I was a complete tool, I got up and limped to her.

"I ain't got a clue about slushy stuff," I said, taking her hands. "But I know that anybody would be lucky to have you."

I pulled her into a hug, something I don't do a lot and if I'm honest, I ain't all that used to affection but I held on and hoped that she'd get the support from my actions even if my words were as useful as a shovel in an avalanche. And, as I don't do hugging, I didn't know how long it was meant to be. After a couple of minutes, I could feel her relax against me, her head resting on my shoulder. I felt a tickle of wet on my neck and realized that she was crying.

"Didn't mean to hurt you, Doc," I told her. "I've spent most of my life locked in an institution. There's a lot of things I don't know."

She met my eyes and searched them. "I'm not sure why I was getting upset. It's not like I'm new to this."

"Maybe it's 'cause you haven't been—well, you for a while?"

She shot me a dark look. "You aren't going to let it lie, are you?"

I shook my head. "Look, Doc. Telling you about my messed up life has gotten me where I am today."

We both looked around at the damp walls, at my injuries, and the fact we were cooking dinner on a camp stove.

"That didn't sound as encouraging as I hoped," I mumbled. "But what I'm trying to say is that it made me feel better."

"I know." She smiled. "And you're right."

"I am?" I frowned. "About which part?"

"Most of it," she said with a sigh. "Thing is, Aeron. Sometimes it's easier to be someone else."

"You're kinda preachin' to the choir there, doc."

She smiled at me and fussed over the dinner once more. I sat back down but decided that Llys needed to talk, so I'd try and act like I got all the love stuff.

"So Susan wasn't pretty enough?"

She laughed. "She was fine, just not—well—not my type."

"You got a type too?" I folded my legs, wincing as my calf ached.

"Yup," she answered and her aura waved around in pretty colors. I hadn't a clue what it meant but it was cool.

"Tell me about it," I said, enjoying the aura light show.

She blushed a little and her aura flickered again. "Athletic, shall we say."

I frowned. "Susan wasn't athletic at all."

She smiled. "I know."

"Then why did you go out with her?"

"I don't know."

Lost again, I sat back, staring at Mrs. Squirrel—who'd poked her head out—for inspiration. "Were you grilling her for information?"

Llys's wide gray eyes met mine and she swallowed something the wrong way and coughed. "'Scuse me?"

"Well, you didn't want to date her and she wasn't your type but you went anyway," I said. "So I figured you could have been trying to find out something."

She dished out and shoved my plate of food into my hands. "For someone so naive, that sounded very cynical."

"So it's true?"

"No." She tapped my hand and pointed to my food for me to eat. "I am not, and have never wined and dined anyone for information."

I chomped on the food as I thought. "Well, if you ever need information off me, just offer to make me this." I looked down at the delicious goodness. "What is this anyhow?"

"A toasted egg, ham, and cheese sandwich," she answered. "Or as you so delicately put it once, croque-madame."

I grinned. "That's your favorite."

She mirrored my grin. "Your dad delivered us some fresh eggs, cheeses, and ham from Mrs. O'Reilly while you took a nap." She looked at her food like it was treasure. "I knew exactly what to do with that."

"Then," I said, lifting up my soda can in a toast. "To fine dining."

She nudged my shoulder and knocked her can to mine. "Fine dining with good company."

"You're only saying that 'cause I have muscles."

With a scowl on her face but a twinkle in her eyes, she shoved my sandwich into my mouth.

Chapter 50

THE SECOND DAY after the storm hit, the river water ran clear. I found being in Llys's company wasn't hard at all. We talked about all sorts of small stuff as we sat and rested up our wounds. We talked about anything but the fact she wasn't who she said she was, the murders of the girls, and my peculiarities. I was finding it hard being cooped up while my wounds healed and I had spent my entire life in a secure institution. Llys looked like she wanted to climb the walls by the end of the day.

"You know, they shouldn't place you in a cult or a mine on your next job," I mentioned as Llys paced the room.

She turned and looked at me with fiery eyes. "Cut it out."

"Why? Who is going to hear us?"

"Just quit it."

I folded my arms. "You getting mad at me?"

"Yes," Llys muttered and then sat in a heap on the floor. "Sorry. You're right. Four walls drive me crazy."

"Try not to tell the institution that. They're already looking for who blew the whistle."

Llys nodded. "No doubt."

"You think it was them who shunted you?"

She fiddled with the rucksack for a moment. "Not sure, not really. It could be a lot of people."

"But they don't know where you are? The people you've dealt with before. Do they?"

She opened the bag and pulled out a very sleek, matte black gun. "No, no one even knows my real name."

I looked down at the gun. "The fact I do is a problem?"

She met my eyes and then looked away. "You don't know my name . . . it's buried beneath every layer I have."

"Renee Black. Colonel Charles Black's daughter."

I was half expecting her to shoot me, the look in her eyes spilled out danger. "He got taken by a storm. My brother Matthew was out on the mountains, training. We both wanted to be like him . . . a hero. Neither came home."

"And Tess?"

She looked up and smiled. "You quoted me the background of my last job. I was Tess, then Tess became Serena's sister. It's how I keep track."

"So, no sisters at all?"

"Nope."

I got up and pulled some of the new clothes Renee, because that's how I thought of her now, had bought me—ones we'd managed to wash out and dry from our pipe tower. "Do you get on with your mother? I mean, Serena and Tess didn't, did they?"

Renee smiled. "I do. I don't get home to see her a lot and she understands. Her new husband is a nice guy."

"And the horses?"

"Mom was a champion at dressage. I preferred pretending to be a cowboy."

I laughed. If I had owned a horse, I would have been exactly the same.

"So you gonna shoot me? 'Cause I need a little help getting out of these rags. The river water made them shrink."

Renee smiled, got to her feet, and tucked the gun into Nan's trunk. A fussing and clattering went on as she muttered until she finally pulled out a pair of tailor's scissors.

"I surrender," I said, holding up my hands. "I'll talk."

Renee shot me a wry smile and snipped the scissors in midair. "Really? Well, now that sounds like an interesting plan."

I eyed the very sharp scissors. "You are going to use them, aren't you?"

She nodded. "How else are we going to get any of it off. It's welded."

I looked down at my outfit. I looked like a very bad advertisement for a retro castaway and one that had stolen a child's clothes.

I closed my eyes as she started to snip away. "So, what am I being interrogated about?"

Renee looked up, gripping the now mini jeans, and smiled. "You can start by telling me how you ever thought these were cool."

Chapter 51

HAVING CLOTHES THAT fit me and shoes which didn't have holes definitely made my job of checking over the cabin easier. As I expected from the storm, there was some damage—half a tree trunk had made its way through the newly repaired roof but it was nothing we couldn't fix up ourselves.

Renee helped me to get the tools back out of the shed and we stood looking up at the cabin in the baking sun.

She pointed to the river. "You need to wash your hands."

I looked at the river and sighed. I knew that Nan was experienced in odd matters but how could the water help?

"Go on," Renee said, nudging me.

I took off my new shoes and socks and rolled up the work pants that Renee had bought me, happy to find they had ties to make them shorts. As I stepped into the cool river, my mind went back to the stone with numbers on it. Nine-eight-four. Was it code? Why had Renee thrown it in the river?

"You okay in there?" she called, and I shoved my hands in the water.

I felt like an idiot just holding my hands in the gentle current. A crazy idiot and I was sure Nan, wherever she was watching from, was chuckling like a good 'un.

"What does nine-eight-four mean?" I asked, wading around so I could look at Renee.

She looked up at the sky and closed her eyes, muttering. "Nothing." She tucked her blonde hair behind her ear.

In the institution, Renee's hair had seemed darker, almost grayish brown, but now it was far lighter and more golden from being out in the sun. I wondered if it was the sun or whether she had been coloring it. I looked at the river water streaming through my fingers. Why the hell did I care what her hair color was? When did I start noticing hair color?

She was a red head when she first used the gun, she had to, it was kill or be killed, even now, all these years later, she can't forgive herself, she'll never forgive herself.

I tried to shake off the information, like a scrolling banner on those twenty-four-hour news channels.

How did she know my name was Renee Black? I've been dedicated, professional, I get the job done, so how the hell can't I just fake who I am to her? How much does she know? Could it be possible that she can read my mind? If the boss finds out, it's over. Then what will I do?

I staggered a little on the rock bed as I stood there. I could see Renee keeping a close eye. Was I hearing her thoughts?

I need to get the job done, hope she won't push it. Oh crap, is that a storm? I hate storms. Oh snap out of it. You're not a child, storms aren't monsters. It's just a bunch of clouds.

My hands started to throb with the cold but I kept them there. I looked up into the sky, it couldn't be Renee's thoughts. There wasn't a cloud for miles.

What the hell is that truck doing? They're going to hit, brakes, brakes! No, No, swerve, swerve, I'm going to hit it, have to jump have to . . .

I winced as I felt the impact from the crash, the bank hit, the rock on my head.

Renee scrambled to the river's edge. "You okay?"

"Stay back," I told her.

"But you don't look too good."

My hands felt numb, the cold much deeper than the water, my eyes watered with the pain from Renee's memories.

Got to save . . . got . . . to . . . The world drifted and shifted, the edges blurred, the softest glow calling from somewhere so very familiar . . . it's all right . . . it's all right . . . so warm and soft, and light . . . warm and soft and—

I lurched forward as my legs gave way, my hands pulsing with pain, like frost bite. I closed my eyes, trying to keep my head above the water.

"Aeron!"

"Stay the hell back!"

I knew if she tried to help, she'd be hurt, badly. My body writhed beneath the agony, burning through every pore. I knew I was drowning, the river sucking the life from me.

"Aeron!"

I could hear my heart in my ears, thudding, the blood screaming for oxygen.

"Rope," I called. "Rope."

I felt the loop over my arms and knew Renee was dragging me onto shore. I was shivering like I'd been entombed in ice. My body felt like a thousand knives were slicing the skin from my bones.

"Don't touch . . . foil . . . don't," I called out, hoping Renee would listen.

I was as potent as a live bomb, the faintest touch would trigger something, I didn't know what, but I knew neither of us would survive it.

"I got the foil. A pillow."

"Don't touch . . . let me dry . . . don't help me till I'm dry."

Renee nodded, I could see her eyes filled with her fear, her concern.

She sat there watching me as I faded in and out of consciousness, in and out of fitful dreams. She'd been hit by the killer and somehow it had forged a connection in my brain. I could hear the darkness in the thoughts now.

When I regained my senses, Renee was dozing by my side.

"Got something to drink?"

Renee snapped her eyes open as I sat up. "What the hell kind of freaky crap was that?"

I shook my head. I felt like the river had been sucking my soul from me. "I've never been so cold in my life."

Renee looked at the river.

"It's fine now. It doesn't hurt nothing living in it, but I'm pretty sure that it would've hurt if you'd entered."

"You looked like you were having a seizure."

I nodded. "I think I was. I don't think I'm supposed to heal. Don't think it's my place."

Renee handed me a bottle of water. "From now on we stick to med kits. Got it."

"Loud and clear," I muttered.

Considering I felt as if I'd been a blood donor for a herd of vampires for at least an hour, in no time my strength returned and I was good as new.

"Weird," I muttered as I tested out my side.

"What is?"

I lifted up my t-shirt and searched for the bruise that had covered my entire ribcage.

Renee raised her eyebrows. "Maybe it was healing you too?"

I looked at the river. "That's how I can heal myself? By nearly drowning? Great."

Renee smiled. "Just make sure you have a healing buddy with some cowboy skills."

She runs, it's too easy, closer, closer, that's it, walk into the snare . . . walk into it . . . yes! Another one . . . oh, I'll have fun with you.

I gazed at Renee and looked around. "Another one . . . killer . . . another one."

Renee pulled out a phone from her jeans. "Where?"

I tried to focus to see the place. "Fields . . . rubble . . . I can't see . . . there's too much damage."

Renee put her hand on my shoulder. "It's okay. Can you see what the girl looks like?"

I cradled my head, trying to will the flash back into my mind. It was too quick, too much of a pulse. "I can't. She's young. She's younger than the others."

I felt sick. Whoever the killer was, there was great joy in the suffering, great fun in the chase.

Renee punched a number on the phone. "It's me. Unsub has another. No location."

"Chelsea . . . Chelsea Borland," I whispered.

"Did you get that? I understand. Will do."

Renee hung up and shrugged. "You want me to explain now?"

I shook my head. "I know you got given an order you ain't happy with."

"How so?" she asked, folding her arms.

"Your aura just lit up like a fairground."

"Oh . . . well, yes. I need to get you into town."

I looked in the direction of Oppidum, no way did I want to go there. I was probably being blamed for the twister.

"I need people to see you . . . in the town."

"Why?"

Renee sighed. "Someone has gone over your father's head. They've called in the Feds."

"How can they? It's not across state lines, is it?" I asked.

"No, but good as. There was another victim during the storms. Apparently she was staying as a guest of the mayor."

"And?"

"She's the daughter of a U.S. senator."

I hung my head. I was in big trouble. There was no way anyone would take my father's word as an alibi and Renee couldn't exactly talk to the Feds. For a start, I didn't know who she was working for and no doubt they would see through her disguise if I had.

"How will being in town help?"

"If they see you and you're right about the new victim, you can't be blamed for taking her."

I nodded and put my shoes and socks back on. It sounded like a bit of a long shot, but it was better than nothing.

AS WE APPROACHED the middle of town, the track of the twister was pretty darn apparent. Main Street was split between one side getting minimal damage, thatched roofs missing and smashed windows but pretty much still standing. A few buildings on the other side had been obliterated. All I could see was sharp daggers of wood jutting out from warped steel and piles of rubble, like something out of a war movie.

The closer we got, the more I felt it, fear and hate pulsing my way. Folks were hurrying indoors, pulling their kids behind them, glaring from inside. Others grouped in huddles, their dark mutterings too inaudible. But I could feel their words, the venom. It felt like I was walking into a huge invisible wall of ice.

Some of the folks I didn't even know—they were new to the place, or maybe they'd changed so much since I'd been inside that I didn't recognize them. Still, that didn't seem to matter. Gossip spread like a mountain blaze. They knew who I was, even if I didn't know them and every last person was firing, "You're not welcome."

My shoulders were so tense, I felt like they'd touch my ears at any second.

"Murderer," a young boy shot at me as he walked past.

I turned and gazed at him. He was a kid. How did he know what I was?

"Come on, Tommie," a woman called.

I looked up and saw a girl I'd known in school. I smiled, and then wished I hadn't.

"Sick. That's what you are, sick," she snarled.

The tiny shred of confidence I'd managed to find with Renee's support shattered on the hard, cold hate of rejection.

"Keep the hell away from my boy. I swear it. I'll shoot you myself."

Renee touched my arm to pull me from the woman's sharp volley, but I pulled away.

"Why do you think that? Why would I hurt your kid?"

"Aeron," Renee whispered. "Leave it."

I walked toward the woman. I couldn't even remember her name, we'd never talked in school. What right did she have to judge me?

"What makes you think I'll hurt him?"

The woman pulled her son behind her back. "Stay the hell away. Keep your sickness to yourself."

I felt myself getting angrier. The hate in the town egged on my already raw senses. "You don't know me."

"I know enough. Jake, those Gyppos, now Darcy. Who's next?"

"Aeron." Renee grabbed my arm. "Just leave it. She's just another fool."

"Fool?" The woman turned to Renee. "I ain't the one keeping a killer company? I heard about people like you."

"Really?" Renee said calmly. "What kind of person am I?"

The woman backed off as I stepped forward, her boy ran down the sidewalk. Renee put herself in front of me with her arms to her side, eyes still fixed on the woman.

"One of them groupies. Like a serial killer, do you?"

"You're pathetic," Renee said. Her voice level, steady, and colder than an Alaskan winter. "Why don't you go get your hair styled, maybe your roots are making you cranky."

The woman covered her head like Renee had revealed a deep dark secret. I tried not to laugh. The anger dissipated as the woman rushed after her son, almost bumping into a startled pair of tourists.

I gave Renee an amused look. "Seriously? Her roots?"

Renee turned around and shrugged. "A lot of women place their entire confidence in looking perfect. One thing out of place and suddenly they aren't worthy anymore."

"Yeah, but she reacted like you'd just wounded her."

Renee sighed as we continued past a bar with frosted glass windows called The Red Dragon. "I did. The woman had major self-esteem issues. Huge. I hit her where it hurt."

"Why? You didn't seem mad."

Renee stopped and turned to me. "These people are despicable. They are yelling at you in the street. Accusing you of harming women. None of that bothers you?"

I shrugged. "I'm used to it."

Renee threw her hands in the air. "And that's what irritates me. It's mob mentality. One of them decides they don't like you, the rest follow—one sheep after the other. Human nature at its worst."

"They're just scared is all," I said as we walked up to Uncle Abe's shop. "I don't think it's a good idea if I go in."

Renee leaned against the wall and shoved her hands in her jeans. "Why?"

"It's my Uncle Abe's shop. He'll have me arrested in minutes."

"Your own uncle?"

I looked down at my shoes. How did I explain how little Abe thought of me? Renee was already in a bad mood and her aura looked like she may sock the next friendly insulter.

"Tell me."

I shifted and kicked a loose stone around. "My father's family are a little, well, stuck in the middle ages."

"And?"

I fiddled with the stone and tapped it against the wall Renee was leaning against. "Women are not citizens. They're possessions. And ones that should be grateful to the men for allowing them to exist."

Renee leaned her head back against the wall. "Do these people still exist? Seriously?"

"Should hear how he feels about foreigners."

"How the hell did you turn out like you did?"

I laughed. "Not surprising I'm a murderer now, huh?"

"You're not a murderer," Renee said. "You're not. I don't care what happened. You did not mean to hurt Jake. I know that and I know you, so quit it."

"But—"

Renee held up her hand. "I'm going in to paternal purgatory.

Wait here. If anyone so much as scowls at you, knock their teeth out."

"Is that a tested therapy, Doc?" I said.

Renee nodded. "Oh, yes. And I thoroughly recommend it."

Renee walked through the doorway, the little bell tinkling inside. I stared out at the busy street. Despite the storm damage, those on the luckier side were happily splashing on new coats of paint, the window fitters shining up the new replacements. Most of them were open for business too with a few tourists taking pictures outside and browsing through the displays on the sidewalk. It didn't stop the hostile looks from the shopkeepers coming my way.

How the hell they could figure that I was to blame for Mother Nature, I didn't know. Faces of people glowered at me from the windows and sidewalks. I had always been treated the same way. I couldn't really understand how it could be any different.

It wasn't just my gifts that bothered them either. I didn't fit.

The girls in town from the age of nine or ten talked about weddings and the cutest boy in school. It drove them crazy that Sam had been my best buddy. None of them could figure out why he wanted to bother with the weird girl who was all arms and legs and unruly hair.

I didn't really get it myself. I mean, I wasn't a princess, I wasn't even interested in him. Not only that but I didn't give a crap who his daddy was.

"Hey, Aeron?"

I snapped out of my daze and turned to find Sam standing in front of me.

"You okay?" he asked.

I folded my arms. I hadn't forgotten the spat in the police station parking lot. "You gonna tell me to get the hell out of Dodge?"

Sam shook his head. "No, and I'm sorry 'bout before."

I didn't answer. Sam would get 'round to what he wanted to spit out faster if I let him talk.

"Mary Goss just accused you of hurting her roots."

I raised my eyebrows. "Can I do that too now? Hell, with all the child snatching, twister causing, and mayhem . . . I'm a busy woman."

Sam laughed. "You're a regular witch. Mary's in fits. Last thing I saw, she was headed for the hairdressers."

I didn't really like to tell him that Renee had fired that barb.

"You ride out the twister okay? Your dad said you were stuck with him."

I nodded. "Two days."

Sam whistled. "Sounds worse than any kind of prison."

I chuckled. Sam had never gotten on with my father. My father hated him by default, because all fathers hated it when their daughters spent time with a boy. Sam hated him right back because he felt my father never stuck up for me and was a useless waste of space.

"After the institution, two days was nothing."

Sam looked away. "I'm sorry you went through that—"

I touched his jacket sleeve. "Don't be. We both live with those scars."

Sam nodded. "I gotta go. Duty calls an' all that . . . but . . . I know it don't mean much . . . I guess . . ."

I waited as he tried to untwist his tongue.

"I'm not sure if anyone said this, or if it matters, but—"

"Spit it out, man. I'm growing cobwebs."

Sam smiled. "Welcome home, Al."

I hadn't heard the nickname in so long it almost swiped my feet out from under me. Sam, not being able to tell his parents just who he was hanging around with, invented a male version of me, using my initials. So Al was born and it was always our way of sticking it to the man.

"Thanks, Sam-o," I called after him as he strolled down the sidewalk.

Chapter 52

RENEE CAME OUT of Uncle Abe's store, and I could barely see her for the groceries. I hurried to her and took a couple of bags. "You feeding the five thousand?"

"The more supplies I get now, the longer I can go without visiting the dark ages."

I nodded, understanding her thinking. The less time in the town the better.

"You know, he even called me little lady," Renee said as she turned to lead me toward the town center. "How does he make it sound like he's hurling the ultimate insult at you?"

I followed Renee, knowing that if we were walking into the hornet's nest, she was probably doing it for a reason. "That's Abe for you. His wife is just as friendly."

"You seem a bit lost in thought. You okay?" Renee asked.

We passed by Mrs. Stein's café, and I looked across the street at Mrs. Casey's shop. "Sam came and spoke to me."

"Sam? Not about the case I hope?"

I shook my head. I could see Mrs. Casey's blonde hair bobbing as she chatted to one of her customers. Mrs. C, as I had once called her, had been kind. She was the kind of woman that all the kids loved.

I turned and saw the worry in Renee's eyes. "He welcomed me home."

"That shop looks a hell of a lot nicer than Abe's. Oh, why don't we take a walk to the lodges and turn around?"

I sighed. "Mrs. Casey was always so nice. Even to me. I mean, I didn't get hugs like the other kids or free sweets but I did get a smile, and once she helped me up when I came off my bike."

Renee matched my sigh and then some. "Was anyone nice?"

"Apart from Mrs. Casey?"

Renee gazed at me for long moments before she simply shook her head and carried on walking.

"What?" I asked, catching up with her.

"How you don't have more issues than *Rolling Stone*, I don't know."

"Are we back to that again?"

Renee nodded. "It's like systematic neglect . . . the complete shunning of a child. It's actually a good thing you are so strong."

"What do you mean?"

Renee stopped outside one of the lodges, or at least it had been a lodge. Now it was a mass of tangled girders jutting upward from beneath the collapsed building. I hoped like hell nobody had been in it at the time.

"If you weren't strong, these people could have broken you. They are lucky you didn't have any of the MacDonald Triad."

My stomach rumbled.

Renee rolled her eyes. "Not the fast food place."

"You want to explain?"

Renee looked at the splintered wood and rubbled remains of the lodge. "Bed wetting, hurting animals, and starting fires."

"I once set the field alight trying to roast marshmallows. Any help?"

Renee laughed. "No, it's compulsive. Otherwise, you would have been their worst nightmare."

"And I'm not now?"

Renee shook her head. "No, you really aren't. You've been their victim your entire life, and yet there's not one shred of bitterness in you, is there?"

I wasn't sure. I wasn't overly fond of the folks around here but then I guess they weren't overly fond of me. Maybe I was naive or stupid. I mean Sam had turned his back on me yet the second he wanted to talk, I listened.

"Just dumb I guess."

"Not dumb, sweet and kind."

Renee seemed to have decided we'd spent enough time loitering and turned around.

I didn't relish a walk to the edge of town. "So what does the triad thing mean, anyhow?"

Renee looked up at the people who were now bunching together in front of shops like I would fire lasers at them any second.

"It's a marker. Red flags that warn us *doctors*."

"Warn you? About what?"

Renee and I turned the corner opposite Abe's on the way to city hall.

"Psychopaths," she said. "Like the one targeting the girls."

CHELSEA BORLAND. THE only child of the Borland family. Your father is such a fool, Chelsea, did you know that? He thinks that his sweet little wife is hard at work all day everyday as he stays at home with you.

What kind of a man stays at home? No wonder you're so mixed up. You don't want to end up like Aeron now, do you? No, she was left with her father when her mother was out of town and look where it got her?

And you're no Aeron, are you, Chelsea? No, you're nobody really, just like Mari, just like Darcy, you will never amount to anything. Why would you? How can you be anything with a father like yours?

He dotes on you, doesn't he, Chelsea. He plays games and cooks and cleans like a good wife while your mother goes off and thinks she can be a man. What right does she have, Chelsea? What right does she have to think she can play the hero?

She even wears a man's uniform. That's right, Chelsea . . . are you ashamed? Of course you are . . . she cleans up that firehouse like she deserves to be there. Can you imagine that? A woman, allowed to be in a firehouse . . . let alone run one. I think we'll have to teach her a lesson, won't we, Chelsea? We'll have to show her that she ain't worthy of anything.

Yes, that's right. We'll show them, and it will be perfect. Especially as we can catch Aeron's attention. You can help me catch her attention . . . she'll see me then, won't she, Chelsea . . . then she'll see just how much of a fool she really is.

Chapter 53

ELI STEPPED OUT of the station into the brilliant sunshine, his lunch in his hand, breathing in the clear air. He didn't get away from his desk most days but today he had his eyes set on a nice peaceful patch in the shade of the old oak tree. He stared at it long enough from his office window with memories of Lilia smiling at him as he carved their initials into it. Somewhere on that old bark, his love for her was still etched. Striding out across the parking lot, he tried not to think how true that was of his heart too.

"Chief . . . Hey, Chief."

He turned around to Skip, knowing that his break was about to be snatched from under his nose. "What is it?"

"Jim Borland rang. Chelsea's gone," Skip panted as he caught up to Eli.

Eli hung his head. Chelsea was his eldest, Ruth's, best friend. "When?"

"He said she was out in his front yard maybe two minutes before he rang. So ten at the most."

Eli saw a US government issue car pull up and his chest tightened. "Skip, handle these guys will you? I'll head over there."

A man got out of the car. "Chief Lorelei."

"Speak to Skip. Got an emergency," he yelled over his shoulder as he ran to his car.

He slid into the driver's seat, started the engine, and sighed as the man strode up to the car and put his badge on his windshield.

"I'm Agent Ewan Fitzpatrick. I need to speak to you, now," the man said.

Eli rolled down his window. "No offense, but I got a little girl who has just been taken. You're stopping me getting there."

Fitzpatrick took his badge off the windshield and jumped into the passenger seat. "In that case, I'll keep you company."

Eli tried not to mutter under his breath. No doubt the mayor had something to do with the kid, half his age, being here.

"So, what's the problem?" Eli asked.

"Senator Evans was visiting Mayor Casey," Fitzpatrick began.

Eli nodded. The senator was a really nice guy and he'd come to survey the tornado damage so he could lobby Congress for support.

"His wife and daughter were with him."

Eli turned the corner onto the main road. "Okay. So where are you going with this?"

"Elsie, his daughter, went missing last night."

Eli stared at Fitzpatrick, narrowly avoiding driving over the sidewalk. "What?"

Fitzpatrick frowned. "You haven't been told?"

"Of course I damn haven't! Where . . . where from?"

"Mayor Casey's reception in the golf club I believe."

Eli rubbed his chin. This was a nightmare, if the daughter of a senator was a victim, Aeron would stand no chance at all.

"Skip, any news?" he radioed.

"Mrs. Stein was on her way out . . . saw a van of some kind . . . she said Aeron was in it."

Eli muttered under his breath. Mrs. Stein would say that, stupid gossiping bat.

"Aeron?" the agent asked.

Eli growled. "My daughter, but you already knew that."

The Borlands lived not far from his own house. Everything about their place looked identical to his apart from the ramp instead of front steps. It wouldn't take a couple of minutes to get there but as he started up the road, he saw Aeron and Doctor Llys walking away from the town.

What the hell was she doing now? He pulled in behind them, slammed open his door, and marched toward them. Were they complete fools? "I told you to stay away from town."

Fitzpatrick got out of the car and strolled up behind him. That was all they needed, a damn Fed eavesdropping.

"We got hit by a storm, remember? We needed supplies."

Eli looked down at the grocery bags in their hands, then up at Doctor Llys who smiled knowingly. He wanted to grab her and hug her.

"Have you seen anything?" he asked.

Aeron gave him a look, which confirmed his worst fears but the doctor seemed to be teaching her some wiles, that was for certain. "Only a big ol' twister carving up the field and trashin' the cabin."

Fitzpatrick stepped forward and the doctor put herself in front of Aeron.

"I'm Agent Ewan Fitzpatrick—FBI. Where were you yesterday evening?"

"We were in the cabin, attempting to clean up the flood water, why?" the doctor said.

"You were together the whole time. Miss—?"

The doctor smiled. "Doctor Serena Llys, and yes, we were. Aeron was quite the hero in the storm along with her father. She's been putting me up."

Eli smiled back at her. Thank heavens she was here.

"Chief," Eli's radio squawked.

"Yes, Skip."

"We got a report of the white van . . . Abe . . . confirmed it's Aeron driving it," Skip said.

Eli looked at Fitzpatrick who nodded. "Aeron is with me, Skip . . . and Agent Fitzpatrick . . . I want you to stop that van."

"On it," Skip said.

Eli nodded at Aeron and the doctor, trying not to grin like he'd won the world series.

He trotted back to the car, got in, and waited for Fitzpatrick to get into the passenger seat.

"Mayor Casey had us thinking your girl was on the run," Fitzpatrick said.

"Mayor Casey hates Aeron. I'm not saying he doesn't have cause to either but as you can see, she ain't driving a van around and she ain't in the habit of snatching girls."

Fitzpatrick nodded. "I think it pretty much showed that, so the next step is to find that van and figure out why someone wants to set her up."

Eli felt a huge weight drop from him. "It's nice to have someone with some sense around here."

Chapter 54

JENNY LORELEI SAT in the chair as her regular hairdresser, Grace, snipped out her split ends. The smell of bleach and lotions was thick in the hot air. Her mind was not on the magazine she was thumbing through but on the conversation between Grace and Mary.

"Just walked up to me an hexed my hair!" Mary wailed.

"Don't you worry 'bout a thing," Grace said, walking away from Jenny and going to the sobbing Mary. "We'll fix those roots right up."

"She's an abomination. Why'd they let her out? Why?"

Jenny tried not to mutter a word. She knew exactly who they were referring to.

Now, to Eli, Aeron was infallible. She could do no wrong and he had just gone on ignoring the nasty little brat's "problems" until finally it cost a boy his life.

Jenny had been the only one who went to him when Iris up and left and Aeron was locked up where she belonged. It was Jenny who had picked up the pieces and given him a proper family, a normal family, and how did he repay her?

Jenny flicked over a page in the magazine irritably. She'd seen little Miss Mischief at work plenty of times. Eli seemed to forget that the girl had stolen and vandalized and delighted in the misfortune of others.

Jenny hadn't. Oh no. She hadn't forgotten the time Aeron stole her father's car and put it into a tree, or the time when she'd thought it was funny to decorate Mrs. Stein's shop with spray. The woman had taken nearly three weeks to get the bats off her windows.

Eli had forgotten what a nasty piece of work the freak was. He was always one to bury his head in the sand, and look where it had gotten them?

The entire town was terrified. After Darcy Toughton had gone missing, no one felt safe. The school had advised parents to meet their kids at the door, the school field trip had been cancelled, and no one was allowing their kids out to play unsupervised.

They were prisoners in their own town. Hiding from Aeron as she waltzed down Main Street like she owned the damn place.

"Jenny, you hear what Mary said?" Grace asked.

"No," Jenny answered.

"She's got one of them groupies following her 'round. Can you believe it? Some woman who thinks Aeron is a good person under it all."

Jenny threw the magazine onto the floor with a slap. "You think she's brought in some con from inside?"

Mary shook her head. "Uh uh, this one looks a bit too educated. But she defended her point blank, like we don't know what she is."

"Just keep your Tommie away from her," Grace said.

Mary put her hands over her mouth, then scrabbled in her hand bag and pulled out her cell.

"What?"

"She saw him . . . please Tommie . . . pick up . . ."

Jenny looked at Grace who bit her lip. "Aeron wouldn't, would she?"

Jenny didn't answer. What Aeron was really capable of, no one knew. She would never have expected Aeron to kill Jake Casey.

"I got to find him. He ain't picking up."

Jenny pulled out her phone. "I'll try and call Eli. Maybe he will go find him."

Mary shook her head. "I'll call Bill instead."

Mary hurried out of the shop, her roots forgotten, and Jenny fought the urge to throw something. This was all Aeron's doing. Would she have taken Tommie? What if she'd taken him? Would Eli just ignore it?

Jenny felt her heart thudding. Her own girls were at her mother's house while she had her hair done. She picked up her phone and called her mother.

"Hey, sweetie, you all right?" her mom asked.

"The girls okay? They okay?"

"I'll go check now."

Jenny paced around in a circle, wondering if her mother had locked the doors. What if she'd let them out in the yard?

"You wanna talk to them?" her mother asked.

"Where are they?"

"Picking daisies, how else they gonna make chains?"

Jenny gripped hold of the salon chair. "I asked you not to let them out."

"Oh, hush. They're just fine. Your father is with them."

Jenny heard the sound of her girls' laughter and nearly fainted on the spot, and she thanked every saint she could remember while she was at it. She looked out the window—she only hoped Mary's Tommie was safe and sound too.

Chapter 55

WHEN WE GOT back to the cabin, we slumped down onto the bench, taking a minute to cool off in the shade. Mrs. Squirrel was having a sniff around nearby and the forest buzzed with activity. I guessed the little critters were busy rebuilding themselves only they were a lot more efficient about it. That, and the wildlife didn't shoot me daggers every two seconds.

I glanced up and saw a beefy guy storming down the road toward the cabin. Looked like trouble. I didn't know who the hell he was but he sure knew me.

"You got any ideas?" I asked.

"Nothing that won't get us both locked up," Renee muttered under her breath.

I sighed and we got to our feet. I tried to brace myself for the onslaught. The guy wasn't armed but by the size of his fists, he didn't really need to be.

"Where the hell is my son, you sick son-of-a-bitch?" he demanded.

I frowned. "Your son?" I hadn't got a flash of a boy, I didn't know what he was talking about.

"Tommie, my son. I know you took him!"

I looked at Renee who stepped forward. "We've only just got back ourselves, as you can see—groceries."

The guy's fear was far more acute than his anger.

"I haven't seen your son. What does he look like?" I asked.

"Aeron," Renee warned.

I waved away her concerns.

The guy looked me square in the eyes, his malice gone. "Tommie. He's seven. Blonde hair. Scar on his cheek."

I looked at Renee and then turned to the man. "I saw him in town with his mother . . . er . . ."

"Mary, yeah. Tommie's missing."

I looked up at the clouds. It wasn't pulsing so I knew Tommie wasn't on the killer's radar but I could feel the man's desperation.

"Hold out your hand," I told him.

"We've got company," Renee whispered.

I looked down the dirt track. My father and Agent Fitzgerald were heading this way.

"Your hand," I urged.

The man stuck his hand out and I touched it.

My ankle . . . oh please . . . it's so dark . . . I hate the dark . . . I want to go home . . . please . . . someone!

I opened my eyes and was lying on the ground. My father, Renee, the agent, and Tommie's father all standing over me.

"The old mine . . . he's fallen down the shaft . . . you need a med team."

Fitzpatrick gave me a blank look, while Tommie's father, Bill, as I was shown in the flash, went whiter than I felt.

"Listen, *Bill*," I said, trying to keep my voice calm. "He's okay, but he needs to get help soon."

Bill nodded. "I gotta let Mary know."

I shook my head and clambered to my feet. "Just go with the agent and my father, okay. Go get Tommie."

"But Mary—"

"No one ever knows. Understood?"

Bill shifted on his feet.

I pulled him into a hug. "Take it as a gift and don't bite the hand," I whispered in his ear.

Bill nodded and he followed my father and Fitzpatrick to the cruiser. My father looked back and smiled at me.

"I think he's thawing," Renee said as the cruiser turned around and churned up mud as it sped down the lane.

I didn't know how to answer. The man had been rejecting me since birth so why should I care now? Why should I care about any of these small-minded people? I did care, I cared too much and that was the problem.

Chapter 56

I SPENT THE afternoon and early evening throwing myself into preparing the wheel and the basic drive mechanism in order to get the electricity working. I soon figured that the windows would be a lot harder to fix and it would take weeks to order in replacements. Renee had suggested wistfully that taking out a section and replacing it with a wall of glass would open up the mill to the beauty around it.

The thought was a nice idea, the reality was pretty much impossible. Even if I'd had that kind of money, which I didn't, renovating the mill was a waste of time. Anything we put in would only fall to the next storm.

I looked up at the sky. More than likely that storm would be heading in within the next day or two. How Oppidum was going to brace itself, I wasn't sure. If the tourist trade wasn't so profitable, I was sure that it would just become another ghost town. Distracting myself only lasted until I sat down as Renee put on the dinner. Then as if the vision had been waiting to pounce, it hit me.

No, please . . . please . . . no more . . . I don't know what you want . . . please . . . let me go home . . . please . . . . no, no . . . NO!

My hands ached and stung, my head swirling.

"What's happened?" Renee asked.

"Chelsea. The killer. God, who would do this?"

I put my head between my legs as each blow rocketed through me.

"Can you see anything?"

I clutched my knees, trying to keep conscious. "No, she lost her sight hours ago."

A cold hand touched my arm and I nearly jumped clean out of my seat. Chelsea Borland, a girl of no more than nine stood before me, trying to offer comfort to me as Mari had done.

"What happened?" Renee asked.

I looked from Chelsea's half-spirit to Renee. "We've got to stop this. I can't just sit here and watch them go through this."

Renee shook her head.

I got to my feet.

"Aeron, you can't. Someone is already trying to frame you. If you start trying to get involved you could play right into the killer's hands."

I looked at Chelsea who sat calmly in the chair I had been sitting in. "I can't do nothing."

"Aeron, if you get arrested for this, more girls could die—"

"And if I don't take the chance? How many more people will suffer? How many more girls?"

Renee sighed. "You have to leave it to the people whose job it is. You'll only get in their way."

I paced around, the movement helping me think. "I helped with Tommie, that has to buy me some kind of leverage."

"To the authorities you are a convicted murderer who is terrorizing a town, or did you miss the entire you're-a-sicko rant."

I folded my arms. I knew Renee was right but I couldn't bear living with another half-spirit, knowing that Chelsea was being played with by the killer.

"I don't care. If I don't do something, I ain't no better than the killer."

"Think about this—"

"I have. You would do the same thing if you were me. We both know it."

Renee looked at me like she wanted to impale me on her tongs but she nodded. "I hate it when you do that," she muttered, putting the hot dogs into buns.

"No, you don't. You're glad you don't have to pretend."

Renee slopped some onions onto the bun, spread mustard on them, and almost shoved the plate into my hands. "Quit it."

I shrugged. "Sorry, I can't help it. You're like a book when you're mad."

"I'm not ma—" Renee stopped and rolled her eyes. "What's the use in arguing when you already know what I'll say."

"So you will help?"

Renee took a bite of her hot dog, but her eyes twinkled as she conceded defeat. "Only if you sit and eat first."

I shook my head, looking at Chelsea still sitting there.

"What? Hell, you look like you've seen—" Renee got up and grabbed the tongs as if they would save her. "You jumped."

"I did," I answered.

"There's . . . is there a . . ."

I nodded chewing on my hot dog.

"Who, where . . . now I'm creeped out," she said, hopping about.

"It's okay. It's Chelsea Borland, she's nine. She went missing earlier. She's staying with us a while . . . till it's over."

Renee put the tongs down and put her hand over her mouth. "Oh, no. Poor kid."

"Yeah," I said, looking at Chelsea. "And that's why it has to stop . . . now."

Chapter 57

ELI FELT THE sheer elation soar through him as the medic team called out that they'd found Tommie. Bill, who had been sitting in the squad car, broke down in tears. It would take them a while to get the boy up the shaft but finding him so quickly had saved his life.

Fitzpatrick maintained a dignified distance throughout the rescue but Eli knew he would want to know how Aeron had known where the boy was.

"You know why Tommie would have been up here?" Eli asked.

Bill rubbed at his eyes. "Yeah. Mary was always telling him that the old mine was where they kept Excalibur. Stupid woman."

"So why did he come to the mine today?"

Bill grunted. "It's Arthur's sword. He loves those stupid tales."

Eli didn't get it. He looked at Fitzpatrick who shrugged. "Why look for it now?"

"To kill Morgana—the witch."

Eli kicked a nearby fallen branch in irritation. "The witch? You mean Aeron?"

Bill nodded, his eyes lingering over the place where the medics were working. "She knew where he was. If it wasn't for her . . ."

Eli walked to Bill and leaned in. "No one ever hears what she did, you understand?"

"She said the same thing. What is she?"

"Not a witch. And not someone your son or any other idiot should take on lightly."

"He's just a boy—"

"And that's when it starts. The gossiping, the tales, the odd girl by the river . . . Yeah, she's the odd one, then before you know it, she's a witch."

Bill stood up. "She *did* kill someone."

Eli shook his head. "She was trying to stop the kid getting hit by the train, she couldn't pull him back in time. She didn't kill anyone, Bill."

Bill folded his arms. "Mary and the others. They said she strung him up, just like the woman from the travelers' camp."

"Mary and the others are nothing but jabbering fishwives, mine included."

"You're her father though. You would defend her."

Eli sighed. Of course he would. She could have chopped Jake Casey into tiny pieces and he'd still love her with every breath in his body. Even if he couldn't show it, even if he messed everything up, even if she never forgave him, he loved her.

"If she's so happy to kill little boys. Why would she help you today?"

Bill smiled. "She wouldn't."

"And that's why you have to keep your mouth shut. Aeron's got enough troubles without adding to them by revealing anything."

Bill nodded. "Least I can do."

The rescue team started moving and Eli and Bill hurried to the mine shaft. Bill was in a fit of tears all over again as they pulled a pale, sodden, and battered Tommie out of the mine. Bill ran to him, dropped to his knees, and cradled the terrified boy.

Eli looked at Fitzpatrick as the medics moved in to take Tommie and Bill off to the hospital.

"Your gal did a pretty good deed," Fitzpatrick said as Eli walked to him.

"Yeah. Aeron is like that."

"She's a psychic?"

Eli frowned. He hated the word. "She's a little different."

"Different? She gave you the exact location of that boy, and if she hadn't, he'd be dead by now."

Eli got in the cruiser, Fitzpatrick following him. He was in no mood to think about Aeron's gifts. Not that there was ever a mood that he did want to.

"Y'know, I've worked with a couple of folks who are psychics but she's somethin' else," Fitzpatrick said.

"Worked with?" Eli asked, driving them in the direction of city hall.

"Yeah, as agents."

Eli rolled his eyes. It was best he kept his mouth shut on that one. He turned his attention back to Chelsea Borland's disappearance. No one had seen her since the mysterious van had snatched her and there'd been no sightings of it since.

"Any news on Elsie Evans?" Eli asked.

The agent shook his head. "We have set up check points on all the major roads and at the airport, but it's chaos 'round here." Eli had to agree. The twister had pretty much blitzed the place. "I guess we weren't as twister proof as we thought."

"I'm surprised there weren't more folks hurt. Good thing they actually listened to the sirens."

"It's not like we hear them an awful lot," Eli said. "So what's the next step for you and your team?"

Fitzpatrick smiled. "Well, I'm just a worker bee. The boss will be on the warpath 'cause we lost the van."

"Ouch."

Fitzpatrick laughed. "You have no idea just how accurate that is."

Eli pulled into the parking lot, and Fitzpatrick smoothed over his trousers, his lips pulling into a thin line. What had gotten him so uncomfortable?

Eli followed his eyes to a woman with spiky blonde hair. "That your boss?"

Fitzpatrick shook his head. "No, that's worse than the boss."

Eli looked at the woman. The small group of agents around her seemed to be cowering like she'd attack at any moment.

"Do I get a heads up before she removes it?"

"Agent Ursula Frei," Fitzpatrick said in a low voice. "Can't tell you where she's from but when she shows up, it's gonna hit the fan."

"All this over Elsie?" Eli asked.

"If it is, it was nice knowing you."

Eli laughed. He thought it funny that this self-assured young man was scared of a woman. He braced himself and got out of the car.

Frei turned and held out her hand in greeting. "Agent Frei. A word, Chief Lorelei."

Eli tilted his head. "Sure. My office okay?"

"Fine." Frei gripped his hand and shook it.

Eli tried not to wince and shake out his hand as he turned, in a daze, toward the building. She'd almost crushed his fingers. There was dominance, then there was this woman. "This about Senator Evans's daughter?"

"No."

He led her into the building and to his office. Frei marched past him into it and told him to sit.

"I'm quite capable of standing," he told her.

Frei folded her arms. "It wasn't a request."

Eli frowned as she closed his door. "Excuse me?"

"The sooner you sit down, the sooner I leave."

Eli went behind his desk and sank into his chair, unsure how the hell to react to the demanding Agent Frei.

"Why is Aeron helping the FBI?" she asked.

"Pardon?"

Frei frowned, her sharp blue eyes like an eagle eying its prey. "Don't play dumb, I know what she is. Why did you let her help the FBI?"

"I think you're mistaken, Agent Frei. Aeron doesn't follow orders from me and I have no intention of telling her she can't help them."

Frei slammed a chair down and sat in front of the desk. "You know what's at stake if they so much as think she might be the killer?"

"I'm very aware they may charge her for a federal offense, yes."

"And with her track record? Did it not cross your mind that they will go for the death penalty?"

Eli's panic thumped through his heart and he pulled his tablets out from his pocket. He needed to see the doctor soon. "I don't know who you are, Agent Frei."

"The senator has an election coming up, which makes this look much worse than a random attack."

Eli frowned. "I'm more worried about my daughter's life."

"You are the only one who is." She glared at him, stoic, icy. "The mayor wants her gone, keeps telling us she'll drive away the tourists. That's a lot of money."

Eli rubbed his hand over his face. The last thing he wanted on his conscience was the entire county's welfare. "I thought Oppidum was Lorelei owned. Why should he care?"

Frei looked at him like he'd told her the grass was purple. "Sure you own the land, but the mayor owns half the tourist trade."

Eli frowned. "That doesn't surprise me. Aeron doesn't know

she's the heir. No one knew we owned anything. Do you think that's why they're targeting her?"

Frei nodded. "It could be and if it is, we need to find out quickly."

Eli looked at the gun she had strapped under her jacket as she sat forward. Same one as Doctor Llys had. Same one that Dan had worn. "Do you have someone taking care of her?"

Frei's eyes cooled even further. "I'm not at liber—"

"It's my daughter, Agent Frei. If you want my help, you'll tell me the truth."

"Fine, yes. One of our best."

"Name?"

Frei's lips thinned as she tensed her jaw. Eli sat back and folded his arms. She could take all night to answer for all he cared. It beat arguing with Jenny.

"Renee Black," Frei said.

"As in Colonel Charles Black's daughter?"

Frei nodded. "One and the same."

Eli smiled from ear to ear. If she was cut from the same cloth as the colonel then they were in great hands.

"Give me the rundown on all you have," Frei said.

Eli nodded. "Okay. So far we have three murders, one adult female Natalia and her daughter Mari were the first two, then we found Darcy Toughton just before the storm hit." He stood up and walked to his window. "The Feds show up and tell me that the senator's daughter Elsie Evans has gone missing." He sighed. "And Chelsea Borland has been taken. She can't be more than eight." What was he going to tell Jim and Kay, her parents? He didn't know where the hell she was. There was no sign of the van, nothing.

"What about the boy? Tommie?" Frei asked.

Eli shook his head. "No, just an accident."

"The Unsub is escalating, two in one day."

"Not escalating, not really. Mari and Natalia were found within twenty-four hours, and Darcy was found not long before he tried to get Doctor Llys, I mean Renee."

"What?"

Eli swallowed hard. Renee had obviously left that bit out of her reports. "Someone tried to run her off the road. Aeron tried to save her. We nearly got sucked up into the twister."

Frei got to her feet and scowled like she wanted to shoot someone. "So, it could well be political if the killer knows who she is . . . the killer knows who Aeron is."

"That could be true, but why not just make a hit on her? Why the game?"

Frei shook her head. "I don't know but somehow we need to keep Aeron away from all this. Maybe we could move her?"

"You'd be lucky."

Frei shot him a dark look.

He nodded. "I mean it. You go marching up to Aeron and demand she run and hide and you'll get the same answer the rest of us get."

"And that is?"

"Where you can stick your badge."

Frei almost smiled, almost. No doubt she was as fiery when cornered.

"What do we do about the Feds?"

Frei looked out of the window in Eli's door. Fitzpatrick was deep in conversation with Jo, a part-time officer working an extra shift. "Fitzpatrick is a great agent. He's pretty by-the-book but he's sharp. He's probably figured out that it isn't Aeron and is looking for whoever *is* responsible."

Eli felt a slither of something cold wriggle through his stomach. "It wouldn't be Renee, would it?"

Frei turned and her eyes shot daggers at him, but he needed to ask it.

"I mean it. She's in the best position. I'm only eliminating the obvious, Agent."

Frei flinched. "I've known Renee for ten years, her father was a war hero. The man was a patriot right down to his boots and I trust her, but I'll look into it."

"Thank you."

"Just keep Aeron out of the limelight as much as you can." Frei opened the door.

"Can you believe it?" Jo said to a bored-looking Fitzpatrick. "I mean who knew the little freak could really harm with her mind."

Eli wanted to crawl into a corner and hide as Frei snapped her eyes to his.

"Y'know, Bill said no, no way did she do nothing, but I heard," Jo continued, "I heard every word from Mary. She said she hexed her roots then conjured up an accident."

Frei glowered. "Bill and Mary?"

"Tommie's parents."

Eli looked out at Fitzpatrick, who was trying to ignore the comments and eat a sandwich. "Jo, go do somethin' useful."

Jo gave him a wide-eyed look and went into the files room.

Frei frowned at Eli. "Hexes? Accidents?"

Eli held open his office door and cast a hungry glance at Fitzpatrick's sandwich. "There's something about Aeron. It'll take a while."

Chapter 58

NOW, IF I thought that helping out and finding Tommie had earned me any kind of reprieve from the folks in town, I was sorely mistaken. The next morning, when I awoke, I could hear Renee getting yelled at by someone outside the front door. Thinking that she shouldn't have to face my problems, I hurried down, only to get stopped in my tracks by what the person was saying to her.

"You were attacked by the Unsub and at no point did you think it was a good idea to report it?"

"No, ma'am."

I snuck up to the crack in the door and peered through. Renee was at attention, a woman nearly as tall as me with the coolest haircut I'd ever seen was dressing her down.

"You could have been killed, you could have blown the entire operation."

"Yes, ma'am."

The blonde woman shoved her hands on her hips. "You even knew she was like her mother, didn't you?"

"Yes, ma'am."

"So why didn't you tell me?"

Renee said nothing for the longest time. I was itching to get out there and support her but I was too curious about my mother—I mean seriously? Iris Lorelei was about as empathic as a stone and about as warm.

"I didn't want to be taken off the case, ma'am."

The blonde woman rolled her eyes. "Have you lost your mind? If you get blown, that's it. You've worked your entire life to get where you are."

Renee's shoulders sagged. "I know, but this is more important than all of us now. Aeron can really make a difference."

"Aeron is a freak of nature."

I tensed at the woman's words. She sounded like every other person in town.

"Aeron is a kind, sweet woman who hasn't got a clue why she's in the center of a storm."

"What if she sees your secrets? Just like her mother did? You want to give her that much power?"

I frowned. I was really confused. Had Renee met my mother? When and why?

"She knows enough, and she's promised not to look further."

"And what happens when she finds out her whole life has been a lie?"

My heart started to thud, and I could hear it pumping away in my ears. My life had been a lie? Why? It was a pretty rotten lie if it was.

"She won't. Can't you trust me enough to do my job?"

"Not when you're emotionally involved. Renee, the father thinks you have something to do with the murders. Hell, I half wanted to search his office for nine-eight-four."

"What?"

The blonde woman nodded. "Oh yeah, he thinks you're here to protect Aeron's position as heir. He doesn't know that we're looking—"

"Did you see it? Nine-eight-four? Was it there?"

The blonde woman folded her arms. "No. Lilia has no idea what it means either."

I gripped the wall for support. Who was Lilia? And what *was* nine-eight-four?

"So what the hell do we do? If he digs around, if he asks around . . . Hell, the whole thing will come out in the open."

The blonde woman shook her head. "It can't. I'm running things on the outside. Why do you think I sent in Ewan?"

"What about Aeron? Doesn't she have the right to know what the hell is going on?"

"No."

Renee was no longer at attention and my brain felt like it was on overload.

"She'd be more supportive than you think, Ursula. She might even help."

"Lilia doesn't want her involved."

"She gave up that right when she abandoned her to join us."

The blonde woman shot Renee a look that made her snap back

to attention. "Just keep her out of sight and out of the spotlight or
I'll pull you off the case."

"She's not just going to sit back when other people are getting
killed. She's too much like her mother."

I stood stunned to the spot. Was Iris my mother? Iris couldn't
see, so who was my mother? Who was Lilia and who were these
people?

"Great, another frickin' hero. Just keep her away from the
case."

"And if the killer targets her?"

"Do what you're paid to."

Renee shoved her hands in her pockets. "And what is that?
You have me blowing the whistle on prison brutality, then follow
Aeron here to Oppidum. Now you're telling me to get rid of a
killer and then what? Aeron will look guilty as hell."

The blonde woman strolled forward, pure ice flowing from
her eyes. She stopped inches from Renee's face, forcing Renee
to look up at her. Her voice was calm but with threat seeping
through it. "Don't push me, Renee. I don't care if she looks like
she's responsible. Just keep her alive and keep her out the damn
way till it's over."

Like hell was I letting anyone talk to her like that. I grabbed
hold of the handle and yanked the door open with such force that
the hinges groaned. I stormed over to the blonde woman and
glared down at her.

"Till what's over?" I demanded.

Renee spun around, her face paling as she met my eyes.

"Till what's over?" I asked again, focusing on the blonde
woman.

The woman raised her chin. "It's none of your concern."

Like hell it wasn't. I stepped closer and pulled myself up to all
six-four. "Who the hell are you to tell me anything?"

Her blue eyes stared into mine, her face stoic. She looked
bored. "Agent Ursula Frei."

"Oh, so nine-eight-four is some kind of code for an arrogant
ass? Maybe it's code for lying through your teeth." I shot a look at
Renee, who closed her eyes.

"I don't know what you mean," Frei said.

I grabbed her hand before Renee could stop me. The flashes hit
my mind like a barrage of bullets.

She was born in Detroit. Her parents had emigrated to the US with their work. She joined the military after graduation and passed every assessment she was given. A field officer for ten years, she was made lead on this case for the first time. Her boss trusted her implicitly, Renee trusted her the same.

"Get your hands off me," Frei warned.

She drank too much when she was on leave, not enough to be a problem, just enough to blot out the dark spaces, the faces and names of the victims she couldn't save, the ones they couldn't get to.

I took my hand off. I didn't know what the hell to think. I walked past them and strode up the road, my boots sinking in the mud. I didn't know where I was headed but I had to do something.

"Aeron, please . . . just wait . . . listen," Renee called after me.

I didn't want to listen. I didn't want to talk. Renee was protecting me, I knew that, and so was Ursula Frei, but why and from what? And why had they lied to my father and me?

"Aeron . . . don't . . . don't go running off . . . please just listen."

I heard approaching squishing footfalls and Renee grabbed my arm.

I spun around and glared at her. Anger pulsed from every part of my body. I felt so pathetic, I couldn't understand the muddle of information I had overheard.

"You want to talk? Then why don't you start with who the hell my mother is? Because Iris Lorelei never saw a damn thing!"

Renee looked back at Frei who got into her car. She was talking on the phone to someone.

I felt like I was about to explode from frustration. "Can't you speak for yourself?"

Renee captured my eyes—hers wide and pleading as she gripped my hand. "Listen to me. I will tell you. I promise you I will, but please, trust me."

I pulled my hand away, surprised that no vision had hit when Renee touched me. "Trust you? Your . . . whatever she is . . . just said how she lied to my father and me and how Lilia doesn't want me involved."

Renee tilted her head. "You can't see it?"

"See what?"

Renee took my hand again. I stared at her. "Nothing?"

I shook my head.

"So it's true." Renee frowned. "You can't see anything to do with yourself."

I pulled my hand away. "I told you that. I'm not the one lyin'."

Renee glanced back at Frei. "She's my boss. We aren't even supposed to be here, but we are, as a favor."

"Why?"

Renee walked to the river bank, scooped up some stones and threw them into the water. "Lilia asked us. We're her team. She handpicked us almost, mentored us, made us a great team."

"I thought you were protection."

Renee nodded. "I am. She sees things. I go in to keep the POI safe and there's a team . . . they investigate while I protect."

I crossed my arms. "So who do you work for?"

Renee shook her finger. "You know I can't say."

"Then who is Lilia?" My heart skipped as I said it. "Wait . . . you said . . . Lilia . . . she sees things." I shook my head and strode away from her.

"Aeron . . . where are you going?"

I stopped and turned around with my hands on my hips. "You comin'?"

Renee looked back at Frei, who was still deep in conversation. "Where are we going?"

I turned back around and marched on as Renee hurried to keep up. "To find my father. He's got a hell of a lot of explaining to do."

Chapter 59

ELI SAT IN the cruiser, dabbing at his mouth. He'd lost his lunch moments before and he hadn't been the only one. They'd found Chelsea. He'd wished like hell that they hadn't. In all his years, he'd seen some things, but this, this was beyond evil. This was . . . well, he didn't know what the hell to call it.

"You got anything, Jeff?" Eli called out.

Jeff peeled his gloves off and threw them on the ground. "Nothing. Shoot. It's too much. Hell, I can't—"

"Then let us." Frei walked toward them with two men.

One Eli recognized as Fitzpatrick and the other looked like an ME.

"Doctor Jeff Deed, I'm Agent Ursula Frei. This is Agent Ewan Fitzpatrick and Doctor Neil Grant. We'd like to take a look."

Jeff stepped away from the body, looking beyond relieved. "All yours."

Eli frowned. "This FBI now?"

Frei nodded. "Yes, we'll need to look at the files."

Eli sighed and looked at Jeff and the other officers. They were all country cops. They did road accidents, tourist problems, mountain rescues . . . Hell, some of them were even smoke jumpers during the summer season. In a few weeks they'd be off, hurling themselves into the line of fire all over the States.

No doubting most of the guys were heroes but this was home. Every one of them knew the Borland family. The smoke jumpers especially. Kay Borland was the fire chief and a damn good one.

Jim, the father was well loved. The guy had been a firefighter too until his accident. There wasn't a nicer family in Oppidum. A nice family, who he would have to find a way of explaining why their little girl, Chelsea, wasn't coming home.

"The files, Chief." Frei had her arms crossed, wearing her impatience like a coat.

Eli opened his mouth to snap at her and met her eyes. He saw deep compassion beneath the steely bluster. "Sure. I'll get Sam to give them to Fitzpatrick."

"That will be helpful. Is there anything you're waiting on?"

Eli frowned and looked at Jeff. "Did you get the results from Michael's find yet?"

"What find?" Jeff called back.

Eli rubbed his chin. "Michael's—the fibers from the tree."

Jeff dropped his gaze to the ground.

"What?" Eli asked.

"Michael was found yesterday. It was a mess."

Eli tried to quell the pang of loss in his heart. Michael was yet another victim, another name. Hell, he needed a whiskey.

He turned to Frei. "Guess there's nothing then."

Frei put her hands on her hips, her jacket pulled back like wings. "Why did he have evidence on him?"

"I'd say you'd need to ask him but in the circumstances . . ."

Frei gazed at the two other Feds who were examining Chelsea. "Do you remember where the evidence was taken?"

Eli nodded. "Sure. You think you might get something?"

Frei shrugged, her hawk-like focus watching every action the agents made. "It's worth a shot."

Eli's radio crackled on his shoulder. "What is it, Skip?"

"There's a disturbance at your place."

Eli's entire body shook and he turned away from Frei. "What?"

"Yeah," Skip said. "Looks like Aeron went to see you and she and Jenny have gotten into it."

Eli flashed Frei a look and headed to his cruiser . "I'm on my way. Keep everyone else on this case."

"Will do."

Eli got into the car and Frei leaned in through his open window. "You can ride along and we'll go out to the spot after, if you want?"

Frei nodded. "Maybe a good idea."

Frei got in the car and Eli tried not to grip the wheel so tightly. What was Aeron doing going to his place? Why would she go there? He hadn't had a chance to tell her about Jenny, or about the girls. This wasn't how he wanted her to find out. He had two days locked up in the storm with her and he hadn't been able to find the words. Now, she was getting it from Jenny of all people. And if there was one person in Oppidum that Aeron had always hated, it was Jenny.

Chapter 60

AS RENEE AND I got to my father's house, I slowed my pace to a crawl. What I was supposed to feel about the place, I didn't know. Everything about it seemed to remind me how badly I didn't belong. My mother, or whoever the woman had been, had never welcomed me. The hedges had always been immaculate, nothing could be out of place. Memories crept into my mind. Memories of being escorted out of the front door and down the path by my father. I'd been a scared, freaked-out kid back then and Iris hadn't given a damn. She'd been more than happy to turn her back on me and walk away. What had I done to her to deserve that?

Renee was hovering behind me, her need to try and calm me pulsating from her. Not wanting to give in, I stared up at the house. I was pretty thankful that he'd spent the storm with us. The entire top half of the house was missing, leaving only the stone ground level.

I met Renee's eyes and she blew the air out from her cheeks.

"Cruiser's not here," I said, looking around. Odd, although my father wasn't inside, someone was . . . well, a few people.

I marched up to the front door and knocked, thinking that it could be workmen or wait, did I sense kids?

The fear and panic shot through my veins like venom. There were two girls in the house, two young girls. Was my father the—?

The door opened. "Yes?"

I scowled at the sight of Jenny McAllister standing in the doorway like she owned the damn place. "Where's my father?"

Jenny folded her arms.

I folded mine.

"He's at work."

"Then why the hell are you here?" I asked, storming past her.

The house was a mess, the wooden floor sticky and slimy. The walls looked no better than Nan's cabin had. The entire place had been flooded out. Weird, the décor was so different. Had he redecorated? I got to the kitchen and stopped in the doorway and stared. Two girls, young girls, the spittin' image of my father, sat at the kitchen table. They stared at me with eyes wide with surprise and fear.

"You're not welcome here," Jenny snapped as she pushed past me and stood in front of the girls.

I shoved down my confusion. "I have more right to be here than you."

"Aeron, maybe we should leave . . . go to city hall," Renee said from behind me.

I stiffened with anger. Like hell was I going anywhere. "No!"

The girls cowered and Jenny knelt between them at the table and put her arms around them.

Why did they look like my father? How could they look like my father? My mother, well, Iris, had been older than him, no way could she have had those girls.

Jenny lifted up her left hand, wedding band in full view. "Oh, I have the right."

"Why the hell would he marry a tramp like you?"

Renee touched my arm.

I pulled away and glared at Jenny. "What did you bribe him with?"

Jenny stood, stomped across the kitchen, and slapped me, hard, across the face. "Unlike you, I don't have to bribe people to get love." She glanced at Renee.

The only thing that stopped me tearing her head off were the two little girls, watching, afraid. I could sense them and what made it worse, they could sense me.

"Girls, go in the other room." Jenny's tone was soft with them, gentle.

The children sat frozen, eyes darting between Jenny and me.

I looked them both in the eyes with a "trust me" expression. I wouldn't harm their mother . . . much.

Jenny shoved me hard out of the kitchen, screaming at me about hurting her kids. Like a possessed woman, she rammed me out of the house onto the lawn before I could get a foothold.

"What the hell are you on about?" I threw the flailing psycho off me.

Jenny straightened and clenched her fist. "You're not taking them too. I'll kill you myself."

She raked my cheek with her nails.

I grabbed her hands. "Why would I harm them?"

Jenny caught me in the stomach with her knee, the wind sucked from my gut.

"Murderer!" she yelled, picking up a rock.

I scrabbled out the way. Renee caught Jenny's hand and wrestled her to the ground.

"She's a lunatic," I said. "What the hell is wrong with you?"

"Murderer!" Jenny yelled louder.

I saw my father pull up out of the corner of my eye as Jenny whacked Renee in the face with her elbow and launched herself at me again.

My father ran across the yard, trailed by Frei. "Cut it out, woman!" He caught Jenny effortlessly and gripped her hands.

Jenny struggled against him like a trapped cat. "Murderer. She was after the girls, I saw her eyes. You were after them."

I laughed at her pathetic accusations, but my father's temper was above boiling point. I'd never seen him talk to a woman like this before.

"Get the hell in the house and not another word!" My father's voice was as cold as his expression.

Jenny wriggled.

He tightened his grip. "Don't think I won't, Jenny."

All the fight drained from Jenny's eyes. "All right. Let go."

My father let go of her hands and she ran into the house, sobbing.

My father turned to me, the anger still pulsing. "What happened?"

"What didn't happen?" I asked. "When did you shack up with a girl?"

My father narrowed his eyes. "You don't get to judge me, girl."

"Don't I? Is that because I'm a murderer or a freak, or maybe it's because you were just waiting to marry a child?"

"She's thirty, Aeron."

"And those girls are what? Eight? You knock up a twenty-one-year-old kid. Nice, Daddy, real nice."

My father picked up the rock and hurled it against the wall with such a force that it exploded.

"Yeah, that's right. Pick someone who is too scared to fight back."

"Don't push me, girl."

I stepped forward, my full height, my anger like a wave of rage crashing from every pore. "Or what? What will you do? Lock me up. Disown me. Lie to me? Or wait, no, you've already done all that."

My father flinched.

"Oh, yeah, Daddy. Lilia. I know all about her."

"Don't you dare."

"Dare what? Pretend that some strange woman was my mother, a woman who hated me. Do you know how it feels growing up thinking your own mother despises you?" I picked up a fallen branch from the ground, swung it at his cruiser, and smashed the windshield. "Do you know how it feels to have a father who can't even bear to look at you!"

I swung again and smashed the side window.

"Jenny. You pick Jenny. Was that for me too? Just to punish me? Was it?"

My father went to grab for me and I hit him, full tilt in the shoulder, sending him sprawling onto the grass.

"Don't touch me. Don't you ever touch me." I swung the branch one last time and hurled it across the road. "You stay the hell away from me."

I strode down the road, tears pumping from my eyes, angry tears, distraught tears, hateful tears. Who was I to ever think anyone could love me?

RENEE GROANED AS Frei checked out her throbbing cheek. She had to give it to Jenny, she had a pretty good right hook.

"Why the shiner?" Frei asked.

Renee flinched. "Jenny objected to me stopping her from killing Aeron."

"What?" Eli pulled himself out of the flowerbed.

"She picked up the rock, she was going to kill her," Renee said.

Frei prodded Renee's face with her thumb and Renee yelped. "She nearly broke your cheekbone."

"She nearly broke Aeron's skull," Renee said.

Frei growled.

Renee sighed. For nearly ten years, she and Frei had been through hell, back, and everywhere in between.

"Why would your wife attack Aeron?" Frei asked.

Eli put his hands on his hips. "Are you kidding me? Apart from the fact everyone thinks she's butchering children? There are times when I'd like to wring her neck myself."

Renee groaned. Baiting Frei was never a good idea, and telling her that you wanted to wring the POI's neck was even worse. She didn't do humor.

Frei folded her arms. "Really? Maybe I should start looking into where you were during these murders?"

Eli held up his hands.

Renee was thankful he didn't push further. She'd had enough confrontation for one day. "That looked like more than a simple spat. That looked pretty personal." Her cheek felt like a balloon.

"It is," Eli said. "Jenny and Aeron . . . hell."

Eli walked to the porch steps and sat down. "Jenny spent most of her days when they were younger making Aeron's life hell. It got to the point where it came to blows."

Renee stared at Eli, wondering just how much of an idiot one man could possibly be.

"And?" Frei asked.

"And . . . Jenny has a scar from her mouth to her chin for a reason."

Renee looked at Frei who shrugged. She'd not seen a scar either.

"Covered in makeup," Eli offered. "But it's there."

"So what did she do?" Renee asked.

Eli rubbed his chin. He looked ten years older than he had a few days ago when they'd met. "Something that made it real easy for everyone to think she's a murderer."

"Which is?" Frei snapped.

"Pushed her through a window. Aeron never apologized or said it was an accident, so it pretty much looked like she was trying to kill her."

"How old was she?"

Eli sighed. "I don't know. Maybe fourteen. Why?"

Renee looked at Frei for the go ahead.

Frei nodded.

"So, what you are saying is that Aeron intended to cause harm to Jenny when she pushed her?" Renee asked.

Eli nodded. "She said as much."

"And she told you she killed Jake. Did you believe that one too?"

Eli blinked a few times while Frei frowned.

Renee's frustration spilled over. "Is it any freaking wonder she reacted? You said Jenny bullied her. You were just lucky she didn't hack her into little pieces."

"Renee," Frei warned.

"He's an idiot, Urs. I'm sorry but he is. They all are. The abuse Aeron has suffered—"

"She was not touched," Eli snapped.

Renee threw her hands in the air. "Well, that just makes it all right then. You tell her you don't love her, you don't want her, that she's a disappointment. Of course that doesn't hurt her, does it?"

"Renee, calm down," Frei said.

Renee walked up to Eli. "If Aeron wasn't such a good woman, if she wasn't so strong, you'd have built yourself a nightmare."

"And you don't think she ain't?" Eli snapped, getting to his feet. "She comes to my house, assaults my wife, scares the hell out of my kids. She trashes my damn cruiser and you think that's okay?"

Renee stood her ground. "Yes. If I had been her. I'd have shot you."

"Renee!" Frei put her hands on her hips but Renee spun on her heels and trotted down the road after Aeron. Frei would kick her ass for this later but there was no way she was leaving Aeron to go through this alone.

"Doing my job," Renee called over her shoulder in a bid to appease Frei. Like hell that was going to work.

Renee hoped that all they'd been through would buy her the dispensation, otherwise she'd be hauled off the case. And she may not have been an Empath but she didn't need to be to know Aeron couldn't survive this alone.

Chapter 61

ELI WATCHED THE fiery blonde stomp off after Aeron and almost smiled. The woman had more fire than a volcano on eruption day and he felt a little twinge of pride that she was defending Aeron. Then he felt the crushing grip of guilt that he couldn't.

"I need to question Jenny," Frei said, her tone icy.

"Jenny? Why?"

Frei looked at him like he was stupid. "Someone who has cause to hate Aeron is trying to frame her . . . you said yourself they have history."

He rubbed his hand over his soaking brow and sighed. "They were children."

Frei stared at him. Her stoic look and folded arms told him all he needed to know. She was unmoved. "Systematic bullying of another child is a precursor. Did Jenny have friends growing up?"

Eli nodded, she'd had a gaggle of followers. "Jenny was the girl everyone wanted to be."

"Until?"

He hated thinking about it. The accusation that he'd abused Aeron in some way rubbing raw his already frazzled senses. What was he supposed to have done? Aeron had said she hurt Jenny, said she'd hurt Jake . . . or had he missed something?

"Until she fell through the window . . . she was going to be a model . . . maybe international."

Frei pulled out her cell and tapped her finger on the screen, no doubt taking notes. "And do you make a habit of forming relationships out of guilt."

Eli's anger boiled and he gripped hold of his belt. Like hell was Frei judging him. "Excuse me?"

"You married Jenny because you felt guilty that you didn't stop the events."

Eli's stomach churned, was she right? "She's a good woman."

Frei's eyes remained cold and formal. "She was a bully, who

then lost her dream. She's bitter, angry, and capable of killing if Renee's statement is anything to go by."

Eli looked at the gold band on his hand. He hated wearing it. He was pretty sure most men must feel that way. Lilia had asked him to get a tattoo instead of wearing a band and he still had it. A golden eagle in flight to represent her native blood.

Shaking his thoughts free of Lilia, he met Frei's eyes. Jenny was mean, nasty, but she was a fine mother. She wouldn't hurt anybody, would she? "Jenny's highly strung at the moment. Storm an' all."

Frei didn't look like she was buying it, neither was Eli in his heart. Jenny was pretty bitter. What the hell had he done marrying her? He was a stupid fool. A stupid, cowardly fool.

"Let me get the girls, take them over to her mother's place. They're probably terrified."

Frei nodded. "It would be better for everyone if she stayed there for a few days."

Eli frowned. "Why?"

"Because, Chief," Frei strolled up to him, her tone as sharp as her eyes, "someone is trying to frame your daughter and if it isn't your blushing bride, then perhaps keeping her somewhere she will be safer, may be wise."

He pulled himself up, puffing out his chest. "She's safe in this house. I can protect my own damn wife."

"Well, you've done such a fine job with your daughter," Frei fired back in a cold, curt tone.

Eli grabbed his hat off the lawn. "You have no right to talk to me like that."

Frei's eyes oozed ice. She was ruthless, that much he could tell. "The only reason I haven't had you suspended and your wife thrown in jail is that you're co-operating. So, if you want to keep your badge and your dignity, do as you're told."

Eli's chest cramped. He gripped at it and fumbled in his pocket. Where the hell were his damn tablets? He looked up.

Frei was holding them out to him. "I want you gone in ten minutes."

He took his medication and rubbed at his sore chest. He wanted to argue. Hell he wanted to put the woman in her place but she had read the label. One phone call and he'd be medically retired.

Chapter 62

AS I HEADED up the road to the cabin I saw smoke puffing out into the sky. My heart sprang into life and I sprinted up the road. A crowd was gathered outside the cabin, including Mary, all hurling abuse as they threw rocks at it. Something felt like it flicked in my head and I lost it. I've never lost it before, but everything came to a head and I picked up a metal bar from the old wheel joint.

"It's the freak!" Mary shouted.

"Murderer!" someone called.

"Child killer!"

"Witch!"

I grabbed hold of Mary, and I swear I was gonna beat her with the bar but the second I touched her, my body shook.

Bill told her the truth but she wasn't going to believe him. Bill was stupid and naive if he thought Aeron wouldn't hurt anyone. Everyone knew she was a killer. No, Mary had to take a stand against the little freak, she'd killed Jake . . . she'd spoiled Sam . . . who could ever marry Sam now after he was tainted by her . . . little freak, little witch.

I stepped back and dropped the bar.

A fist caught me in the face. I fell onto the ground. Another blow landed, then another, the pain phased out by the agony in my heart. These people hated me, they had always hated me and why, all I had done was be myself.

I curled into a ball as the blows kept coming, unwilling to fight anymore, unwilling to feel anymore . . . and so I just waited . . . waited for it to be over.

RENEE RAN DOWN the muddy lane and stopped when she saw the crowd around Aeron's house. She pulled out her cell phone and pressed the alarm button. The flames were licking from the windows on the bottom floor and Aeron was nowhere to be seen.

"Son of a—"

Renee pulled her pistol from her belt and fired into the sky. She saw Aeron on the ground, barely breathing, barely moving.

"Get the hell away from her!" Renee pointed the gun at the mob.

One of the men lurched toward Renee. She pulled the trigger and the bullet kicked up the dirt next to his foot.

"She's the other one . . . get her," Mary shrieked, prompting the mob to edge forward.

Renee pointed the gun at Mary's head. "The next person who moves, I pull the trigger."

The crowd stopped. Mary stared at her with wide-eyed fear.

"Oh, you scared now? She saves your boy and this is how you repay her?"

"She caused it," Mary almost screeched, her eyes locked on the pistol.

Renee shook the pistol. "No, you did. Bill back up your story, Mary?" She pulled out her phone. "Why don't we get him down here?"

Mary shifted her feet in the dirt.

Renee switched the loading mechanism back. Click. "Uh uh. Your roots will be the least of your troubles."

Renee heard Aeron splutter on the ground and walked to her, gun still trained on Mary. Sirens rang out through the dead silence. Renee pulled Aeron toward her with one hand and brushed a hand through her hair, trying to let her know that she was there, that it was her. "It's okay, I got you."

The mud kicked up as the fire engine plowed up the lane, followed by a police cruiser, the ambulance, and Frei's car.

Mary and the others glanced at one another, a few backed up, whispers, mutters filled the air.

"Now we'll see how brave you are," Renee shot at Mary.

The fire crew jumped from the truck and sprinted into the cabin to tackle the blaze. A woman, who looked like the fire chief, was pale and her eyes empty. Renee looked at her uniform name tag. *Borland.*

Chief Borland hurried to Aeron, pulled her medical kit out, and worked on her. "What the hell did they do to you?"

Renee kept her gun trained on Mary. "They believe she's the killer."

Chief Borland shook her head. Renee could see her brimming tears. "No woman could be that way to a girl."

The simple sentence broke Renee's heart. A mother, the one who had just lost her precious child, was able to see, yet the mother whose son had been saved was the orchestrator of this mob attack. Where was the justice?

"What's going on?" Frei barked as she stormed over to them.

"These people tried to burn down Aeron's home and beat her," Renee said.

Eli put his hands over his head, looking helpless.

"Officers, I want everyone here taken in," Frei said.

Skip and Jo looked at each other, then at Eli.

He narrowed his eyes at them. "You heard the agent, round every damn one of them up."

Jo sighed then started forward and Skip opened up his arms to corral the hate mob.

"We need to get her to the hospital," Chief Borland said.

Frei nodded. "Get her moved."

Mary shook off Jo's grip on her arm. Renee trained her gun on her. "What are we being charged with?"

"If Aeron doesn't make it . . ." Frei said in a deep, dangerous voice that made even Renee shiver. Her eyes hardened. "I'll see every last one of you charged with murder."

The mob stared at them terrified and let the officers escort them to the waiting van.

The EMTs lifted Aeron onto a stretcher.

Renee watched them work on her and her stomach twisted up into a knot. She gripped hold of the gun as Mary was led away by Jo.

A hand gently took hold of the barrel "It's okay . . . she'll be fine," Frei said in a calm, soothing voice.

Renee blinked back the tears. "God, I hope so."

Frei smiled—brief, curt but nevertheless comforting. "Me too . . . me too."

Chapter 63

"YOU'RE LUCKY," THE doctor told me as he strolled into the pokey hospital room.

I lay beat up on the plastic-covered bed and turned to stare at the wall, the chill from wearing the stupid gown making my skin get bumps. Lucky? Uh-huh. No, lucky was a world away from my life. The sound of shoes squeaked on the floor outside and Renee popped her head through the doorway.

"I got away as soon as I could." She walked to me and sat on the chair next to the bed as the doctor clipped the X-rays up onto the light-board on the wall.

"You haven't broken a thing. Not one bone. Remarkable, isn't it?" He grinned, waving a finger at the board.

I didn't care. I was past caring.

"Will she be okay?" Renee asked. She glanced between me and the board.

The doctor chuckled. "She is just fine. A few bruises but nothing some painkillers won't fix." He squinted at Renee. "You, on the other hand, need to see about that cheek."

I turned to her and my self-pity vanished. Her cheek looked a kind of blue and purple. "What happened, did they—?"

"No. No, I'm fine," Renee said to the doctor. "And it was Jenny. It's fine." She gave me a "no argument" look.

"Doesn't look fine," the doctor and I said together.

"At least check if it's broken," I added.

Renee held her hands up as he tried to examine her. "I'm fine, I've been checked out." She turned to me and lifted her hand as if she wanted to touch the cut on my head but stopped. "Really, I'm more worried about you."

The doctor shook his head and took the charts off the wall. "Clean bill of health."

I got up from the bed, the room swayed as I tried to focus. My ribs felt like someone had shoved a load of razors under my skin.

"Where's your shirt?" Renee made me sit down and helped me

to dress myself. I was half ready to grumble, but there was no way I could figure to get my arm in the sleeve without help.

"I ain't helpless." My voice sounded like I was—wobbly, crackly, and feeble.

Paying me no mind, Renee took hold of my arm to steady me. As I wobbled my way out of the room and started to hobble down the corridor, my left leg felt all numb and buckled every now and again.

"He give you anything for the pain?" she asked.

I shook my head but the corridor wiggled before my eyes. "Didn't want nothin'."

I took a breath, trying to clear the fog, and stepped forward only for Renee to steer me to the right.

"Wall," she said as I tried to focus on her. Go figure how woozy an ambulance ride could make you feel. "Guess we should be glad of the muscles, huh?"

I tried to laugh, to smile, anything, but I couldn't. I didn't have anything vaguely close to emotion in my body. I felt tired, drained, and defeated.

"After all this, you should think about a vacation . . . or maybe just moving away." Her tone was cautious. I knew she was trying to help and I could feel her worry fizzing until it became an annoying buzz in my head.

I shoved my finger in my ear and waggled it to fend off the sound. "Where would I go? Where would be different from here?" I was a freak, it didn't matter where I was, I'd never fit in.

Renee helped me down the steps as my body groaned and moaned at the effort. It hurt, really hurt.

"There's a big world out there. Maybe you could come on a road trip with me." She took a shallow breath. I looked at her. "Let me show you the Rockies?"

I stopped trying to walk.

Renee furrowed her brow. "Okay?"

I leaned against the metal guardrail. The buzz from her got louder. "I thought you were here to protect me?"

"I am." She puffed herself up, a fake smile plastered on her face. I could see through it, her insecurity rolled off her. "Well, not that I'm doing a great job. I nearly got you sucked into a twister and beaten to death by a mob."

I didn't smile at the humor. Somewhere inside I appreciated it. She was trying to help, at least for now. "You're only here until whatever it is you're protecting me from is over, right?"

Renee nodded.

"So then why pretend like you care?" I pulled away from the guardrail and staggered my way down the steps. My left leg felt so foreign I wondered if it was still attached.

Renee took my arm. "If you think you can get me to leave you alone by pushing me away, you're mistaken." Her voice was so soft and soothing.

Still, I didn't get her. Why the pretense? "I'm just a client to you, another person in a long list to protect then forget like I never existed." I folded my arms, feeling like I was on a boat. "Serena will be someone's sister and you will be someone else."

Renee shook her head, her smile so warm that I had to fight not to return it. "I'll be Renee to you." She rubbed her hand over my arm and fussed over my sleeve. "I hope you're less grouchy on long drives than this."

I didn't get it. Everyone hated me. I had felt how much with Mary's touch. Why was Renee different?

"Stop trying to figure everything and shove it in a box." Her eyes twinkled, the gentleness in them easing away any insecurity I had of her leaving. "You're starting to remind me of Ursula."

Renee took my arm and helped me down the rest of the steps.

"She backed you up though, that has to mean something?"

Renee sighed and her weariness ebbed over me. "If I still have a job after this, I'll be pretty amazed."

The world waved around before me again and I stopped on a step. It took a couple of seconds to catch my breath as the pain in my ribs jabbed at me. "Why? I'm still walking around, ain't I?"

Renee rubbed my back, but her gaze flicked to the floor. "No thanks to me."

Hating that she was feeling bad on my account, I nudged her and then winced at the contact. Great, another bruise. "Don't do that to yourself. It's not your fault I'm a freak."

Renee gripped my arm tightly as she tensed. The sharp pain shot right up through my shoulder, and I yelped.

"Sorry," she mumbled. "Stop saying you're a freak. The next person who calls you it, I swear I'll shoot them." She put her hands on her hips. "I will."

Her frown was so deep, her tone so serious that I knew I was probably gawping at her. The little glitter showing the truth sparkled around her and I guess the sentiment got to me a little more than it should have. Why someone getting shot warmed my heart I didn't know, but I caught myself smiling.

"There you are," Renee whispered, her gray eyes as warm as her smile. "Can't keep that heart down for long."

Clearing my throat, I tried to ignore her soft chuckle. The soft light from the windows bounced off the floor as I limped along, Renee beside me. Her words seemed to switch something back on inside me and I became aware of the hospital. The noise, the worries, the busy lives—I shivered, I needed to get out of there, fast.

She watched me in silence as we walked, her eyes making my cheeks get all warm.

"So, what next?" I asked, hoping to make her quit staring.

My own question got me thinking. For someone who was supposed to know so much, I had no idea what to do, how to act, if the cabin was still standing—

"Mrs. Squirrel!" The panic thumped through my veins as I gripped Renee by the shoulders.

Two doctors on their way past looked up from their discussion and one peered over his glasses at me.

Renee put her hands over mine and chuckled. "She's fine. I attached the box to the willow for now."

I let out a breath from somewhere so deep, I coughed, bent over, and gripped my side to stop my ribs from falling out. When did breathing get so hard?

"You okay?"

The answer was no, I was a long way from okay and my feet seemed to zoom in and out of focus. "Sure."

Renee waved to the doctors. "She's fine."

The doctors shook their heads at me, one of them still taking a look over his shoulder as they continued on their way. He was about as convinced of me being okay as I was.

Renee took my elbow and helped me to straighten up. "Back to the question. What do we do next?"

I nodded and wished I hadn't as the ceiling pinged to and fro like a pinball machine. Not good.

"I'll tell you what we're going to do." Renee's voice next to my ear helped to ground me. Her tone like back in the institution, confident, clear. "We're going to walk into town. We'll show them you aren't going to slink off into the sunset." She squeezed my elbow, making a shot of pain rocket down to my fingertips. "You deserve to be there the same as them."

I flexed my fingers to fend off the tingling and tried to roll my throbbing shoulder. I knew from the doc's examination that it was deep purple. I guessed that must be why my fingers felt like marshmallows. "I don't want a return visit."

Renee slid her hand into mine. She rubbed her other hand over the top. I frowned and looked down. Our skin was touching. I met her eyes.

Her brow was wrinkled up. "How don't you get any visions anymore?"

Weird. Had I lost the ability to feel? I stood still for a moment and the din of the busy hospital bombarded me like hailstones. Nope, still a freak. "I guess maybe . . . I can't see nothing to do with me?"

Renee's aura wiggled about around her, her energy like a warm cozy blanket. "And?"

The thought made me smile. "And other than that, I guess, you're not hidin' from me?"

Keeping her hand in mine, she led me out into the sunlight. Air, fresh air was good. I didn't really want to chance sucking in a deep breath, but even the feel of the sun on my face made a difference.

"I didn't get much of a choice. You kinda found my hiding place," Renee said as she helped me over to her very nice looking new car.

I ain't a big one for makes or fancy rides but this one was slick and shiny and fitted her somehow. Weird how a car could echo the person it belonged to. Ignoring her curious gaze, I opened the door and attempted to bend down to move the seat back.

"Wait, I'll do that." Renee hurried around, fixed the seat, and helped me in. "I forget you need more space sometimes."

Even with the seat back, I still had to bend my knees a little but the smooth leather seat against my aching back provoked a sigh deep inside. Man, that felt good. The new car smell filled my nostrils as I lay my head back, enjoying the quiet, the soft, sweet quiet. "Is this yours to keep?"

Renee murmured something. I peeked an eye open. She was smiling, again.

I grinned back. "In that case, a road trip sounds like fun."

Renee started the car. She was pretending to be cool and Frei-like but her aura was jigging around like it had sat on a termite mound. "I'll hold you to that."

Chapter 64

RENEE TOOK ME to the out-of-town store to get some new clothes. The only pair she had gotten me were now pretty ripped and bloodied from the mob attack. I hate shopping with a passion. If you're someone like me—big and tall and well just not a tiny waif, nothing really fits. It was even worse with the bumps and bruises. Renee had made me eat at a café to stop me from fainting. I was happy to go along with it—anything to delay going back to the town.

As we were driving back to the cabin, my stomach got more and more tied up in knots. I didn't know what state the place would be in and I didn't know if I had the energy to start all over again. Maybe Renee was right. A road trip—a permanent one— sounded good.

We pulled onto the Main Street and Renee's phone rang. She flicked her eyes to me as she picked it off the dash and held it to her ear. Odd, she'd rambled on at me about how she could connect her cell to the car and talk on speaker—something she was pretty proud of so I guessed the call had to be business.

"What? Now? Of course." She slowed the car as she spoke. "I'll be there in five."

Renee cut the call and I smiled. "Drop me off here. I'll walk the rest of the way."

She gazed out at the street, and I could see that she wanted to do anything but. Her aura fizzed and wobbled. "Are you sure?"

Sure? Not even close to it but she needed to be someplace else and I needed some time to figure out what the hell I was going to do. "Not like I haven't gotten a beatin' before."

Renee's eyes darkened but I shrugged. Sad fact was I'd spent a lot of my childhood hiding from baying mobs. Sam had stopped it all. His friendship, however brief it had been, however ill-fated, had pretty much ensured I survived.

I sat and watched her fight with herself. If I was honest. I didn't really want her going anywhere. "Just remember—"

"Road trip—yeah, I got it."

Renee pulled the car over, her thoughts rumbling around her. I got that she didn't want to ditch me in the middle of town alone and although I appreciated that, I wasn't scared of nobody. I found every sense of dignity I had left and puffed my chest out with it and tried not to cough and splutter.

"I'm not completely helpless, you know?"

Renee looked at me, her mouth scrunched up in one corner. She could probably see through the facade but I'd spent most of my life fending for myself, I wasn't about to get all needy now.

I took a deep breath and got out, trying not to wince, trying not to just get straight back in and ask her to get me out of there.

"See you at the cabin."

"I won't be long." She leaned over to look up at me through the passenger window. "Be careful, okay?"

"Sure." I made a show of straightening up. The pain jabbed me right in between the shoulder blades. "Take as long as you need."

Renee pulled off and my confidence withered. The fear of being in this place made me feel like a soldier behind enemy lines. Soldiers had a cause to be there, all I was doing was existing.

I tried not to hobble too much as I walked past the shops. When I was injured or ill, I seemed to be even more open. The huge cloud hung overhead. Its slimy, dark tentacles stretched into every building and looked like a pillar of doom. The voluminous column of hate seeped into the people, the fear building to frenzy. And I could feel it all.

Every face, all eyes—hostile, unforgiving, judging like the barbs of a poison dart piercing my heart, crushing it.

"Murderer!"

"Witch!"

"Child killer!"

I could almost hear their thoughts. The venom punched me from all sides, smashed into me like waves. My heart ached with it as I stumbled on. The tenser I got, the more the pain crushed me, my chest tight, wheezy, my heart hammered, my skin soaked. I couldn't breathe, I couldn't keep going, I—

I collided with something. I found myself staring at Sam.

He raised his eyebrows. "Hey, you okay?"

I nodded but my hands trembled and Sam wasn't stupid.

"I heard what Mary did." He scowled, his eyes hardening. "Took great delight in booking her in."

Not sure if I'd just not heard him right. I blinked a couple of times. "You ain't on their side?"

Sam laughed, like he always had when we were kids. A laugh that always stripped my defenses. "You think I care what a bunch of small-town yokels think of you?"

Was he just teasing me? Did he really mean that, after Jake, after everything? "Don't know, been a long time."

Sam pulled me into a hug, he seemed careful not to catch my bruises or touch my skin. I sunk into it, relief rushed over me. He knew me. He knew me enough to give me space, to guard me from seeing. I was so thankful for it, I could have stayed there forever.

"How 'bout now, Al." His tone was light, playful. "I good as said that the next idiot who targets you will get my world famous uppercut."

I clung on. Sam had been such a good friend and I'd brought him nothing but pain. "Even Mary?"

"'Specially Mary." His hearty laugh rumbled through him. "I just got back from telling Bill." Sam's heart beat steadily in my ear as I listened to him recount the tale. "I don't know why the idiot bothered to marry her. I mean sure, he knocked her up after high school but everyone knows he don't love her."

I dug Sam in the ribs. "When did you turn into a jackass?"

He grunted and squeezed me gently. "Oh come on, Al . . . if you were a guy, would you have stuck around?"

The question made me pause. I felt like a scared teenager again. I felt like that little girl who was too small to put up a fight and went running to the one friend who could shelter me. "I wouldn't have been drunk enough in the first place."

Sam's laughter flowed from him like light. The cloud overhead shook with it. It couldn't get him. No, Sam was too strong. "See, that's what I love about you. You get it."

He smiled down at me, his puppy dog charm oozed out. "You need a ride? Or you just gonna hobble on home?"

I straightened myself up. "If I got legs—"

"You can walk, yeah, yeah . . ." He rolled his eyes and tucked his thumbs in his belt. "Some women would be happy to catch a ride."

I launched myself forward and hugged Sam once more. "*Most* women more like."

Sam lifted his dimpled chin, posing, which just made me laugh and nudge his shoulder. "Get gone, you arrogant ass."

Sam took his hat off and bowed low. "As you wish, ma'am."

I stared for the longest time after him as he strutted off down the street. I sure as hell couldn't figure out why he bothered with me, but he did. I guess the saying "love is blind" was pretty true in his case.

Not for the first time I felt a twinge of regret that I couldn't return it. What would life had been like if I could have?

I looked at the hairdressers, full of women preening and perming and desperately trying to cling onto youth. Nah, that wasn't me. I was never going to be one of them.

Sam had told me many times that was why, that was what caught his attention and his heart. I wasn't them and I wasn't going to stick him on a pedestal, no matter how handsome he was.

I turned to walk toward the cabin, the red sun now painting the evening sky in color. The whiff of a storm danced on the breeze, the clouds of darkness loomed overhead. But, for this moment, I wandered alone through the town and felt that in spite of it all, Sam was still on my side. And just that thought alone oozed the strength back into me.

Chapter 65

RENEE PULLED UP to the trailer that her team had commandeered. She checked in her mirror for the hundredth time to make sure she hadn't been followed.

"You're acting like a rookie," she muttered and forced herself to get out of the car.

The site was a couple miles out of town and in a perfect spot for the team to work from. The road would be under surveillance and Frei would have warned her if they'd seen anyone.

With a last glance down the dirt track, Renee headed to the trailer and knocked on the door. The fact they were risking her being seen near them said something was wrong. Her vein pulsed in her throat and she soothed a hand over it. Why would Frei call her in? She lifted her hand to knock again and jumped as Fitzpatrick opened it up with a nod.

He stood back to let her enter and Renee glanced over her shoulder, one last check to make sure that no one was watching. "I came as soon as I could. What's happened?"

Fitzpatrick opened his mouth to speak.

"Close the door, Renee," Frei said from somewhere behind him.

Renee joined the team at a table they had turned into a command center of sorts.

"Now you're all here," Frei said, tapping her pen on a pad. "We can sort out where we are."

Renee sat beside Fitzpatrick and took a mug offered to her by Donovan, the nerd.

Renee inhaled the rich smell of strong, black coffee as she scanned the others at the table. All eight members in her CIG team were present—not that they were ever in the same place at the same time normally. She pretty much spent her time with Fitzpatrick and Frei. Very rarely did she see Donovan and even rarer did she see the others in the team who worked out of headquarters.

The fact all eight of them were in the trailer confirmed to

Renee that Frei was worried. This was, after all, off the record. A favor for Lilia, who no doubt was keeping an eye, somewhere.

"Ewan, you want to take first pitch?" Frei asked.

Fitzpatrick nodded and picked up his tablet. "We got word that Elsie Evans has been found. Turns out she took a trip to Kansas City for a party. Local police picked her up."

Renee rolled her eyes. She was sure the senator was really proud of his sixteen year old.

"Will?" Frei asked, turning to Donovan.

He pushed his glasses up his nose and rapped his fingers on his tablet. "No hits on the M.O.—it isn't a copycat, no similar cases in any other part of the country."

Frei turned to the two guys who Renee had never met. Intel, she guessed. "What you got?"

The more stocky of the two shook his head, his brow was shiny, his eyes wide. "Nothing. The traces for the scene on the forensic guy . . . you know . . . er . . . the one with the fibers?"

Frei nodded but her eyes hardened. She had never been one for patience.

"Looks like it could have been tampered with," he said, dropping his gaze to his notes. "DNA . . . is . . . er . . . missing." He sighed. "But whether that was . . . well . . . intentional or not . . . maybe we'll never know."

Frei's scowl made Renee shudder. Sometimes she swore that the woman could shoot ice from her eyes.

"Maybe? You will *never* know?" Frei asked in clipped tones.

Renee lowered her head and sipped her coffee, thankful she wasn't in Frei's crosshairs.

"I'll go back over it." He exchanged glances with the other Intel guy who nodded.

"Good to be thorough," the other man added, flinching under Frei's steely glare.

Renee sat back. She wasn't an investigator like the others, her skill lay in the field, in protection but nevertheless, it sounded like they were stumped.

"Ben? Daniel?" Frei looked around the table, blue eyes glinting as if to dare them not to give her a satisfactory answer.

Renee looked at the profilers. The identical twin brothers were fidgety, awkward with shaved hair at the sides and slicked over sections on top. They were the best, and good guys, no doubt about that. But, the fact they could read people as well as Aeron, and without the abilities she had, freaked Renee out. Her job, her survival depended on her being able to conceal who she was. These guys, with their facts and figures decoded people like they were computer programs. At least Aeron was more naturally blessed.

The twins were pretty weedy guys and the more awkward one, Ben, cleared his throat. "It's too wide a base. The killer likes inflicting pain, treats the victims like they are animals." He flicked his hair back into place and slapped it downward. "It all appears pretty straightforward that our Unsub is a man who hates women."

"But?" Renee asked, earning a look from Frei.

Ben offered her a toothy smile. "But, the age ranges are all over the place. You had Mari sixteen, her mother—"

"Which we could put down to her being in the wrong place." Daniel pointed at his notes and slid them over to Frei.

"Exactly," Ben said as he leaned over and used his pen to show her. "Then there was Darcy, again sixteen—"

Daniel leaned over too until both were almost in Frei's personal space. Renee gripped her mug, hoping that they would realize. "Then the Unsub goes for Chelsea. Why?"

Ben nodded, his enthusiasm bringing him within inches of Frei's face. Renee clung to her coffee. "Yes!" He thumped the table. "Why change M.O.?"

Silence.

Ben looked up and jerked backward as he locked eyes with Frei. They scrambled back to their seats, Frei's unyielding stare fixed on them.

"Could it be a different killer?" she asked, her voice calm but icy.

"No," Ben and Daniel said in unison, then with identical gestures, twitched their shoulders in shrugs of apology.

"Didn't you say that the Unsub was trying to frame Aeron?" Renee asked Frei, trying to ignore the freaky and, to her mind, over-excited men. Who the hell thought Unsubs were cause for excitement?

Frei nodded. "I think so but these boys don't." She shot them a look which made them fidget. "And Jenny didn't pan out."

"How so? She tried to kill Aeron in front of my eyes." Wasn't that a pretty damn good motive? Jenny hated Aeron. That sounded like motive to her.

Frei frowned. "The POI was fine. Jenny has an alibi for the Chelsea murder. She was in the hairdressers."

Renee got up, her mind whirring. "So, what are you saying?"

"That we need to look at this logically." Frei's tone was bored as always. Renee fought the wish to shake her into life.

"Aren't we already?" Renee put her hand through her hair as the panic rumbled in her stomach. "What about Mary or one of the other loons in town."

Ben and Daniel wrinkled their noses at her term.

"It has to be someone strong," Ben said, folding his arms.

"And with practical skills," Daniel added, pointing to his notes.

"Not to mention knowledge of the area." Ben's tone said that he felt that settled the matter.

Renee put her hands on her hips. "Which means?"

"Maybe Lilia got half a picture," Frei said.

Renee raised startled eyes to Frei. She could not be serious about this.

"It's happened before."

Was Frei really going there? Renee shook her head. Oh no, not this time. No, they were wrong. "I was with her when the murders took place."

"Were you awake?" Frei asked.

Renee felt her cheeks flush. Frei hadn't meant it in that way but her stupid feelings made her react. "Probably not, I don't know."

Frei didn't yield. "Did the POI leave your sight?"

Renee hated being under scrutiny and her neck itched with the blush. She sighed. Hell, she needed therapy. "Yes. I couldn't exactly get in her tent with her."

"Then how can you be sure?" Frei's tone was less curt but Renee still felt exposed, still felt like all eyes were on her.

She wrung her hands together. "I was there, she was in my sight when Chelsea was taken." That was as good an alibi as Jenny's was.

Frei lifted her eyebrows, her lips pursed, which told Renee everything she needed to know. The team had discussed this. To them Aeron was not only the POI, but the Unsub too. She didn't need Aeron to read their feelings. Who was she to tell them how to catch a killer? She was there to protect and shut the hell up.

"What does Lilia say?" Renee stomped through the trailer and slammed open the door at the back. "Do you believe it's Aeron?"

Lilia looked up from her desk, her gold pen in her long elegant fingers. She placed it down, taking her time to answer, as always. Renee flexed and clenched her hands, willing the tension to calm, willing sanity to prevail.

"I don't know." Lilia reclined in her chair and studied her. Renee fiddled with the hem of her t-shirt. She hated that it felt as though Lilia knew everything about her. "I saw Aeron as the center of the storm."

How could she do that to her own daughter? She'd given birth to her. Surely she, the woman who saw so much, could see how good Aeron was. "So, you're telling me that you are going to sit back and watch her be framed for something she didn't do?"

Lilia's eyes, so much like Aeron's, studied Renee for long, heavy moments. Renee lifted her chin in defiance. Lilia may have let Aeron go to prison for Jake Casey but Renee was not going to abandon her. Not now, not ever.

"What makes you so sure that she isn't?" How could Lilia do that? How could she even entertain that Aeron was the killer?

Renee leaned on the desk. "I *know*—with every single part of me—I *know* she wouldn't."

"Like you knew about Yannick?" Frei asked from beside her.

Renee turned. "Don't throw that at me. He got one over on me." The past wriggled up from the place she had buried it. She swallowed it back down, closing her eyes to slam shut the doors on him, on the pain.

"And what if Aeron has too?" Frei's hand touched her elbow, making Renee open her eyes. "Lilia said herself that Aeron can see more than she's telling you."

Renee turned to Lilia. "She sees what I let her see."

Lilia's eyes wrinkled with her beaming smile. "You and I both know that isn't quite the truth."

"Oh, so you saw that too." Renee felt a blush ripple through her cheeks once more. She hated feeling so exposed, so helpless. "You sure as hell could have told me."

"Tell her what?" Frei asked Lilia. "What are you talking about?"

Renee met Frei's eyes. "How I feel, Urs."

Frei looked at Lilia and then folded her arms. "Just frickin' wonderful, Renee. That's all we damn need."

"I didn't do it on purpose." Now she sounded like a dumb teenager, she felt just as out of control. She'd tried. She'd tried every way she could think of not to feel anything.

Frei narrowed her eyes. "The decision's made. I'm sorry, Renee, but even if you love her, I can't just ignore the facts."

Renee blinked a few times. Wow, so that's how much they valued her. After everything they'd been through, her word meant nothing. She threw her gun and badge onto the table. "Then you don't need me anymore."

Frei tried to grab Renee's arm, but Renee swerved around her.

"If you can't trust my judgment now, there's no point." Renee stormed out of the trailer, her heart raging. Her stomach like a tombola, swirling around and around. She'd just quit, she'd just given up nearly fifteen years of her life.

Did she trust Aeron that much? She got in the car and slammed it into gear, the tires screamed as she spun off. She'd never been more certain in her life.

Chapter 66

ELI WALKED OUT of city hall and wandered toward the oak tree. His head throbbed with a mammoth headache. Jenny was at her mother's with the girls and not only wasn't she talking to him, it was all his fault. He slumped down in the shade, pulled his meds out of his pocket, and smiled at them. Aeron's voice called out in his memory. "Take your damn tablets." She was some kid that one.

He had wanted all day to go and see Aeron in the hospital. He'd called and been told she was fine but there was so much he hadn't said to her. So much he wanted to explain, but she'd told him, in no uncertain terms, to stay away. He'd run roughshod over her feelings her entire life, it was the least he could do to honor that.

The sight of her lying helpless in a heap on the ground tore at his heart. Why did they all hate her so much? She never did a damn thing to them. He scowled. He'd charged every damn one of the cowards, backed up by the Feds each step of the way. Mary was the only one who had wriggled out of the loop because, like always, she hadn't done a thing. All he'd had on her was inciting violence. Even the thought of her crocodile tears made his chest ache. She'd always been the same. Stir the pot and watch it boil. Witch.

He rubbed his stinging eyes and tried to blink back the tears. He could have lost Aeron today, he could have lost her and never told her the truth. He needed to right that. He needed to tell her, even if she never talked to him again. No more lies.

"Chief?" Skip ran up to him.

Eli pulled out his hanky and wiped his tears away. "What now?" What the hell else could they throw at him?

Skip bounced from one foot to the other on the sidewalk as if he didn't want to get too close. "Jenny called." He thumbed to the city hall. "She's gone back to the house, get her things."

"Good riddance," Eli muttered. "Anything else?"

Skip shook his head then nodded, then shrugged. "You know about the Feds skipping town, so pretty much nothing."

With nothing useful to offer Skip, he pocketed his meds. "No news is good news."

He looked up and saw Aeron hobbling down the street. Was it Aeron? He blinked a few times, it had to be. Without thinking he hurried to her, forgetting his vow to stay away, forgetting everything.

"What are you doing out?" His voice shrill to his own ears. It wasn't meant to sound like an accusation.

Aeron looked at him, then looked through him and started to walk past.

Eli's heart crumbled, and he gripped hold of his chest. Her cheek was swollen, her forehead sported a Band-Aid. He couldn't bear it, her indifference, he had to make it right. "Please . . . Aeron, let me explain."

Aeron kept walking and he caught hold of her hand. "Please."

Aeron turned to yell, to scream at him. He could see the explosion ready to erupt but instead her eyes rolled back and she dropped to the ground.

He caught and cradled her. "Get a medic. Now!" he called to Skip, who ran into city hall.

"Aeron, sweetheart." Her body was limp. "Oh, God . . . please . . . please." He brushed her hair from her face, his fingers trembling. "What's happening?"

Aeron started to spasm and twitch, her body writhing like she was being hit by electric shocks.

Eli clung onto her, praying help would come quickly. "Aeron!"

WELL HELLO, JENNY . . . must have thought that little scar on your face stopped me seeing you . . . but it's all right, I'm watching. I see you. I've been waiting, waiting for just the right moment. Do you remember the fun we used to have? Do you? Before you got so ugly? Oh yes, Jenny . . . You even thought I cared, didn't you?

I'm going to show you some fun now. I'm going to give you just what you deserve. Oh, yes . . . Marrying an old man, how pathetic. Did you really think anyone could love you? With a face like yours? Come now, even before you got all sliced up, you were always so dull, so tight, narrow, so . . . ugly.

I'll change that for you right now. You can be special now, you can help me to achieve greatness. Yes, it's the least you could do, Jenny. You owe me so much . . . you do, for taking the time out to collect you. Yes, we can have some fun . . . you can even bring the girls.

ELI TOOK OFF his belt and fed it in between Aeron's teeth, hoping like hell it would stop her biting off her tongue. The hospital must have missed something.

"Aeron!" Renee shouted. She ran down the sidewalk and slid to her knees on the other side of Aeron. "What happened?"

Eli shook his head, helpless. "I wanted to explain, I told her. I grabbed her hand and she went to yell." What had he done, what had happened to her? "Her eyes rolled."

Renee pulled off her jacket and tucked it under Aeron's head. Eli looked up to see folks pour out of the café, the shops and the hairdressers as Aeron lay having an epileptic fit on the street.

"Don't you have something better to do?" he shouted. These people were sick. Were they just going to stand and watch?

His tears pulsed down his cheeks. She was getting worse. He stroked her forehead and kissed it softly. His baby girl, his beautiful baby girl. He'd failed her, failed her so bad.

Abe sauntered across the street to them, and the smile on his face tore at Eli's heart. "Let's hope she doesn't make it. Safer for us all."

Eli shot to his feet and hit his brother so hard that his own knuckles cracked. "You sick son-of-a—"

"Eli, she's . . . I don't know . . . she's getting worse," Renee called to him.

Eli looked down at Abe sprawled on the sidewalk. He'd been obedient and silent when the family turned their backs. He'd listened to everyone. How could Abe say that about Aeron? How?

"God, I'm sorry, I'm so sorry I listened to them," he said, returning to Aeron's side.

He only prayed that one day he could tell her that, tell her everything.

JENNY OPENED THE door. The last person she expected to see. "What the hell do you want? Eli send you?" She looked down at the gun. "What are you doing?"

The trigger squeezed, the flash from the barrel. Agony ripped through her stomach, agony and panic. The girls, not the girls, no.

"Run . . . Run!"

Crack, the gun fires. Scream, the pain spread. "Run!"

The girls run, oh no . . . No! Ropes around their arms and legs, squeals and screams, sobbing and wailing. The vase on the table . . . reach . . . reach . . . bloody fingers . . . you will not take them . . .

"What are you doing, Jenny?"

"*No!*"

Crack, the gun fired again. Breathe . . . no . . . the girls . . . no . . . The vase so far away . . . in the dark . . . the pain . . . the pain . . . it's so . . . it's too . . .

RENEE GRIPPED HOLD of Aeron, trying to show her, through her fit, that someone was there, that she wasn't alone in this. The crowd was around them, blocking out the last rays of sun. A morbid fascination. As if they were willing Aeron to lose her fight.

"Jenny, Jenny in trouble . . . girls . . . trouble . . . now . . ." Aeron mumbled and thrashed about.

"What?" Eli ducked Aeron's flailing arm..

"It's a vision." Renee only hoped it wouldn't kill her. It was worse than it had been on the roof, so much worse. "She can see." Last time she'd had a vision . . . Renee's heart hammered. "Where's Jenny?"

"She's in the house," Eli answered.

"Why? She was meant to stay—"

Eli sighed. "I know . . . she went back for her things."

Renee held Aeron's hand tighter as she twitched. Was it calming? "Maybe you should go . . . Go to her?"

Eli shook his head. "I'm not leaving her, not here." He glanced at city hall. "Where the hell is Skip?"

"Run . . . no . . . run!" Aeron spasmed, her back arched, and Renee tried to shove the coat back underneath. If she'd not gone to the cabin first, if she'd not walked into town, she could have been here sooner, maybe stopped it.

The crowd moved back in fear. Renee glared up at them. Why weren't any of them running for help? Why weren't they doing something?

"Eli!" Skip barged his way through the crowd. "Eli! First response is at your house."

Eli looked up at Skip, then down to Aeron. "It's a vision? It's really a vision?"

"You need to go," Renee said again.

The crowd rumbled with the realization that Aeron *was* seeing something, but what?

Aeron opened her eyes, just the whites showing. "*No!*"

Eli fell back onto his knees as Renee tried to restrain Aeron. Her heart pounded with every agonizing scream. It was horrific.

Aeron sobbed, wailed, and screamed. "No . . . please . . . no . . . reach the vase . . . please!"

Skip went to Eli's side. "Eli, you gotta come. Come quick." He yanked at Eli's arm. "It's Jenny. The response couldn't get there in time."

Eli's face drained of color. "Jenny?"

"Yeah." Skip's chin wobbled as he took a breath. "Gun man, there were shots."

Eli stumbled to his feet. "Skip, help Renee get Aeron back home." He rubbed a hand over his chest. "Get her home, away from here."

Skip nodded, and Renee felt Aeron shiver underneath her. She fell limp.

"Go," Renee whispered to Eli.

He nodded and staggered through the crowd.

"Help me get her up," Renee told Skip.

"Course—"

"Let me help." Bill pushed his way through the crowd. "Let me help her."

Renee nodded, rubbing away her tears as he took Aeron into his arms.

Bill glared at the crowd. "What the hell's the matter with y'all? She saved my son!" He stormed at the people and they stumbled out of his way.

Skip took Renee's arm and guided her past the shocked crowd.

Her whole body shuddered with sobs and worry so intense it hurt to breathe, to move, to think.

"My truck's on the corner. Hospital?" Bill asked.

Renee shook her head. "There's nothing they can do. All we can do is pray that she makes it."

Bill nodded and headed down the street. The distant sirens rang out in the evening air.

"Jenny. She didn't make it." Skip's eyes filled with tears. "She fought." He cleared his throat. "Same van spotted."

"If you tell me Aeron was driving—"

"She was." He shook his head and wiped his eyes on his sleeve. "I don't know what the hell is going on, ma'am, but she didn't shoot nobody."

Renee touched Skip's arm. She could see the depth of mourning in his eyes. Every death was like a nail in their hope and safety. Every victim taken like a rip in their souls.

"What about the girls?" Renee held Aeron's head as Bill placed her into his truck.

"Unless they're with Jenny's mom . . ."

Renee looked down at Aeron, who was crying and whimpering like a child.

Fear rippled down her arms, through her body, churning in her stomach. "Come on." She climbed into the back and lifted Aeron's head onto her lap. "Wake up." She brushed the hair from Aeron's face and stroked her forehead. "We need you. We need to know."

Chapter 67

MY BODY WAS weak, wobbly, spent. The pain of moving, only small to the pain of knowing, of feeling. I had breathed every moment of Jenny's final seconds. I had lain there with her in the hallway, the breeze of the storm tickling her legs, the warm blood from her wounds pooling around her.

I had made a choice to be there with her, in that moment, I had somehow lent her my strength, I had absorbed the pain she should have felt into my own being. I stayed beside her, singing to her, talking to her. She spent her final moments, her hand gripping mine, her eyes on mine.

"I'm sorry," she told me. "I'm sorry."

"It doesn't matter, it doesn't matter anymore."

"The girls . . . please, save them," she said.

Before I could answer, she was gone. Her eyes flickered shut, her chest ceasing to rise. I rubbed my hand over her forehead, stroked it, stayed until the police hammered up the porch steps. How I'd been there, I didn't know, but it had taken more from me than I had left to give.

Now I watched Renee stroke the back of my hand with her thumb, her tears soft, silent in the light of the campfire. Bill was with her but Skip had left to be with Eli. They would be looking for the girls.

If I could have spoken, I would have tried to tell them but I had no more energy, no more fight.

So I watched as Bill set up the campsite for Renee and she bathed my forehead with cool cloths. The sun had set and the stars sprinkled out across the black canopy of sky. The half moon was ringed with a halo, a peaceful night, a calm night, as though the world were at rest in spite of the madness.

Renee's eyelids drooped when Bill left us but she would not leave my side and so I didn't leave either. She talked to me and sung gently, same as I had done for Jenny. Her eyelids drooped a little more as her tears wore out her shattered mind. She rested her head on my shoulder and fell asleep.

I was about to leave, to unchain myself, but a movement from the distance stopped me. The dust kicked up over the road and stirred Renee. She hovered over me, gun out, eyes focused on the approaching car. The black hood came into view and she lowered her weapon as my father stumbled out of his car. His face white, his hand rubbing at his chest.

"Any news?" Renee asked.

My father shook his head. He looked wrecked in body, mind, and spirit. His guilt seemed to circle him like a vulture, picking at him. From my position I could sense so much of his pain.

His eyes on me, he hurried to us. "Any change?"

Renee bit her lip and raised her hand as if she wanted to comfort my father, then she dropped it and sighed. "Not for the better, she's barely breathing."

My father collapsed onto his knees beside me. "Oh God, please." His face screwed up and he let out a howl of agony from deep inside. "Please!" His roar at the night sky echoed out. He buried his head in my shoulder and gripped my arms. His desperation poured out of him. "Please . . . baby . . ."

I went to touch him, to comfort him, but my hand moved through his arm. Too weak. His violent sobs shook through him, the raw pain unbearable to watch.

"Please . . . don't leave me . . . don't leave me."

His pain shot out of him, hitting me like a blast of icy air. I couldn't bear to watch. It was torture to see him like that.

He dropped his head back and screamed at the sky. "Please."

He dropped forward, gathered me up, cradled me as he rocked me.

"Please, God . . . Please . . . please bring her back to me . . . please." His wracked sobs filled the silence as he rocked. "I need to tell you . . . I need to make it right . . . don't leave . . . please."

Renee looked up to the sky, her hand over her mouth as she lingered in the background. Her silent tears streamed down her face as she stared at the river. Then she took her hand away. "Do you trust me?"

My father looked up, his eyes wide, his nod desperate. "You have an idea?"

Renee was still fixed on the river. No, that was a stupid idea. No, I tried to make a noise, do something, but she couldn't see me. I was powerless to stop her.

She took a breath and met my father's eyes. "Help me get her in the river."

My father frowned. "What?"

Renee went to him and placed her hand on his. "She healed herself in the river."

In a fit of frantic movement, my father gripped my arms. He grunted as they tried to lift me up, his face reddening. I could see the pain in his chest glowing. He shouldn't be doing it. He needed his tablets. Renee helped him get my limp body upright. I tried to stop them, but I had no energy to make contact.

"Stop. You need to stop." My voice made no sound as the breeze stole it away.

They half-carried, half-dragged me as they slipped and squished through the mud to the river bank.

"I'll go in," Renee said.

My father held me steady as he frowned at her. "Why?"

Renee sighed. "We have to find your girls. Aeron told me that no one could touch her, that it was too dangerous."

"It is," I screamed, praying somehow they would hear my voice but it was no louder to my ears than the river lapping against the rocks.

My father's eyes hardened as he struggled against slipping in the mud. "Then it'll be me." Renee opened her mouth but he shook his head. "Listen, I've failed her in every way I could but no more." He hoisted me up as the mud gave way under his shoes. "If it costs me my soul I'll get her back."

And the truth glimmered from him, falling, sparkling, vibrant colors shooting out like fireworks. The words warmed me, seeped inwards, and filled my heart beyond any feeling I'd ever known. Why couldn't he have said that to me? Why didn't he tell me?

Renee nodded and let me go as he hauled my limp body up and waded out into the river. He let me down gently into the water so that I floated onto my back and turned to Renee. "What did Aeron do?"

Renee closed her eyes, hugged herself, her brow wrinkled with concentration. "Her hands." She smiled and looked at him. "Nan told her to wash her hands."

He raised his eyebrows until his receding hairline twitched. "Nan?"

Renee gave a tilt of her head as she shrugged. "Long story." She glanced at the cabin. "Wait."

As my father bathed in the cold river with my body, Renee bolted into the cabin. I went after her, trying to catch hold of her arm, anything to stop her. This was a dumb idea. She sloshed through the water from the fire hoses, coughing at the thick smell of burning in the air.

"Stop. Don't do this." I grasped for her hand as she took the creaking safety stairs two at a time. "Stop."

Renee scrabbled around in the dark until I heard metal scraping as she dragged out Nan's trunk. She yanked open the lid and I tried to slam it shut again. My hand slipped right through.

"Renee, please. His heart."

I was helpless. I watched her dig through the debris inside until she found a book. It had to be Nan's diary.

"No!" I tried to snatch for it but she turned and hurried straight through me. I felt like no more than mist as she did it, displacing and reforming.

All I could do was listen to her footsteps on the stairs, then the sloshing of water as she made her way to the door. I gathered enough to run after her but she was already at the river bank bellowing instructions.

"Nan says that you need to hold her under, you can't let go until she opens her eyes."

My father scowled. "Nan wants me to drown her?"

Renee glanced down at the book. "No, yourself."

I tried to knock the book out of Renee's hands. Ghosts could do stuff like that couldn't they. I focused on it, trying to push all my energy through. I heard a splash and I snapped my head around to the river. My father was already sticking his head under the water.

Renee looked into the sky. "Nan says you can see me, Aeron." She nodded as I looked around me. Was Nan here? "She says that you don't want me to do this. She says it's your choice." Her eyes misted over. "It's your choice if you live and your choice how long he stays under there."

"No!" I tried to grab the book. Straight through again.

Renee continued, she couldn't hear me. My father was still under the surface. "If you don't come back, you forfeit his life too. You forfeit your sisters' lives. Is that what you want?"

"Please, stop it. His heart. Please." I touched Renee and she shivered.

"You're the only one who can do this." She gripped the book. "Aeron, if you don't, the killer wins."

I looked at the river. The pain in my father's heart was visible from under the water. The frantic pumping escalated. His heart. It would give out at any second. My own body started to look cold and as I stood there, I felt more solid. We were both drowning.

"Aeron, please." Renee's voice cracked. "Don't make me stand here and watch you both die."

I touched the tears that streamed down Renee's cheeks. I couldn't do that to her, to him. The tears felt warm on my fingertip. I stared down at the teardrop, it seeped down my finger, spread up over my hand, my arm, my chest. It spread all over— my feet, my ankles, my legs, my waist, I was being suffocated by it, my heart pounded, the blood screamed in my ears. The water freezing, drowning me, arms holding me down. I opened my eyes and pushed, sending me and my father to the surface.

He coughed and spluttered. His heart still glowed as he gripped hold of his chest. I hacked up the river water from my lungs, spluttering, wheezing, shivering, trying to suck in the cold night air.

My father looked at me, bent over at the waist, head nearly in the water. His face drained of color as the glowing in his chest became a blast of pain and his knees buckled.

I grabbed for him, placed my hand on his chest, and sucked the pain from him.

"Stay with me."

His breathing stopped.

"You're not going anywhere, you hear me." I squeezed him to me with my other hand and put every drop of love I could from myself into his pores.

Silence. I held him there. I was not letting go. This stopped now. The cloud wasn't taking him too.

Truth, love, hope. I needed to believe. "Daddy, please. I love you. Don't go."

Believe. Don't give up. Never give up.

The river water lapped at the edges. Renee's gentle sobs from the bank. The forest sounds, the trees rustling. The stars glimmering above. I put my hand inside his shirt and touched my hand to his chest. Never give up.

"Come back."

Faint at first, was it there? I had to believe. Believe. Louder, yes, there was something. Something was there. Harder. *Thump, thump, thump.* His heart burst into rhythm against my palm. His gasp in my ear. I held on. He gripped me back. My legs buckled with the effort of healing. His arms wrapped around me. The love pulsed back from him. Energy bounced to and fro, back and forth, building. We were healing each other.

"God, girl, you scared me half to death," he rasped in my ear. I could feel his joy.

I buried my head in his shoulder, holding fast, every desperate need being answered. He didn't hate me, he'd risked everything to get me back. He loved me.

"I thought you didn't want me." Tears dribbled into my mouth. "I thought you hated me."

My father gripped me so tight that I felt like a precious treasure. He'd risked everything for me. "I love you, baby." He rubbed my back. "I've always loved you, baby girl." He kissed my forehead and looked me in the eyes. "Never forget that, no matter what a jackass I am, I love you."

He pulled me to him again and something shifted inside me. A wall shattered and the pain burst out of me, the loud sobs released the past. All the years that I thought no one had cared, that no one had wanted me, that no one loved me, and all along he had.

"I thought I'd lost you," he said. "I thought that vision had taken you from me."

"I thought your heart gave out." I clung to him. "But I believed. I weren't gonna let you go."

We stood there in the bitter water. The healing radiated every ounce of love that had remained hidden and buried beneath a life of lies. The flowing of forgiveness, restoring, healing, strengthening.

"I felt you." His breathy whisper in my ear shimmered. "I'll never doubt you again."

Chapter 68

RENEE STOOD ON the bank, watching father and daughter wrapped in a hug in the middle of the river and she said a silent prayer to whoever had been listening. Her head ached, her jaw ached, her stomach was clenched almost as tightly as her grip on the blank notebook in her hands. Nan's diary was burned and so she'd grabbed the first book she could find. It had been one hell of a risk.

Even so, Renee had felt Aeron, she had felt her in the air, in the wind all evening. It was almost as though Aeron's voice had been whispering to her when she searched through the trunk in the cabin. Yes, the river had been a gamble but something inside her just knew. She could not explain it, it wasn't logic, but if anything was going to bring Aeron back, it would be the display of complete love from her father.

She'd banked on everything she knew about Aeron to save her, and thank God, she had been right. She shivered with the cold and that glaring truth. The fear of just why she knew it raged deep inside. She was logical, she didn't believe in what she couldn't see. Even with Lilia, most of the time she put it down to science or a good instinct even when the obvious was there for her to see for herself. It was one thing for someone else to feel all the freaky stuff, then excuses could be made, plausible explanations, but now she was doing it, and it terrified her. There was no logic other than the fact that she just knew. She shook her head. *How did she know? How* was she so sure that Aeron was not the killer?

She watched as Eli and Aeron clambered up the bank, shivering, jaws chattering.

She wanted to hold Aeron, keep her safe, shelter her, the relief of seeing her present, real, moving, it made her throat close. She hurried to them with two blankets from the camp, anything not to stare like a fool. "What is it with you and new clothes?"

Aeron cocked her head, her eyes lingering over the space around Renee and smiled gently. "At least they ain't ripped this time."

Aeron swept her up. Her chuckling filling Renee's ear as she shrieked at the cold, sodden, heartfelt hug.

"Thank you." Her whisper was so gentle, so good to hear. She was alive. She was okay.

"For what?" Renee whispered back, her voice hoarse.

"Not giving up on me."

Tears threatened once more. Renee pulled back, not daring to meet Aeron's eyes. She felt too much, she was too exposed. She busied herself with the stove, they'd need hot tea.

Aeron's gaze seemed to follow her, her big brown eyes watching her work and, no doubt, she was reading her too.

"Quit it." Renee handed the steaming tea to her, ignoring Aeron's lopsided grin.

"Have you got your meds?" Renee handed Eli his tea.

He rubbed his hand over his chest and rolled his shoulder, his tea jumping about in the cup. "No, but considering I just nearly drowned myself . . ." He glanced at Aeron. "I feel better."

Aeron flicked her eyes away and Renee didn't miss the avoidance. So that's what she had been doing.

"You lost your badge," Aeron said, cutting off Renee before she could ask her own question.

Tensing, Renee shoved her hands in her pockets. "I . . . well, yeah." She shrugged, reminding herself of a naughty preschooler. "I quit." Aeron and Eli stared at her but all she could do was shrug again. "Difference of opinions."

"Like they think I'm the killer." Aeron's voice was calm but the words, the truth still stung.

"I don't. That should count for something." She tried not to think about the fact her own team didn't trust her judgment.

Aeron met her eyes. "You know it does." She smiled. "So, where does that leave us?"

Eli stared desolately into his tea. "The girls are missing, they don't have a lot of time." He bowed his head. "And, well . . . Jenny is—"

Aeron touched Eli's hand. "I know, I'm sorry." She turned to Renee, something was rippling across her eyes, something she wasn't saying. "Your people ain't gonna help?"

Renee tried to understand what she hadn't said, had she seen more in the vision? "No, not unless they get something solid that changes their mind."

Eli groaned. "Wonderful. So what did they have?"

Renee closed her eyes, trying to remember the things Daniel and Ben had said. "They said it was made to look like a man who hated women, that Chelsea was a decoy of sorts." What did she know? It sounded to her like they didn't have a clue. "They think it was a set up."

Staring at his tea, Eli rubbed a drip from the rim. "So, someone is attempting to make it look like a serial killer?"

It seemed like it to her at least. "I guess so. Investigation isn't my strong suit but I got the impression they felt that Aeron was trying to cover her tracks."

His hands turned white as he gripped the cup. "Why? Why would they?"

Renee met Aeron's gaze but was unable to hold it.

"Lilia," Aeron grunted.

"Lilia?" Eli said. "Your mother? Aeron, she dis—"

"Is Renee's boss." Aeron's voice carried such hurt, such bitterness that she spat the words out. "You've been fed a load of lies by her." She downed her tea. "She's part of Renee's people."

Renee felt her cheeks color, the warmth of the fire cool in comparison. Some hero she was.

"What? She's alive?" Eli's eyes misted, his jaw trembled, and he ran his hand over the back of his neck. He looked beyond exhausted, the poor man had gone through hell. "She's alive and she didn't say a word? She just left?"

Renee couldn't bear the sound of heartbreak in his voice. "She had her reasons." She tried to capture both their eyes. "None of it to do with either of you." How had Lilia done it? How had she left them? "I'm not going to sit here and defend her because right now I want to give her a black eye but if she hadn't become . . ." How did she say it, explain it? "Well, what she is . . ." What would have happened? Without Lilia's sacrifice what price would they all have paid? She shuddered. "It's just unthinkable."

Aeron and Eli exchanged a look. Aeron squeezed Eli's shoulder as he took gulps of his tea. "What about your side?"

He finished his cup and took Aeron's from her. He stood and went to the river to rinse them out. "Nothing, no evidence. Well, Michael found some but the killer found him."

Renee shook her head. "Our guys thought the evidence had

been tampered with but they couldn't prove it. Was there anyone lurking about? Anyone on the edges?"

Eli shook his head and wiped the cups with a cloth. "The forensic team, about five of the sheriff's and my guys. None of us paid much attention, we were in the forest." He sighed. "Most of us were just trying to get through it, you know?"

Renee nodded. She doubted even a hardened ME would have found the scene easy to work.

Eli placed the cups in the box. "You think the killer could have been watching?"

Renee stared at the camp stove. No doubt he had watched them every time. No doubt he knew he'd left evidence. "Must have been."

"I've got an idea," Aeron said, softly. "It could work."

Anything was better than just sitting there. "What is it?"

Aeron took a deep breath. "We're running out of time. None of us is Sherlock Holmes but we have me."

Renee's heart started an ominous thudding rhythm. Oh, that didn't sound good. "What do you mean?"

Aeron stood up and wobbled a little. "Maybe I can get somethin' off the girls. Maybe where they were?"

"You mean the bodies?" Eli said, his face paling.

Aeron nodded. "It's the only card we have left to play."

"I can't risk losing you again." Eli got to his feet and also wobbled. "I can't just drown you every five minutes either."

Renee bit her lip. Aeron was right. Without her, those girls would be dead before anyone could get to them, without Aeron, the killer was going to get away.

In no uncertain terms should she ever recount what Lilia had told her. She'd signed a clause, she'd pledged with her hand on her heart. It was a golden rule. "Lilia said you were the center of the storm."

Eli put his hands on her shoulders like he would shake her. "What did you say?"

Renee swallowed. What the hell had she just said? "Lilia, she said that Aeron was the center of the storm."

Eli threw his blanket off his shoulders. "Damn crafty sneak." He strode to the car, slipping on the muddy grass as he fished his keys out of his sodden pocket. "Let's go."

Aeron shook off her own blanket and followed.

Renee dumped water on the fire as she wondered what the hell was going on. "You gonna explain what I said?"

Eli looked at her in the rear-view mirror as she clambered into the back seat with Aeron. "Lilia always used to say that her gifts made her the center of any storm." He smiled. "And the only one who could stop it from the inside."

Renee folded her arms. "So she got me to quit on purpose?"

Aeron chuckled.

Renee pursed her lips. It wasn't funny.

"You really think they would ever doubt you?" Aeron asked. "You said yourself that they trusted you."

To protect maybe. It had been quite clear how little she meant back in the trailer. "They told me—"

"They used your weak spot," Aeron said.

She didn't get it. "Why?"

Aeron touched Renee's hand. "Because maybe I'll need my trusty knight."

Renee looked out of the window. She hoped Aeron was joking, she hadn't exactly been at her best lately.

"You said you trusted Lilia, didn't you?" Aeron whispered to her.

Renee nodded then growled, infernal woman. "I do."

Aeron grinned and leaned closer to her. "And you trust me?"

There was no doubt in that at all. "Of course, you know I do."

Aeron nudged her shoulder. "Then the only thing left to do is trust yourself." She flashed an adorable toothy grin. "Like you told me, you're good at your job."

Renee sighed. "I *was* good at my job." Long ago, before Aeron unraveled her. "Before . . . everything."

Flexing her mammoth biceps, Aeron flashed her another grin. "I'm still here ain't I?"

Renee tried to frown but it was half-hearted. Hell, she was incorrigible, completely incorrigible. "No thanks to me."

Eli pulled into the sheriff's department parking lot in Ironton. They got out into the cold, the breeze starting to pick up. The stars overhead encroached upon by clouds.

"No one else knew me well enough to know I wouldn't sacrifice him for nothing." Aeron trailed her eyes over her father striding to the front door.

Oh hell, Aeron knew. She knew exactly how Renee had bluffed her way through it.

"You know me," she whispered. "You believe I can do this, right?"

"Of course." Renee couldn't exactly say no. No, where was the logic? Touching dead bodies won't find a killer. But then, talking to ghosts didn't happen, or visions, or healing. This was insane. "I believe in you." Considering what they were about to try, she had to.

Chapter 69

AS WE WALKED down the corridor of the sheriff's department, it took every bit of will power I had not to turn around and run out of the building. All I could think of was how I'd have to see the girls' dead bodies. My biggest fear was Natalia. The other girls, well, I'd seen their spirits, they'd spent time with me and Renee but Natalia—I shuddered—I really didn't want to get anywhere near her. The closer we got to the coroner's office, the more I thought about why we were there. It was my dumb idea to try and touch the victims, not my father's not Renee's, mine. What the hell had I been thinking? What if I couldn't do this? What would I say to my father then? He needed me to find my sisters, he was counting on me.

We stopped outside a door. A sign next to it read Coroner's Office.

"The girls are in here," my father said. His hands trembled as he reached for the handle and I wanted to ease his pain, his worry. Those girls meant everything to him.

"We can do this, we can get them back," I said, touching his hand and wondering how I was going to make good on it.

A flash of me fixing Mrs. Squirrels' box made me stop and stare at him as he opened the door. A rippling wave of pride flowed from him to me. His eyes met mine and he smiled.

He walked into the office to the counter where a man in a white coat was sitting at a desk.

"Jeff, Aeron's gonna take a look at the girls," my father said.

Jeff raised his eyebrows. "You what?"

My father set his jaw. "You want to argue with me right now?"

Jeff shook his head, shooting a furtive glance at me as he got to his feet. "No. They're over here."

He let us behind the counter to a door, which he opened. I braced myself and walked past him into the cold room. I stared at the metal tables where the five victims lay. I glanced back at Renee. She seemed to understand what I wanted and gently kept my father from entering any further.

"I need space." I hoped my father couldn't see the mess Jenny was in.

"Why don't we go and get some coffee?" Renee said to Jeff and my father. "Let her work."

Jeff gave me an uncertain look.

Eli grabbed his arm. "Just do it."

I waited until the door was closed behind them and looked around the morgue. The stench of chemical disinfectant mingled with what I guessed was the smell of corpses. The stark, fluorescent light glinted off the metal tables. The victims were each covered over with a sheet.

I kept getting flashes of the women sitting up and screaming at me. Alone in the silence, my hands trembled, the fear dribbling sweat down my neck.

It was quiet. These bodies were empty shells now, the spirits long gone.

"They ain't here no more," I told myself. "Just walk on over and touch them."

I went to Mari first and pulled back the sheet. She was gray, neatly sewn up by Jeff. He'd taken great care of her, tending the wounds that had been inflicted on her. The gentleness he'd shown after all Mari had been through welled up in my heart. For every creep there was a caring soul.

I didn't really know what to do, so I touched Mari's arm. She was like ice. Nothing happened. There was nothing but a shell. I touched her hair, but the result was still the same. Maybe she'd been gone too long. I hoped that she'd made it to where she needed to go, that she was at peace. I covered her back up and walked over to Natalia. I stood staring at the sheet, terrified that she would spring up and strangle me. Her fury still haunted my dreams, her rage-filled cries still rattled through every inch of me. My heart pounding in my ears, I reached out for the sheet but dropped my hand away. I couldn't do this, I couldn't get near her.

"Come on. You can do this. You gotta do this." I danced about on the balls of my feet, my hands in my hair. I had to touch her, somehow I had to.

I glanced at the door. There wasn't time to waste on freaking out. My sisters needed me. Baby steps.

"You can do this."

I took a deep breath and edged forward.

"Please don't get mad, Natalia, please. I'm tryin' to help."

My hand trembled as I grabbed the sheet and yanked it back. I dodged backward. Slammed my eyes shut. Ready to run. My heart pounding like it wanted to get out. Ready for her to start wailing.

Nothing.

I peeked one eye open and saw her body. She was gray like Mari had been, sewn up. Still, my heart hammered away and my hands dripped with sweat.

"I just gotta touch you," I whispered to her. Flashes of her jolting upright and leaping at me pulsed through my mind. "Please, just quick. I can save other folks." I shoved my hands in my back pockets, my stomach clenching up. "My sisters, I gotta help them, please."

Before I bottled out, I put my hands on her face and arm. Expecting her to scream, howl, thrash about, I could hear my own breath shuddering in my ears.

Nothing.

No trace of anything. No way to read her.

"No, I need to read you. I need to know what happened."

Panic pouring off me, I went to Darcy, nothing. Chelsea, nothing. Finally Jenny but nothing. There was no energy to tap into, they were gone. What the hell did I do now?

"Any luck?" Renee asked from the doorway as I placed the sheet back over Jenny.

"Nothing," I answered. "I can't get a thing."

What the hell kind of use were my burdens if I couldn't save nobody?

Renee walked to me, nestled under my arm, and patted my back as she smiled. "The grandmother, Mari's grandmother, is back at city hall in Oppidum. She's got an idea."

I went to the sink to wash my hands and tried not to panic. How could I not see anything, now, when I really needed to? I could feel the churning sickness in my stomach, the worry that I couldn't help after all. What if I had to watch my own sisters suffer too? It was too much.

My knees wobbled but Renee was right there beside me. "They're in the meeting room."

"They?" I asked.

Renee smiled. "Bill did some rounding up after he left us. Went to Mari's family for help but when he got there, her grandmother had him pick up the cavalry."

"Bill?" I remembered him at the campsite. Mary's husband was helping?

Renee beamed at me, her eyes intense. "Yes."

I shook my head, not sure what to make of it but I didn't have the time to ask questions.

I STOPPED AT the double door of the meeting room, not sure if I should enter.

Renee smiled at me. "I'm right here. I'm not going anywhere."

I glanced at my father. "I'm here too. You can do this."

Buoyed, I opened the door. The families were seated in the rows of chairs and the grandmother was seated behind the council table. I couldn't do this, I couldn't face them—

"Take a seat, I'm going to teach you something." The grandmother nodded to the chair next to her.

I wanted to turn around and run but Renee nudged me forward. The Borlands were there, the Toughtons, and so was my father. What if I couldn't see, what if it didn't work.

Renee steered me around the rows of chairs and the watching eyes to the seat and made me sit, then sat next to me. What if I couldn't get anything off the victims? How was I going to help them? They needed me to help them. They needed me to do this.

"We believe in you," she whispered.

The grandmother laid out jewelry on the table. "Skin loses its memory when there is no life in it but metal or objects that are precious to someone's heart, keep them for longer."

"Okay," I said, looking down at the table. Was that why I'd got nothing? Maybe it was the skin?

Her lined face wrinkled up in a smile. "First we need to see if you can read it properly." Her smile faded. "Mistakes aren't an option."

Great confidence booster. I swallowed the lump in my throat. "Can't you do it?"

"Most of us only see glimpses of what's to come, child. You are a special case."

"Center of the storm," I muttered.

"Your mother is right." She held up a watch. "Now, try this, tell me what you see."

I took the watch from the grandmother and held it. Nothing happened. "I can't see nothing." It was no good. When I needed my burdens they were gone. What kind of mean trick was that?

The grandmother handed me a second watch. "And this?"

I held it and closed my eyes. I could do this. I could do this.

The warmth pulsed off it and the smell of thick smoke surrounded me, men yelling and running, the heat of the flames, there wasn't time, there wasn't—

I opened my eyes and looked at Jim Borland. "It's yours . . . you wore it in your accident."

Everyone stared at me like I'd struck gold. My stomach lurched with the pang of hope and tension. A pain shot up my spine and I rubbed at my neck. "You saved that family but your neck?"

Jim nodded. "They can't see what's wrong with it . . . keep losing my eyesight."

"It's not your neck. It's your nerve, your ulna nerve." I had no idea about names and medical stuff so I sure as shoots didn't know how I knew it. "It's trapped." I walked to him and pressed the spot. "Here."

Jim flinched and yelped.

"A doctor in the city will help."

He looked at his wife who held his hand. "Thank you."

"It's just returning the favor." I sounded pretty darn confident about it, so confident that I pretty much convinced myself. Go figure.

I smiled at Chief Borland and returned to my seat. I looked at the pieces, stopping myself from asking Renee if there really was such a thing as an ulna nerve.

"This one," the grandmother said.

I picked it up—

Air whooshed past me. The fall was in slow motion, the ground hard, the crack severe, breathing was painful, but there was no money to fix it, not now, no insurance—

I looked at Frank Toughton. "Yours, your back, it's broken?"

He nodded.

"They can fix it but you don't have the money, right?"

He nodded again.

"I'll pay for you." I didn't know how the hell I was going to do that. What was I saying? "I have money." My mouth worked like someone else was in charge.

My father smiled and turned to Frank. "I'll get on it."

He would? How? What? I didn't get it? Did I have money?

The grandmother pointed at one of the remaining objects, a bracelet. "Now this."

The second I touched it, fire erupted in my head.

PERFECT, THIS IS just so perfect. The two sweet little girls. Ruth and Louise, you're such precious little angels. There's no point in struggling, you have to be brave, that's the least you could do for me.

Such sorrow from the little one, why are you crying? Didn't I make it perfect? Make your mother a worthy target? I could have let her know what I'd do but that will be our secret won't it? We won't tell anyone what I have planned for Aeron.

No, you see, sweet children, Aeron thinks she's special, she's so clever, that it makes her better than us . . . we'll show her though. We'll show her.

I COULD SEE the trees, tall, high, the smell of pine around me. The ground was mulch and muck, my feet sliding on it. I could smell the rain of the storm, the oncoming storm. It would be big, nasty.

I opened my eyes. "Darcy's."

Her parents leaned in.

"Yes, do you know?" her mother asked.

Her father held her hand. "Can you see?"

I swallowed. No way could I tell them what their girl had been through. I closed my eyes instead. The pain of her injuries jabbing and stabbing at me.

"The lodge . . . a dirt bike. . . I hear . . . the river . . . the river!"

Renee pulled the map off the wall and spread it over the table. My father and the others got up and looked at it.

"Okay, the river stretches near the lodge," Renee said as she marked the area.

The grandmother handed me a ring.

I saw a field and howled as my neck jarred from the impact of the rope. I rubbed at my throat. A dirt bike sound, just like before. I got a flash of the lodge, the smell of pine, and the glimpse of stained wood.

"A dirt bike . . . the lodge . . . pine trees . . . stained wood floor . . . old."

My father marked the map. "We got about five cabins around the lodge. All near the river."

The grandmother handed me another necklace with a heart on it and my breath caught. Chelsea's, the emotion caught in my throat, the memory of her spirit sitting in the cabin.

Pine, stronger this time. Her feet got wet . . . the steepness. She couldn't climb fast—

"It's across the river . . . it's . . . up the mountain?" I opened my eyes and placed my finger down on the exact spot. "The pump house."

My father nodded and hurried from the room. The door opened seconds later and my father, with a hardened expression, walked back in with Mayor Casey behind him.

"I'm confining you all to this room," Mayor Casey said, with a sly smile.

"You haven't the authority," my father said.

Mayor Casey laughed. "Meet Agent Frei."

My heart dropped as Frei walked in with her team and closed the door behind them.

"We're taking over," Frei said.

I jumped to my feet.

"You're under arrest. Please sit back down." Frei's voice was curt, cold, and cutting.

I shook my head. "We have to get to the girls."

"She's found them," Jim Borland said. "What are you doing? Let them go."

Frei narrowed her eyes at me. "It's just part of your game. We found the evidence that you thought you'd gotten rid of."

Not knowing what she was talking about, I looked at my father. "What evidence?"

"The hair, *your* hair. Darcy fought back, didn't she?" Frei's voice gained an edge that made my hackles rise.

I frowned. The flash of Darcy pushing out at the killer flickered in my mind.

Frei walked up to the table and leaned across it—her face close to mine, her eyes hard and narrowed. "Did you hope they'd let you go, so you and your partner could finish the job?"

"Partner?" I looked at Renee. "What is she talking about?"

Renee shook her head. "I don't know."

"As for you." Frei glared at Renee. "I want to question you, alone. Your story about being on leave doesn't seem to have worked out."

Renee met my eyes, something flickering across her gray ones. "It's okay. We can straighten this out."

I stepped back. I had to trust her. The agents walked out of the room with Mayor Casey, who looked extremely pleased with himself.

I turned to the parents. "I swear to you, I did not harm your children. I swear it."

"We know," Maggie Toughton said. "You told us about Frank's accident and Jim's. We know you can see."

I looked at the grandmother who smiled. "That was why you did it?"

She nodded at the small round windows in the doors. "Now, I'm figuring they're going to be a while."

I looked out a window and saw Renee follow Frei into the glass-walled office across the corridor. "The door is guarded. What do we do?"

"We're on the second floor, it's too much of a drop to get down."

"Not if you got a ladder," Jim said, looking at Kay.

Kay pulled out her cell phone and thumbed in a text. "Easy when you got friends," she said and a second or two later she nodded.

I looked at my father. "You comin'?"

He stared long and hard through the window in the door at the mayor. "I've had about enough of that slimy bastard to last me a life time."

I looked across the hall, Renee met my eyes. I wasn't sure if she could read me, like I could read her but we needed a distraction and it would have to come from her.

Chapter 70

RENEE LOOKED INTO Aeron's eyes and an odd flashed image hit her mind like a gunshot. She frowned.

A ladder up against the wall, a fire truck.

She smiled. Had Aeron shown her that? Aeron nodded as Renee lifted her eyebrows in question.

Freaky. That's what you are, freaky, she thought.

Aeron shrugged in response which almost made Renee laugh out loud.

Frei yanked the blind down and cut Renee's connection to Aeron. Renee scowled at her and Frei gave her the "don't even think about it" look. "The evidence is all there, *Doctor.*" She stepped between Renee and the glass wall. "You need to distance yourself, now, before she drags you down with her."

Renee lifted her chin. "Are you that much of an idiot?" She turned to Mayor Casey and wanted to smack off his smug grin. "Are you all that blind that you can't see she's innocent?" She threw her hands in the air. "Why would the victims' families be on her side?"

Mayor Casey's thin lips twitched. "I couldn't care less what a bunch of nobodies think. What I do care about is the image of this town." He smiled, the kind of slimy politician's smile that made Renee want to thump him. "It's business." His smirk vanished. "Do you have any idea how much revenue I'll lose?"

Renee scowled, the idiot could cost lives with his greed. "You? As the mayor you mean? As the public servant who cares about the little people?"

Mayor Casey laughed. "As the owner of several lodges that won't be full if there's a freak on the loose."

Renee got the strange feeling that Aeron was ready for her to do *something.* She grabbed Frei's gun from her belt and pointed it at the mayor.

"I don't like fat cats," she said as loudly as possible, hoping like hell Aeron was listening.

"What the hell are you doing?" Frei sounded no more worried than if Renee was brandishing a rule.

Renee met her eyes. "Protecting my patient's interests." She made sure she was out of arm's length. Frei was faster than she was, more deadly with or without weapons. There was no way that Renee wanted to pull the trigger on her, ever. She motioned with the pistol as she edged toward the door. "Get over by the mayor."

Renee heard the commotion outside, then Fitzpatrick and Jo ran into the room.

Renee primed the pistol. Mayor Casey was not so smug now. "No one move."

Frei grabbed her radio.

Renee shook her head. "Don't think I won't."

"Have you lost your mind?" Frei was as deadpan as always. "You know they'll shoot you the second you pull that trigger."

Why was she so calm? Renee shook the thought away and nodded. "Yeah, but it'll be too late for Mr. Mayor here." She held out her hand. "Now hand over the radio."

Frei held the radio out, her ice cold eyes devoid of reaction or emotion. Renee snatched up the radio and ducked backward, sure that Frei would try something. She didn't. Renee tucked the radio onto her belt. "Now get over by the chair and tie him up."

Frei did as she was told. Renee glanced out of the door and hoped the great escape was in progress.

"Now you," she said to Frei. She raised an eyebrow. "Do it."

Frei rolled her eyes and did as she was told as Mayor Casey shunted about in his seat.

"You'll regret this." He glared at her. "I swear it."

Renee looked out of the door as Fitzpatrick and Jo stood with their guns ready. "Unless you want me to shoot, hand them over and get in here."

Fitzpatrick looked at Frei who muttered, "Just do it." Jo followed Fitzpatrick into the office and they placed their guns on the table.

Renee heard Skip curse as the door across the hall slammed open and the families spilled out.

"In here!" Renee called.

Kay, Jim, and Maggie Toughton ran into the office, picked up the guns, and aimed them at the agents and Jo.

"Keep them here. No one moves."

They nodded.

"Map," Renee said as she ushered Skip back into the meeting room. The window was open, no sign of them. Hopefully they were on their way. *You can do it,* she thought. *You can find them.*

Skip went over to the map on the table. "Are you all crazy?"

"Listen to me, Skip, Aeron and Eli, they've gone to the pump house." She looked down at the map. "You saw Aeron in the street yourself. It wasn't her. They need to get the girls out."

Skip stared at her and then nodded. "You think . . . you think they can?"

Renee tied her hair back. "Skip, I know I'm asking a lot but you got to buy us time. How long will it take to get to the pump house?"

He looked blankly at her, rubbing his hand over his dimpled chin. "Hell, I don't know, been there once up the Blackbear ridge." He wheezed out a breath. "An hour, maybe two."

Renee looked out the window. The sky was black, no stars now. The smell of a storm building. "I'm gonna go after them. I want you to wait one hour and call in the medic team. Do you understand?"

Skip rubbed his chin harder and glanced at the doorway. "Hell, what am I going to say. What if Sam comes in?"

That was a great question and one she couldn't answer. "If he loves Aeron as much as he says he does, he'll be on her side."

Skip took a deep breath, still rubbing away at his stubble but at least he didn't argue.

Renee looked at the map. "Now, I've got to find the co-ordinates."

"I'll help with that," Kay said from the doorway. "And I'm coming with you. I know that mountain like my own face and I got the equipment ready." She grinned. "Mountain rescue an' all."

Glad of the help, Renee smiled back. "We'll need a truck, do you have Bill's number?"

"Sure thing." Kay pulled out her cell.

As Kay filled Bill in on the situation, Renee studied the map. Mountains were tricky to the people who knew them. She'd lost her father, her brother to the weather on them. The sky outside was rumbling. They'd at least have rain, maybe mist. Kay would no doubt have the best equipment for the job but still, Renee felt that swirling of fear wriggle its way up from inside her stomach.

"So what are we looking at here?" Kay asked.

There was no way to sugar-coat it. If Kay was going to put herself in danger, she needed to know. "Well, the killer has a gun, he has the advantage, and he has time." She put her hands on her hips. "There are two girls so it could take longer."

"Okay, do you have vests, Skip?" Kay was in rescue mode, her focus on the task. It shook Renee into doing the same. She needed to look at it like it was another rescue. She'd do Aeron no good getting emotional.

They followed Skip to the supply room. He opened a locker and handed them vests. "You'll need these too." He pulled out the rifles. "In for a dime an' all that."

Renee strapped her vest in place, took the rifle, and checked it over. "Thanks."

With a shrug, Skip led the way back to the meeting room and stared into the room where Mayor Casey was being held. "Just go get 'em, girls."

Kay looked out the window. "He's outside. We'll pick up my gear on the way. You ready?"

Renee glanced at Frei through the doorway and the usually stoic woman flickered a little with something, the corner of her mouth twitched.

"Ready."

They hurried out of the room and down the stairs, the cool air thick with imminent precipitation. What was that in Frei's eyes? Renee shook her head as she got into Bill's truck. In all their time as colleagues she had never once got the switch on Frei. No one was as fast as her. Renee sat in the truck, staring out of the window. She'd never even gotten close to getting the switch on her. The realization made her laugh to herself. Maybe she hadn't this time either.

Chapter 71

THE SKY WAS enveloped by clouds as we drove to the lodges. I stared at the plume of black blocking out the moon and stars. Was Mother Nature on the killer's side? Was it angry?

It took us no time to reach the bottom of Blackbear but it would be a trek on foot from here on up. We didn't have supplies. My father's weapon was back in the station and neither of us had a phone or radio to make contact with the outside world. We were on our own.

I looked up at the trees swaying in the wind. I could just about make out the tops of them as they rustled warnings and my mind drifted back to Renee. I wasn't sure what she had done to distract the officers but it had worked. Nevertheless, the rest of the force, the sheriff department, and anyone fit enough to lend a hand, including Sam, was out hunting for the girls.

Still, we wouldn't have long before the alarm was raised. They thought I was the killer.

As we started our climb, a thick mist swept over the top of the mountain and I pulled my father to a halt. "No way we can navigate up there, not without help."

He started to walk. "We can't afford to wait." He glanced at me over his shoulder. "There's no time."

I eyed the mist. "The killer could have laid out traps . . . anythin'. We don't even have a flashlight and there's no moon."

My father looked up at the mist and then back to me. "What other ideas do we have?"

He would hate it but it was our best option. "Sam."

My father shook his head.

I gripped hold of his shoulders. "Listen, I know you don't like him but Sam knows this mountain better than anyone." We needed Sam. "I can run down to his place and catch you up."

My father sighed and took off his wide-brimmed hat. "What if he doesn't believe you?"

That was the question. Did he? Did Sam trust me? Did that love he professed still burn in him enough to help me now? "If he doesn't, then at least I can send help."

My father met my eyes and ran his fingers over the hat's brim. "You trust the boy that much?"

I wasn't sure. Sam *the boy* would have been there like a shot. I would never have doubted him for a second but I didn't know Sam *the man*. I didn't know whether duty would override his loyalty or whether the fact I was on the run would matter to him. All I could do was try.

"What else do we have?"

My father nodded. "I'll take the green route. No use trying to hurtle up the red in this."

"I'll catch you." I gripped my father and hugged him. "I'll be there."

"You'd better," my father mumbled, slamming his hat back on. " 'Cause I don't want to put my back out carrying them home."

I squeezed my father's shoulder and hurried off along the river to the Caseys' place. They lived a little further downstream in a converted lodge the size of a hotel. I didn't dare look back to my father, now trekking up the mountain blind. I couldn't, I had to focus on getting to Sam.

Crunching and sliding through the mulch to the lodge, I ran through my plea to Sam. Although I wasn't sure what the hell I was going to say when I got there. Back on Main Street, the last time I'd seen him, Sam was every bit as loyal as he had been before everything happened. Would he trust me after Jake?

My heart soared as I saw the lights on. Hopefully, Sam had stopped for a break, or I could convince Mrs. Casey to somehow reach him. Hell, as long shots went, it was going to be a mammoth one.

I hurried up the wooden steps of the stilted residence and frowned. The door was a little open. I knocked. Nothing. "Mrs. Casey? Sam?"

I pushed open the door, something gloopy under my fingers. I looked at my hand. Blood. My heart tripled in rhythm. "Sam?"

I hurried into the house and skidded in the pool of blood. No, not Sam, please no. I searched, scrabbled through every room finding nothing, no one.

"Sam?"

Please, he had to be okay, he had to be. I headed to the back and saw the light on in the kitchen. I rounded the corner. I ejected the bile from my stomach. I sucked in the air. Tried not to heave again. My eyes watered. So much blood. Mrs. Casey, or at least it had been. I turned away. The bile rose up once more. Who could do that? Why would they do that?

Her spirit seemed to linger, the faint sound of unearthly sobbing echoed around me. I needed to find Sam, I needed to get back to my father. What the hell was I going to do?

Just touch her, I told myself. *Reach out and touch her.*

There was blood everywhere. Where the hell did I put my hands? My stomach lurched and rolled. Breathe, slow, deep, just breathe. I glanced up and heaved at the sight. Slamming my eyes shut, I gulped in the air. Slow . . . deep . . . breathe. I opened them and retched again. There was no time for this. No time.

Just touch her!

I held my breath and held her hand. Nothing. I touched her watch. Nothing. I looked down at it. It was a fake watch. Mrs. Casey didn't do replicas.

The thought made me shiver. Someone knew I'd be here. I'd touch—

I looked down at my hand, covered in Mrs. Casey—or Sam's blood.

Sirens blared in the distance. No, no, I was being set up.

No, I needed to find the girls. I hurried to the kitchen units. "I need something to touch. I need to know. Come on." Nothing in the cupboards. Plastic tubs fell out at me as I fumbled through the cupboard. Nothing in the drawers, the cutlery, the plates, the mugs, nothing. Nothing gave me a damn thing.

The sirens grew louder. I spun around. I needed something Anything. I looked at the floor. What was it? Something, something was there. Yes, what was—?

"Sam!" Lying there covered in blood was Sam's badge.

I dived for it and skidded in all the crimson goo. I picked it up and fell as the vision hit.

Waiting . . . yes . . . waiting for him to come . . . for her to come . . . I have set my little game in motion . . . come and get me . . . come and find me . . . what will you do to save those you love?

I heard the footsteps in the front of the house, threw the badge, and hurtled out through the back and down the steps. I stumbled at the bottom and tried to steady my breathing. The killer knew. The killer knew about me and I had to face them, whoever they were, I had to face them to save my father, my sisters, and Sam.

I looked to the left and saw the dirt bike. The killer wanted me to use it. Wanted me to go tearing from the house on it. The police could see me. What other choice was there? My father was climbing in pitch black. He was heading into the trap. I had to get to him, to them.

There was no other way.

I kicked the bike into gear. The wheels roared into motion. I sped off. Gun shots rang out. Dirt kicked up beside the bike and I swerved. I clung on, wobbling, the bike screaming underneath me. I slammed my foot down, stopping myself from flying off.

Chase me, I thought. *Chase me, follow my lead . . . the girls, my father, Sam, they need your help.*

Chapter 72

RENEE ZIPPED UP her windbreaker as the rain started to fall—soft at first but the sky held an ominous bank of black which meant a cloud burst at any minute.

"Wind's picking up," Kay said. "Mist has dropped so visibility is poor. We'll need to keep together."

"Ties?" She looked at Kay and Bill who nodded at her.

"Kay, you lead. You know the mountain." Bill stared up at the sky. "I'll head up the rear, that way if anyone comes from behind, I can cut you girls loose." Bill raised his hand before Renee could protest. "No arguing, ma'am. If the killer is up there. He's waitin' on us." He puffed out his chest. "An' I don't know 'bout you but I don't want to be on his list."

Renee looked at Kay. "What routes do we have?" She tied the rope around her waist. "How much can we risk?"

"We can risk the yellow, just." Kay fixed her helmet in place and twisted the light on. "But no way are we heading up the lee side. If there's gonna be a slide, it'll be there."

Was that quick enough? Renee put her own helmet on. "How fast is yellow?"

Kay cocked her head. "We can make it in maybe forty minutes, to an hour." Kay met Bill's eyes, then Renee's. "Anyone who ain't fit needs to back out now."

Renee knew that the question was directed at her.

"I didn't serve in the marines to get beat by a mountain," Bill said.

Renee flinched. Her father had been a hero, nature could be merciless. Kay and Bill looked at her. She had the choice, she could lie, she could protect herself but what was the point? They needed to trust her. In no uncertain terms should she tell them a thing. Ever. "Commander Renee Black, Agent for the CIG." She smiled. "That and I grew up in the Rockies."

Kay and Bill stared at her, eyes wide, then at each other, then back to her.

There was no need to be *that* dumbstruck. She was good, but surely the scene at city hall should have gone some way to making them think she wasn't a doctor. "Don't look so surprised."

Bill pulled a confused face, his eyebrows tilting. "You're kinda small for an agent."

Renee put her hands on her hips. "Small?"

Kay nudged the big guy. "Petite, is what Bill means."

Small, petite, seriously? She took a few steps up the steep slope. "Low center of gravity." She stopped and folded her arms. "And I'm not small. I'm just not over six foot."

They climbed as quickly as they could up the slope. The rain got heavier, the mist thicker, surrounding them like a cloak. Kay's radio crackled. She picked it off her coat and listened to it, swearing.

"What's wrong?" Renee held her hand over her eyes and peered through the rain.

"Aeron. She must have gone to get Sam." She shook her head. "They think she's killed Mrs. Casey."

Renee sped up and reached Kay. The radio chatter crackled over the growing wind.

"Covered in blood . . . footprints . . . dirt bike . . . SOS."

Renee knew the voice. Fitzpatrick. What the hell was Aeron thinking? Why go to Sam's? Why get on a freakin' dirt bike?

"SOS?" Kay asked.

Renee met her eyes, then Bill's. Crap. "CIG code." She sighed. "Shoot On Sight."

"But they're your people. Tell them she ain't no killer," Bill said.

Taking a breath, she tried not to let her panic show. "I can't. They won't listen to me now."

Bill folded his arms. "Why?"

Renee continued to trudge up the slick path, the others following. "The Criminal Investigations Group has rules, regulations—"

"Yeah, you can't so much as breathe without a command, I get that," Bill answered.

Renee frowned at him. "How do you?"

Bill shrugged. "Marine. We see a lot of people that don't exist."

That made sense. "Then you get that the SOS probably applies to me right now too."

Kay spun around. "What do you mean?"

She fought every instinct that demanded she keep her identity, her duty from them. It was so ingrained that she swore CIG would appear from the undergrowth and riddle her with bullets. She'd broken so many damn rules, what the hell did secrecy matter now? "I disobeyed a direct order, I quit, and in their eyes I'm helping a killer get away."

Kay and Bill exchanged glances.

"And are you?" Kay asked.

"No." Renee heard her own curt tones and offered a smile to smooth it over. It wasn't their fault. These people were risking their own lives now. They had the right to ask questions. "Aeron's innocent, I promise you. She can find those girls, she will find them."

"Good enough for me," Bill said.

"Me too," Kay added.

Good to know. Her "Thank you," didn't quite seem enough. The climb was starting to wind her. She just prayed she was right. What the hell was Aeron doing at Sam's? Why had she taken the dirt bike? Why would she—?

The realization hit her like thunder through her soul. Adrenaline poured through her as she stormed ahead. They needed to get there, *she* needed to get there. Hell, Aeron wouldn't see it coming. "We need to push the pace. There's not much time."

Chapter 73

ELI TRUDGED UP the slope, his boots sliding in the mud. He'd lost the green route twenty minutes ago but turning round wasn't an option. He'd headed up, that was all he could do, but the ground was getting softer and the mud sucked at his legs as the rain pinged harder off his hat. His heart pounded in his ears but he hadn't felt any pain. He supposed it was the adrenaline or maybe Aeron had really fixed him back in the river. He prayed it was. He didn't have the time to have a heart attack now.

Eli focused, focused hard on the slope, his foe, his little girls were up there and he should be nearing the ridge by now. That's if he was going the right way.

He'd have felt a damn sight better if he had his gun or maybe a flashlight. Scrambling through the foliage was slowing him down and sapping at his energy. The air was thinner up here too and the mist was pretty much like blinkers. Every step was perilous, the back of the ridge lay somewhere off the green route. That, and a hundred foot drop if he stumbled over the edge.

Eli felt he was climbing in a straight line but that didn't mean a thing on the mountains. They were odd creatures, he'd always hated them. Always hated going anywhere near them. Beautiful to look at but more predatory than the mountain lions prowling them. How people did this for fun, he didn't know. Dumbass people who wanted to get frozen to death or fall from great heights. Idiots who made other people hike up and risk their lives to get them.

Stupid dumb hikers, stupid mountain, stupid rain. Eli tightened his jaw. Yeah, yelling at hikers and mountains and idiots made him feel better.

And so he continued, scrabbling through the undergrowth, cussing at every fool he'd ever met, and trying not to think that some lunatic had murdered his wife and taken his girls.

ELI, ELI, ELI . . . dear, dear. What shape are you in? What a way for the chief to make his entrance. I never knew how

*incapable you were, should I have left a trail of lights for you?
Are you that stupid that you couldn't stay on the path?*

*Never mind, Eli. It's okay. I've left my little tricks out there, I
saw you coming, I heard you coming. Does it make you feel less
afraid to face me? Whining and complaining about your pathetic
life?*

*I have always wondered just how you, ignorant, pathetic you,
could possibly have Aeron for a daughter?*

*You, the man who lets women walk all over him. Oh dear, Eli,
try not to fall to your death, won't you? I am trying to make a
masterpiece here and it won't be half as much fun if you don't
attend.*

*That's it, a little more . . . come on, old man . . . that's it, just
that little bit further . . .*

ELI YELLED OUT in agony as something sunk into his calf.
He looked down, blood oozed out. A huge maw of metal grasped
his leg, the flaps of his skin pulled back to reveal bone.

"Son of a—" He gripped the trap with trembling hands and
hitched back the lever. It snapped open. He dragged his leg out
just before it clamped shut again. His eyes watered as he lay on the
ground whimpering. That was all he could do. Long . . . deep . . .
breaths, the wooziness making stars pop in his vision. He rolled
onto his side and glanced down at the wound. Hell, it was deep,
real deep.

"I hate mountains." He swore, tearing the sleeve of his shirt.
"I hate rain." He growled with the agony as he tied it above the
wound. "I hate traps." He yanked it tight, screaming through the
agony.

Eli grabbed a nearby tree and hauled himself up. He tested the
leg out. "Son of a—" He bit his knuckles, the tears streamed down
his cheeks. It was at least broken. "Gotta keep moving. Gotta find
them." He sucked in more breaths, chanting it like a mantra to get
through each excruciating step. "Gotta keep moving. I'm coming,
girls." He hobbled on, knowing he must be close. "Daddy's
coming, hold on." He had to keep going, he had to.

THAT'S IT! I haven't had so much fun in a while, Eli. Did it hurt? Oh I bet it did, didn't it. How did it feel to have metal rip through your leg? I bet it was agony.

I've tears of joy in my eyes, Eli . . . especially now you're still trying to win. What do you think is going to happen, Eli? That I'll just let you walk away? That I'll stand back and let you take them.

Now, don't get me wrong, old man. I thought about rigging the place, so that when you opened the door, the whole thing would blow and Aeron would feel it, every second. It's so beautiful how she feels it. Every murder, Eli . . . she's felt it . . . felt my power.

I HOPPED THE bike over the dead tree on the track. I was nearly at the top. It had taken me too long. My father must be there by now and my skin prickled like I was being stung by hornets. I'd come off the bike a couple of minutes back and rolled around on the ground as white hot daggers dug through my leg. Lucky for me I'd only grazed up my arm and my hand when I'd jammed my hand out to stop myself hitting the ground head first. My hands were raw from the grazes, knees too but it was nothing like the pain that had ripped through my leg.

I didn't know what the hell had happened but by the time I'd got back on the dirt bike I felt sick with fear. My skin was fine. I weren't injured enough to account for the pain. That meant somebody else, somebody close had suffered the wound. A flash of anger shattered my thoughts into pieces and I slid the bike to a stop. I could feel the killer. I could feel their hate, I could feel the darkness in them radiating like molten lava.

I ditched the bike, stepped over the wire the killer had left trailing across the track, and closed my eyes. If I was going to survive, if any of us were, I needed to tap into them. I needed to connect.

ELI GOT TO the pump house but he was dragging his leg. He'd ripped off another piece from his shirt as a tourniquet. He may lose his leg but his girls, no, he'd find them. He'd get them out.

He opened the door to the old structure which had been used to control the man-made stream down the mountain. Inside smelled like rot and the unmistakable stench of death.

This was the place all right. Aeron was right. Why hadn't he believed her all along? If he'd just listened to her, trusted her, maybe Jenny would have been alive, maybe his girls would be safe in bed.

Eli fumbled through the dark, not sure if he should risk calling out the girls' names or to wait until he knew the coast was clear. A whimper reached his ears.

"Ruth, Lou, you there?"

"Daddy!" Ruth's voice. Thank God.

He strained to listen, to hear any movement. "Ruth . . . baby, where are you? Where's Lou?"

Eli felt for the walls and guided himself through the pitch black, his leg dragging loudly behind him. He swallowed and fought down the wooziness, fought down the pain.

"Daddy, Lou ain't waking up." Ruth's sobs filled the air. "I can't get her to wake up."

He limped toward Ruth's voice, sending something crashing to the floor as he collided with it. "Keep talking, Ruth. Keep talking." He focused everything he had on listening for her voice.

Up ahead, he saw the faint glow of a gas light, Ruth and Lou lay strapped to an iron bed.

"Daddy, I can't wake her."

He went to Ruth. She looked unharmed at first glance. He moved around to Lou. She was breathing, shallow breathing. "It's okay, I'm here, sweetheart." He smiled down at her, trying not to show he was hurt. "What happened?"

"I did."

Something hard hit the back of his head. He knew that voice. "You?" He dropped to his knees and the room faded out.

Chapter 74

I CROUCHED DOWN as I approached the pump house. It was in darkness, quiet, nothing moving. I gripped my head and dropped to my knees as white hot pain ripped through my skull. I bent over, catching my breath. Someone was hurt, badly. Where? There was nothing but bleak wilderness, the mist cutting us off from the world. The killer could be anywhere. Were they in the pump house? Were they lurking in wait for me?

As I approached the building, the desolation flowed off it like dry ice, stretched out, and tainted the land around it. I could hear the screams of past victims, the crying, the wailing. The big black cloud sucked at the shack like a colossal parasitic beast. Its power throbbed toward me like fiery claws, daring me to enter, daring me to walk into its jaws.

Come, come closer, you'll never win, you'll never get them back, you'll fail, you are nothing but a failure.

It hit me like a wall, a wall I couldn't walk through. It was too hard, too much.

The claws shot out at me. I grabbed my side as it stung my ribs. I ripped at the clothes but my skin was fine. Another strike. Another stinging, burning, ripple in my shoulder.

You will never save them. You're no one, nothing, you don't exist.

It would not win. "I do exist." I hurled myself through the doorway.

The darkness, so black, was thicker than the mountain fog, the desperation coated the walls, the blood, the pain, the hopelessness.

You are nothing, you will fail, you are the one causing this, it's you. Do everyone a favor and end it. You're nothing.

Never give up. Never let it win. "No." I forced myself to shut down. To visualize the armor. Baby steps. One. At. A. Time.

The belt—*Truth*—I was different. I could sense in more ways than I knew, different for a reason. One step forward—*Different* enough to get here, to see.

The breastplate—*Righteousness*—I had seen it, so I could stop it. Another step—I could heal whoever was hurt.

The boots—*Peace*—I could bring peace. I needed to tread, soft, steady, one step at a time. I could bring peace to the victims, to the town. I could do this.

The shield—*Faith*—Renee, Nan, my father. They'd had faith in me. I needed to believe in myself. I could stop the killer, I could free the town from the cloud.

The helmet—*Salvation*—I was the only one who could save my family now. Another step forward. I was here for a reason. I saw for a reason. I could pierce the clouds, sever the dark tentacles.

The sword—*Spirit*—I had gifts, gifts no one else had. Gifts I could use to help and stop anyone getting hurt again. It was in my hands now, this was my fight. And I could bring light back to my world.

"And I will."

I swore to whoever was up there that I would. I was gonna take down that cloud once and for all.

I recited the passage from scripture and I repeated it, over and over and over until the madness calmed.

"I can do this."

The whispering, the pains still jibed at me but distantly. I moved further in. What was that sound? I stopped and listened, listened hard. Whimpering? Yes, it was. I could feel my father and my sisters. I opened my mouth to call but scuffling and crashing echoed out.

"No . . ." My father's voice. Crash, slam, where were they? "No . . ." My father was wounded. His voice faint. That's what I'd felt on the roadside. The cloud was trying to stop me getting to him.

Silence.

My pulse thudded in my ears. Whimpers, sobs, my sisters' energies, my father's energy but there was no one else. Maybe they'd run?

"Dad? Are you there?"

I heard a spluttered reply, moved to it, and saw him in the dim light up ahead.

"Dad . . . Oh, God . . ."

He was on top of a table, his neck tied up with a rope, his injured leg limp and his good leg slipping on the wood. His blood dribbled down his face, his side burned.

"Aeron . . . Run . . ." No one else was here. No one but my father and the girls.

"They've escaped. There's no one here. I need to get you free."

"No." My father shook his head. "Run!"

I felt the cloud overhead pulse like it had erupted. I took a step toward him and froze as I heard a crack next to my ear and felt a cold hard muzzle touch my cheek.

MY HEART CRUMBLED like sand. The last person on earth I'd expected it to be. "I couldn't feel you . . . How? Why?"

All I got in return was laughter, soft, inhumane laughter. The cloud pulsed with it.

"I trusted you, I cared about you, why?"

My father slipped a little further and I went to help him only for the killer to tut. "We don't need the old man. He's not good for you."

"What?" My father needed my help. He needed me to stay calm.

"He's been holding you back. The coward left you to go to prison," the killer whispered in my ear and stroked my cheek with a warm hand. I'd trusted—how had I not seen, not known? It was right in front of me.

The voice whispered into my ear again, the familiar voice, the trusted voice, the breath tickling my neck. "I'll make him pay though. Just for you. It's all for you." A soft kiss touched my cheek. "He left you to rot. He abandoned you."

I tried to pull myself free. "And you didn't?"

A hand gripped my bicep and spun me around to face the daggers of truth. Sam stood in front of me and laughed, his manic eyes twinkled. "No. I know you saw, you saw my work and you took the blame." He opened his arms to me and beckoned me forward. "You gave me the time to get it right."

I shook my head. "I . . . what?" No, no that wasn't true.

Sam took me into his arms and forced my head to his chest. "You saw how much my brother got in the way. I was gonna make you special but he didn't like it. I know you saw."

"Sam, I was there," I said. "I tried to stop him."

Sam ran his fingers through my hair. Fear made my limbs spasm, I couldn't move. I couldn't take it in. No, I had tried to help

Jake. "There's no need for lies now. I made a mistake with Jake but you helped me." He kissed my neck. "Helped me to learn."

The nausea rolled upward from my stomach, burning its way through me. Helped him? But I'd been there? I'd killed Jake? I'd tried to stop him falling into the train. Hadn't I? Sam trailed his hand over my shoulder—

Such a pest of a brother, always hanging around. She puts up with him, why, I don't know and he thinks he has a chance with her. If only she knew about his little crush, as if she'd look at him when she was blind to me? Oh no . . .

"*What are you doing, Sam?*"

"*None of your business, you runt.*"

His weasel twitching, eyes trailing over my plan. "*What you doing with that rope? Where's Aeron?*"

Oh wouldn't he like to know. He will, just like everyone else, she'll know. If I can't have her, I'll collect her.

"*Why do you have Papa's gun? I'm telling . . .*"

So easy to catch, ain't you, you little runt. Why the squirming? Oh dear . . . what's that? The signal box is out? Oh dear . . . so the high-speed train will just whip on through?

"*What are you doing? Let me go?*"

So easy, this is too easy. Why haven't I done this before? "*You like trains, don't you?*"

"*Sam . . . no . . .please . . . let me go!*"

"*Why don't you take a closer look.*"

One push, so easy, the little runt is gone.

Tears streamed down my face. Sam held me to him, his gun in his hand. He'd let me believe I killed Jake or he thought I knew. My heart tore in two as I realized. He thought I had taken the fall for him, that I must be on his side. He'd killed Jake. He'd killed his own brother.

"See, baby." The cocky tone, once so comforting, shot ice right through me. "You and me, we played a little game. I know you enjoyed seeing them didn't you?" He kissed my neck again. I tensed. How could he do that? How could he think that? "Enjoyed how I outfoxed the others? Did you feel it? Did you feel all the pain?"

I closed my eyes. My whole body trembled and shook. Enjoyment? He really was crazy. How had I not seen? How didn't I know? Where was the cloud over his head? Why was there only one over the town? Was it using him? Where were the tentacles now?

He kissed my forehead, his hands in my hair. "I'll show you, can you see?"

Mother, oh how useless you are. You just sit around and let that arrogant fool use you. Surely you see his affairs, the way he fritters away your money and you say nothing.

You even know about me, don't you? So you'll understand why I'm going to collect you too, don't you?

"There are many things I've regretted, but none as much as giving birth to you."

"Well, how ungrateful. Mom of the year. Why don't we take a walk."

"I don't care what you do to me—"

"Good. I like a choice."

My knees buckled as I relived her final moments. Sam forced me to stand and take it. Every slash, every blow, I gripped his shoulders, the pain unbearable.

"Feels good, doesn't it?"

I could hear my father slipping, Sam laughing, the whimper of my sisters and somewhere in the distance the cloud rejoiced in my agony.

Never. Give. Up. "I won't let you win." I grabbed for his gun.

Chapter 75

RENEE SUMMONED UP the last of her energy to haul herself over the crest. They had spent most of the time sliding and slipping as the rain battered their faces. Renee dropped to her knees, gulping in breaths.

"How far?" she asked.

"Up ahead," Kay said between gasps of air.

Renee heard voices, from her left, lots of voices. "Must be CIG. You need to stay out of sight or surrender." She fixed them both with a stare. "No heroics. Do not try and stop them."

"Why? Where are you going?" Bill asked.

Renee got to her feet. "I've got to do this alone. Neither of you needs to be harmed."

"I can't let you go in there alone." Bill pulled the rope from his waist.

Renee slipped off the rope. "You've helped me get here. When it's safe, you can help me get the girls down the mountain." She wobbled from exhaustion and shook it off, willing her focus to come back. "Stay here, please."

Kay and Bill hurried into some undergrowth as Renee crouched low. She saw the dirt bike next to a tree and the trip wire in front of it. It was almost as if Aeron had known it would be there.

Cut it out, she told herself. Doubting Aeron was the last thing she needed to do. But what if? What if she had been like Yannick? What if Aeron had fooled her?

She'd been so sure about him. She had banked everything on his innocence and she had been wrong. He'd nearly killed her in the process.

Renee blinked back the memories and glared at the pump house. No, Aeron wasn't Yannick. Aeron was a hero, Aeron was good and right and wouldn't harm anyone.

Renee believed in her with every part of her soul, and right now Aeron needed her.

She took the rifle off her back and loaded it. The pump house was silent as she approached. Then shouting and clattering filled the air.

"Aeron!"

Renee bolted toward the pump house and hoped like hell she'd make it in time.

AS I TOOK hold of the gun, the visions of Jenny howled through my mind. I kept hold and hit Sam in the side with my elbow. He grabbed my hair as he fell. We clattered down, my grazed palms scraped on the wood floor, the gun slid away. He laughed and slapped me across the face with the back of his hand. Stars flashed in my vision.

"You have to try harder than that, come on."

I brought my knee up sharp, caught him in the stomach, and ripped myself from his grasp. I dived for the gun, Sam's hands dug into my waist. He rolled me away.

"That's it. I love it when you fight. Let's have some fun."

I snapped my elbow back and hit him in the stomach again. My father struggled on the edge of the table. I scrabbled to my feet and pushed his foot back onto the flat. A hand on my shoulder, I turned and caught a fist in my jaw.

I cradled my head with my hands to stop from cracking it on the wood. Blood oozed from my lip, my jaw was on fire. Sam laughed, so devoid of soul, so lost. It tore at my heart, burning like a wound. How could he do it? Why? I flicked my foot out and caught him in the ankle. He went to raise the pistol. My father swung out and kicked the gun with his free leg.

Sam turned, eyes blazing, and shunted the table away.

"No!"

I dove into Sam and rammed him into the wall. The place shook from the impact. I staggered to my feet and dragged the table back to my father.

Sam clamped his hands over my mouth and my neck, his breath hard and fast in my ear. "See, ain't this fun, love."

I tried to break his grip but his arm pulled tighter, the blood squealed in my ears, the panic thumped in my chest.

"Watch him hang there, sweetheart." He yanked my chin up to force me. "Watch him, the life fading from him, same as you. Shush now."

I lunged forward, bent over, and threw him over my shoulder. Sam slammed onto the floor with a groan. Where was the gun? Where the hell was the gun? I looked at my father. The table. I hauled it back. A small foothold.

My father's eyes widened. "Watch—"

Sam clattered into my side, my ribs crunching with the contact from his shoulder. The wind ripped out of me as I thudded to the floor. I couldn't breathe. I gasped for air but Sam pulled me onto my back and gripped my neck with his hands.

"So you choose him? After all I've done for you?"

I kicked out but he trapped my legs with his own. I clawed at his face but he squeezed tighter.

"I made it perfect for you, can't you see?" His eyes bulged. Manic. "It's all for you!"

The room swayed violently as my lungs tried to contract. I hit out, flailed, but the oxygen was leaving me. The life being squeezed from me.

"I'm gonna make it look like you, Al." His spit hit my face as he ranted. "I'm gonna make it all your fault."

No. I reached out my hand and ripped at his shirt. He laughed. I hit his chest with everything I had.

Sam screamed and rolled onto the floor, writhing. I scrabbled away, gasping for air as he convulsed on the floor.

Sam opened his eyes. He kicked out at the table, the leg snapped. My father dropped on the end of the rope. I crawled to him. A boot hit me in the side. Wheezing, I glanced up. Sam was on his feet. His face red, the vein in his forehead prominent. He was in agony, writhing agony but his madness overrode it. He raised the pistol in his trembling hand and laughed. "I win."

Chapter 76

I LOOKED INTO Sam's eyes. My father wriggled helplessly, twitched, the girls screamed and cried somewhere nearby. Sam, the boy I had trusted, the boy who I had gone to prison for, stood grinning at me like it was all a game.

The rumble of thunder made me realize. It was not the cloud controlling him. No, Sam *was* the darkness, the cloud. There was nothing malfunctioning like the girls back in the institution. There was nothing to blame. Sam was evil. He was just evil.

"They'll know it was you." I needed to help my father. I needed to stop Sam hurting my sisters.

"No, they won't. It's all in your prints, your DNA. I'm the hero." His hyena-like giggle burst from his lips. "The one who killed the freak."

His words stung more deeply than all I had discovered. He'd been playing me all along, he'd bided his time. Jake had died because of me. All those girls had died as if I had killed them myself. Sam was soulless and always had been.

"Hey, Al. Maybe they'll give me a medal."

It had all been a show, a face, I couldn't read him or sense him because there was no feeling to sense. He was hollow, an evil hollow shell, and I'd helped him stay free. Helped him kill others by lying.

"I don't care," I told him. "I don't care no more."

"Yes, you do." He sneered, spit flying from his lips. His hair wild. "You care. You feel."

I glanced at my father. He was fighting. His foot had found the leg of the table. He was trying to push himself up. I needed to draw Sam from him. "Not anymore." I edged away from my father and Sam followed me. "Kill everyone for all I care. I've been inside, I'd rather you pull the trigger."

Sam hesitated. He narrowed his eyes.

I stepped back as I glanced at the pistol aimed at my head. "Anythin' is better than that place."

Sam waved the gun around. "You're lying!"

The grandmother's words came back to me in that moment. I'd know, I'd know when I held the killer's heart in the palm of my hand. I knew what I had to do. Sam was the killer, the beast, the cloud. It was up to me. I had to finish it.

"Am I?" I shrugged. My father pushed himself up if only a bit. "Tell me, how well do you really know me?"

Sam's eyes flickered as he processed my words. "What?"

"You think you know me?" I asked. "You think I got four more years for being a good girl?"

Sam twitched. "No . . . you . . . no!"

I smiled the slyest smile I could conjure. "Yes, we're similar, so similar." I nodded. "You may have won the game but I'll always beat you. Always."

Sam growled. "You won't. I win! I win!"

He sounded like a petulant child. How had I not seen it? How? I shook my head. "No matter what you do to me. I never wanted you. I never cared about you. You are nothing." I forced a cocky grin to my face. "That's how I feel, Sam-O." I spat at his feet. "You're a nobody. Do you know that?"

The gun swayed a little as Sam shook his head. "No. I am better than you!"

My father opened his eyes. He was holding on. I had to keep going. "You know, I laughed at you for being such a fool. A pathetic fool. Every single day."

I kept my gaze locked with his. The tears poured from his eyes. Renee was close. I could feel her. I had to keep him there. I had to squeeze, squeeze that bitter heart.

"I mean, you just let your daddy beat you. What a loser."

"No," Sam spluttered through his tears. The gun swayed. He swayed.

"You let him bully you. You watched him beat your mom." I snorted my disgust. "What a coward."

"She deserved it!" Sam rubbed at his tears with one hand. "You're a freak! A witch!"

I took a deep breath. There was one more thing, one more declaration that would break him. I had to. There was no other way.

"Maybe, but you know why I'm better than you?"

"It was for you. It was all for you." The vein in his forehead bulged as he screamed.

I had to. There was no other choice. I never wanted to hurt nobody, Sam least of all. I took a deep breath. "It was for nothing." I focused every ounce of energy I had and locked eyes with him. "I'll never *ever* love you."

His eyes flickered. His shoulders slumped. He lifted the gun. The door slammed open and he pulled the trigger.

KAY BORLAND LOOKED down the road as the flashlights came into view and glanced at Bill. "If we don't do somethin', Aeron's gonna get flayed for somethin' she didn't do."

Bill nodded. "So what do we do? The lady said to keep our heads down."

Kay waved it off and stood up. She was sick of crouching anyhow. "When did you start listenin' to advice?"

Bill got to his feet. "Since I married Mary when my ma told me to stay the hell away."

Kay smiled. Bill deserved better, everyone knew that but the daft tool adored that messed-up Mary like no other. "I don't know 'bout you but whoever's in that pump house killed my girl." She straightened her shoulders. "Like hell is he gettin' away."

She could hear him mutter behind her as she marched down the path toward the sounds. This was for Chelsea. Her little sweet Chelsea.

"Drop your weapon!" a voice called out.

Kay dropped her rifle. "I don't want to argue, but Aeron ain't your killer." She thumbed in the direction of the pump house. "An' they got the son-of-a-bitch cornered."

The agent, the blonde woman from the police station, stormed into view. "We know."

Two men hurried forward and took the surrendered weapons.

Kay frowned, surprised. "You do?"

The agent nodded. "Where's the pump house?"

"This way." Kay started up the path.

Shots rang out.

One.

Two. Three.

Silence.

The agent tore up the path past a stunned Kay.

RENEE DUCKED AS the bullet splintered the wood next to her head. She shot twice. Sam Casey dropped to his torn-up knees and gripped them, his gun clattered to the floor. Aeron scrambled across the floor and kicked it toward Renee. She launched herself to her feet and shoved her weight under her father. Eli was hanging there. He looked limp.

"I can try shooting."

"No," Aeron said. "The girls, they're in the back somewhere."

Aeron was covered in blood and bruises. Her neck red raw, her face swollen. Renee hurried over to her, took one of Eli's legs, and helped to support him. Sam was still whimpering and wailing on the floor.

"Don't give up on me. Come on," Aeron muttered to her father.

She was slurring, she looked so pale, her eyelids drooping. Renee could see her knees trembling even in the dim light. "You okay? You hurt?"

Aeron shook her head. Her sole focus on her father. Renee heard voices and tensed. The unmistakable bark of Frei.

"Unarmed!" Renee called.

"Coming in!" Frei called back.

CIG burst through the doorway. Lasers zipping through the dark. Frei stormed in, the CIG team moving past them, clearing the building. Renee breathed out in relief as Bill and Jo hurried over and took Eli's weight off her.

"Cut him down," Kay said, passing Bill a switchblade.

Eli fell forward, Bill careful as he lowered him down. Renee took Aeron's arm and pulled her away as Kay knelt beside Eli.

"He's breathing." Kay drew the med kit to her. "Gonna need to stabilize him before we move him."

"Is he . . . ?" Aeron shivered. "Will he . . . ?"

"Let her work." Renee took her hand. "Give her space, okay?"

"In here!" Frei's voice echoed out from the back.

Fitzpatrick, Bill, and several officers, trampled over Sam. Frei appeared a second later with one of the girls in her arms, Bill had the other.

Aeron stumbled to them. "Are they okay?"

"Thanks to you." Frei's voice was gentle. The most gentle Renee had ever heard it.

Aeron nodded, then she wheezed out a breath as her shoulders slumped. Her eyelids drooped as she tried to talk. Her eyes on Sam. "He wanted to kill me all along." She wrapped her arms around herself. "He even killed Jake."

Frei met Renee's eyes. "Get her out of here. Away from him." She snapped back to the action. "Get the girls out. Now."

Renee took Aeron's hand and led her to the doorway. She glanced behind. Frei had given the girl to Fitzpatrick and was shoving the uniformed officers toward the door.

"We don't need an army. Unless you have medical training, get out." Frei scowled at the wailing Sam. "And someone . . . shut him the hell up."

The freezing air made Renee shiver. Aeron needed warmth. Renee led them to a patch of grass.

"You got foil?" Renee asked Fitzpatrick.

He took the pack off his back and pulled one out before leaving them alone.

"I thought you'd kill him," Aeron said as Renee wrapped the foil around her shoulders. "I thought." Her words shuddered from her, slurred, heavy. "I thought he'd kill me."

Renee pulled Aeron to her. She held on as sobs wracked through Aeron's body. The eruption built and built, the sobs louder and louder. Aeron dropped to her knees, Renee with her.

"You saved my life," Aeron whispered into her ear. "You saved us all." She clutched at Renee's shoulders. "I knew you'd come. I just knew."

Renee's heart thudded with the whispered words. She held Aeron's head in her hands and swept the hair from her bloodied face.

"I'll always be there," she said, wanting so much to tell her the truth.

The chaos of the police, the CIG, and Sam's wails carried on all around them but they were cocooned in a protective bubble as though her arms could keep out the world.

"You're safe now," she said, kissing Aeron's forehead, wanting to take her pain away. "I've got you."

Aeron buried her head into Renee's shoulder. Renee looked up to the sky. "Thank you. Thank you."

Relief that Aeron was safe, that she'd gotten there in time, that she had her safe and sound in her arms, cooled her frazzled senses. In her mind she said the words she couldn't say out loud, knowing that Aeron was too distraught to read her. *I love you. I love you so much.*

Chapter 77

I DON'T KNOW how long it took to get down the mountain, I was so disconnected from everything. I saw my father carried down on a stretcher, I saw the two girls being carried by Bill and one of the other officers. Renee held my hand the whole way down, murmuring gentle words, soft words to console me.

Bill even suggested to the others that they tie Sam to the dirt bike and haul him down the mountain. The locals were on his side but Kay told them no, that they were better than him. So Sam was stretchered by the Feds as none of the locals would look at him. He wailed the whole way down, his cries like a siren ringing in my ears.

When we finally got to the bottom, it seemed like the whole world had come out to see the commotion. Mary ran to Bill, Jenny's parents took the girls and went in the ambulance with them. Jim was there waiting for Kay, tears in his eyes. My father was taken in another ambulance. I stared at him. I wanted to go with him but before I could ask, the doors slammed and it screeched off.

"You can see him later, I promise." Renee squeezed my hand. I didn't have no energy left to argue. As I looked up, I noticed a sea of faces looking at me.

"Good for you, girl," someone shouted.

"Hero, that's what you are," another added.

"Saved the girls, she did!"

"Hero!"

"Savior!"

I wanted to hide behind Renee, I wanted to bury my head. My aching, splitting head.

"'Bout freaking time," Renee muttered under her breath.

My Uncle Abe stepped forward and grabbed me into a hug as if he'd loved me all his life.

"My niece!" he said to the crowd.

I pulled away. Abe had his nose bandaged. Renee had told me why.

"Just milk it," he snapped.

I shook my head. "You're no family of mine. You or Sara."

Abe gripped me into a hug once more and my body tensed—

Get rid of the little witch, that's what we need to do. Yes, get rid of some of the dead rot in this town. Help out the boy, that will be for the best. Yes, the boy needn't do it alone.

I dropped to the ground with the vision. The realization hit me, sucking the breath right out of me.

Abe scowled at me. "Cut it out. Stand up. What the hell are you doing now?"

Frei and Renee were at my side, placed their hands on my arms, and helped me back to my feet.

"What is it?" Renee asked.

Focus on Frei. Focus. You need to tell her. I blinked a few times, waggling my finger in my ear. The nauseating high-pitched sound made her face swim in front of mine. "You said he couldn't do it alone."

She frowned. "I did but we have—"

"It's Sara."

Everyone turned to look at Sara. Gasps and muttering rippled through the crowd.

Sara stared at them and put her hands out. "Oh come on, you all know she's a freak. As if I would—"

Summoning every ounce of energy I had left, I stormed forward and slapped her clean across the face. "You did that to your own family."

Abe grabbed my arm but I shook him off and threw myself onto Sara. We slammed to the ground. I didn't care. The puddles, the mud, the crowd. I didn't care. I gripped hold of her shoulders and rammed her down. I wanted to grip her neck and squeeze the life out of her. I wanted her to know what she'd done. What pain she'd caused so many other families.

"What did he promise you? Huh?"

Sara kicked, squealed, her nails digging into my hands as I pinned her in place. "Freak!"

"What did he tell you? Did he tell you he loved you? Did he bat those eyes? Was it worth it?" I shook her with every word. "Was. It. Worth. It?"

"Yes!" she screamed out, her eyes glinting.

The crowd gasped. Hands hauled me off her before I did wring her neck. She lay panting on the ground. "You should have seen you all." She roared with laughter. "So easy. It was so easy."

Kay charged forward.

Frei put a hand on her arm. "Get her out of here."

Sara giggled manically as she was hoisted off the ground and thrown, head first, into the back of a police car.

Abe shook his head. "Tramp."

Was that it? Was that all he had to say?

"Aeron, leave it." Renee dragged me away before I could say anything and took me to another police car.

"We need to get you checked out," she said, wiping the rain-sodden hair from my eyes.

Not paying her much attention, I fixed my glare on Abe. He was being consoled by someone. He lapped up the attention.

"Nothing the river won't fix." Maybe I could "heal" him too.

Renee pulled my face down to look at her. "If you haven't noticed, we're in the middle of a monsoon." She stared into my eyes. "No river drowning for you."

"But—"

"No." Renee opened the door and pushed me down by my head until I sat. "No buts." She picked up my legs and placed them into the car then turned to Skip. "She goes to the hospital and doesn't leave until she's been seen. Got it?"

"Yes, ma'am."

"I'll be there as soon as I can." She knelt beside the car. "I won't be long."

"Promise?" My voice sounded feeble and pathetic.

Her eyes filled with gentle affection. "Promise."

"Doctor Llys, get your ass over here. Now."

She sighed at Frei's bark and got to her feet.

"Coming." She rolled her eyes. "There was a please in there somewhere, I'm sure."

She shut the door and I heard her tap on the roof. The vehicle rumbled and bumped onto the road.

I shivered, feeling cold now I was away from her. I stared out the back window. Renee was striding toward Frei. I rubbed my arms, the bumps raising all the way along them. I hadn't even realized it was raining. Now I was cold and so far beyond exhaustion that my brain felt as though I'd eaten too much candy. I knew that I wouldn't be able to sleep even if I'd wanted to.

The lights of the town faded as the squad car headed out onto the highway. My heart ached with the loss of a friend as much as the horror he'd caused. Sam. I'd taken the sword that I'd been given and stabbed him so deep that he'd never recover from it.

Skip was silent. He kept his eyes focused on the road ahead as his radio hummed some kind of jazz tune. I looked in the rear-view mirror. The cloud was gone now, gone for good. But at what cost?

If this was winning, it sure as hell wasn't the same as they showed in movies. I didn't feel like I'd saved anyone. Instead, I'd just ripped out the only shred of humanity Sam had owned. I'd held his heart and crushed it.

That made me no better than him.

I felt something beside me and turned. I wasn't alone in the back seat no more. Mari sat there and smiled, the wounds that Sam had inflicted on her faded before my eyes. Then Natalia appeared. I tensed, but she didn't howl with rage or scream in agony. No, she smiled too. Then Darcy, then Chelsea, then Jenny, and finally Mrs. Casey. Each one of them nodded to me.

As they started to fade, my breath caught. Jake, little Jake Casey sat beaming at me, his eyes so full of hope, peace, and love. I burst into tears at the sight of him. It had been so long. He was just the same, just like I'd remembered him. He looked so . . . so . . . happy.

I reached out to touch him, his hand moved through mine. He giggled, oh how I missed that sound, and it lifted my heart. He wasn't scared of Sam, he wasn't chained by the cloud no more. I realized that was what I'd done for them all, I'd freed them, I'd set them free.

Jake held onto his mother's hand and the others reappeared for just a moment, a brief affirming moment.

"Thank you," they whispered in a strange slow slur. "Thank you."

Chapter 78

RENEE WOKE UP and stared at a strong cup of black coffee under her nose. She looked up at Frei and nodded thanks. Her back creaked and cracked as she stretched. The sound of the beep, beep of the heart monitor soothed her.

When she had gotten to the hospital, she'd been told that Aeron had been taken into surgery. Thankfully, the procedure had been to reset her jaw and she'd suffered no head or neck injuries. Still, Renee hated the thought that Aeron would need metal in her mouth until it healed. She looked at Aeron's bruised face and tried not to think how close Sam had come to harming her.

"How is she?" Frei sat watching her from the other side of the room. Normally, she wouldn't bother with hospital visits or even ask about a POI once they were done. Renee cocked her head. Maybe Miss Ice Queen herself had a soft spot for their little Missourian.

Breathing in the rich aroma, Renee smiled. Frei didn't do cheap coffee. "Considering she was nearly strangled to death, fell off a dirt bike, and had her jaw smashed. She's great."

Frei frowned. "The op took a while. It should have been shorter." She got up and took the charts off the end of Aeron's bed. "Under observation for concussion." She flicked through the pages. "Not surprising."

Renee sipped the coffee, knowing Frei didn't expect her to say anything.

Frei tutted her way through the charts, returned to her seat, and picked up her coffee. "Lilia wants to know if you're coming back." She stared into the Styrofoam cup.

"She's so clued up. Why doesn't she tell me?" Lilia and Frei had played her, they'd used her fears and weaknesses. She'd thought of Lilia as a mentor, a hero, and Frei, hell Frei was meant to be the closest thing she had to a friend. How could they do that to her?

"You know it doesn't work like that." Frei stretched out her shoulders and glanced at Aeron as the machine beep missed a beat. "Besides, you knew I was on your side."

Renee sighed. Did she? No doubt Frei had helped her out in city hall and had no doubt backed her up by ordering an SOS. It was an order they almost never used. Sam, even as dangerous as he was, didn't warrant it. An SOS was bordering national security level. "Did I?"

"I don't do nice." She sipped at her coffee. "But, I'll always have your back."

From Frei that was a glowing stamp of approval. Renee took a long drink from her cup to hide her smile. "Did you get the evidence on Sara?"

Frei twitched her eyebrows in a "You think?" look. "Apart from the very public confession?" She nodded. "Her husband gave us everything we needed. He'd bought a van for the deliveries but it had been stolen." The corner of her lips twitched. "Or so Sara said. It was pretty much covered in both their DNA."

Aeron had nearly been framed for it all. Sam had nearly completed a perfect plan. Renee watched Frei sit there like she was on guard duty—the woman never seemed to sleep or tire or get emotional about anything. Oddly, she found that comforting. Frei was always Frei—stoic, cold, efficient. A machine. A dependable machine. "How did you know it was him?"

No matter how Renee had tried to figure it out, she couldn't understand how the CIG team had gone from thinking Aeron was the Unsub to the truth. "Nine-eight-four." Frei's tone told her that, no doubt, someone felt her wrath. "We found his badge on the floor. It was his number."

Renee closed her eyes. "Why didn't the team look at that?"

"They did." Frei drained her cup. "But Sam Casey had an alibi for every murder."

Renee snapped her eyes open. "Who?"

Frei crushed the cup in her hand, her blue eyes sparking. "Sara, and his mother."

Renee looked at Aeron who was still out from the anesthetic. "And Jake's death?"

"I got our forensics on it, and Sam pretty much confessed to the whole thing." She nodded. "Aeron's a free woman."

Renee smiled and leaned back in her chair. "About freaking time."

"Now we just have to convince her to join us." Frei's matter-of-fact tone didn't make it any less jarring.

"What?" Were they completely unhinged? Aeron? Why would she want to join them? They'd thought she was capable of murdering young girls for a start.

Frei gave Renee one of *those* looks that normally meant "duh?" "Why do you think Lilia took a back seat?" Frei got up and walked out of the room.

Renee stared after her. Was she serious?

How much she wanted Aeron to join her in CIG—her heart thudded at the thought—but what if Aeron didn't want that? She'd been through so much. She had to come to terms with so much. What right did they have to demand she join the cause too?

Being part of CIG wasn't something a person did for an easy life, or *any* life at all. It was an unnoticed, unappreciated endless battle to help, stop, or rescue people from events that hadn't even happened yet.

For Renee it had been a conscious decision, knowing all that it entailed—well, most of it—but then if all she'd seen in recent months hadn't convinced her that no one held all the pieces of the puzzle, she wasn't sure what would.

Renee brushed the hair from Aeron's forehead. She was such a hero, such a pure-hearted soul—Renee sighed—and she was in way over her head.

She sat back, careful not to wake Aeron, and pulled a crumpled envelope from her pocket. *Dr. Serena Llys—No peeking, Shortstop.* She smiled at it and pulled out the letter from Nan.

> *Dear Renee, (an' yes, I sure as shoots know who you are.)*
>
> *Now I know that you ain't used to things not being logic and reason but I know that you got the gray cells to get what I'm telling you in this note.*
>
> *My Shortstop is real special and I know that you got it bad for her. I ain't the worldly sort but I know what I seen in my visions. We both know that the dimwit ain't got one iota of how she feels and after everything is all tied up an' toasted, she's gonna need some time to figure out that she ain't made of stone.*
>
> *You got to give her that time to realize she has a place in the world, that she is important. She's got*

to figure it out all on her own. She's got to learn she is worthwhile again. Careful how you handle her though, cos she's got a lot going on in that dimwitted head and if you say too much, she'll just bolt like her mother.

Renee skipped over the section where Nan talked about the storms and the murders. She'd read and re-read the note a thousand times since Aeron had given it to her and every time it had given her goose bumps. Here was a woman that she had never met talking to her through words like she was an old friend.

At first, the letter had terrified her. She'd ignored the rest and focused on the storms, on the murders, on something she could grasp but over the nights locked in with Aeron after the tornado—and every one since—she had turned to the words to help keep her steady and strong.

Nan even talked about after, about now. At first Renee hadn't understood but today as she sat there, listening to Aeron's steady breathing, the words spoke to her so deeply and she would cling to them—in hope—that Nan was right.

Now, when Shortstop has realized her gifts mean she can't just sit an' play her fiddle all day, everything is gonna change in her world an' yours.

It ain't gonna be easy and I can tell you clear as crystal that it ain't gonna be smooth but you know better than for me to tell you that your paths are as twisted together as a wicker basket.

So, just stick with it—an' her—an' you'll get there.

You're a good 'un an' I know you'll listen, so take care of my Shortstop cos she's real precious to me.

Nan xxx

Renee smiled at the words and wiped a tear from her eye. God, she hoped it would all work out but she really couldn't see how Aeron would want to join CIG, an organization that would steal the very freedom she'd just secured.

Renee tried not to worry, tried to keep faith that somehow Aeron might realize, might feel *something*. She turned over the letter to put it back in the envelope and spotted a line of text she hadn't seen before.

PS I couldn't have picked anyone better to protect her myself. So quit fretting already.

"Thank you," Renee whispered to the empty room, "that means a lot."

A gust swept around her. Renee looked up and saw that the windows and door were shut tight and for the first time it didn't scare her.

Renee continued to watch Aeron sleep. The beep of the heart monitor as steady as a clock ticking. If there was one thing she'd learned, it was to trust in the things she couldn't see.

Chapter 79

BILL MARCHED INTO the town hall and was pretty pleased with the turnout. He wasn't sure how much he could rally everyone and he, Kay, and Jim had worked tirelessly to convince the town. It had taken some doing, even though Aeron should be hailed as a hero.

Bill figured if she'd been in the military, she would have more medals than space but the townsfolks' minds weren't easily changed.

Bill glanced at Mary who sat begrudgingly with their son on her lap. She was sucking lemons at the moment but after what she did to Aeron, she could scowl and mutter all she liked. He knew she would too. One thing about the daft crow he knew was that she loved him, same as he loved her. So Mary would do what it took to climb back out of the mutt house and into his affections again.

"Y'know why you're here, so I'll cut straight to the point," he began in his best impression of a politician. "We messed up big time and it's up to us to set it right."

"She brought it on herself," Mrs. Stein heckled from the back.

Bill folded his arms. "Ain't you in church every Sunday?"

"Sure am," she yelled back.

He opened his arms out to the crowd. "Then you been sleepin' through the whole thing?"

The crowd laughed and Mrs. Stein muttered darkly but shut up. *There's a first time for everything,* Bill thought.

"Now, you seen the plans and I know a lot of you are strugglin' yourselves at the moment."

"That's talking pretty light," one of the guys yelled.

"You can say that again," another added.

Bill raised up his hands. "I know, but we can do this." He summoned his best grin. "And maybe, if we work together, we can fix ourselves up as we go?"

There were a few skeptical looks, a few "no way am I doin' that," and a few nods. It was a start at least.

"Where we gonna get the money from?" someone called out.

Bill looked at the doorway. Agent Black had introduced him to Lilia a couple of days ago. Agent Black had said that Lilia waltzing in would give them the answers they needed. Bill wasn't sure how but after seeing Aeron at work, he was good as ready to believe anything.

"Ma'am?" He held out his arm to welcome her and Lilia strode out onto the stage. Some people gasped and stared at her wide-eyed. Bill wondered if some movie star had just wandered onto stage. He furrowed his brow, she did look kinda familiar. There was something about her that made him feel like he'd met her already.

"I don't need introductions. So I'll make this clear." Her tone was warm but pretty clear she wasn't fooling around. "As all your properties are on my land, I'll foot the bill."

Bill folded his arms across her chest. She had a pretty neat ride and some kind of fancy clothing. *No shootin'*, he thought. *She owns the damn place.*

"On one condition . . ." Lilia looked at Bill.

He rubbed his crew cut. "What condition is that, ma'am?"

Mrs. Stein barged forward, her eyes as scrunched up and mean looking as always. "You show your face and think we'll just forget you ran off and left."

Lilia's smile made Bill feel a little warm all over as she peered down at the dotty old bat. "Yes, Aunt Gertie. I do."

He opened his mouth, then closed it, then opened it again. Huh? "She's related to you?"

Lilia smiled at him and squeezed his shoulder. "For my sins." She turned back to the crowd. "The condition is this. All the houses will be designed and built to withstand storms. If your property is near the river, we can work around it so you're not getting flooded every year."

"You rolling in it?" someone called. "'Cause I ain't seen no gold."

The crowd agreed. Bill had to too. It sounded like it would cost a pretty penny. Sure, she looked pretty rich but enough to fund the whole of the repairs?

With a knowing smile, she seemed to charm everybody in the room. "Now I've recuperated the money the mayor has been embezzling. That will more than cover your expenses."

He what? Bill scowled. The Casey men were a sure-fire pain in the ass. What a load of crooks. First Sam, then his father. *Good freakin' riddance.*

Kay stood up and Lilia smiled at her warmly.

"Ma'am, I don't really know who you are." Kay shrugged. "But you sure as hell look like Aeron."

Several people laughed. Bill and Kay looked at each other in confusion. What was so funny?

Kay cleared her throat. "See, Aeron . . . well . . . She kinda promised the Toughtons—"

"That she would pay for his operation?" Lilia said in a soft voice

Kay's face softened and she nodded. She motioned to Frank and Maggie Toughton. Maggie took Frank's hand, her eyes intense. Bill wasn't sure how Aeron could help nobody with money. It wasn't like she was rich or nothing. Why had she promised it?

"Aeron will keep her promise." Lilia held Kay's eyes. "And I will pay for Jim to see that specialist she suggested."

"You will?" Kay just stood there, blinking at her.

Lilia smiled and Bill couldn't help but smile with her. The woman was like a warm summer's day.

"The Lorelei family always keep their word."

Bill finally twigged. "Damn, you're her mom?" That's why she was so familiar. "Figures."

The crowd chuckled and he took that moment to rally them. "So who's with me?"

The roar of affirmation was so loud that Mrs. Stein covered her ears.

Chapter 80

I CAME AROUND feeling like my jaw had been set in concrete and spent most of that week sucking my food through a straw. Renee had been in the room with me most of the time, and I'd had to pretty much force her to go and get some rest. I knew that she was trying to keep me from thinking too much. Thinking 'bout Sam, thinking 'bout all he'd done. Thing was, I blamed myself. There was nothing she could really say that would make that any better. No matter how much she tried, no amount of words would really heal the wounds he'd inflicted because of me.

One thing that kept me from needing a permanent visit to Serenity was my father. He was up and about, his leg set and his throat healing. He was lucky not to have snapped his neck, Renee told me. I was thankful for that thick ol' rind of his for the first time.

He'd been in to see me a few times but as he could only croak and I wasn't much better, we'd sat in silence. The only time he had spoken, he'd told me he was sorry. Sorry that he'd never said nothing about Lilia and sorry that he'd messed up so bad. I'd tried to tell him that it weren't his fault but I guessed we had come out of the same tree and if I was feeling responsible, nothing I said would make him feel no different.

Seeing his injuries made me want to hate Sam. I wasn't sure why I didn't but I couldn't, same as Sara. Sure, I hated what they did—I really hated it—but hate them? I guess I just wasn't capable of it.

So, with nothing better to do, I sat there stewing, staring out at the top of a green tree and trying to block out the nurses' aching feet, an elderly lady's desperation as she tried to find her dentures, and the woman next door's infatuation with the junior doctor. Good thing I'd been in a mental institution already or I would have thought I was crazy.

The door opened and I lifted myself up ready to give Renee an ear-bashing for not resting. I stared at a woman in my doorway. She was me, or an older, more ladylike version at least. Even the hair. That's why my father couldn't bear to look at me. We were like clones. Heck, I was so much like Lilia that it was a mirror image. Sure, it was a freaky funhouse mirror but wow, it was unreal.

"Can I come in?" she asked, hovering in the doorway.

I shrugged. My brain warred with my heart. I mean, this was my mother, my real mother, the woman who gave me life, the one who I was bonded to in gifts and some pretty strong genes. But she was my *absent* mother. She weren't my mom. She was just somebody I had known nothing about, a mother who had abandoned me and sat back while I went through hell, alone. Renee had said she saw stuff, so did she know? Had she seen what damage her running off had done? Could she see how much it had crushed my father?

Still darkening the doorway, she hesitated. "Your jaw looks better."

I shrugged again. I hadn't seen my jaw. To me it was twice the size of Blackbear and not half as pretty.

This woman, this stranger, walked in and sat in the visitor chair. "When you were a child, I saw something that forced me into a choice." She stared out of the window. "I could either ignore it, stay with the family I loved." She met my eyes. "And I still adore." She flicked her eyes away again. "Or I could stop the horrific from happening."

I cleared my throat, which felt like I'd swallowed a cactus. Talking weren't easy with the metal in my jaw. "Renee said you stop things happening."

"Not quite," Lilia said. "I learned long ago that I must never tamper with fate, only heed its warnings."

I looked down at my hands, picked at my fingers, wondering how much I'd see if I touched her, how much she had held back from me. Would I finally see the truth?

"That's what the group does. I see a person who is instrumental in an event—"

"The center of the storm?" Trying not to glare at her, I picked away. Norah had picked back in the institution. I had told her off for it so many times. Had Lilia seen that? Had she let me spend over a decade of my life in there and done nothing?

"The center of the storm, yes. I'm not sure what they are doing there, or why." She was trying to catch my eye but I didn't want to look at her. "But I know that they are either the cause, the victim, or the one who breaks its grip."

It sounded about as useful as my gifts were. It sounded like she was grasping in the dark. I didn't like it. Going in blind and messing around with folks' lives didn't seem right or fair.

"That's what the CIG team does." She leaned forward, crossing her legs all ladylike. Guess we weren't clones in mannerisms. "Renee protects the person while the others try to discern what role they play and what will happen."

It sounded dumb, even if Renee was a hero. What was she doing with those people? "May as well hang seaweed out to predict rain."

My mother met my eyes, I expected her to argue but she smiled. I was irritated with myself for responding to it. One, 'cause it hurt like hell to smile and two, 'cause she didn't deserve a smile. "That's why we need someone who can read people."

I lay my head back and closed my eyes. This must be some kind of a delusion. Mothers, even long lost ones who'd just up and left, would maybe engage in small talk or ask forgiveness.

But no. Here was my mother, my betraying, abandoning, lying mother sitting in my room and trying to guilt me into being what? Another her? "I don't mess with stuff. I'm done seeing." That sounded like I was in kindergarten.

"It doesn't work like that, Aeron."

Uh uh, she didn't get to use that "I'm your mother" tone with me. No way. Iris had tried it and gotten nowhere, like hell was Lilia. "Doesn't it? The only thing I'm planning on doin' is gettin' in the car with Renee and heading the hell out of here." I glared at her. "An' as far away from you as I can get."

I wasn't shocked by the bitterness in my voice but I was shocked at how much I wanted to hurt my mother back. At how much I wanted her to feel all she'd put me and my father through.

"Renee will be back at work as soon as I ask her to be," she said. Curt, cutting, and pretty much like Frei. Who the hell did these people think they were?

"She promised me." I folded my arms. Renee would do like she promised. She would. She said so.

My mother smiled again, like I hadn't snapped at all. "Renee is an agent first, and above everything else."

Short of sticking my fingers in my ears to block her out, I made do with picking the blanket. "No, Renee ain't. Did you miss that part? Miss the bit where she is desperate to see her mom?" I hung on the word mom, just so she realized what real mom's made their kids feel. "Do you know that she has been so many people that she doesn't know who the hell she is no more?" These people didn't care about nobody and I didn't want Renee nowhere near them.

Lilia tilted her head. "Renee is a wonderful agent and an incredible woman." She ran her nails over her skirt and picked strands off it. "That's our problem. We don't have anyone like you. You see through covers and lies, you see the truth. I see pictures of the future."

Yeah right. "You see a bunch of symbols and try to figure out what they mean."

She sighed. "We're a lot more alike than you realize—"

"We ain't nothing alike."

She reached across the bed and touched my hand.

I didn't want to leave, I would have given anything, but I could see them, feel the fear, the screams, I couldn't ignore it . . . Dan listened to me. He headed off to his people . . . they were waiting on the tracks, the medics at the ready when the train left it. I had the choice . . . let them live or die . . . but I'd seen it for a reason.

Telling Dan meant I had to leave, I had to leave my baby, my love . . . I had to go far away from them, never tell them, never contact them. I had to watch him marry other women, watch my baby in someone else's arms. The only person who really knew where I was, Nan, vowed never to speak another word as it broke her heart in two.

I had to . . . I made that choice. I stand by that choice.

"I don't expect you, or your father, to ever forgive me."

I was reeling. I could see the vision she'd had, like mine but of the future. She'd been terrified and it had driven her almost to madness. Telling my father's best friend, a man who she knew worked for CIG, had been the biggest risk of her life. She'd risked everything, but on that train, hurtling off the track was a young man. That man had made a breakthrough in science. That breakthrough had saved hundreds of thousands of lives around the world.

She'd done it to save lives. Would I have done that? Would I have left? What the hell kind of a curveball was that for life to throw at you? "Why couldn't you say nothing?"

Eyes still locked on the imaginary fluff she was picking off her skirt, she sighed. "The people I see. Persons of Interest—"

"Yeah, I heard Renee mention POIs."

My mother smiled. "Well, they can be anyone, from someone important to the future of society, a mass murderer, a criminal, or a normal average everyday person who just happens to do something extraordinary."

"It's nice to know I was under the murderer marker . . . thanks, *Mom*."

My mother shook her head. "I never believed you would harm another soul for a second. If I thought you would, Renee would not have approached you."

Not sure if I bought that. I narrowed my eyes at her. "I thought she was a rough and tough agent."

My mother's nod was so enthusiastic that I couldn't help but smile. Darn it. "Oh, she is." Her gaze drifted to the window again. "But I made a mistake once and she will live with the scars for the rest of her life. Never again."

My stomach did a back flip into my throat. "Scars?"

"I want you to think about what I have said." Her changes of subject sure as shoots weren't subtle. "Aeron, you could save more lives than you realize."

Two could play at that. "Have you spoken to Dad?" Take that one. Hah.

She shook her head, her eyes narrowed. "No, and I won't either." Her lips twitched in a smile. "I can't until I know what you're going to do."

Oh that was sneaky, throw it out there and wait for the bite. "Why?"

Again, a smile, a challenge in her eyes. "I'm not going to tell you."

I grabbed her hand. The truth hit me like a crowbar. In short, if I didn't go, my mother would have to stay with the team. If I didn't go, my father and my half-sisters would have to go it alone.

"I thought you weren't using your gifts anymore?"

Sneaky, conniving . . . "I don't get why." Why couldn't she see them? Folks knew who she was in Oppidum. "I don't understand."

"We're dealing with fate, with nature." Her eyes sparkled with her belief in the cause. "I believe we're being guided, I truly do, but the team, no matter how skilled, they can't go it alone." Her sad smile said it all. "One of us needs to be there."

What the heck kinda use would I be? "But I can't see the future."

Again her eyes narrowed.

I folded my arms. "Can't."

She pursed her lips. She had perfected the "You're not being truthful, are you?" look that Nan had worn so often. "You *can* but not like me. I will still give you the cases but from here."

That gave me a lot of choice. "So, you'll stay, raise the girls?"

"I missed out on you, so yes." It sounded like she meant it, the truth even shimmered from her but I still found it hard to believe.

I looked out of the window. "And Dad?"

Her aura lit up as she smiled. I guessed she felt as lost without him as he had without her. "I'll make sure he never worries again. Promise."

I laughed, a helpless beaten laugh. What could I do? What could I say to that? No? I didn't want to go hiding who I was, I didn't want to play around with peoples' lives, hoping that I was helping. What was the use? She'd probably seen our conversation before it happened anyhow. "I guess I was never going to be free, was I?"

My mother's eyes flickered with guilt and pain. Sure, I was mad at her but I couldn't say I wouldn't have done the same thing. What choice had either of us had?

Maybe I was just a sucker but I couldn't sit there and make her feel worse. "Can I at least take Renee back to see her mother first. She needs a vacation."

The light shone back into her eyes. "Of course." She squeezed my knee through the blanket. "Sometimes the visions take months anyway."

I touched my jaw. It was aching with more than just the operation now. It was aching with the responsibility I'd just heaped onto my shoulders. From one institution to another. At least I wouldn't be in orange. "Then I guess it's a deal."

Chapter 81

ELI PAID THE cab driver and hobbled up his driveway. His head was so full his brain felt squashed in. He hadn't been back since Jenny had been killed and the front door still had crime scene tape plastered across it. He ripped it off and opened up the door to the dark stain on the floor.

"Oh, hell."

He threw the tape down and slumped onto the front step. He couldn't bear to go in, he couldn't even look at the place.

Jenny had been leaving him, she hated Aeron and he was sure she hated him but her death left his emotions in some kind of deep freeze. They'd parted on the worst terms. She'd gone against his advice to stay at her mother's and the last thing he'd thought about her before the attack was "good riddance."

That resentment hadn't changed, and he hadn't loved the girl. He rubbed his hand over his face. Why the hell had he married her? He should have seen what Casey was, he should have stopped him. Jenny's death nagged at his conscience. His girls would grow up without their mother, just like Aeron had. Jenny had been a good mother. So why didn't he feel a thing? He should be distraught, she was his wife, the mother of his children. Why didn't it tear him apart? He rubbed the bridge of his nose. He felt odd. That was the only way to describe it. He felt out of touch with the world, with himself.

He knew what the reason was too. Stupidly and selfishly he felt it cleared the way for some hopeful reunion with Lilia. It always came back to that infernal woman. She was alive, she was out there, she owned his heart and he was pretty sure half of his being. It didn't matter that she'd run out on him, that she was a betraying, deserting, heart-breaking vixen who probably hadn't given him a thought. If she was in town, she hadn't been to see him and if that wasn't a clear message, he didn't know what was.

Growling up at the sky, he tried not to think of her, to banish her from his thoughts but that little voice kept on talking. Lilia

could come back, she was under the same sky that he was. The
fact she'd gone and left him years ago didn't seem to bother his
foolish heart. There was a chance.

Eli put his head in his hands. What kind of man was he?
His wife had just been murdered by Sam Casey, his girls were
traumatized, Aeron was due out of hospital any day but his
thoughts were on Lilia.

"An idiot," he told himself. "A complete idiot."

"Still talking to yourself, huh?"

Eli's heart nearly leaped out of his mouth and hopped down the
road. "Lilia?"

He didn't trust himself to look up, his body shivered with his
nerves. Oh hell, she was right there.

He felt her sit beside him, making him feel the way only she
could, simply by being there. He stared at his hands and picked at
the skin on his finger. She was there, she was really there.

"You passed on your habit. She does the same."

Eli picked a little more, not sure he could trust his voice, not
sure he could trust himself. He wasn't a strong man, the last
few months had confirmed it. He was a poor excuse for a father,
husband, and he'd been the police chief in a town ripped to pieces
by his own deputy.

Long, elegant fingers smoothed down over his hands and
stopped him. "Don't beat yourself up."

Eli fought the tears in his eyes. He was not going to weep but
the emotion pushed at him till he felt he was going to burst. He
sucked in the air. He would not cry.

"I told Aeron why I left." Her fingers lingered over his—long
elegant fingers. "I told her and I'll tell you."

Eli stared at the hands he'd seen in his memory every single
night, the beauty of the woman he'd tried and failed to forget. He'd
loved her ghost as much as he'd loved the woman. It didn't seem
to matter that she was here, next to him, he still didn't believe it.
He was too scared to.

Lilia, *his* Lilia, *here* next to him, her hands linked with his, her
voice in his ear, her smell. She smelled the same, she smelled like
the summer blooms and lavender.

"Do you remember the Amtrak crash?"

Who didn't? It had been big news. "That scientist was on it,
talks about a guardian angel."

"Eddie Carmichael, he was twenty one at the time."

Eli wasn't sure why they were talking about small things, when there was so much to say but any words, any moment with her, even if he looked up and she faded, he'd take it.

"I saw him, Eli." Her hands drew gentle circles over his. Her voice so much like home that his heart hammered with it. Don't cry. Don't cry. "I saw the train."

Eli closed his eyes, trying to force the tears not to fall, breathing as deep and slow as he could.

"I went to Dan. I had to leave when they knew. I couldn't come home."

Eli let out a choked breath, his throat raw. "You should have said—"

"I couldn't. You know that Dan never even got to see his mother."

His anger jarred at him. How could Dan do that? His own friend? He knew how Eli felt about her and he'd taken her away anyhow. Traitor. "The poor woman died of heartbreak." His anger bubbled. "I know how she felt."

The smell of summer wafted into his nostrils again as Lilia leaned on his shoulder, her silky hair fell over his forearm. He looked up to the sky, anything not to look into those eyes, into her face. Please, don't cry. Keep it together.

"I watched over you. I mourned as you did." She sighed and his heart ached worse than before Aeron had fixed it. "I had to go."

Eli nodded. What could he say? To hell with the world and Doctor What's-his-name, you should have been with me? He didn't care about rules or the CIG. He had died the day that she left. What good would it do? What did it matter now?

He had managed to destroy everything he'd touched and there was no hope she would come back. This was goodbye. A parting torture to torment the rest of his days.

"You should see Aeron," he managed, although his voice had a wobble a mile wide.

"She told me the same thing about you." Lilia chuckled.

Oh hell, not the laugh. Anything but her laughter. Eli's tears trickled down his cheeks as he stared up into the blue sky. He couldn't take this. His heart couldn't take it.

"She's joining CIG."

A sob fell from his mouth. He would lose them both now, lose them to secrets and silence. Heroes behind closed doors. Heroes he would never see again.

"She won't have to stay away, Eli. She can come home."

How could he watch them leave, how could he say goodbye all over again? "Why would she want to? After everything? She must be itching to get gone."

Lilia pulled his face gently around to look at her. Amber eyes of warmth—lines where she'd laughed a million times and he wasn't there to hear it. A line in her forehead, where she'd frowned a million times and he wasn't there to soothe her. A wisp of gray in her hair, where she'd worried alone for long lonely years and he wasn't there to hold her.

Lilia was so beautiful, her clothes so elegant, her skin tanned as always. It was torture, sweet, savage torture.

Helpless to stop himself, he touched her hair, still silk under his fingers, her cheek still soft under his touch. She turned a little, kissed his palm, her hand holding his to her.

He felt the wedding ring and saw it was the one he'd given her. She'd never taken it off by the look of it. It seemed as bonded to her hand as she was to his heart.

Eli pulled out the gold chain from round his neck, a chain he'd worn even when another woman's ring was on his finger. A chain she'd given him when they were all of fourteen. Lilia's eyes twinkled in the sunlight as the tears spilled down her cheeks. Eyes that had seen a lifetime without him.

"How long do you have?" he asked, not wanting to know but needing to.

Lilia took his face in her hands, leaned in close, and whispered the words he'd dreamed of, prayed for, begged on his knees to hear fall from her lips. "The rest of our lives."

Chapter 82

I LEFT THE hospital nearly a month after. The doctors needed to fix pretty much every part of me from my run-in with Sam. Normally, I would have been allowed home a lot quicker but the doctors weren't happy that I was living in a tent.

Renee picked me up in her shiny new car. She'd already brought in more clothes. Clothes, which she told me my mother had paid for, and so I had my first pair of fitting jeans in well over a decade. I don't much care for fashion or appearances but I had to say it felt good not to be walking around in work clothes. Neither of us had talked much about what had happened in the pump house. Renee had kept her silence and I'd kept mine. I thought she was letting me process it, then I guessed that she was probably doing the same thing.

The silence was pretty awkward as we drove down the highway. I could feel that she wanted to talk but for some reason didn't. She drummed her fingers on the wheel as she glanced at me, and I guessed it was gonna have to be me who went first.

"So, what did you decide?" She didn't know nothing about Lilia coming to see me but if Lilia had been right then Renee was CIG through and through.

I could see her worry, her sadness pouring off her. "I don't know what else to do with my life, Aeron."

The highway was pretty quiet, the sunlight bounced off the windshields of the cars that we passed. There was something cheery about the lush green on either side and I was relieved to see no signs of the cloud. It was just clear deep blue. It was kind of a shame to have Renee feeling so down when it was so beautiful outside. "Why do you have to do somethin' else?"

Renee glanced at me, her scowl so deep that I tensed, making my jaw twinge. Next time, whatever Renee said, I was using the river. "I'll be gone, from here, no contact, not even a phone call."

I rubbed at my aching jaw, definitely the river. "Who you plannin' on calling?"

"Don't be a wiseass." Her tone was nearly as icy as Frei's. Her aura flamed with her words and I couldn't help but smile. She'd been fighting my corner every step of the way.

I didn't get what I'd done to deserve it but I weren't gonna argue. "Would it help if I said my mother roped me in?"

Renee's mouth fell open and she yanked the wheel. I clattered into the door as we swung across the lanes. We were headed straight for a tree as I reached across and pulled the wheel back to the middle, steadying us.

"Sorry," she murmured, taking control back. "Lilia did . . . I mean . . . really . . . you joined CIG?"

I wouldn't so much say joined as corralled but either way, that's where I was. "She wants me to work out in the field, help you I'm guessin'." I shrugged. "Well, more like you rescuin' me."

Renee's grin matched the smile in her eyes. "You're not kidding? You wouldn't joke about that, would you?"

"Not unless I had a death wish." I thumbed to the tree we'd nearly gotten acquainted with.

"Are you sure, Aeron?" Her gray eyes were so wide that I could see the flecks of darker blue around her pupils. "I mean, with the life." She turned back to the road, thank Blackbear. "It's not easy." Her hands were tight on the wheel. "What about your freedom?"

"I never had it. An' the only taste I got . . . Well, I was miserable." Fussing with the hem of my new t-shirt, I felt dumb. "There is . . . well . . . another reason."

"What's that?"

I couldn't look at Renee. She'd probably think that I needed re-committing. "I'd kinda . . . well . . . I guess . . ." I sighed. "I mean . . . I maybe . . ." I took a deep breath. "I'd miss you if you weren't around." I blurted it like I'd lost control of my mouth. She was staring at me again. I could feel it on my cheek. I cleared my throat. "I mean . . . how would I eat?"

She chuckled and I focused with intent on the sign for Oppidum. "We can't have you go hungry now, could we?"

The joy from her felt like I'd been wrapped in a warm blanket.

Steeling myself, I turned to her. "I did give my mother one condition though."

Renee raised an eyebrow. "Oh, what's that?"

I gripped the wheel—just in case. "We get to have a road trip to the Rockies first."

Chapter 83

OUTSIDE NAN'S CABIN, in the beautiful summer sun, Kay heard Bill cursing from around the corner. She gently lowered her sleeping cargo into the little blue box on the wall and shot a smile at Jim. They were nearly ready, nearly.

"You okay there, Bill?" Jim called out.

"Damn, if I ain't hit my thumb once, I hit it every damn time."

Kay rolled her eyes and kissed Jim on the cheek. Finding little moments to smile wasn't easy. Every single second she thought about her little girl but doing something different, something with Jim, even if he was just shouting out instructions, was keeping them together.

She'd been told by the shrink that a lot of couples didn't make it through losing a child, especially a wonderful, adored child like Chelsea. Kay was sure it was true because in the few days after, until the night Bill rounded them up to go help Aeron, until then, they could barely look at each other. Jim for the guilt he felt, he blamed himself for not watching her every single second. Kay blamed herself for being at work, for leaving her baby at home and heading to the station. Guilt had nearly ripped them apart *but* helping Aeron, helping to catch Sam Casey had done something for them both.

They'd helped Chelsea get justice, together, Jim holding down the fort at the station, keeping the mayor tied up, and Kay heading up Blackbear. Together they'd helped, just a little.

Kay didn't think for a second that they were out of the woods. Neither did she pretend that she would ever get over losing her baby. What mother could? Doing something good instead of letting the grief suck her down was the best way. Chelsea, her little baby wouldn't have wanted it any different.

"I can see a car!" one of the guys yelled.

Kay closed the lid on the box and flashed a smile at Jim. "Quick. Finish up. Down tools."

Bill's bellowing, "You heard the lady!" catapulted everyone into life. There was a manic scramble to tidy and wipe and hammer in the last of the nails before every member of the party hurried, chuckling and hollering to each other, and hid out of sight.

Kay looked at Bill who grabbed hold of Mary as she ducked round the corner.

"Stop screeching, woman. You'll scare the damn squirrel."

Everyone looked at the painted blue box and laughed as the squirrel stuck her head out in annoyance.

Chapter 84

ELI GOT INTO the car, not having a clue where Lilia was taking him. They'd been staying in one of the hotels that hadn't been flattened in town since she'd come home to him. It would have to do for now. He didn't want to go back to the house he'd shared with Jenny. Not now, not ever.

"For the last time, I am not telling you. You're useless at surprises." Lilia started the engine and checked her make-up in the mirror. She didn't need to, she got more beautiful every time he looked at her.

She caught him staring and he smiled. "Some things never change."

Lilia held his gaze and ran a polished nail over his cheek. He sat back and pulled the belt away from his neck.

Lilia frowned and squeezed his knee. "Is it sore?"

He stared out the window. He didn't want to tell her that the belt itself was enough to make him feel faint. The repeated dreams of ropes, of his life wrung out of him, of Sam's laughter, of watching as Aeron fought to save him, the girls, and herself.

"That agent of yours is quite the firecracker." There was no need to talk about the scars now. It was a beautiful day. "Kneecapping Sam. That's some skill."

Lilia's eyes warmed in the same way it did when she spoke of Aeron. Miss Renee Black was dear to her heart. "You should see her hand-to hand skills." Her eyes turned mischievous. "One of the male agents went to take her on in self-defense once." She winced.

He did too. "What did she do?"

Lilia laughed—that heart-warming, soul-lifting laugh that made his stomach wriggle like he was a teenager again. "Let's just say his voice was higher for a few days."

Eli covered himself up and sucked in his breath. Poor guy. "Sounds like Aeron."

Lilia nodded. "One of the many reasons I am so fond of her."

With a smile he looked out of the window. The town was really taking shape again. Builders and contractors from all over the county, and locals were rebuilding Main Street. "Guess you wanted to rebuild faster."

Lilia hummed her agreement as she pulled her sunglasses from her head and slid them on. "We need to get ready for tourist season. At least if we can get the basics done, then people can still earn money."

Eli looked at Casey's Mart and felt a twinge for Mrs. Casey. She'd suffered for so many years in silence at the hands of her husband, only to see her son kill his brother and then turn on her.

"What are you going to do with the shop?"

"Toughtons," she said.

Eli smiled. "You're a good woman."

Lilia laughed again. Eli's heart skipped again.

Lilia pulled past the city hall and their oak tree. The streets faded into country roads and Mrs. O'Reilly's farm sat on the hill in the horizon.

"We going to the cabin?" he asked.

Lilia tutted but did turn down the dirt track, the golden field swayed and danced in the sun.

"Aeron isn't back till later." Why were they were heading there now?

She peered over her sunglasses at him. "Renee picked her up. She'll be a couple of minutes behind us. It'll give us time."

"Time?" Eli looked at Lilia, the mischief in her eyes glinted like jewels. He turned back to the road. "Great Blackbear in a box!"

The cabin looked immaculate. Its odd jutting roof tiled perfectly and uniformly, no sign of the patchwork that Aeron had started. The walls were painted cream, the windows blue trimmed, the sills white and gleaming in the sun's rays. The doorway was painted blue, the flowerbeds trimmed and planted up with pinks, purples, and whites.

Lilia stopped the car.

Eli got out and walked to the cabin, lost for words. Even the water wheel was churning.

Lilia took his hand and led him around the back.

Behind the corn store, Bill, Kay, the Toughtons, Skip, well, most of the town were setting up tables and tents. They turned and waved at him.

Lilia handed him a party hat.

He stared down at it. "You remembered?"

With a chuckle she tapped him on the tip of the nose. "It's not something a mother ever forgets."

Eli smiled and dipped his head for her to tie the band to hold it on. "I'm not sure if she will remember though."

Lilia kissed him and placed her own hat on. "Then maybe it's time we showed her the famous Lorelei tradition?"

Chapter 85

I GOT RENEE to pull over as we reached the end of the road at the turn off to the cabin. I didn't know why, but after the last time—being in the river with my father, the place burned out—I wasn't sure if I could go back. Renee sat on the hood as I walked to the pole that had been replaced—the memories of Renee in the river, the knowledge that Sam had tried to kill her and so nearly had were still strong.

"I'm still here," Renee said from her perch.

I touched the pole and smelled the scent of new wood varnish. The ache of what *could* have happened swamped my mind with guilt. "I think it's best if I go." I couldn't deal with it. "Can we just go, now?"

I turned around.

"Let me just get the camping stuff." She nodded toward the cabin. "Plus, don't you want to check on Mrs. Squirrel?"

I looked down the road. The field I'd sewn was blocked out by the gold of Mrs. O'Reilly's crop. "Can I wait here?"

Renee got off the hood and walked up to me. "What is it?"

I didn't know how to explain. "I've felt so much pain, so much fear. I don't think. . . I just want to run. Can we do that?"

Renee's eyes filled with concern. "Running won't stop the past finding you."

"Then how can I forget? How am I supposed to just carry on when everyone died because of me?"

She rubbed my arm. "You? Aeron this isn't your fault, none of this is your fault."

I hugged myself. That familiar numbness of loss settled over me. The tears that had flowed so freely for a time, now trapped in my stone heart. "He killed them, because of me." I looked at the river. "He rammed you off the road because of me."

"He rammed me off the road . . ." Renee pulled me into her arms and held me tightly. "Because he was damaged. Sam Casey could have flipped at any time."

I wasn't so sure. "He waited for me to come back, bided his time, all those years just waitin'." I closed my eyes, trying to fight the guilt that gnawed at me. It was unbearable.

In the hospital I'd kinda been in limbo, been removed from the devastation left in Sam's wake. Now, I was back here, it battered me, gripped me like a giant fist, squeezed the breath from my body.

"He is ill, Aeron." Renee put her hand on my arm. "You didn't make him ill."

I hadn't told a soul what I'd seen in the pump house. "There was nothing wrong with him."

"What?"

It wasn't something I wanted to let out. It felt so hard to explain. What had Sam been? "You remember I told you—back in the institution—that I could see when folks had things goin' wrong in their head?"

Renee nodded. "When you realized Aimee was lying."

"Yeah, well . . ." How did I explain? "There was no leechin' cloud over his head like Lori, no flickers of someone talkin' to him, no dead areas like the psychos." I shrugged. "There was *nothing* wrong."

Her warm hand on my arm gave me the strength to continue. She knew me, she believed in me. "Sam was plain evil, Renee. That was it, no rhyme or reason, just evil as hell."

Renee took away her hand and I opened my eyes.

She tucked her hands in her pockets for a moment and paced. "Didn't you see a cloud?"

I nodded.

She glanced at me. "So that cloud didn't control him?"

I shook my head.

She stopped pacing and frowned. "Then, what was it?"

I looked up into the big old blue canvas above me, that nasty parasite long gone. "Fear. I realized that there's a big fight goin' on that's way over our heads." It sounded so unreal, so strange to say out loud. "Seems like fear doesn't much like hope. Fear likes to feed off folks till they got nothing left to give."

Renee's eyes veiled much in the same way they always did when I freaked her the hell out. "Fear and doubt?"

I nodded. "Yeah, doubt too. I got it figured that somethin' sure don't want folks to succeed in life." I smiled. "And then somethin' else does."

"Now you sound like you're talking about good and evil."

Maybe it was, maybe it wasn't, it was way too complicated. Even thinking about it tied my mind up in knots. "I got no iota of what it is . . . but I know I just pretty much stuck a target on my back."

"Why?"

I felt a chill wash over my shoulders, which seeming as it was eighty-five degrees, felt a little odd. "All my life, it's like I was being hidden, kept safe, that by being in the institution, I was kinda under the radar."

Renee paced the blacktop again. "And now?"

I looked up at the sky. "Whatever's out there knows, and it ain't happy."

Renee walked to me, chin out, defiant. "Well, that cloud couldn't hurt you. Sam tried to, but I was there. When Mother Nature tried to suck you up, your father was there. Whatever the bad things are out there, there's a hell of a lot more good."

I cocked my head. "That your medical opinion, Doc?"

Renee narrowed her eyes. "Damn straight it is."

I felt like another of Renee's carefully built-up barriers dropped, which forced me to drop one in return.

"I knew what he went through at home," I said, burying my head in her shoulder. "I saw the bruises, I saw Jake's. But I didn't know what to do."

Renee squeezed me tightly. "You were a child, what could you have done?" She rubbed soothing circles over my back. "Honestly, Aeron? After all I have seen of this place, who could you confide in?"

I didn't know. Back then my father wouldn't have listened, would he? Mayor Casey was in control of everything back then too. Even if my father had believed me, he wouldn't have been able to prove a thing. "I should have tried."

Renee pulled back to look at me. "Even if you had, you think Sam would have been any different?"

Would he? Would Sam have been a good husband or father? Even if I'd seen it was him on the track that day, even if I'd been able to prove it, would it have stopped him? The killing would have started when he was released, wouldn't it? Was he always destined to be evil? Were some folks just born that way?

"I guess we'll never know."

Renee led me back to the car. "All you can do is deal with what did happen. It's not going to go away today or tomorrow. Scars take time to heal and sometimes even then, they still show."

I got into the passenger seat. "My mother said you had scars."

Renee's knuckles turned white as she gripped the wheel. I wanted to say sorry, that I hadn't meant nothing by it but she took a few breaths and nodded. "Can I just say that I know what you're going through and I'm going to be there every step of the way?"

I hated how much the past had hurt her. I hated that someone or something had wounded her so bad. "It's probably the best thing you could say."

Renee started the car, and I closed my eyes as we headed down the dirt track. I guessed one last time to look at the place, even in such a state, was best. I did worry about Mrs. Squirrel too. She kind of liked living indoors and popping in and out.

Hell, Nan must be raging at me for trashing generations of hard work.

Renee stopped the car, and I wasn't sure that I wanted to open my eyes. I didn't know how to feel. I felt so unstable, like a weather vane in a tornado, swinging around in circles from one emotion to the next until I was numb from the exhaustion.

Renee squeezed my knee. "Come on, help me. It'll be quicker."

I took a deep breath and opened my eyes.

Now, I don't cuss much but a long line of them fell from my lips as I looked at the cabin.

"Nice," Renee shot at me. "Very ladylike."

"How?" I got out of the car, my jaw although wired up, felt like it was dragging on the ground. "When . . . How?"

Renee took my hand and walked me to the door. She opened it and we walked inside. I blinked around in astonishment. It was as modern and done out as a model home, like the ones I'd seen in magazines.

"Look at that!" I walked to the range cooker in the middle, the set out so different yet so homey and . . . well, fancy.

I ran up the stairs and wandered around in shock. The floors were divided up, partitioned out in some places, the paint smell lingered in my nostrils, the shock, the awe flooded my veins. I found where my old bed had been. Now it was a large room, new windows, big windows looking out across the fields at the back.

At the foot of the biggest bed I've ever seen was Nan's trunk. It had been spruced up same as the rest of the place.

"I . . . How?"

Renee led me out of the cabin and I stopped to look at the wheel, working just fine, the creaking sucked me back into my childhood. No wonder Nan had loved it so much. It reminded me of her, it reminded me of how much I missed her.

"Thanks, Nan," I whispered, getting a gentle breeze tickle my arms in reply.

A scuffling drew my attention and I went to the blue box and picked up the lid. Mrs. Squirrel peered up at me. If I didn't know any better I'd say she'd been worried. I got a lengthy sniff and a swish of her tail.

"Hey there. How's the home?"

Mrs. Squirrel dug about a little and I noticed a round hole in the wall. "What's that?"

"Tunnel, into a box in the house—for the winter," Renee said behind me.

Mrs. Squirrel looked up as if to affirm Renee's words. I smiled when I saw some furry things wriggling in the corner.

"I'll leave you in peace," I whispered, closing the lid.

"Come on, round the back," Renee said.

I frowned. Huh? "Of the cabin?"

She rolled her eyes. "Where else, *Dimwit*?"

I followed her around the corn store . . . "Sweet Blackbear in a box!"

The tears erupted from me. I cried so hard that my breath shuddered, my shoulders juddered. I couldn't control it.

Renee took my arm. "Hey, it's okay. You want to leave?"

I bent and waved off the concerned looks from all the people sitting in party hats. I *couldn't* cry twenty minutes ago. Now I couldn't stop.

"I'll be fine . . . I just . . . I'd forgotten."

Renee rubbed my back in soothing circles. "Happy birthday, Aeron."

I was crying so hard. Why the hell was I crying? That's it, I was losing it. I must have looked completely crazy. Picturing myself hunched over and wailing, I started laughing at myself. Heck, if people hadn't thought I was crazy before, they sure must think it now.

"Just take deep breaths . . . Slow, deep breaths."

I did as Renee told me, feeling some kind of sense return to me.

I glanced up at her. "I've never had a party."

My mother and father waved at me, they looked so happy, like liquid joy was spraying out from them in all directions.

Oh, heck, they looked so sweet. My eyes blurred with more tears. They were gonna take me back to Serenity, I knew it.

Two familiar girls ducked into my view in party dresses, holding gifts.

"Happy birthday," the taller girl said and nudged the younger one who nodded. "Happy birthday, Ire-yon."

"It's Aeron . . . Air-on." I rubbed my tears away and smiled down at them. Considering the hell they'd been through, their auras were full of light.

"Papa says Mamma's gone away," the smallest one said. "That she needed to help the angels."

My heart ached and squeezed in my chest. "Yeah, she's okay though. She's gonna look after you."

"Oh, I know," the little one said. "I see her all the time."

I cocked my head. "You do?"

The older girl scowled and poked her sister. "Lou, cut it. You know Mamma hated that nonsense."

The little one folded her arms. "She does not so." She stamped her feet, making me chuckle. She was kinda cute. "Not no more. She said Aeron would help." Her nose wrinkled up as she concentrated. "And . . . um . . . Lollipop."

"Lilia," the eldest muttered.

I knelt down and took both their hands in mine. Lou's glowed hotter than a fire in wintertime and Ruth's wasn't far behind it. Seemed my mother wasn't the only one with a gift or two. Thankfully, it was just a perception, not a full blown burden.

"Lilia is my mom but she was gone when I was growin' up. So, as you need someone to help you take care of Dad—"

"Papa," Lou corrected.

"Well that Hopalong over there." I pointed at my father and the girls giggled. "How 'bout she helps you?"

Lou folded her arms and stuck out her bottom lip. "Does that mean they're gonna yell now?"

"Lou!" Ruth muttered.

"Ruth!" Lou muttered back.

"Girls, come get your food," my father called.

They kissed me on the cheek before I could object and hurried off, leaving the gifts in my hands.

I got to my feet. Renee nudged my shoulder and walked ahead to the tent. I looked out across all the tables—the Toughtons, the Borlands, the gypsy families with the grandmother, Bill and . . . "Mary?"

"Bill's orders, don't ask," Renee whispered.

There were quite a few of the townspeople there too, some I knew, some I didn't but to my surprise Mrs. Stein was even there, in the back and sour faced as always.

"What did you do, put a spell on them?" I asked my mother as I sat at the table.

Renee plonked a hat on my head and one on her own.

"She's always been grumpy. It's her thing." My mother handed me a present. "I've wanted to say this for so long. Happy birthday."

I put the girls' gifts on the table and took my mother's present. By my father's grin, I knew he had been in on the present too.

I shook the box and stuck my tongue out. I hadn't had presents in . . . well . . . When had I last had a present? "What is it?"

"Tradition," they both answered.

I unwrapped the box and opened it up. I stared at a necklace of solid silver with a picture of someone engraved on it. "What is it?"

My mother pulled it out of the box. "St Christopher's, patron saint of travelers. Nan was given it by her mother and she gave it to mine, then to me." She held it out to me. "Now, it's yours."

I wasn't sure I should touch it. I was terrified I'd get several lifetimes of flashes thudding through my head.

"Just love and protection," my mother reassured me.

I picked it up and felt such a wave of love crash over me, that it chased all the pain away, if even for a moment. Renee helped me put it on. I clutched it in my hand and noticed something inscribed on the back.

"Ephesians?" I asked, reading the passage about armor. Had Nan, my mother—had they all worn the same protection?

"One and the same," my mother said.

My jaw ached as it trembled, my tears threatening yet again.

"See, told you that you were a hero," Renee whispered to me.

I raised an eyebrow at her. "How'd you figure that?"

Renee pointed to the necklace and winked. "All heroes have armor."

Heroes? I was no hero. "That so?"

She folded her arms and gave me a satisfied nod. "Yup."

Her aura danced around like it did when she was in a playful mood.

"I thought heroes did the saving." I pointed to my jaw. "And you were the one in that role." I looked down at myself and chuckled. "Not quite the image of a damsel, am I?"

Renee's eyes twinkled but she said nothing, so I poked her.

"Don't you go picturing me in any dress," I said. "It ain't ever gonna happen."

She had a cheeky glint in her eyes. "Sure about that?"

I narrowed mine at her. "Crystal."

Renee handed me a burger and squirted a flower pattern on the top. "Shame it wasn't pink."

Pink? Now she was asking for it. "Don't think I won't dunk you in the river."

"You'd never catch me." She squirted ketchup at me and hit me in the cheek. "Besides, as the hero I'd more likely dunk you."

I put down my burger and wiped the ketchup off with my fingertip. "You think so?"

Renee backed away from the table. "Oh, I *know* so."

She ran a few feet but I caught her. She struggled but I had a lot longer arms.

"Aeron, now be nice," she warned. "You need me to watch your back, remember?"

She squirmed and I hoisted her off the ground. "In that case maybe we should get you all healed up, huh?"

I carried her to the river as she wriggled like a hooked fish. I could sense everyone watching me but the river was beckoning.

She tried to push away and unclasp my hands but I wasn't letting her go nowhere. "Aeron. Don't you dare."

"Too late." I readied myself to throw her.

She spun in my arms and dropped to her feet. I hurtled over her shoulder as she threw me.

Splash.

I sat in the cold water and spat out the river.

Renee stood on the bank with a smug grin. "You need rescuing?"

I held out my hand. She took it. I grinned. Got you. I gave her hand a yank and heard my sly laugh echo out.

Splash.

She surfaced. Her hair plastered across her face.

"That was sneaky." She flicked her hair back and splashed me.

"I thought you were a doctor," I said with a smile. "You said you could read minds."

She slapped the top of the water and sent it crashing into my face. "Maybe I let you do it."

"I *know* you didn't."

"Thought you couldn't see anything about yourself?"

I opened my mouth and then closed it, which made her laugh as she pulled me to my feet. "Besides I'm a hero, it's my job to know these things."

Her eyes met mine and I pulled her into a soggy hug. "I can't argue with that. I reckon you've proved beyond doubt that you're good at your job."

Chapter 86

THE DAY PASSED by in a blur, I was told of all that Bill and the others had done, how even Mrs. Stein helped out by catering for the workers. I had never felt so loved, so included, so . . . well, happy as I did that afternoon. My birthday, the day my life had begun all those years ago, seemed to have begun all over again that day.

My parents and the girls were going to move into the cabin. Although it was mine, I was happy for them to share it. I wanted the place to be filled with love and laughter, I wanted the girls to know what joy and happiness were. I wanted the walls coated with it and the love flowing through it.

I knew they could do that together.

After much celebrating, the night was nearer morning, the smell of dew hanging in the air, we finally wandered into the cabin to sleep. Renee helped me up the stairs as my head felt like it was on backward with laughter and hope.

Hope, now there was a feeling I didn't know well. It wasn't even hoping for something, just an odd little flicker of optimism that somehow the sun had burst through the clouds in my life. Not that I was expecting an endless summer. No, just a few dry days here and there.

"Y'know," Renee said as we got to my floor, "you never did explain to me how your father healed up his heart. The doctor said it's better than a man half his age."

I tensed and concentrated on getting to the bed without stumbling too much. "Must be Lilia."

"Uh huh." Renee grinned at me and nudged me in the ribs. "So you telling me that you don't know anything?"

I shook my head and nudged her back. "Oh no, I'd never say that."

Renee raised her eyebrow. "And what do you say?"

Her gray eyes twinkled like her aura all over again. It felt so weird how it was hers above everyone else's that enchanted me. Even her eyes, like the color of a stormy sea ringed with the sky on a cloudless day. I couldn't help but wonder why no one had tied her down to domestication but I was kinda glad they hadn't.

I thought about telling her that but she'd gotten so tense when we talked about her date, after the twister. I didn't want her to get all upset again.

So, realizing I was pretty much gawping at her, I cleared my throat. "Nothing."

I tried to untie my boots. I struggled, exhausted from the day. Renee knelt down and helped me to pull one off.

"You need a good rest," she scolded, untying the other one. Her eyes flicked to mine often, like she was wondering what I'd been thinking about for so long.

"A road trip will fix that right up."

Renee beamed at me, and the tears started to bubble over. I laughed at myself. I'd been spun around by my emotions most of the day. They were good tears this time though. I'd never experienced good tears before today.

"Are you okay?" she asked softly, pulling me into a hug.

"Think so," I mumbled into her shoulder. I was pretty sure I'd soaked her shirt several times over the course of the day.

"I have a present for you," Renee said as I rubbed my stinging eyes. Go figure how crying could make you so tired.

"You do?"

Renee nodded with a mischievous look. "I know you wanted to get them but I thought I'm more of an expert."

"You did, huh?" I didn't know what she was talking about.

"Don't get mad though, I used your money."

I raised my eyebrows. "What money?"

Renee laughed. "You telling me no one's told you that you're an heiress?"

My mouth opened and closed in my best fish impression. "I'm a what?"

"The entire town," Renee said. "Oppidum, it's owned by your family."

After everything that had been thrown at me in the last couple of months, I wasn't sure what the hell to do with that information. "So, you tellin' me, I've ended up Ivy League too?"

Renee winked. "Don't worry, I won't tell a soul."

I should hope not either. What would they think? I sucked in the air. "Especially not the girls. What the hell would Aimee make of it?"

The thought of the girls back in the institution made me restless, but I got an idea of how I could make it right. "So, are we talkin' rich or really, really rich?"

Renee put a wrapped box on my lap. "Even richer."

"Enough to make sure the girls will be okay?"

Renee beamed. "More than enough. They won't be out for a while though."

It didn't matter. I wanted them to have somewhere safe, somewhere people cared for them when they were released. "But they will, get out, won't they?"

She flicked her gaze away. "Aimee is continuing her recovery. I made sure the new psychiatrist was the best."

I was glad of that. I got a little picture in my head of Aimee twiddling her ring on her necklace. I hoped one day she'd be able to take it off, to let it go.

Renee pulled off her own shoes and wiggled her toes. "Nora is much better. If the new doctor can continue to convince her to take, and keep taking her medication, she'll be okay."

I chuckled at Renee's mis-matched socks. Go figure the Doctor Llys I'd met back in the institution wearing mis-matched socks. "Will she get out?"

She looked at me as if she was trying to figure out what was funny. "That's really up to her. Tiz will be with her for a while yet though."

I looked down at the present. I'd never known why Tiz was in the institution. All I knew was how much she loved shiny objects. "What she do?"

"It's more what may happen again," Renee said. "It's for her safety, Aeron, and everyone else's."

I didn't like the sound of that. "That bad, huh?"

"Let's just say that if she gets out, she'll be watched very, very carefully."

Tiz? Renee was making out like Tiz was some dangerous psycho. Sure she got the fluctuations, something whispering in her ear, but that bad?

"Open." Renee tapped the box.

I ripped the wrapping off and lifted the lid. My breath caught as I pulled out a very shiny, sparkly set of golden high heels.

"For Yasmin," Renee said.

I hugged her half to death and planted a kiss on her cheek for good measure. I couldn't speak, they were perfect.

Renee took them off me as I wiped my eyes with my sleeve. I hadn't noticed the display case on the wall before Renee placed them inside.

It was just like I'd seen in the dream. They glinted and glimmered and shone like jewels. Yasmin would have loved them.

I sighed as I watched Renee fuss. "You are staying with me, right?"

She looked up, eyebrows raised.

I felt like a dumb kid again. "I mean, I'm used to you being near and after everything—"

"Of course I will." She pulled her bed clothes out of her pack. "I'm here for you."

"You know that works both ways, right," I said. "If you need me."

She beamed at me, her aura once again like a firework display. "What are you looking at when you do that?"

I shrugged, feeling like a snooper. "Your aura."

She cocked her head. "I have an aura?"

"Everyone does." I felt a wave of guilt wash over me and shrugged. "I see your mood an' well . . ."

"What?" Her gray eyes studied mine.

Ah heck, she must already know I was crazy. "It's kinda pretty."

Her smile lit up her face. "It is?"

My cheeks were so hot they got itchy. "Right now it's all warm, red mixed with purples swirling 'round."

She bit her lip. "Do you know what it means?"

"Not a clue but it's more pink when you're talking to me." I met her eyes again and the aura display continued. "Like I said, I didn't get an instruction manual."

I lay back on the bed.

"Do you find it hard being in here with us all?" Renee whispered as she turned out the light. I felt her get in on the other side of the gigantic bed. "Considering how alone you've been, it must be an onslaught."

Maybe she had a point, I guess with five other people in the same place I could feel battered but I didn't. "I guess after the institution, I'm used to it."

There was ruffling and the cover flicked off my feet. "Is it a problem?"

I listened to the stillness. Renee's soft breathing, I could feel the glowing love of my parents, the peaceful dreams of my sisters as they were watched over by Nan. I could even sense Mrs. Squirrel's care and tenderness for her new arrivals.

I felt lucky, I felt . . . blessed for the first time. "It used to bother me. I thought I knew too much."

A feeling of deep peace and joy washed over me. It felt good, really good.

"And now?" Renee asked.

I touched the necklace and smiled. "No, no, it's not a problem anymore."

About the Author

Jody Klaire started writing in 2011 and although she had been writing music and lyrics for fifteen years, becoming an author had never been something she aspired to. However, the moment that she began to compose the story for her first novel, she was hooked. Jody has been many things from police officer to singer/songwriter and tries to use her experiences in life to evoke vivid pictures. She aspires for her characters to touch the hearts of the reader. She lives with a host of furry friends: her golden retriever, several gerbils, some sneaky house mice, and a neighbour's cat. She loves writing, sport, music, art, and teaching herself new subjects. Jody is a proud member of GCLS, The Writer's Workshop WordCloud, and is delighted to be a part of the Bedazzled Ink family.

BLIND TRUST

TEASER

Renee looked at Evan and signaled to him. He started to back up the ATV. The other members of our rescue crew carried on in the distance, digging around a car on its side. The snow underneath us shifted and I got a warning flash.

"Stop!"

Evan did as he was told and Renee lifted her eyebrows in question.

"I'll have to pull him from here, the whole thing is shifting."

Renee didn't argue but took Duke and moved him back. "Aeron, can you pull him up?"

I nodded. I hoped it looked convincing.

"Then I'll bring a rope out to you too," she said.

"There's no time." My heart thudded, my skin clammy against the cold weather gear. I shivered and Renee frowned.

"Aeron, you don't look to great . . . maybe—"

"I can do this. Get everyone back." I turned to the edge. "Charlie, I'm gonna pull you up,"

"Hurry." His faint cry shot adrenaline through my veins. Renee met my eyes, all manner of thoughts flashing across her face.

"Hey," I offered her a smile. "I'll be okay . . . what's a little snow, right?"

She hesitated.

"Nan didn't get you saving my butt back in Oppidum to see me hurtle over a snowy edge." I met her eyes, trying to send every bit of reassurance I could her way. "Trust me."

"I do," she said. It was such a strong statement that I swore it could have knocked me backwards with the force. Renee had always been kinda intense. I guessed that's what happened when you lived the life she did, but there were times, like now, when I wondered how much of a toll it took on her.

"Good. Back up and let the snow expert do her thing," I said, my throat feeling like it had a snowball wedged in it.

Renee did as I asked and I turned back to face the edge. Another flash had warned me that I was sitting on the top of a huge slab of snow, which was going to give way, soon.

All I had to do was haul up a fully grown man with a tow rope and not get me or him hurt.

No problem, I thought as I gripped hold of the rope. No problem at all.

Lightning Source UK Ltd.
Milton Keynes UK
UKOW04f0601240118
316742UK00001B/38/P